D1433124

THE PROVING FLIGHT

The Proving Flight

A NOVEL

BY

DAVID BEATY

Readers Union
Secker and Warburg
LONDON 1958

This Readers Union edition was produced in 1958 for sale to its members only by Readers Union Ltd at 38 William IV Street, Charing Cross, London, and at Letchworth Garden City, Hertfordshire. Full details of membership may be obtained from our London address. The book has been reset in 11 point Fournier type and printed by Butler & Tanner Ltd Frome and London. It was first published by Martin Secker & Warburg Ltd in 1956.

CHAPTER ONE

FROM the noise-bound cockpit of an aircraft, the wide circle of London on an early spring evening looked as quiet as a bank of windflowers. Thinly scattered on the surrounding elevations, they clustered thick and white around the rich financial soil of the Thames embankment. Here and there, a neon-lighted pink pimpernel glittered, a buttercup flashed yellow or a bud unfolded the bright freshness of its green. It was seven o'clock. Bellamy moved the control column to the left. Obediently the Emperor turned port on to final approach, momentarily tucking away the brilliant colours under an outstretched starboard wing. Then, like a dragonfly, the plane swept towards the bank, dropped her legs cautiously, and left the dark sky with a whine of throttled-back engines, a whisper of brakes.

Gently, the sound of the tyres on the runway grew softer and softer. The noise of the engines died. The Emperor settled down to a comfortable little jog trot at the speed of a bicycle, till two blue lights on the right announced the beginning of the taxi-track back to the ramp. Slowing down almost to a stop, the nose-wheel angled over to point at the dark gap between them.

Wobbling her tail with a self-satisfied little flourish, she left the footlight glare of the thin straight stage of the runway and nosed into the dimly lit maze of the taxi-track which would eventually lead her back to the huge hangar near the Staines Road, which for the moment was her home.

Inside the cockpit, the crew turned the lights up a little. They shone down on to a small, rather cramped cave in which five men were working. Captain Bellamy, sitting in the left-hand driving seat, let his eyes shift for a second from steering the aircraft between the row of taxi-lights, and glanced back at the engineer behind him.

'Mr. Rawlings!'

'Sir?'

'You've started the air-test report?'

The bald pink head of the engineer inclined in a formidable affirmative. 'I have, sir! I have!'

'Controls and boosters seem all right. All anti-icing and de-icing equipment serviceable. Lights okay, auto-pilot okay, nose-wheel steering okay. My instruments are working well, but' – he turned towards the man sitting beside him, separated by the two-foot-wide throttle box between them – 'your artificial horizon is acting up, isn't it?'

The young face of First Officer James Seawood, still and statue-like in the holy glimmer of the subdued instrument lighting, suddenly jerked into life. 'Yes, sir . . . definitely . . . my horizon, sir. No good at all.' His fair hair flopped over his forehead in staccato emphasis of his words. 'It took a long time to erect, Mr. Rawlings, and now – '

Hooper chipped in with, 'All radios okay,' and at exactly the same time, Douthwaite made a laconic comment that the Loran, the black box of radar tricks that could give them accurate positions way out in the Atlantic, was unserviceable.

'All right, all right!' Rawlings irritably licked the stub of pencil that was conveying these observations in uncertain grey on a printed form in front of him. 'One at a time, *please*. Now, Vic – '

'The radios,' Hooper said very slowly, 'have been tested and found serviceable.'

The pencil laboriously indicated as much on the paper, as outside the four idling engines gossiped to each other in undertones, and the wheels scrunched on towards the hangar.

'Thank you. Now, Alex – '

'This Loran receiver is a bit on the blink.'

'You want a new one fitted?'

'I want a new one fitted.'

'Reason for change . . . bit on the blink?'

'Reason for change . . . unserviceable,' Douthwaite said shortly.

'Wish that was all I had to put down,' Rawlings grumbled, 'when I wanted an engine changed.' His blunt pencil went on writing, squeaking slightly from the pressure that was applied to it.

Airily unconcerned with this human picking of holes in her, the Emperor glided out of the darkness and stamped her silhouette against the 3D screen of the lighted hangar, its doors gaping to admit her.

She was a curious shape for an aeroplane. Her undercarriage legs were very short, almost as if they had given way under her seventy tons – but to make up for this down-to-earth stance, her tail soared to heaven with a flat and graceful majesty that riveted all attention to her rear. The swept-back wings, in which her fuel was stored, were surprisingly small for her size and seemed there just to be an inflammable parasol to cover her four mighty turbo-prop engines. And underneath her long cylinder fuselage, right at the front, the cutaway effect of the nose-wheel well gave her the appearance (so the *Daily Mail* said) of smiling a curiously enigmatic Mona Lisa smile. Could this mean (the *Daily Mirror* asked) that she was quietly confident of capturing for the New Elizabethan age of England the lordship of the air above Drake's captive seven seas?

It might more likely mean that her designer had found that was the best sort of nose-wheel well to have. But it *might* mean that. For this was the newest, the biggest and the most unusual solidified dream of British aeronautical manufacturers, the only aeroplane (according to her makers) capable of *always* operating non-stop, London-New York, against the heavy head winds of the Atlantic, the sole survivor of a post-war civil aeronautical era of abortion and disaster, of high-sounding names making low-sounding noises, of big boosts-up and Humpty Dumpty falls, as one after the other, and to the tune of millions of the taxpayers' pounds and golden yards of hard-won prestige, the British ideas of a fast, long-range, passenger-carrying aeroplane flopped back on the ground, dead beat.

This last hope now seemed splendidly aware of her isolation in the race. Taking her time, as she neared the hangar and the waiting ground engineers, the Emperor began to mince forward delicately, as though, now she was out of the cover of darkness, she must (mannequin-like) display the royal metal of which she was made to the very best advantage.

She slid to a stop beside a tractor. Bellamy called over his shoulder, 'Shut them down', and Rawlings, momentarily relinquishing the pencil for his awesome array of levers, selected four with red-topped handles and slammed them forward. Cut off in the middle of a sentence, the engines gave a creak of protest, the propellors free-wheeled round eighteen complete turns. Then all four stopped together.

A voice called up hopefully from the ground, 'Everything okay, sir?'

Nobody answered from the flight deck. The voice, rather more shrill than before, changed the question to: 'Is she all right, sir?'

And as there was still no answer (for Rawlings was laboriously finishing off the test report, while the pilots climbed out of their seats), the voice, now hoarse with anxiety, asked, 'Nothing *much* the matter with her, is there, sir?'

Up in the crew compartment, Bellamy leant over the engineer's shoulders. 'Satisfied?'

'Well . . .' The blunt pencil left the air-test report and swept over the innocent instruments. 'They're reading okay . . . No roughness. Power's there. Everything *must* be all right, sir.'

Ignoring the crust of doubt round the engineer's voice, Bellamy said, 'Good.' He knew perfectly well what was at the back of Rawlings' mind. When anyone is brought up in the sweet religion of piston engines, practises their teachings professionally for twenty years, a brand-new way of making a propellor go round, using a modified form of jet propulsion, is naturally regarded (especially after only a couple of months' indoctrination) as a very likely runner for the heretic's stakes.

As Rawlings' pencil once more returned to its secretarial labours, Bellamy observed, 'Looks like we're all set for the proving flight tomorrow!'

He said the words with an encouraging off-handedness, as any leader of an expedition might say them after all the preparation had been made, and then, finding no answering gleam of enthusiasm, added, 'I must say . . . she went very well.'

But still nobody said anything. Among all the dead instruments in the silence around them, only the clock ticked.

Looking at the faces of his crew, it struck Bellamy what unlikely pioneers they were. Beyond an interest in aviation, comparable to other men's interest in their jobs, there was nothing to distinguish them from the millions beyond the airport who were now relaxing from today in preparation for an almost identical tomorrow. And yet, fate had haphazardly scooped up these four into the small net of the Emperor's cockpit – and the proving flight was to be (in Rawlings' own words) 'our lot'.

A smile, not without sympathy, deepened the lines round the pilot's mouth. Not many years over thirty, Bellamy had, by hard work and a real flair for flying, reached the position of Senior Training Captain amongst the other Company pilots. Now, as the silence persisted, the smile widened – 'And she handles beautifully . . . doesn't she, Mr. Seawood?'

'Beautifully,' echoed Seawood. 'A treat . . . a real treat to fly, sir.'

'The lack of vibration,' Douthwaite quoted drily what all the air correspondents in the papers had most enthused over, 'is something *out of this world.*'

'Which gives you,' Bellamy put in promptly, 'a steady table to work on . . . for a change.'

'And let's hope,' Rawlings said, diverting from his cares to have a crack at the navigator, 'it'll keep him from grumbling that the engines are out of synchronisation!'

Hooper, hearing the compliments flying about the Emperor and not to be outdone, mentioned modestly that 'the radio set-up's good, too, sir', and in a more confident frame of mind, hailed the approaching future with, 'New York . . . *here we come!*'

A thump against the Emperor's side brought them all back to the fact that there was, after all, a world outside this small metal cell. The ground engineer, who had waited in vain for an answer to his queries and mistrusting the almost church-like quietness that hung around the nose of the aircraft, had hurriedly made off for the crew steps and was now clanging up them, one by one, to find out the worst.

He had expected a strained and prickly reception on the flight deck. Instead, the atmosphere could even be called friendly. When Bellamy said, 'Nothing much . . . just a few instrument changes,' it took a little time for the relieved beam to dawn across his face.

'Not bad,' he called to his waiting mates below. 'Couple of hours' work . . . at the most.' And not even Rawlings contradicted him. Instead, the flight engineer produced the long piece of paper, an unimpressive, pencilled parchment of approval for the Emperor's baptism in North Atlantic air. 'Ready if you are, Captain.'

The pilot leaned over the small six-inch-wide table that skirted the engineer's panel, and watched by his crew of the morning, he struck out the bottom alternative of the conclusion – the air-test is considered {satisfactory / unsatisfactory} – and with a certain flourish signed himself below, in rather large handwriting, as *Andrew Bellamy*.

That signature was only one of thousands in the Emperor's young life – on bills, cheques, patents, lawsuits, letters, appeals, writs, contracts, penalty clauses, labour agreements – but it was one, rather more than the others, that set in immediate motion that attack on the future of flying for which the Emperor had long been scheduled. From the Air Enterprise Operations office, the telephone wires rang out the good news in a number of assorted houses, widely scattered over Inner and Outer London, where lived the other Britons destined to accompany the crew over the Atlantic on the proving flight.

Captain Cavendish was the first one informed. As soon as he'd heard the news in his home at Ascot, he demanded, 'Has *everyone* been told?'

'Well . . . Captain Bellamy and his crew know, of course, sir. And now we're – '

'You mean . . . Captain Bellamy and *my* crew!'

'Of course, sir.' Hastily, the Operations Officer corrected himself. 'I'm sorry, sir. Captain Bellamy and *your* crew. And now we're getting in touch with the others.'

In a semi-detached villa near Harrow, a pair of tartan-wool carpet slippers slip-slopped towards the telephone, and the man who had designed the mighty turbo-prop engines of the Emperor, Mr. Cruttwell, took up the receiver and cradled it against the curiously hairy ear that projected from the egg-shaped baldness of his head. 'Going tomorrow?' His voice sounded surprised. 'I was under the impression they were going to give the controls system another looking over.'

In a bachelor flat in Kensington, the swish of a crimson silk dressing-gown, to and fro, to and fro, seemed to be trying to soothe the irritation in its master's voice, as Mr. Eastlake, the chief designer of the Emperor's airframe, asked the Operations Officer, 'Are you *sure* there are only a few instrument changes? I was told yesterday they were changing the two outboard engines!'

In a Maida Vale maisonette, a little girl fetched her father from the lighted garage, where he was polishing the powerful bonnet of a silver and grey 1955 Jaguar. He put away the cloth, washed his hands carefully in the cloakroom, and then, as though he were announcing a guest at a diplomatic soirée, called into the patient receiver: 'Chief Steward Hamilton!'

He listened for a minute. 'Don't send the crew transport for me!' he advised the Operations Officer authoritatively. 'I shall be driving to the airport in my own little bus.'

The long white fingers of Dr. Enderby-Browne, the Company's medical adviser, lifted the telephone out of its cradle. 'Four o'clock at the airport? I shall not fail to be there.'

All Riley, Air Enterprise's public relations officer, said on the telephone in the Cockatoo Club was 'Consider me as having been . . . warned,' and then went back to the bar, where the boys and girls could – better than Operations Officers – appreciate his dry, ironic wit.

Not far away, Captain Payton was contacted at Primrose 9824. The big hand that held the pearl-grey earpiece was very slightly nervous. 'The Chairman will be delighted.' Instinctively, he was practising on the piece of coloured plastic that slightly fawning manner which had helped him to propel an office desk to far greater heights in the aviation sky than he would ever have reached in an aeroplane. Now the tentative Line Manager of Air Enterprise Emperors, he smiled down at the carpet, watching himelf being confirmed in the appointment.

'Thank you, Smith,' he said smoothly. 'Thank you for your good wishes. I'm sure we'll bring it off.'

But it was not so much the proving flight he was thinking about. Vividly on the carpet beneath his feet, the designs were changing. As he put the receiver down, he caught a glimpse of himself as Director of Operations. By the time he reached the drawing-room, the patterns were spelling *Vice-Chairman*; and when his wife said to him, 'I do think the

Chairman might have invited us to his party tonight,' it was for the moment difficult to remember that she wasn't talking about himself.

By the time Bellamy came into the Operations office from the aircraft, everyone, including the two stewardesses, Miss Knight and Miss Greenacres, as well as Mr. Brocklehurst, the Under-Secretary of State who would be accompanying the flight, had been warned. There had been one abortive notification – quite the most important, and the Operations Officer was sweating a little as he looked up from his list. 'Oh, Captain Bellamy – '

'Yes?'

'There's a message for you, sir.'

'Who from?'

'The Chairman.'

'Well, what is it?'

'He wants you to report to his home, sir. As soon as possible.'

'Say why?'

'I rather gather he wanted a personal account of the air-test. He said – '

'You told him she was serviceable?'

'I said there were only a few minor instrument changes.'

'Was he pleased?'

'I don't know, sir,' the Operations Officer said doubtfully. 'He just told me to phone back when *everything* was serviceable.'

Bellamy appeared to be on the point of saying something. Instead he turned abruptly on his heel. 'Thanks,' he called over his shoulder, and then, 'Good night.'

He stood for a moment in the doorway, a thickset, square-looking figure, with his cap shading his face, and his coat collar turned up against the damp and cold.

'Hell!' he said, thrusting his hands deep in his pockets and stepping out into the light-splashed darkness between the concrete buildings. He walked with his head thrust slightly forward, moving on the balls of his feet, with a curious quiet deliberate movement. The Chairman's message had brought him up sharply against that transition between the air and the ground which always irked him. In the cockpit, black was black and white was white. None of the muddy greys and in-betweens that passed for them on the ground. You had to go from A to B and with careful planning you got there. Each flight represented to him a geometrical theorem. The problem was to complete it safely, and *engines off* at London or Idelwild was the equivalent of writing Q.E.D. on the bottom of the paper. And if the job was all in the air he would have been one of the happy few who could go to bed at night with *that* problem solved, and with a clear-cut formula for solving the next.

But it wasn't. Once on the ground, the trust between men, which was so important that (paradoxically) it was never questioned, disappeared faster than the free liquor at an unscheduled night-stop. The need to soothe the public, to impress the taxpayer, the Ministry, the politicians, to outfly their rivals, not to mention the smaller, more interesting, personal ones of building the odd empire, ditching the next man, pleasing the boss, or even showing a little friendly preference for the husband of your wife's best friend, made the going as complicated and as tricky as the New York holding-pattern.

Bellamy walked over to his car – its long green bonnet now a dark grey shape in the deserted parking place. He started up the engine, and leaving the airport, nosed his car into the London-bound stream. His hands automatically adjusted themselves to the feel of these different controls, but his mind was still making the necessary change. It was only in the air that he felt himself – stripped of all inessentials, as the aircraft was streamlined for flight. And now, very much like the aircraft again, those attributes that helped him in the air made him a far slower progressor on the ground.

He eased the car abstractedly, creeping up through the traffic. The lights stopped him at Hammersmith, and the sight of a telephone box reminded him that he'd have to let the stewardess know he wouldn't be looking in at her party. He lit a cigarette, letting it hang out of the corner of his mouth, his eyes screwed up against the smoke, and as the signal changed to green, he steered the car towards Mayfair.

The increasing elegance of his surroundings made the vision of Sir James overlie the clinical mental analysis of the

Emperor that had been occupying his mind for the last fifteen minutes: prosperity, success, good living, the ornamented façade that disguised the heavy stone and steel structure of the man. Bellamy frowned.

Everyone had been told that the Emperor had been found serviceable. And so it had. By Bellamy himself. And yet, like Rawlings an hour before, now he hesitated over the word. He went over every test he'd put her through. Over every satisfactory result. On paper, they added up to a good aeroplane – built as cheaply as possible, certainly, but apart from a few modifications he would have liked done, a good aeroplane, nevertheless.

But in Bellamy's mind, there was a mysterious quantity 'x' that confused all the calculations. The same hunch that often told him he was north or south of a track when there was no navigational evidence either way, now gave him a vague warning that all was not well under the Emperor's sleek skin. Through years of flying, he had acquired a little of the same aerial instinct as birds.

That, or it was his body's way of showing the strain of this impending flight. Bellamy brought the car to a stop outside the Chairman's home with an unusual jerk.

There was a telephone box a hundred yards up the quiet road. He could make his call to Lalette Greenacres before going in. For a moment, Bellamy sat with the engine switched off, his gloved hand still resting idly on the wheel. He stared up at the long lighted windows on his left. Behind the blue curtains, Sir James was having an intimate party with people of influence. In there, many stars and constellations would be glittering expensively. With a thin smile, Bellamy wondered how the Chairman was guiding the Emperor through *that* particular sky.

Impatiently, he swung himself out of the seat, and slammed the car door shut behind him.

The first arrival at Lalette Greenacres' party was the other stewardess. Angela Knight stood just within the small hall pulling at her gloves and smiling politely at the obvious party clothes that the attic flat was wearing.

'It all looks very nice. Quite a spread!' She advanced into

the large room with the sloping ceiling that was the living-room-cum-lounge, and peeped at the plates of sandwiches and sausage rolls and savouries on sticks.

'And the bar's over there.' Lalette waved at the table covered with a sheet and laden with beer and a few bottles of spirits and glasses that had been specially bought from the nearest Woolworth's.

'Am I the first?' Angela followed Lalette into the bedroom and laid her coat down carefully and neatly folded her gloves and scarf. In the mirror, she re-powdered her rather long well-shaped face and combed her hair.

'Just had it set?' Lalette asked, watching the dark sleek waves fall prettily into place. 'Looks very nice,' she added politely.

'Well, it's rather a special occasion, isn't it? It's up to us to look our best.'

'Oh, it's special, all right!' Lalette patted her own short blonde curls behind Angela in the mirror.

'I hope I'm not too early,' the other girl said stiffly. They neither of them knew each other very well, although they had flown on the same route for six months. Most of the stewardesses, unless they lived in the same house, were on just hello and nodding acquaintances with each other. And their real knowledge of one another's personalities was supplied by the powerful grapevine, which distilled a strong essence of romance about each and every girl on the Line. And with the property of wine it acquired volume with the hands that pressed it, and added strength and flavour with time.

Now the two of them were thrown together for a week, on an enterprise of importance and among a varied and rather difficult selection of men. Both of the girls stared for a moment thoughtfully at the other's reflection in the mirror, sizing her up as friend or foe, and wondering just what the grapevine had said about the other, and (not unkindly) why she had been chosen.

Simultaneously, they both became aware of the other's eyes and smiled. 'Would you like to come in the lounge and have a drink before the others come?'

'Who are you expecting?' Angela's brown eyes watched Lalette over the rim of her sherry glass. She moved a little nearer to the fire and held out her free hand to the warmth.

'I'm expecting whoever comes!' Lalette sat down on a leather-covered pouffe, and clasped her hands round her knees. The firelight scooped out the hollows and highlighted the planes of her pointed, well-boned face. It was a young face. Pretty and piquant under the short fair curls.

Angela smiled and shrugged her shoulders. 'That's one thing I find difficult about this life! You never know who's turning up, or where or when.'

'Oh, but that's the *fun* of it! Anything might happen!' Lalette laughed. 'And usually *does*.'

Angela wet her lips again with sherry. It was not the kind that she was used to in her father's house and she was not now surprised that most of the bottles had their labels turned away.

'Well,' Angela said slowly, finding conversation difficult and wishing now that she hadn't persuaded herself that it was the right thing to do to make her own small contribution to the send-off by attending Lalette's party. 'If you don't know *who's* coming . . . do you know *when*?'

'Oh, any time now, I should think.' She looked at her wrist-watch. Then she added casually, 'D'you know any of this crew . . . *well*?'

Lalette looked into the fire and Angela watched her face carefully. There was no sort of expression that she could define. Lalette's profile in repose had that sad sweet air that she supposed some men found appealing, tinted prettily like a nineteenth-century water-colour. Not really the sort of person she would have chosen to partner her on this responsible trip. The sort of person her father would describe as not a good stayer.

'Captain Bellamy has taken me out several times,' she said slowly. 'If that's what you mean. We have . . . well, quite a number of tastes in common.'

'Nice for you,' Lalette said, nodding her head gravely. 'What did you do?'

'Oh, the usual things that one *does* do. Dinner and the theatre. And then a concert once.'

'In London?' Lalette looked only mildly interested.

'Yes, of course. But we did a trip together to Montreal. And there I took him to see some friends of Daddy's.' She smiled. 'They liked him tremendously. They were English, of course. Ex-army, like Daddy. They wrote afterwards and said they thought he'd go far. I think he will, too.'

'And does Daddy?'

'From what he's heard, yes. But of course they haven't met.'

'More sherry?' Lalette walked over with the bottle and poured some into Angela's glass.

'Well' – she raised her glass – 'here's to the happy day.'

'Which one? Tomorrow?'

'No. The happy day . . . when he does . . . meet Daddy.'

'Oh,' Angela laughed. 'We haven't got around to that *yet*!' She clasped her hands in front of her, suddenly not at all averse to a quiet girlish talk. 'But he does seem . . . what shall I say? . . . reliable and hard working and – ' She closed her eyes to help her to think of the right word.

'Deadly dull,' Lalette finished for her.

'Don't you like him?' Angela's eyes flew open. 'I thought he was quite a friend of your family or something.'

'He was in the R.A.F. with my brother. And I don't *really* think he's deadly dull.' She paused. 'It's just that you make him sound so.'

'I'm sorry *you* don't like the qualities that *I* like in him. I find – '

Lalette cut in as though closing the subject. 'Anyway, I'd rather fly behind him than anyone else.'

'Except, of course, for the most senior pilots.'

Lalette looked across at the other girl speculatively. 'Did you say your father was retired Army?'

Angela nodded. 'Brigadier,' she said reverently.

'Well, you've certainly absorbed its seniority tradition!' she said, but with a kind of pert gentleness that disarmed Angela.

'I suppose I have. On the other hand, there's a good deal to be said for it.'

Lalette was just going to express her doubts when downstairs the bell started to ring. It pealed four times. 'Here we go!' she said, jumping up and skipping out on to the landing.

She peered over the well of the staircase. 'There's a whole lot of them,' she called back over her shoulder to Angela. The bell rang again. 'And now they're all coming up at once!'

Very slowly, accompanied by a soft sizzling of conversation and laughter, a small stream of people were making their way up the five flights of stairs like a lighted fuse to the party preparations upstairs.

Half an hour later, it was all fully ignited. People had mingled and then divided into groups. Drifts of tobacco smoke hung like flat grey islands of scum above the jampot bubble of the party underneath. Lalette squeezed her way in and out, filling glasses, handing round plates of sandwiches and opening boxes of cigarettes. She didn't know how long the phone had been ringing when she first heard it. There were so many high-pitched ingredients to the steady, sustained clamour in the room. She picked the receiver up quickly, sticking her finger in one ear to keep out the too audible success of the party. 'Freemantle 5050. Yes, it's me. Don't I sound like me? You sound just the same Andrew.'

Andrew Bellamy's voice at the other end sounded faintly exasperated. 'Look, Lalette, I'm awfully sorry, but – '

'You can't make it, eh?' Her voice sounded light and pleasant. She frowned at the receiver and bit her lip.

'I'm afraid I'm about to be tied up at the Chairman's. Terribly sorry, Lalette. Have a good time and all that. Oh, and don't keep the boys too late!'

'I'm sorry too, Andrew,' she said flatly.

'And Lalette . . ."

'Yes, Andrew?'

'Apologise to Angela, would you? There's a good girl.'

'Apologise for what, Andrew?' Lalette said gently. 'That you can't come to . . . *my* party?'

'Yes. I said I'd see her there. Thanks, Lalette. That's fine, if you would. Good night.'

'Good night,' she said softly to the empty receiver. 'Good night. Sleep well.'

She walked away briskly from the hall table and back into the lounge. Her eyes were smarting with the cigarette haze and the room felt stuffy and stale. She saw Angela talking to two of the pilots in a corner by the fireplace. She moved over towards her. 'I wonder' – she nodded and smiled at the two men – 'Angela, if you'd help me serve the coffee? No,' she said firmly. 'Just Angela. Yes, of course we can manage! They're not so keen to help on the aeroplane, are they?'

As soon as they were in the kitchen, she said, 'It was really just to give you a message. No, don't bother with the coffee. It's all ready anyway. I'm just going to let everyone grab. You'll be disappointed. Andrew Bellamy phoned that he can't come and asked me to say sorry to you. I think he'd have spoken to you, but he was pretty tied up.'

'Oh,' Angela said, 'and why?'

'He's going to the Chairman's. I gather he's about to dive into the midst of one of the old gent's *get-togethers.*' Lalette smiled.

'Really!' Angela smiled, too. 'He's to be there all evening?'

'So I gather. A pity! This sort of a party would have done him a world of good.'

'But I couldn't agree less!' Angela's well-shaped eyebrows flew up. 'You can't mean it. When he's going to Sir James'?' She tapped Lalette's shoulder with her forefinger to emphasise each word. '*That's* what'll do him the world of good!'

The party in the Chairman's world was sumptuously under way by the time the Operations Officer phoned back.

As was right and proper, it was the butler who answered him, but Sir James Joliffe was hovering (as he had been this last hour) not ten feet away. He was standing a little on his rather plump toes, hands in the pockets of his dinner-jacket trousers, a careful smile succeeding in stowing away ninety-nine per cent of the anxiety of his bright shrewd eyes into the deepening lines of his face.

With a deliberately unconcerned gesture, he took the receiver from Underwood. And 'Joliffe,' he said slowly, and then, 'Perfectly serviceable now? Every instrument . . . every engine . . . the controls . . . the radios?' and after that, 'Just what I expected!'

He grinned at Underwood, smacked his small square hands together, and in reply to the butler's solicitious 'Everything is satisfactory, I trust, Sir James!' said with an explosion of boyish enthusiasm, 'Perfect . . . perfect!'

'My felicitations, Sir James.'

'Thank you, Underwood . . . thank you.' The Chairman of Air Enterprise rubbed his chin thoughtfully. 'Captain Bellamy will be arriving any time now. Show him straight up, would you?'

Then leaving the butler in the hall, he walked up the wide shallow staircase. His progress, in the world, so far, had been rather like those stairs. Slowly, measured step by measured step, each one richly carpeted against knocks and jars, he had risen almost annually. Now, he was starting to take the lift. His own engineering business had brought him in a comfortable fortune; but more than that, it had brought him in contact, through building aero engines, with what his enemies described as a resurrected desire to play with trains, and what his friends described as the irresistible challenge of that untamed element, the air. He had given himself to civil aviation with more passionate abandon than any woman to her loved one. And when Joliffe gave there was no refusing just as, when Joliffe withheld, as many people left behind him in the dustbowl could testify, the arid wind did not cease, nor did the sun shine.

The war had brought him a baronetcy. The airline business might bring him anything. As Chairman of Air Enterprise he had sponsored this entirely new aeroplane for the lucrative North Atlantic route. If this came off (and it would) his world-wide reputation was assured; a barony, a peerage, the establishment of a modern steel-founded dynasty were not only on the cards, they were practically in the contract.

For years, he had watched the Sleeping Beauty of the British aviation industry being lulled into Nirvana by its friends – the Press, the Government, and the Chancellor of the Exchequer. And then, timing his entrance, some said as the Wicked Fairy, some said as Prince Charming himself, Sir James Joliffe had burst into the centre of the stage, bringing with him what a friendly journalist described as his 'uncanny ability to drive a wedge into the future through all the fears and difficulties of this all-too-human present'.

And now, reaching the very top of the stairs, he still knew what to do. He opened the door to what Lady Joliffe called the *Reception Room* very slowly. The noise and chatter of the party died down a little. People stopped to turn their heads and smile and nod. It was always the same when Joliffe entered a room.

Lady Bartle said, 'Ah, there you are!', and came over towards where he stood, savouring the sweetness that filled his well-trained senses: from the restrained voices of his guests, from the mingled smell of cigar smoke and French perfume, from the well-matured brandy, and (most important of all – the ingredient that like the alchemist's stone turned all the others to gold) from the deference that was so plentifully accorded to success.

He sighed, half closing his eyes, so that the lounge became a blurred picture of rich colours and gentle movement. Beside him, Lady Bartle chattered on, while her voice, as wet and harsh and splattering as a waterfall, made an almost pleasant sound-track to his thoughts. Besides, even the pleasure which his round red face could not quite contain was not wasted. It leaked out around his mouth, embedded itself deeply in the lines that skirted his plump cheeks, and was hunted down and devoured by Lady Bartle's hungry and dissatisfied eyes.

The two of them were still in that happy companionship when Captain Bellamy was at last announced. Across a good yardage of Aubusson carpet, into an air that was lit and warmed and scented, and well insulated against trouble, came a man in uniform – the blue colour clashing with the well-cut dinner jackets and the kaleidoscopic silks and laces of Balmain and Dior. The still-young face, tanned and clean-cut, gave the impression of being out of place, out-dated like a new wine by the seasoned flesh of the other faces around it.

Not seeing anyone he knew, the pilot stood still. Sir James, both fat competent hands outstretched in welcome, came striding across from the other side of the room. By the flick of a master-switch, the benign pleasure which had been flowing through him all evening was canalised into a bumper welcome for Bellamy.

'Come,' he said, with a bubbling heartiness, his right arm making an arc behind the pilot that was only a degree or so less warm than an arm on the shoulder. This was *his* man. The whole gesture seemed to imply it. Here was a young man with ability and a sense of duty. Recognising both, Sir James had not even troubled to consider the second commandment in the Book of Pilots – seniority. Way above his seniors, this man had been promoted Chief Training Captain as the Chairman's instinctive choice for the right man for the job. 'Now I want you to meet everyone . . . we've all been waiting for this moment.'

His voice smoothly split open the groups of two and three, whose segments turned to meet Bellamy like fruit prepared for his delectation. Noble names, influential in business, in flying, or in finance, were exchanged for the down-to-earth, unknown one of Andrew Bellamy while Sir James, as though conscious of the unfair market rate, was adding the odd makeweight here and there of, 'A fine war record', or 'One of our crack pilots.'

Then as they moved away, and the few small groups behind them returned to cosier subjects. Sir James walked Bellamy slowly towards the library door. 'There are a few things I'd like to talk over.' He smiled genially at the others. 'And I'm sure you don't want to be bored with shop. So, if you'll excuse me . . . Bellamy and I . . . a little *get-together* – '

Sir James turned the handle and they walked into the darkness together. The baize-covered library door closed behind them. The Chairman switched the lights on and illuminated a dun-coloured, sober-sided world, where the air (very faintly) smelled of the vault, and where row upon row of books had turned their stiff, straight Puritan backs on the champagne and the laughter.

But Joliffe tonight was carrying his own party round with him. Like an invisible lava, his enthusiasm simply poured over the cold library air. In a great wave, it burst over Bellamy, as he stood (not unlike a very large blue-covered book taken down from the shelves) on the bearskin rug by the side of the empty fireplace.

'So the air-test was a great success, Bellamy?'

'Everything important worked, sir.'

'Excellent!' Sir James clasped his hands together as though his right hand was wringing congratulations from his left. 'So now . . . we're all set to go?'

'Yes.'

'Everybody on the top line for the trip?'

Bellamy said drily. 'Operating crew looks fit enough.'

'Fine . . . fine! All just like me . . . rarin' to go.' His eyes left the pilot's face and looked up at the ceiling, where the golden future was painted. 'It'll be years before any other Company can get hold of Emperors. We'll have a clear field on the Atlantic. And think of the loads!' Coming down to earth again, he smiled at Bellamy. 'And she's got looks! Unorthodox, of course. Unusual. But all the same . . . handsome, wouldn't you say?'

'Looks like an aeroplane.'

'Quite. She *looks* as though she can fly. And she handles beautifully, doesn't she?'

'Smooth enough. Controls are easy.'

'And the immense power of those engines, Bellamy!'

'Needs it, sir. Big aeroplane.'

'And the interior! Bright . . . comfortable.'

'Cockpit's cramped. A little more room there – '

The Chairman laughed. 'You pilots . . . never satisfied, are you? But I know you're as proud of her as I am.' In an easy, confident way, he stretched his arms. 'However . . . better get down to business, I suppose.'

He talked of the programme for the proving flight, the send-off ceremony, the welcome that might be expected in New York and later in Bermuda. As the conversation proceeded, on one side, there was the brief staccato of Bellamy's remarks; on the other, the full rich flow of carefully modulated eloquence.

Gradually, the Chairman began to notice how one-sided it was. Bellamy today was showing a regrettable lack of enthusiasm. As he talked, he searched his mind for a reason. The pilots had been piqued that their advice was not called for in the Emperor's design – had at one stage even sent a deputation.

Perhaps it was that—just another of those difficulties that had cropped up during the Emperor's building. There had been many others: fights between airframe designer for more weight (and therefore more strength) and engine designer for lightness (and therefore more speed): trouble over this, trouble over that – the suggestion only yesterday from the factory that they should postpone the proving flight to fit the almost completed Mark II hydraulic booster cylinders.

In all those times, the Chairman's confidence had cleared the air, blown away the fog so that everyone could see the way *he* wanted things done. He'd given out. They'd given in.

And he was still giving out today.

With his bright eyes flashing out energy like electricity, he was just saying, 'And all this publicity, we've got – ', when Bellamy suddenly interrupted. 'Yes, sir. This *publicity* – '

The pilot paused, as vision after vision of the Chairman in action slid through his memory: Sir James on television, a symbol of confidence in a listless, uneasy world: Sir James smiling up at a row of bathing beauties, kicking up their heels at the ecstasy of sitting on the Emperor's leading edge: Sir James gravely escorting Royalty over this new and gigantic example of the ingenuity of the British peoples – 'Certainly sold the Emperor to the public.'

'They've taken her to their hearts, Bellamy.'

'Made them think the proving flight's a formality.' The pilot's eyes went straight to the newspaper, open on the Chairman's desk. 'I'm interested tomorrow in seeing what she can do, sir. Not in fulfilling her publicity claims.'

So that was it. Sir James had seen Bellamy's attention wander to the large picture of the Emperor in the paper, with at one side a photograph of himself – on the other, an impressive portrait of Captain Cavendish.

'We're very fortunate,' he said, 'in having a pilot of Captain Cavendish's reputation coming along with us tomorrow.'

Bellamy said nothing. Sir James was satisfied he'd hit the nail on the head. Two captains would be on board tomorrow, partly to lessen fatigue, mostly to fit in with the Chairman's publicity plan. Bellamy was at his prime as a pilot – but he was unknown. Cavendish was a household name – but he had passed his flying prime a very long time ago. Adept at picking out the assets in a man, Sir James intended to get the best out of both generations.

'And of course,' the Chairman went on, to smooth Bellamy's ruffled feelings in his rôle of ghost pilot, 'we're very fortunate indeed in having a pilot of your exceptional ability.'

Bellamy again said nothing. He doubted whether Sir James realised quite *how* fortunate they were – and out of his loyalty to a fellow pilot, he felt no inclination to tell him. As part of his Training Captain's job, he had given Cavendish one of his bi-annual check flights only a week ago. The man flew as though he was controlling an aeroplane built in 1935, with no inherent stability. Never let the controls alone once. His whole attitude implied that no aircraft was going to be allowed to fly itself while Captain Cavendish was in the cockpit.

'Well . . . I think that's the lot, Bellamy. Unless you've got anything to add?'

'Nothing, sir.'

'In that case, shall we join . . . I was going to say the ladies! . . . the other members of the party?'

They walked beside each other to the door. This time, Bellamy opened it. 'After you, sir.'

The outward appearance that the Chairman gave his guests when he came back into the room was exactly the same as he had given them when he left them, half an hour before. He was just as full of enthusiasm: 'Champagne, Lady Bartle?' and 'Ah, there you are, Sir Lionel!' and 'I was speaking to the Minister the other day – ' but all the time, his mind was chewing over the two new facts that he had just learned, and which would now have to be taken into consideration.

Bellamy resented Cavendish's appearance in the crew. More important still, Bellamy was not so much *his* man as he had supposed.

'It's midnight!' His wife plucked at his sleeve. 'It's the day of the proving flight. Don't you think a toast – '

'Of course . . . of course!' He raised his hands up above his head. 'Ladies and gentlemen . . . *please.*'

There was a brief period of undertoned silence, while the hired waiter, knowing his cue, went round with the champagne.

Everybody obediently waited, with a full glass a few inches from their lips. In the sudden hush, a stillness lay over the room, broken only by the sound of the wind and the rain in the unseen darkness outside.

Sir James raised his glass on high. There was no need to say much. In eight words, he could tell them the plain, unvarnished truth.

'Ladies and gentlemen . . . I give you . . . *the Emperor!*'

Snug from the rain, in her hangar at London Airport, the

Emperor snoozed away the hours of darkness, watched over by three men. On Sir James' orders, they were on vigil in the glass-fronted office beside her – a human insurance against fire, theft or sabotage.

Pordige, the airport policeman, was shuffling the greasy pack for the umpteenth time. Huggett, the foreman, yawned. Only the third man, Trickleby, the odd-job hangar man, had preserved an interest in the endless game they were playing. His eyes, very large and burning bright, watched every movement intently as Pordige dealt them a hand.

Huggett raised his head and wearily looked through the glass. 'She's still there,' he said unnecessarily. 'Will I be glad when the bastard's hopped it!'

The policeman nodded in agreement. 'It'll be a load off *my* mind when she's gone.' And, then, as though the strain was already pressing on his nerves: 'What wouldn't I give for a smoke, 'Uggett!'

'You had my last.'

'You got one, Trick, old man?'

' 'Aven't.'

'Think I'll bust if I don't get a smoke!'

Pordige morosely picked up his hand, looked the cards over, and threw them down on the table. 'I've 'ad this game,' he said. He looked at the absorbed white face of Trickleby beside him. 'You got the ace up your sleeve again?'

Trickleby stared at him and said nothing.

'Does he always talk as much as this, 'Uggett?'

'Oh, Trick's a deep one . . . Trick is!'

Pordige said. 'If you want to lose to 'im again that's your affair, I'm off to do my round.' He got up, left the office, made one complete circuit of the Emperor, and returned.

'Caught anyone?' Huggett asked amiably.

'Trouble with you, 'Uggett . . . you got no sense of responsibility! What the Russians wouldn't like to do to that million quid's worth!'

'Cost a million quid, did she?'

'So the papers say.'

Huggett's face remained unimpressed. 'Company still turned down our pay claim last week, didn't they, Trick?'

'Did.'

'Makes you see why now.' He winked at Pordige. 'Don't it, Trick?'

'Does.'

'Says in the papers,' Pordige went on, 'that she flies like a bird. Bit of an expensive bird, if you ask me!' He gave the foreman a great nudge. 'What d'you say, 'Uggett?'

But before Huggett could answer him, Trickleby burst out with a rush of unaccustomed words, shrill and sharp. 'A million quid can't buy a bird!' The man included them both in a look of evangelical ferocity. 'There ain't a man living can make a bird!' He glared accusingly at Pordige. 'Can you make a bird that can fly in the sky?'

Pordige's honest eyes went wide with astonishment. 'What the God Almighty . . .?' he began, when Huggett whispered to him behind his hand, 'He don't know nothing! Don't take no notice of him!'

Pordige looked at Trickleby's face with an added interest. The man had relapsed now into his usual silence, flicking the cards one by one on the table and studying them closely.

Huggett walked over to the window and looked out into the streaming rain. Lights had suddenly begun one after the other to dart out of the darkness opposite. He looked at his watch. 'Early shift's arrived at the Astroliner hangar,' he said to Pordige. 'You could scrounge a smoke from one of them.'

'But I dunno any of 'em! Wouldn't be right.'

'You know Tompkins, the Inspector.'

'Only seen him once or twice.' A wheedling note crept into the policeman's voice. 'If you'd come over . . . be better. More proper.'

Huggett looked distastefully at the rain.

'It's not far,' Pordige pointed out. 'Only a few yards.'

'All right, all right!' Huggett shrugged his shoulders good-humouredly. 'Got to have a word with Tompkins, anyway.' He stood up and took his mackintosh off a hook behind the door.

'You be all right, Trick?'

An almost beatific smile made an unexpected appearance on the hangar man's face. 'Don't worry about me!'

'Won't be long, Trick.'

'You take your time, Mr. 'Uggett.'

Together with the policeman, the foreman stepped from the office into the hangar. As their steps on the concrete clanged round the enclosed darkness, Pordige remarked, 'Very affable, all of a sudden, your mate.' They walked past the Emperor, leaving her alone and silent, and entered the damp, awakening world outside.

High above them, an aircraft's engines grizzled disconsolately into the rain-filled sky. 'Queer sort of bloke,' Pordige went on. 'What is 'e . . . a Communist?'

Huggett laughed. 'More likely the other way! Bit simple, you know! Bit too religious!'

Pordige steered his big boots round the perimeter of a puddle of black water. 'I'm surprised,' he said lugubriously, 'I'm *very* surprised, at the Company employing a man like that!'

'These days, we take what we can get. He tightens a nut perfectly well. He's not half bad at cleaning out the Elsans and polishing up the skin.'

Pordige nodded his head. 'I get you! I get you!'

They had reached the Astroliner buildings. Huggett pushed the glass-panelled door open and they hurried inside.

There, for a moment, they stood just inside the hangar, wiping the rain from their faces, aware that already the darkness was dissolving. Through a crack in the clouds to the east, the sun was poking its light fingers down low over London to gather up the windflowers, one by one.

Huggett said suddenly, 'But mostly, Trick just makes tea for the boys, and brings it round. Brews up a nice cupper tea, Trick does!'

As they moved together towards the sleepy voices in the Astroliner's maintenance office, Pordige observed profoundly, 'Takes all sorts . . . when you come to think of it . . . takes all sorts to make the wheels go round!'

CHAPTER TWO

For a ten-mile radius, the subdued excitement encircled London Airport like a halo round the moon. Traffic thickened all along the Great West Road, clotted into irritating blockages at the Hounslows, and then flowed swiftly and surely towards the open-mouthed airport gates. Extra guards were on duty. Aviation's aristocrats, the Very Important Persons, were being stood aside for and saluted with highly organised confusion. In the middle of the stream, hemmed in on all sides a dark green car with a long bonnet impatiently tried to edge its way ahead.

Just before the airport, it turned sharp left and shook itself free of all company. But the main sluggish current continued onwards. The Rolls-Royces and the Bentleys slowed down at the first gate – then, recognised by policemen, in swept the managing directors of the Emperor's manufacturers, the members of the Board, foreign experts, business bosses, insurance men, bankers, and among the politicians (but in a modest Hillman, a governmental example to the taxpayers of the economic situation) the Minister himself.

The cars were stopped at the second gate. Technical representatives, the salesmen of the firms who had done the cabin decor, the designers of the feminine elegancies with which the Ladies' Powder Room was so heavily armed, members of the Press, caterers – all showed their pink passes.

The third gate was the public enclosure and everyone was paying sixpence.

But over on the far side of the airport, at ninety degrees to the herd, Bellamy swung the green car on the rough-roaded short cut to Operations through a gap in the hedge, watched only by an old man in hitched-up corduroy trousers who was suppose to be clipping it.

Out of the corner of his right eye, he noticed that the Emperor had already been towed out to the tarmac to stand just beside a dais full of microphones and ciné cameras. Men in overalls swarmed like white ants over her silver surface: coming and going from the cabin: in and out of the cockpit:

up and down from the wing – while florists' girls were arranging hot-house blooms in pots to give the impression she was walking on flowers.

Bellamy transferred his attention to the bleak nakedness of the concrete Operations building, now getting nearer and nearer. Just beyond its double swing-doors, he put on brake and parked. As he was rooting round in the car for his luggage, he saw out of the back window that Captain Cavendish had already materialised, and – very erect and terribly tall – was standing on the steps, waiting for him.

He locked the car up, and humping his bag and brief-case, walked slowly towards the Grand Old Man of Air Enterprise Airways.

Captain Cavendish had entered civil aviation thirty years ago, when a pilot, if not quite a God, was a Number One Superman. Since then, what with the war and the advance of social equality and science, times had changed.

But Captain Cavendish had not.

Rather, as his contemporary airmen left him – a great many killed, others grounded, some intermarrying in spirit with Bellamy's generation of proletarian pilots, trained by tours of military operations – the responsibility seemed to fall even more on his shoulders to maintain the old ways and the old attitude. Immaculate, his brass buttons gleaming like a geometrical constellation against the dark blue heaven of his greatcoat, he was (on the ground, anyway) the symbol of an almost extinct race – a lord-of-the-manor, still solvent after taxation and undaunted by death duties, of vast estates in the sky.

His unblinking eyes watched Bellamy approach, but gave not the slightest sign of recognition. He waited until the younger pilot had come right up to him and had dumped his bag and brief-case, like two offerings, on the ground by his feet. Then – 'Ah, Bellamy!' he said.

'Ah, Cavendish!'

The older pilot frowned at the sound of his naked name. 'You checked everything on the air-test, Captain? Ab-*solutely* everything?'

'Everything, Captain.'

Cavendish paused to scrutinise the Training Captain from top to toe. 'Now, Captain Bellamy,' he said, 'I have been giving some serious thought to this problem of dual command.'

'Captain Cavendish . . . *so have I*.'

'And what I have decided,' Cavendish continued, 'is *this*. We shall share the take-offs and landings between us. You will do the westbound. I will do the eastbound.'

'And while we're airborne?'

'When it's your turn, Captain, you will take the decisions in the air.' He rubbed his chin for a moment reflectively, as though brooding over the wisdom of such generosity. Then he added, as a comfort both to himself and Bellamy, 'After all . . . I will always be available to you in an advisory capacity.'

'Thank you, Captain,' Bellamy said gravely. 'And when it's your turn . . . I will always be available to *you*.'

'Quite, Captain, quite,' Cavendish meticulously flicked a piece of fluff off his great-coat with his long, gloved fingers. 'An admirable arrangement! And now . . . since I see the rest of my crew has arrived . . . shall we stroll over to discover what the meteorological officer has in store for you?'

On the far eastern side of the airport, Lalette Greenacres pushed open the door of the Catering Section and came in with a rush of cold air, the last of the pale sunlight and a little flurry of smiles and apologies. Like a subdued echo behind her, Angela Knight followed her in.

'Oh, we *are* late, Mr. Hamilton!' Lalette rustled forward. Even in her uniform, she seemed to move as though wrapped in silks and laces and taffetas. 'I thought we might be. The traffic – '

'*I* got through the traffic,' Mr. Hamilton said.

'Oh, I *know*.' Lalette beamed up at him. 'We saw you, didn't we, Angela? In your *enormous* Jaguar. Driving like the wind.' She patted her forage cap more firmly on her head and looked up at him with her big blue eyes. 'We thought it was the Minister, at first!'

Not displeased, Mr. Hamilton said, 'Well, it's all done! Food's checked. Bar's signed for. The works!' He swept a hand over his big bony jaw. 'Yes,' he went on, 'that car of mine can certainly move. Where did I pass you?'

'Osterley Park,' Lalette said. 'The driver did his best. But you must have been *here* before we got out of that jam.'

The Chief Steward lit a cigarette and puffed at it contentedly. 'Cars like that certainly don't grow on trees.'

'What *do* they grow on, Mr. Hamilton?' Lalette asked innocently.

It was the 64-dollar question to which all Air Enterprise, mindful of a steward's salary, would have liked to know the answer. But Mr. Hamilton was not to be drawn out. He gave a little smile of secret satisfaction, and then suddenly re-galvanised, stubbed out the half-smoked cigarette into an ash-tray. 'Now's not the time for chitter-chatter. Miss Greenacres! We haven't got all day! Duty calls!'

Angela had gone to the window, and was now looking towards the main airport building. She said, in an almost gratified voice, 'I'd no idea there'd be quite *so* many people.'

Lalette turned, and walked over beside. her 'A bit *too* many.' She stood on tiptoe, craning her neck. '*Many* too many!'

'Well' – Mr. Hamilton came bustling firmly towards his charges – 'they won't have come to see you girls. Now, Miss Knight . . . Miss Greenacres! Transport's been waiting these past twenty minutes!' Like a good sheepdog, he gently propelled them through the door and into the van outside. 'They'll have loaded the stores by now . . . but we have to get the cabin ready.'

As the van slowly wound its way round the perimeter track, Mr. Hamilton went on talking. This had to be done, that had to be done. Sir James liked dinner at eight. When Captain Cavendish was on duty, he insisted on tea *on the hour*, *every hour*. Not just a cup. The pot on a tray, and the cloth better be clean. Captain Bellamy liked his steaks well done, and often had a craving for orange-juice in the early hours. Engineer Officer Rawlings could never be satisfied, and must not be allowed to come poking round the galley. The future Line Manager, Captain Payton, liked a lot of magazines beside him, and as for the Public Relations Officer, Mr. Riley –

They were near the apron now, just passing the crowds that strained against the ropes of the public enclosure. The

Emperor seemed to be a great silver magnet, drawing them all towards her.

'Wonderful publicity man . . . Sir James.' Hamilton eyed the multitude with complacent approval. 'Never seen such interest. You'd think they'd come to see a hanging!'

The van had stopped in front of the carpet. As they got out, Lalette whispered, 'Makes you feel that your slip's showing,' and the two girls self-consciously followed Hamilton up the red road to where the Emperor stood waiting for them among its banks of flowers – an oasis in the grey desert of the tarmac. 'Lovely flowers,' she went on, keeping her eyes away from the sea of faces. 'Just like a wedding!'

It felt strange to be walking across the carpet, to feel people stop talking in order to stare. The aircraft, now that they were beside it, curved up and away from them, looking like a primitive monster idol laden with gifts of propitiation; but one that might, at any moment, lift a huge emu-like leg, or blow fire and smoke through its wide nostrils and hurl them and their gifts and their flowers to the self-same destruction.

Mr. Hamilton stopped at the steps and politely allowed the girls to precede him. As their shoes clanked against the metal stairs, they were conscious that hundreds of pairs of eyes, tired of waiting for the big brass to make an appearance and start the ball rolling, were watching them closely.

Inside the cabin, it was warm. There was a smell of newness and disinfectant and now the sweet scent of fruit from the galley. The aisle carpet was a thick velvety pink, the seats bright red, and the inside of the fuselage was quilted and tinted the same colour as the carpet.

'I said from the beginning it looks like a boudoir,' Mr. Hamilton said and sniffed. 'Bit too fancy, if you ask me!' He walked up and down the aisle a time or two, as though to get the feel of it. 'This carpet'll get trodden down in no time.' He put a pink linen head-rest cover straight, tested the comfort of the Chairman's seat, and checked that it was unobscured by too much of the wing. 'Miss Greenacres, you stack the stuff in the galley! Miss Knight, get the folders out and the cotton wool and the sweets! *With* the paper bags! And see the books and magazines are ready! No watching the ceremony till the work's done!'

He peered out of one of the portholes at the dais and microphones. 'We'll get a grand-stand view from inside here. Best seats in the house . . . and all with the compliments of the management!'

'*East*, Captain Cavendish,' said Bellamy.

'*North*, Captain Bellamy.'

There was a moment's silence while the forecaster nervously fingered his tie. 'It's a difficult situation,' he said. 'What with bad radio conditions and so few reports, it's impossible to forecast accurately *which* way this Low will move.'

He put his finger on the trouble. Drawn on the chart of the forecast folder, a big depression covered most of the central Atlantic. Through his thick spectacles, he looked first at Cavendish on his left, then at Bellamy on his right. 'I only wish we could be more help.'

Sandwiched between them, he did his best with the deadlock. 'Perhaps north-east – ' he was suggesting mildly, when Cavendish interrupted: 'I have seen this sort of weather before.' He paused. '*Many* times.'

'Then you've been unlucky.'

'When you've flown the Atlantic as long as I have, Captain, *luck* doesn't come into it.'

'At present it does.'

'I tell you it doesn't!'

'Until forecasting's a hundred per cent . . . it's bound to.'

'Look at the temperature at Weather Ship Charlie!'

'I've looked at it.'

'There's your clue, Captain. The warm air is moving north, so we may expect – '

Bellamy said softly, 'Let's cut out the meteorological lecture, Captain.'

Over the head of the forecaster, Cavendish glowered down at him. He was not used to this sort of treatment. He was beginning to regret his generosity over the question of command. Turning to the forecaster, he demanded, 'What's the head component on the Great Circle?'

The Great Circle is the shortest track across the earth's curved surface.

'Well . . . we *estimate* minus 55 knots at 24,000 feet.'

'There you are, you see!' Cavendish transferred his attention to the now silent Bellamy. 'With strong winds like that . . . we shall have to do a composite to latitude 58 North.'

A composite is in effect a huge dog-leg – a kind of tacking to avoid flying into the teeth of the wind.

Bellamy said, 'Those winds might be a good deal stronger.'

'Unlikely, Captain.'

'And *much* stronger on a composite.'

'Captain Bellamy!' The enormous dignity of the older pilot had been unnecessarily ruffled. He pulled irritably at his iron-grey moustache. 'You've done nothing but contradict me ever since we came into this office!'

'And you've done nothing but contradict *me*.'

'I happen to have . . . *rather more experience* – '

'Not on Emperors.'

'One aircraft is very much like another to the Atlantic.'

'Not when we're flying so high.'

'We have more fuel . . . a greater range – '

'Not when we lose so much more than piston-engined aircraft by descending lower.'

The forecaster shuffled his feet uncomfortably. More used to being at the receiving end of digs and punches from know-all pilots, his present neutrality seemed strange. It occurred to him that they might get further towards New York if they used their energy in fighting the elements instead of wasting it on each other. He glanced behind him sympathetically at the two shadows, the First Officer and the navigator, who waited, just as silently as the unknown Atlantic three hundred miles away, for their commanders to make up their minds. Then, as though to try a new topic on which perhaps agreement could be reached, he turned over the pages of the forecast folder and said, 'Shall we take a look at the other side?'

Both pilots examined the forecast map of surface conditions. A blue and red line – meaning an occlusion of warm and cold fronts – trailed all the way down the Canadian eastern seaboard. Goose, Gander and the Maritime airports, so useful in an emergency, were all border-line to out.

The met man said apologetically, 'That's not very good either, I'm afraid.'

Cavendish cleared his throat. 'They've been too pessimistic over Gander . . . as usual.'

Bellamy said nothing.

'And New York! At least New York's good.'

'Too good,' Bellamy murmured, thinking specifically of the fog that a clear, cold calm so often produces in the early hours.

'The trouble with you younger pilots, Bellamy, is that you're never satisfied.' Cavendish gave a cluck of impatience. 'Well . . . that's that!' He turned to Douthwaite behind him. 'You've got that straight for the flight plan? A composite up to 58 North?'

'Yes, Captain.'

Cavendish was just saying, 'Now for alternates, we'll use – ' when Bellamy cut in, 'I believe I'm in command on this leg?'

Surprised and put out, Cavendish drew himself up to his full height. 'I was just telling Mr. Douthwaite, Bellamy, what we'd *already* decided to – '

'*We've* decided nothing.'

'Then perhaps we can decide something' – Cavendish opened his eyes very wide – '*now*.'

'I have already decided.'

'A composite, no doubt, Captain?'

'A Great Circle.' He turned to the navigator. 'Got that?'

'Yes, Captain'

Cavendish's face went almost white. 'In my advisory capacity, I most strongly recommend – '

'I heard your recommendation, Captain Cavendish.'

'And yet you're not acting on it?'

Bellamy shook his head. 'I've got to fly this leg. Not you.'

'On the contrary, Captain, we shall *all* be flying this leg.'

'Shall I put it, then – that it'll be *my* responsibility?'

Cavendish shrugged his shoulders. 'You can put it that way . . . if you want to. You've had my interpretation. You've had my advice. Now' – he started to fit his fingers into his gloves – always with Cavendish a signal of adieu – 'is there anything else we want to grumble to the forecaster about?'

'That's the lot.'

'In that case,' Captain Cavendish was leading in the walk to the door, 'perhaps *we* could proceed to Operations to make up *your* Great Circle flight plan.'

Just before he went out, Cavendish turned towards the forecaster and nodded 'Thank you.'

Bellamy wished him, 'Good afternoon.'

Then, followed by Douthwaite and Seawood, they walked out into the corridor together. The meteorological officer watched them go. He smiled timidly at their broad blue backs.

'Have a good trip, Captains,' he said.

When the three catering crew had finished, the Emperor's passenger cabin looked like a schoolroom awaiting a group of scholars. The chairs, identical and dead in line, had each in front of them a small folding table, and they all dutifully faced the square board on which from time to time (in coloured lights instead of chalk) their master would write varied instructions. Each seat had a sheaf of papers and pamphlets of geographical and aeronautical information, a card to write their comments on, and a complimentary Company pencil. There was a little air sickness bag in case they weren't quite up to the weather, a button marked *Steward* to press when they felt like it, and underneath (discreetly out of sight) a saffron-coloured life-jacket.

But despite the examination they were about to sit (or maybe because of it) the pupils and their friends were playing high carnival in the playground outside.

'If you come over here, Miss Greenacres,' Hamilton said, 'you'll be able to see very well. And as you're a bit taller, Miss Knight . . . you stand a little behind.'

Pressing her face against the porthole, Lalette watched the procession of important people, headed by Sir James and the Minister, slowly cross the carpet and mount the dais.

As the first two stepped on the platform, their feet seemed to set off a specially prepared cheer bomb that sent the dais and its surrounds and the public enclosure up in one great burst of sound. Sir James smiled deprecatingly at the Minister to emphasise the power of public enthusiasm. The newsreel camera-man got busy and the B.B.C. interviewer moved his microphone nearer. A small girl, her little fat limbs the colour of liver sausages in the chilly wind, wavered across the carpet and presented the Minister with a buttonhole.

'The Chairman's niece,' Hamilton said. 'Nice little kid.

Should have longer socks on than that! Mrs. Hamilton never let's ours wear short ones until June.'

Repeatedly, the Chairman had to hold up his hands for silence. After bowing to the Minister, he eventually started his speech. '... and fellow air-minded citizens of this great enterprising country, there never was a time when any enterprise that conquered any element was not dear to the hearts of Englishmen. And today, as generations of your forefathers have done since time immemorial, you have come to wish yet another enterprise Godspeed.

'You all know the Emperor ... the masculine majesty of her name, the muscular beauty of her powerful lines. You have come, I think, to regard her ... as I do ... as a *symbol* of new discoveries, new conquests that await us in the vast domain above our heads, the three-dimensional continent of the sky. The British designed her. The British built her. The British will fly her. But' – and he shielded his eyes with his stout right hand, as though the vision in front of them was blinding bright – 'the *World* will be our passengers.'

Sir James paused to let the cheering die down before going on, 'Within a few more minutes, you will be waving us goodbye. You will think of us in your hearts tonight. And tomorrow, all of you will be reading of us. For we shall have crossed the Atlantic in the first prop-jet aircraft, prototype of many more to come, inaugurating the first *scheduled* non-stop London-New York service. And this trip will be more than a trial. For although only a few technical passengers and myself will be accompanying the crew, it has been my wish to share with other business enterprises the splendid prestige of this historic flight, and the Emperor's holds are filled to capacity with twelve tons of British goods, newly designed to capture the vitally important American market.'

He stopped. He looked at the waiting faces. Then he said, almost in a whisper, 'And who has made this possible?'

The Minister prepared a deprecating smile to fit his thin face. But it was not, after all, required. Sir James drew a deep breath. He waved at the public enclosure.

'You,' he said softly. '*You* have made it possible. You have backed this enterprise ... with your interest, your pennies and your pounds. You have shown you have faith in us. And we shall not let you down. If other airlines can't be run economically, Air Enterprise will show them how it's done.'

Mindful of the listening ears of the nationalised companies, the Minister stirred uncomfortably. But by now, Sir James – buoyed up by his own words and driven by the emotion in his heart – had been carried away well beyond the pale. 'If other airlines can't keep to schedule, I'll promise you we'll come in and out like clockwork.'

The Chairman swung himself back and forward on his heels, conscious that the crowd were with him. 'It used to be said . . . a horried little jingle . . . if you've time to spare, go by air. Now I say to you: *Don't mind the Met, go by jet.*'

Inside the aircraft, Hamilton swept his fingers over his jaw. 'Very fine talker, Sir James! Now here's Captain Cavendish He's taking off his gloves. He's going to say something.'

Cavendish had withdrawn from the Flight Planning early in order to make this appearance before his public. Recognising him, they gave him a cheer. He spoke very briefly, but with immense dignity about 'this honour, this climax to my long career'. The crowd cheered again as he replaced his gloves, and walked across the dais to stand at Sir James' right hand.

Mr. Hamilton leaned forward. 'It's all over bar the shouting, *I* would say.' He pursed his mouth. 'Well!' He sighed and stretched. 'That was a short speech of the Minister's.'

'Didn't even know he'd started,' Angela murmured.

'And well you might not, either,' Hamilton said. 'Over before it began. There they go!' He peered down. 'Leaving already!'

The Minister was stepping down from the dais, bracketed behind by Sir James' hospitable arm and accompanied by Captain Cavendish. As they went, the long line of airport officials jerked into life. Five pink heads bounced gently up and down like small balloons on a warm breeze across the few paces to the edge of the carpet and the waiting cars. Just in time, as the Minister reached his Hillman, the line reformed. There were handshakes, so well timed, so similar, that it looked as though the same pink communal hand had been passed from one to the other all the way down the line.

Hamilton got up and smoothed the sleeves of his jacket. 'Now for business,' he said.

Down below, the B.B.C. man looked round. Like a long, black mother-snake with millions of eager ears to feed, the microphone looked too. They seemed suddenly to have been left very much on their own. Then slowly across the tarmac came the blunt-nosed crew car from Operations.

'Ah,' said the commentator with relief into the microphone. 'Here come the rest of Captain Cavendish's crew! In less than twelve hours, they will be standing on American soil. There's that air of quiet confidence about them . . . almost, one would say, nonchalance. To them, of course, this is nothing but a job of work. I'll just ask the relief captain if he has time to say a few words to you . . . '

Bellamy was climbing the third rung of the crew steps. The Great Circle to New York with the fuel available had, after all, worked out. But only just. It had meant using Boston and Washington as alternate airfields, both of which were so close they might well be affected by exactly the same weather, if New York suddenly started to deteriorate. And he didn't like that front along the Maritimes. And as for that huge Low at 35 West –

He felt someone tugging at his leg, and looking down saw it was Seawood. 'They want you at the mike, Skipper.'

Bellamy swore under his breath, climbed down and walked up the dais to the microphone.

'And your name, Captain, is . . . is . . . is – ' The commentator hurriedly scanned the briefing notes he'd been given.

'Bellamy.'

'Of course . . . of course! Captain Bellamy,' the commentator explained into the microphone, 'will be standing by to give Captain Cavendish a helping hand when he's tired.'

Bellamy stood stock still, looking at him.

'And what sort of a trip does it look like from the weather point of view, Captain?'

Bellamy opened up the met folder, ran his tongue over his lips, and seemed just on the point of speaking at some length. But the commentator interrupted. His training had taught him to recognise a subject likely to strike a wrong note on a programme. Most people obliged by saying the words he more or less put into their mouths: but sometimes you got a man with a mulish attitude, and then you had to be careful.

The commentator said hastily, 'The Captain's opened his folder for me. I can see there's going to be a few showers . . . a bit of rain. But I don't suppose little things like that will worry the Emperor. Thank you, Captain Bellamy, thank you.' He gave a great big smile as an indication that the interview was over, 'I expect you'll be wanting to start your engines, Captain?'

Bellamy said 'Yes,' left the microphone, and finding the crew steps had been removed joined his passengers who were now clustering round the main gangway, preparing to embark.

There were still a few minutes to wait before the engines could be started.

The commentator was left alone again. Rather nervously, he told the listening millions that the day was nearly over, and filled in the sudden silence that now hung expectantly over the Emperor by describing the shadows of the evening that stole across the sky.

The life was going quickly from the late afternoon.

Already at the farther side of the airport, the white mist was softening the hard lines of the hangars, waiting until the sun finally disappeared to roll across the grass between the runways, and blur the lights and cover the bare spaces with a thin, deceptive layer of fog.

The band still playing in the public enclosure and the constant rise and swell of roaring engines could not quite dispel the essential sadness of an airfield. Somewhere in the flat lonely spaces, in the wide patiently waiting arms of the runways, in the sight of an aeroplane rising majestically to become little by little a small silent speck, and then nothing in the sky, was a melancholy in keeping with the time of day. A time of day unkindly to airmen. A time when the indefinite light obscured distances, slightly altered the shape of objects, made heights difficult to judge, and gave a feeling of nervousness and insecurity. A time when at home the curtains would be drawn, the fire stirred into a blaze, and the tea-trolley with its muffin dish and its home-made chocolate cake would be wheeled within a hand's reach.

Standing very straight at the top of the steps, Lalette had a wonderful view of the seven embarking passengers. First the top of their heads, then their faces, then the whole of them. She looked down at a grey trilby, the brim of which came gradually upwards to reveal a red face with a rather saggy chin.

'Good afternoon, Captain Payton,' she said. 'Your seat is thirty-four, fourth down on the right.'

'Thank you, Miss . . . er – ' She remembered he always made a point of not knowing the names of the catering crew.

'Greenacres, sir,' she said brightly, as he handed her his coat and moved on down the cabin where Hamilton was settling people into their seats. In a spare moment, he came back to lean confidentially towards Lalette. 'Don't forget about Mr. Brocklehurst, will you? Here he is now.'

Lalette looked up. 'What about him? The V.I.P. treatment, you mean? There's a note about it here.' She held up her square board with its papers pinned to it.

'That's right! But' – said Hamilton, not to be done out ot his piece – ' what it *doesn't* say there is this – ' He paused. 'They say he has the Minister's ear.'

A gleam of humour momentarily sparkled in the deceptively clear blue eyes, but she extinguished it before it disturbed the set composure of her mouth. She glanced back at the other passengers, whose names did *not* appear on her board. Mr. Riley, the Public Relations Officer, now staring nostalgically out of his porthole at the world he had just left. Several seats before him, the airframe designer, Mr. Eastlake, was looking around the cabin with satisfaction. He was the clever, younger generation scientist who likes to look as little like a man with a brain as possible. Catching her eye, he smiled.

And away on the other side of the aisle, as if to draw attention to the cleavage, which the grapevine described as enormous between them, sat Mr. Cruttwell, the designer of the Emperor's engines. With his high domed head, his pale, dried-up mouth, he looked like men's wisdom through the ages.

Hamilton stopped beside her again. 'Time the doctor was here!' He peered beyond her, down the steps to the jumble of heads on the tarmac. 'There he is, now! There he is! In the black homburg.'

The Company's director of medical services detached himself from the group of well-wishers and came slowly up the steps. Dressed from head to foot in black, with a footfall as quiet as a sleeping patient's pulse, he looked like a diplomat spy making away with the plans of the fortifications. The only colour was in his face, in the reddish cheeks, the thick pointed eyebrows like sun-filled corn stukes, and the eyes, pale and round and murky green as goldfish bowls.

'Good afternoon, Dr. Enderby-Browne,' Lalette said, and smiled. 'Your seat is number eighteen. Yes, that's right! Seventh down on the left.'

Hamilton came forward and took his hat, and showed him to his seat. He refused to be parted from the heavy black leather brief-case, but he allowed Hamilton to take away the black overcoat with its old-world velvet collar, revealing, like a black onion, a lounge suit of the same colour and the same masterly tailoring underneath.

'Getting near!' Hamilton looked at his watch. The only excitement he showed was to sweep his fingers over his big, bony chin. 'We'll be bang on time. Just you see! Sir James is coming on board now.'

Lalette saw Angela, still standing on the tarmac by the steps, tuck a stray lock of hair under her cap and give a little nervous tossing of her head. Looking down, she watched the Chairman climb. First, his impressive iron-grey head, from this unfair vantage point thinning visibly in a circle at the top, as though even in his present worldly state, he had yet been set aside for the tonsure. Then the forehead (even larger from here than in his pictures) and his eyes, exaggerated by the angle of her vision, so they seemed to look out of little blown-out bags of crumpled jewellers' tissue paper. Half way up the stairs, he paused and turned. All the uniformed company staff were at the salute. Everyone else cheered. He waved in acknowledgment and then put up his thumb. He paused for a moment like that to allow the cameras a steady shot. Then he turned and walked slowly into the cabin.

'Good afternoon, Sir James,' Lalette said reverently, her voice trembling with nervousness.

'Good afternoon, Sir James,' Hamilton bowed low, taking the Chairman's hat and coat with exaggerated care.

'Thank you, Miss Greenacres,' the Chairman smiled. 'Thank you, Hamilton.'

Surprised that he knew their names, Lalette smiled back, but the Chairman was already hurrying towards Mr. Brocklehurst.

'Well, that's that!' Angela pattered quickly on high-heeled shoes up the steps. The doors were closed. Angela's face was pale, her laugh high and nervous. 'We're off,' she said breathlessly.

Lalette nodded. Now that the doors were fastened, and the cabin had become an airtight shell, she felt as though she had been clamped inside a giant oyster. The engines started up one by one. She looked out of the window, and watched the chocks being pulled away. The officials and the ground staff stepped back as though now they were washing their hands of the whole enterprise. For half a mile back, the slipstream bent over the short winter-browned grass, and sent pieces of paper and clouds of dust jumping and scurrying away out of sight.

The engines sounded slightly different from the ones she was used to. Instead of the angry rough shout, the clattering and banging, the noise stopping and starting and falling over itself like a toppling wave, these had, somehow, under their deep bass drone, a weird banshee wail. It made her think of rain-filled clouds that marched endlessly from a blurred distant point where the sea and sky became one troubled mass, of failures and emergencies, of fear and trouble. Even the lack of vibration seemed unmasculine and suspect. For the first time today, although briefly, she was afraid.

Then she rubbed up her buttons with the sleeve of her jacket, adjusted the angle of her forage cap, and walked up the aisle and through the door to the flight deck.

In the cockpit of the Emperor, she reported to Bellamy in what she hoped was a most military manner: 'Passengers strapped in and rear door shut, sir!'

CHAPTER THREE

THEY took off to the west, into a green horizon. It was as though, now the light was dying under the rain-filled clouds, the colour of the darkening fields had run into the sky, making it luminous as wet grass. Gradually, while the Emperor climbed, the countryside below became faint and faded. The green air thinned to the width of a sword-blade that had just sliced clean the base of the heavy cumulus above it, and then suddenly was itself smashed to atoms, glowing round the wispy edges of grey vapour – bright bits of lime-colour that grew smaller and smaller until they were stamped out into nothing by the cold blackness of continuous cloud.

'Prop anti-icers on,' Bellamy said. On the right hand side of the cockpit, a switch clicked down to send alcohol over the airscrews. Shuddering a little in a bumpy element, the Emperor hauled herself blindly upwards. Rain rattled against the wind-screens. The airspeed indicator read 190 knots. The hands on the altimeter followed each other slowly round the clock. The course on the compass held steady at 295°. But there was no change outside, no evidence of movement, no alteration. The same black air was the only view from the windows.

Nobody said anything. Even in the passenger compartment there was complete quiet. As always on the climb to cruising altitude, everyone seemed to be waiting. This was a no-man's-land forty minutes – in the lift between their existence on the ground and a life that awaited them at 24,000 feet. The light blazed on the strawberry-red upholstery of the many empty places. A daffodil that Riley had plucked from the flower banks before coming on board and had planted in the join between the two rear seats, now the sole survivor of the reception left behind them, jiggled its soundless bell every time the Emperor heaved and swung in the uneven air. Now and again, the hydraulic pump let out a wail like a female foghorn, as though to hark all attention back to the invisible depths of this wet world that licked at the portholes.

Sir James, seeing Brocklehurst beside him look round every time the pump sounded, finally said, 'It's the boosters.'

'Oh?'

'There is no antiquated wire and pulley arrangement for operating the flying controls on *this* aeroplane.' Sir James pursed his lips with pride. 'Too big, you see. So, in common with other aircraft – but in much greater detail – hydraulic cylinders activated by the pilot's control column do all the pushing and pulling of the rudders and ailerons and elevators.'

'Oh?'

'Even the emergency system has to be hydraulic. A pilot would find it *very difficult* to move the controls manually.'

'We live, do we not, Sir James,' Brocklehurst observed, 'in a highly mechanised world where man's strength is gradually being superseded – '

'Look at that!' The Chairman leant right across the Under-Secretary to point a well-padded finger at the new scenery outside. The Emperor's nose had pierced through the layer cloud. Now flying in undiluted air, she was still going up, but higher still, surrounding her on all sides, gigantic heads of cumulus had butted through the stratus, looking like the mushroom explosions from a pattern of hydrogen bombs, dropped from outer space, that had straddled across her path.

'Very beautiful, Sir James,' Brocklehurst said, ever mindful of the brief war-time career in the R.A.F. that had given him his only flying experience. 'Reminds me of looking back on the target, one time we bombed Wilhelmshaven, just at dusk.'

Watching the near misses around them, they both stared over the plump engines and the curved wing, out at the gathering darkness beyond. Then the Chairman put his hands in his pockets and leaned back. The seats were quite definitely comfortable, but he had his doubts about the fabric. He had a mind to let his cousin, who was a heavy woollen manufacturer, give it a look-over. It was smart enough, looked really quite plushy, but he'd bet anyone a pound to a penny that it wouldn't wear.

Sitting like that, his head tilted back, he could get an off-the-record look at Brocklehurst. When his face wasn't split open in a frank, clean-toothed smile, or composed into an I-follow-you-through-all-these-arguments-and-I-sympathise-more-than-I-dare-say look of the junior politician, it sagged badly, just where, Sir James sighed, it should most burgeon out into bone and muscle and tensity. The hair at the back of his neck was also an unpleasing sight. It grew in an anomaly of soft, brown hen's feathers unexpectedly sprouting from the red-grained skin of a turkey.

Sir James closed his eyes. The engines filled his ears with a strong sustained sweetness, his nose drew in the smell of new leather and polish and expensive cigarettes, all mixed and compressed in the cabin to a good strong masculine odour. This flight was going to be a piece of cake, he told himself again and again. After all his careful planning there wouldn't be anything to it. He toyed with a few points for his quarterly message to the staff; mastery of the air, conquering the weather, nothing impossible to determination and efficiency. Inspired by the forward thrust of the airscrews, together with the power of his own thoughts, his lower lip cupped its partner and his jaw visibly pushed behind all seventy tons of mighty machine.

Under the sanctuary of his lowered lids he went over what release he should make to the press. From there it was just a short jump to salaries, from salaries to finances. His mind was filled with intersecting patterns of figures, like coloured pieces of an intricate mosaic – but moving, not static, and each movement setting off countless others, which absorbed and excited him. Deep in his favourite contemplation, a small smile relaxed his face.

Then suddenly, a frown drew together the strong brows but his eyes remained tight shut. His nose the first to give warning, continued an independent investigation. It breathed in the air more often than it needed. It twitched pleasantly. He opened his eyes, and they were similarly delighted.

'A magazine, sir?'

The Chairman allowed his ears this small share of the pleasure. Miss Greenacres, his nose told him, was a walking advertisement for the bottles and jars so lavishly contained in the Ladies' Powder Room. Nevertheless, as a change of scene from Brocklehurst, she was invaluable.

He pulled himself up with the little groan of protest allowed to the middle-aged and successful. He looked her up and down frankly. Their eyes, like two advance posts of opposing armies, crossed each other as she also completed her equally frank and undisguised survey.

'Thank you, Miss Greenacres.'

He smiled. Nevertheless he made a small mental note to see Miss Carey, their Lady Personnel Officer, about the qualifications the Selection Board were on the look-out for in choosing their flying catering staff. Efficiency and utility must, he felt, take priority on the list. Nubile stewardesses, isolated for anything up to two weeks with young men were apt to represent a debit to the Comapny by leaving to get married almost as soon as they had completed their expensive training. But he could still congratulate the Catering Officer on providing for this flight sufficient prettiness to distract his tired eyes.

'What have you got there?' He looked at the pile in the stewardess's hands. '*The Economist*, I think.'

Brocklehurst chose the evening paper in order to look for his name in it. They both sat there, silently reading, no longer concerned with the turbulent air outside.

The aircraft was, in any case, riding more smoothly now. Bellamy was doing his best to avoid the clouds. As he climbed, he banked away from them, making the Emperor run the gauntlet, weaving and turning between the bursts. But sometimes in this half-light haze that still filmed over the stars, a cumulus loomed up out of nowhere and snatched at her wing, tipping it up and making the metal shiver, the engines thump in their mountings, and the whole fuselage shake from an impact like bomb-blast, as the Emperor shied away.

'Turbulent north-westerly air-stream,' was the way Bellamy described the phenomenon to Seawood. 'Damn difficult to see the things. Let me know if you spot another.'

Screwing up their eyes, they both peered out of their windscreens. But the cloud-tops were fewer now. The altimeter was reading 21,000 feet and there was clear darkness ahead. Somebody suddenly switched on Orion, low down in the southern horizon; then the Pleiades; Deneb and the glittering Arcturus; the Plough; Sirius; Aldebaran; and the smudge of the Milky Way. When they reached cruising altitude, five minutes later, all the stars were already there to meet them.

Level, her speed building up rapidly, high in the clear, the Emperor's dark shape decked out from nose to tail with glittering lights moved boldly westwards towards her first rendezvous with North Atlantic air.

'No moon!' Rawlings grumbled to Hooper as he throttled back the engines to cruising power. 'Black as the ace of spades outside!'

Back in the cabin, Sir James put away *The Economist* and boomed out to Brocklehurst, 'Enjoying yourself?'

The Under-Secretary would have wished that the Chairman had not sounded quite so like an uncle to a favourite nephew he'd taken out on a treat from school. But he fished around for the party political smile and adjusted it precisely over his rather angular face. 'Very much, Sir James.'

He had not wanted to come. It had been the Minister who had suggested it, on the grounds that his appearance on the passenger list would give the lie to the too-often-spoken rumours that the Ministry was hand-in-glove with the nationalised airline corporations. He had been even less keen when the Minister had hinted that this private enterprise Emperor would inevitably follow the same primrose path that had already been blazed by other British long-range airliners designed since the war. But a man had a duty to do; and if ever he was to succeed in the party, he jolly well had to do it.

'Will you have a' – for a moment, Brocklehurst had a vision of being about to be offered ice cake, milk or a chocolate ice-cream – 'sherry?'

'I think sherry would slip down very nicely.' He had rather a dry, old-fashioned way of speaking, as though he kept in his mouth, instead of a tongue, a whole collection of china ornaments, all badly in need of dusting. The interior of the cabin, designed with the modern emphasis on psychological colours to promote warmth and cheerfulness to its occupants, could do little with Brocklehurst's black and white pin-stripe suit.

Miss Knight was standing attentively beside them. 'Two sherries, please,' the Chairman said, and then seeing Payton across the aisle glancing expectantly towards him, corrected himself with, 'Make it three.'

The future Line Manager slid as near to the other two as he could. This would be the time to talk of schedules and operating costs, of delivery dates and training programmes. Above all, of future plans for the organisation of the Line.

Behind them, the other passengers gingerly took a taste of

these first few minutes of the eleven-hour span they would be at this altitude. It didn't seem too bad. Newspapers and magazines remained the same as they had been on the ground. The daffodil was now quite still. Below their feet, the floor was rock-steady. Right at the back, Riley pulled the pink curtain over the black sky and the stars and asked Lalette for whisky. From the galley floated the smell of dinner, as Hamilton bent over the enamelled electric stove.

Everybody followed Sir James' example and relaxed completely. They watched the three pieces of high brass up at the front take their sherries, and heard the Chairman say, 'Smooth.'

'*Very* smooth,' Payton put in quickly. 'You'll notice no vibration on the Emperor, Mr. Brocklehurst.'

'No?' The Under-Secretary was busy studying the continuous waves of brown sherry that lapped against the side of his glass. From somewhere in the background, perhaps from the cabin, perhaps from outside, came a thudding uneven whine. 'Is that the hydraulic pump again, Sir James?'

His sherry glass half-way up to his lips, the Chairman said, 'I can't hear anything, dear fellow.'

Payton said decisively, 'I can't hear anything either, Sir James.'

Thud-thud-*whee*. Thud-thud-*whee*.

'Just a bit of wax, singing in your ears after the pressure change on the climb, Brocklehurst. Take a deep breath . . . and *swallow*!'

But three rows further back, the same noise interrupted Eastlake, as he sat reading a detective novel. Black hair was sleeked over his high forehead as though purposely to hide it. The brown check suit and the yellow waistcoat suggested the horsy set rather than the Chief Designer's office.

He lifted his eyes from the pages and listened. Then he bent down and put his hand against the metal skirting board over the heating system. At the tips of his fingers, he felt the tingling of vibration.

He glanced across at Cruttwell. The engine designer was shifting uneasily in his seat, trying to get as good a view of the starboard outer engine as he could.

Eastlake called across the aisle, 'Cruttwell!'

The other designer turned his head and regarded him coldly, 'Yes?'

Very slowly, Eastlake lifted his thin, dapper body off the seat, and walked over to Cruttwell. In a low voice, he said, 'Something up, eh?'

'I don't think so.'

'Awful lot of vibration.'

'I can't feel it.'

Eastlake looked disappointed. 'Bit better now. But it was coming from Number Four.'

Thud-thud-*whee.*

'Awful,' he went on, 'if we had to return to London . . . after that send-off!'

Cruttwell said nothing. A few more wrinkles had tagged on to his already wizened skin.

A smile was now twisting up the corners of Eastlake's narrow lips. 'Bit longer on the test-bed. That's what your engines needed!'

A goaded look had come into Cruttwell's anxious eyes. He was a patient man. Normally a timid one, too. But Eastlake had an uncanny facility for getting under his skin. 'They're only out of synchronisation,' he said, in an unusual burst of nervous irritation. 'This flight engineer we've got on board . . . he's as bad as those half-wits in the hangars!'

'Isn't there only a small reduction of r.p.m. from climb power to cruise?'

Cruttwell said abruptly, 'Very small!'

One of the engines suddenly raced away into a powerful high-pitched scream. Then it died just as quietly away into a muffled beat of drums that gradually disintegrated into a half-hearted flappy thumping.

Cruttwell got up. 'I think I'll go forward to see what he's up to.'

The smile on Eastlake's face had widened. 'I think perhaps you'll *have* to.'

As Cruttwell passed the threesome on his way to the front, the Chairman called out, 'Has someone just sat on the propellor switches, Mr. Cruttwell?'

He replied politely, 'I don't know, sir.' He knocked on the

door of the flight deck, and slipped on past the rest-compartment, where Captain Cavendish sat, perfectly unmoved, reading the *Evening News*.

Just at the entrance to the cockpit, he heard Bellamy say to the engineer in a voice full of exasperation, 'You haven't got the damned things synchronised *yet*.'

'Perhaps I could help, Captain.'

The pilot turned in his seat. 'Oh . . . it's you, Mr. Cruttwell. Yes, I wish you would.'

Rawlings sat in front of his fifty-six dials, beads of sweat already glistening on his forehead, his huge fingers tripping over themselves on the throttles and the switches, like an organist eager to catch up with a hymn that an enthusiastic congregation was running away with.

'These damn switches!' he was saying, as the R.P.M. indicator on Number Four again sagged back too far. He glowered at them. Dainty little things, very artistically designed, more suitable for the lights in the Ladies' Powder Room than for the split-second movement up and down to control the pitch of the propellors.

Cruttwell suggested, 'It's Number Four, isn't it?'

'I know! I've got eyes, too!' The engineer was hotter than ever. 'What I'd like to know is why there isn't automatic synchronisation on board.'

'No need for it,' Cruttwell said, rising to the defence. 'Enough complication on the panel *now* without adding to it unnecessarily.'

'And these switches!'

'Ah, there I agree with you. I told Mr. Eastlake more than once that his idea of uniform switches throughout – '

Bellamy cut abruptly into this designing discussion with, 'I can still hear Number Four.'

Cruttwell said to Rawlings, 'I wonder, could I . . . for a moment?' The huge blue-covered shoulders grudgingly shifted to one side. The engine designer, bird-like, turned his egg-shaped head perched on its skinny neck, slightly to one side. He listened, while his hairless hand touched the switches as though they were white hot. Then he said, 'I think . . . I think that's it, isn't it?'

Everyone on the flight deck listened. The sound of the

motors now was sweet and even. Bellamy flashed his torch over the two propellors on the right, and watched the shadow of their blades march exactly in step like twin sentries on parade. 'That's it,' he said.

Feeling he had been shown up, Rawlings' face reverted to the bleakness of a red sand-stone moor as he frowned at Cruttwell, and received in return a nervous beam back through the thick spectacles.

The rest of the flight deck relaxed back into routine. Bellamy was just suggesting to Seawood that a cup of tea mightn't be a bad idea if he wouldn't mind pressing the bell, when a gruff voice spoke from the back of the cockpit.

It was Captain Cavendish.

The *Evening News* was finished, consumed. Now he stood, framed in the doorway to the rest-compartment. There was so much of him that his head had to hang forward over his chest, as though he had lowered it to charge them. His grey eyes, at full travel upwards in their sockets, regarded the scene in front of them – Cruttwell, Bellamy, the rest of the crew against a background of the clear black night – with evident disapproval.

'We took a long time to get those propellors sorted out, didn't we, Captain Bellamy?'

'Yes, we did, Captain Cavendish.'

Cavendish started to adjust his gloves on his hands, and took his cap off its present position on the top of the spare radio transmitter. 'Now everything has at last settled down . . . I shall go aft to talk to the passengers.'

'Tell them it was just synchronisation trouble, will you?'

The head had to bend even further forward so that the uniform cap could crown it. 'I shall certainly apologise to the Chairman, Captain.'

'Thank you, Captain.'

The head followed the shoulders in a dignified backward withdrawal into the rest compartment, and then the whole big body of Captain Cavendish turned a hundred and eighty degrees towards the rear of the aeroplane. He entered the passenger cabin very slowly. He could stand up quite straight now, and he made the very best use of the opportunity.

He took the glove off his right hand, so that there it was

ready, unpeeled, waiting, to consummate his introduction to the Under-Secretary of State. 'Good evening, Sir James,' he said.

'Ah, good evening, Captain Cavendish.' Here was his prize exhibit, and the Chairman presented it with pride. 'I don't think you've met Mr. Brocklehurst.'

'I have not had that honour.'

'Of course, I've heard a great deal about you, Captain.'

The meeting was thus effected with mutual satisfaction. 'That noise you heard just now,' Cavendish said. 'I must apologise – '

'Somebody sat on the R.P.M. switches, eh, Captain?' the Chairman said again, and the pilot joined in the general forgiving laughter. 'Something like that,' he said.

'Smooth now,' said Sir James.

'*Very* smooth,' said Payton.

'And a beautiful take-off, Captain,' Brocklehurst put in, just to show he understood the finer points of those sorts of things.

'And now the weather, Captain,' the Chairman said, just a shade anxiously. 'I haven't had the time – '

'There is a big Low in the Atlantic.'

A little more anxiously: 'There is?'

'A heavy head-wind component.'

Much more anxiously: 'But you'll be able to do it direct?'

'Well, Sir James – ' Cavendish paused. He could never resist a moment like this. The hush as he stood there, seemingly holding up the ceiling with the top of his hat, was packed to the brim with the many things a pilot had to cope with – ice, storms, headwinds, control, maintenance, fog, fatigue, forecasting, fuel consumption – all clinging like little Old Men of the Sea tightly round his ample shoulders. The suspense of his audience increased as the silence continued. They were all agog now. The Chairman could hardly sit still. Then suddenly, from away up above them, through the now smiling grey moustache came a voice so calm and quiet that all the elements would have to cease to hear it, 'I think I shall be able to promise you New York non-stop.'

All the air in Sir James' lungs was employed in the one word: 'Excellent!'

'The weather at our destination will be ceiling and visibility unlimited.'

'Excellent!' The Chairman had no breath left this time. It was Payton who had deputised.

Cavendish stood there, a maypole round which the others executed a three-step. The schedule for the proving flight was discussed. For Brocklehurst's benefit, Sir James outlined the plans: 'There will be a welcome committee waiting for us at New York. We'll be a bit late, I'm afraid. I know a dinner and a cocktail party may well be on the programme of our four days there. Perhaps more . . . it all depends on the showing we can make. Down we go on Thursday to Bermuda – to show the flag for a couple of days. And we start back on Saturday, arriving home church-time on Sunday morning.'

'Makes a nice week's holiday for you, Mr. Brocklehurst,' Payton suggested, craning his neck round Cavendish's bulk so he could see and be seen.

'Makes a nice week's holiday for *all of us*,' the Chairman corrected him. Then he looked up at the pilot. 'Except for Captain Cavendish.'

The pilot did not contradict him. They had started talking about operating costs, and Brocklehurst, whose sherry had sharpened his appetite, was looking round to see how dinner was getting along. Cavendish started to put on his right-hand glove. 'If you will excuse me, Sir James . . . the other passengers – '

'Of course, Captain.'

Cavendish moved majestically forward, allowing Payton at last an uninterrupted view of his superiors, and proceeded further down the cabin to have a word with Eastlake.

Right at the back, Riley had finished his third whisky, and deciding to promote himself, advanced three rows to slip into the empty seat beside Enderby-Browne, who was busily engaged in making notes in an exercise book.

'Don't you find the noise of the engines too distracting to concentrate, doctor?'

The cornstuke eyebrows quirked up above the bright eyes. 'I should find their silence even more distracting, Mr. Riley.'

'Yes . . . of course.' Riley gave a tolerant smile. 'Still on the thesis, doctor?'

'Still on the thesis, Mr. Riley. Original research takes a great deal of time. And I have so little opportunity.'

'If I could help at all . . . I mean, with the writing – ' There was one thing in which Riley excelled. He had a wonderful fertility for writing advertisements, and he combined this work with his usual P.R.O. duties. He was also a rake. Furthermore, he was unreliable. He alternated between the flesh-pots of commerce and the frugality of what he called his artistic conscience. But, remembering the way, in a couple of hundred words, the man could make the hungry's mouths water for Air Enterprise's seven-course dinners, the lonely pine for the gentle attention of Air Enterprise's stewardesses, the thrifty avid to invest in Air Enterprise's cut-price fares, and the weary ache for the foamy comfort of Air Enterprise's luxury bunks – the Chairman had so far been persuaded that the operating cost of Mr. Riley per million passenger miles was just above the break-even factor.

'It's very kind of you, Mr. Riley, but – ' The doctor shook his head, and applied himself once more to his notebook. How the P.R.O. expected to help prepare a thesis on the effects of altitude, noise, exposure to cabin atmosphere and carbon monoxide, fatigue, vibration and irregular meals in relation to the airborne human body was difficult to perceive.

'I know what you're thinking, doctor.' The florid face looked wounded. 'You're not trying to lure people into being airmen. What you put down is the cold scientific truth. And what I put down – '

'I'm sure, Mr. Riley,' the doctor said gently, 'you write very well indeed.'

But Riley was not to mollified. The whiskies (Enderby-Browne had noticed all three of them) at this cabin altitude had had *nearly double the usual effect. The eyes were already a little blood-shot.* An interesting observation, well worth noting.

'You don't believe the stuff I write, doctor. I'll tell you something . . . neither do I.'

The effect of alcohol on the barriers of the conscious mind, inducing confidence and at the same time laying bare the reasons for a lack of confidence.

Interesting again.

Riley's voice grew higher. 'And now you think I couldn't write the truth if I tried!'

The desire to pick a quarrel, fight. Curious that a few drops of yellow fluid could wash away thousands of years and disclose the primeval lust for the jungle, sieved out by modern civilisation.

'Not at all, Mr. Riley.'

'But I can, doctor! And one day, *I will* !'

'I'm sure you will.' Enderby-Browne looked up from his notebook, and saw that a few feet in front of him Cavendish had apparently finished all he was going to say to Eastlake. 'Excuse me, Captain,' he said. 'But could you oblige me with the cabin altitude?' It was essential to get it exact for that note on Riley.

Cavendish took a few more steps rearwards. 'We're cruising at 24,000. Pressurisation is at maximum. That'll make the cabin pressure equivalent to 5,000 feet.'

'Thank you, Captain.'

Cavendish inquired with grave courtesy, 'Is the thesis finished, doctor?'

'Not quite, Captain.'

'I heard you were coming with us to give a lecture on your findings to the New York Canford Institute.'

The doctor laughed self-consciously. It was, as a matter of fact, his ambition to lecture to this world-famous gathering of the world's medical brains. But so far, there had been no signs that it would ever be realised. 'Oh no! I'm coming in the course of my ordinary duties with the Company. They . . . the Canford Institute don't even know I'm coming over.'

'I expect you could give us some surprises, doctor.'

'Yes, Captain,' he was specifically thinking of airline operators and airframe designers. 'I could.'

Eastlake heard him, and turned round to give out with his spick-and-span smile. 'If you had your way, doctor, no aircraft would leave the ground!'

Enderby-Browne said in reply, 'It's a pity, Mr. Eastlake, that you haven't designed a pressurisation system that would bring the cabin at cruising altitude down to sea-level.'

Irritation flashed across Eastlake's face. 'That isn't practicable.'

'Still a pity . . . for many reasons.'

Any remark that criticised his work was enough to knock Eastlake off his horse. He reddened. This man knew nothing of engineering. He hadn't designed the combinations of cheap chemicals which it was his job to maintain as living human beings. The airframe designer had just thought of a suitably biting retort, when a brisk voice announced, 'Dinner is served, gentlemen.'

Hamilton always seemed to know his cue. There he stood, in this difficult atmosphere, gleaming in his white coat, a tray in either hand on which was tastefully arranged a bowl of turtle soup, a dish of olives and celery and sliced tomatoes and a glittering array of tools to tackle further delights to come.

Eastlake got back on his horse again. He produced a party quip, 'Just what the doctor ordered.' And Enderby-Browne nodded good-humouredly as he noted down *deficiency of blood sugar as a cause of irritation.* Then he put his exercise book away on top of the life-jacket under his seat, and in its place, accepted the plastic tray on his lap.

Captain Cavendish continued right to the back, to wash his hands preparatory to his own meal. And up at the front, the Chairman had got through his soup, had got through as well nearly everything he wanted to impress into Brocklehurst, except the way Air Enterprise worked.

'It's the *get-together* that does it,' he was saying. 'Co-operation. Team spirit. Singly, each of us is a thin twig. But bound one to the other – '

It was unfortunate, Payton thought, that the Chairman should hit upon the Italian symbol of fascism. 'What Sir James means, Mr. Brocklehurst,' he said quickly, 'is that we all stand or fall by the Emperor.'

Brocklehurst looked out of his porthole. It was beginning to clear a little, and through the darkness, several miles below the aircraft, could just be seen the irregular grey shapes of scattered clouds. 'I can understand that,' he said.

Those same grey shapes were studied by Bellamy, out of the pilot's left-hand window. He identified them as fracto-cumulus, height 8,000 feet: five-eighths cloud above: temperature – 25° Centigrade. With a ball-point pen, he wrote it all down in the weather proforma – the oblong card which chimed the hours on the darkened flight deck – and passed it back so that the engineer could add the fuel available, the navigator could put in their position, and the radio officer could send it to Control.

Emperor Able Dog was running easily now. Her motors hummed their monotonous tune in perfect harmony. Under the dimmed green lights, the instrument panel, with its phosphorescent sparkle of lines and figures, stayed still and steady on its rubber mountings. The compass needle never moved from 295°.

Seawood, sitting in the right-hand seat, was smoking. The red glow of his cigarette reflected in the dark mirror of the side-window beyond. 'Nice night, sir,' he said.

'Not bad so far.'

'Want your dinner now, Skipper?'

'No. Never have mine till late. You go back and have yours, if you like.'

'Thank you, sir.' Seawood started to get out of his seat. The red glow of his cigarette was replaced by an alternating flash of light, bursting out yellow into the darkness and then dying away again.

'Isn't that Fastnet Rock to starboard?'

Seawood turned and looked out. A great illuminated line, like a searchlight half-smudged by intermittent cloud, pierced the darkness below. Like a powerful farewell signal from the ground in morse, it flashed out at them three short lighted dots and a long dash of darkness.

'It is, Skipper. Dead on our beam.'

Bellamy said, 'Tell the navigator, will you? Might as well get a ground-speed check on it.' But Douthwaite had already taken one. He came up between the pilots with an alteration of course – 300°.

'Those winds, Captain,' he said. 'You were right.'

'We're falling behind flight plan?'

'Fifteen minutes late already.'

Bellamy swung the aircraft round the required five degrees to starboard. All he said was, 'And another ten hours to go!'

Gradually, the flickering beam from the lighthouse, last outpost of Europe, moved further and further behind the aircraft till it was no more than a spark on the line of the horizon. Then it, too, vanished into the night, and Emperor Able Dog, cutting her lonely road steadily west against the resisting wind, was abandoned to the dark Atlantic.

CHAPTER FOUR

ALONG the narrow pink-pile carpet, Hamilton walked the cold Atlantic air. With the two girls behind him in the galley, doing the jobs that were suitable to their femininity and lack of seniority, he transformed this microscopic foreign body, that had now been floating in the orb of the sky for over three hours, into a well-orientated British society.

He was not displeased with the stewardesses who had been assigned to him. Indeed, more than anyone else, he had been responsible for their choice. Their prettiness, which he viewed with the dispassion of a man whose values had passed to more enduring things, fitted in pleasantly with the dainty newness of the cabin's interior. And their well-behaved efficiency meant that he could forget about them, and not have to worry his head about the usual complications that the more scatter-brained of the girls would have brought with them on to an otherwise all-male outing.

Dinner had been served with a polished precision that had rejoiced him. And now, with the ladies withdrawn to the galley for the washing up, there remained only the serving of the coffee and brandy and liqueurs, and the mysteries of the after-dinner masculine half-hour.

Delicately savouring the incense-like aroma of cigars, and with his body slightly bowing over the napkin-wrapped brandy bottle, Hamilton watched anxiously as the Chairman slowly raised the balloon glass to his nose, and then to his lips. 'Excellent, Hamilton! Excellent!'

Hamilton sighed with pleasure. Then Angela appeared at his elbow and whispered. 'Captain Bellamy has just rung from the rest-room. He doesn't want dinner yet. Just orange juice. Shall I take it along to him?'

Hamilton pursed his lips. The whole atmosphere of good living and maturity would be shattered by the sight of a tray with a glass of orange juice going through the cabin, and at this hour too. But on the other side of the flight-deck door was another hierarchy for whose well-being Hamilton regarded himself as equally responsible and in there, for the time being, Bellamy was king.

'Certainly, Miss Knight! Right away! Oh, and don't forget your clean napkin! Hurry now! Don't keep the Captain waiting!' He sighed gently and rubbed his jaw, reflecting sadly on the difficulties of a man with a foot in two worlds.

Back in the galley, Angela prepared the tray carefully. And then in the few seconds that Hamilton would have used to check his tie and the folds of the napkin, she dabbed some cologne behind her ears and renewed her already immaculate lipstick. Lalette, the last of the washing up done, stared gloomily out of the window.

The aircraft was ploughing on steadily into the night.

Ten minutes later, she looked at her watch and frowned. Time seemed to be simply crawling along. She was quite glad when Hamilton came in and said, 'Captain Cavendish's tea, Miss Greenacres! He'll have finished it now . . . if you would go and get the cups. He'll be wanting another pot in a minute!'

She got up and walked through the cabin. Up front everything was cool and shadowy, as different from the world that the closing door had just sliced away from her as an undeveloped negative from a coloured picture-postcard. To the left, with a metal door rimmed like a party invitation in gold light, was the crew rest compartment. Two paces in front, lit only by the phosphorescent green lights from the instruments, was the flight deck.

Lalette edged her way past Rawlings' massive shoulders to stand behind the dark silhouette of Captain Cavendish. 'Have you finished, sir?'

'Ah, yes, thank you.'

Lalette took the tray and paused for a moment outside the door of the rest-room. There was no reason, she supposed, why Angela shouldn't stay and chat to Bellamy if she wanted to. He was off duty and there was only enough work for one in the galley.

But all the same, she thought, she might as well save herself a journey to fetch his empty glass. She knocked and went in.

There were two seats on either side of the narrow room, with a table that could be put up between. Bellamy sat on one, Angela on the other, and the girl was holding a packet of photographs in her hand. 'I just thought,' Lalette said to Bellamy, 'that I'd collect your glass, and get it done with.'

'Not quite finished. You can have it in a moment.'

'We were just looking at these photographs.' Angela seemed to be almost apologising, as though she wasn't sure that sitting there was quite proper. 'Some of them are really quite good.'

'May I see?' Lalette took the packet that Angela handed her. 'They're very good!' She looked at them vaguely, until she saw that one was of Bellamy. 'This is very nice of you . . . sir.'

Bellamy said nothing. He just raised his eyebrows and gave a faint smile.

The next one was of Bellamy, too. Lalette reddened. He was in a sports jacket and flannels and was looking into the camera and laughing as though he was enjoying himself hugely. Then there was another. This time of an old gentleman in a well-ordered garden, nipping off some buds with a pair of secateurs.

'Ah,' said Lalette, 'and this one? This must be . . . er . . . Daddy?'

She did it, she knew, with quite deceptive gentleness. All the same, Bellamy looked up at her sharply. He finished off his orange juice and put the glass down with a smart click on to the tray. 'I've finished now, Lalette,' he said, 'You can clear away, if you want to.'

'Thank you, sir,' she said, picking up the other tray in her free hand. 'Will that be all?'

'Yes . . . thank you.' He gave her a direct look that outstared her own unblinking one.

'What about that other one? The one I took of you?' she heard him say to Angela, as she let the door snap shut behind her.

There was one thing, she thought, washing up with too much soap powder, too much hot water and too much violence, neither of them would do anything but chat politely, look at photographs and do the proper thing. And with everything done and cleared away, she stared out once more through the porthole beyond the sink.

Intermittently, a star appeared from behind the overcast

and was swallowed up again in a world without colour or dimensions. Sitting alone on a high stool in the tail, Lalette watched out for them to keep her company. In front, from the mighty engines came a low sustained roar, and quieter, but just as thrustful and determined, from the cabin came the lesser human noise. And here she was, an isolated unimportant female, riding pillion as it were, unnoticed through the night. She watched the red navigation light dip itself into a pool of cloud and emerge blurred, to dry itself bright and clear against the next stretch of open sky.

'Miss Greenacres!' Hamilton came bustling up, one eye on his watch. 'It's on the hour! You're forgetting Captain Cavendish's tea!'

'Do you take sugar in your tea, Mr. Cruttwell?'

'Please, Captain Cavendish.'

'One or two lumps?'

'Two lumps, please.'

The tray that Lalette had brought up now rested on the flat rear of the throttle pedestal. Cavendish, now beginning his second hour on watch, had sent Seawood back to the rest compartment and had replaced him in the right-hand seat with Mr. Cruttwell. Behind them, Rawlings and Hooper were sharing a second pot of tea with Douthwaite.

Under the dimmed glow of the instrument lights, the flight deck made a peaceful domestic scene, like a family gossiping in an evening drawing-room beside the dying embers of a green fire.

Outside, it was black. A dark marsh of cloud had swamped the stars to the north. Every now and again, the tea-cups rattled as the Emperor's wings got caught in an isolated cumulus top. But most of the stuff was still below them, and the occasional shimmying was nothing more than the gentle up and down movements of a rocking-chair, as the automatic pilot did its silent corrections.

Rawlings lolled back, contentedly eyeing the perfect behaviour of all the engine instruments. Certainly they were a little late on flight plan – but his particular babies were as healthy a set of quadruplets as had ever been constructed. And there was nine hours' fuel left in their tanks.

He lapped up a mouthful of warm tea. Then he nudged Hooper. 'Cigarette?'

'Thanks.'

'How's the weather on the other side?'

'Couldn't get the last reports. Radio conditions are pretty bad.'

'Last lot you got all right?'

'Not too bad. Maritimes are still out. But Boston and New York were okay.'

Rawlings grunted with satisfaction. Here was the missing third line, good destination weather, to fit in with fuel and serviceability to complete the airman's eternal triangle. 'New York's the one we want.'

'Smooth trip,' Hooper said. 'You know, when you come to think of it, these semi-final jet jobs aren't half bad.'

'My seat's hard.'

'I could do with a bit more room. My elbow – '

'They should have put the fuel system control valves nearer . . . so I could reach 'em.'

'The way people park their hats on the top of my spares! I tell you one day I'll – '

'That man Douthwaite's working too hard. Hey, Alex!' Rawlings leant across the small space to the navigator's table. 'Your tea's getting cold!'

But the navigator took no notice of him. With infinite precision, he was drawing a thin line on his chart that he topped off with an arrowhead at each end.

Not persisting in his effort to make the conversation three-sided, Rawlings turned back to Hooper. 'You got anything to read?'

'Only Cavendish's *Evening News*.'

'Might as well take a gander at it.'

The paper rustled as it was being passed across the flight deck. Cavendish interrupted himself in his monologue with Cruttwell. He turned round. 'Is that my *Evening News*?''

'Yes, Captain.'

'Thank you very much.' Cavendish leant back to collect it. 'Now I wanted to show you this article, Mr. Cruttwell.'

Cavendish was enjoying himself. He was playing the age-old game of pilots with aircraft constructors: how the perfect aeroplane should be built, and where every one of them was going wrong. He spread the paper out in front of him. 'Just look what this man says about the Emperor!'

Mr. Cruttwell looked. He was a modest man, a scientific intellectual, and as such he was inclined to be a little over-awed by the enormous presence of Captain Cavendish.

'You'll notice,' Cavendish continued, 'that he calls the lay-out of the cockpit a pilot's paradise. Now, often a pilot has to act *immediately*, and in this particular cockpit – '

'Of course,' Cruttwell suggested mildly, 'so many instruments are difficult to arrange.'

'Now *even I* have the utmost difficulty in reaching some of the controls quickly. Look where the A.D.F. is! And as for the de-icer boot switch – '

'Minor things, perhaps, Captain, wouldn't you say?'

'Minor! That's the trouble with you designers! You've never *been* in a passenger-carrying aircraft when quick action is *imperative*.'

The paper was still spread out in front of them, held out by Cavendish's arms. 'Captain,' a voice said behind them. But Cavendish was still lecturing.

'Captain Cavendish!'

The flow stopped abruptly. 'Yes, Mr. Douthwaite?'

'You were right about that Low. We've hit the bottom of it.'

'So it's shot up north, has it?' There was a certain satisfaction in Cavendish's voice. 'I told Captain Bellamy it would. That temperature at the weather ship – '

In scrupulous fairness to both his captains, Douthwaite pointed out, 'But Captain Bellany was right about the winds. *Much* stronger than forecast.'

Coldly now, Cavendish demanded, 'What *is* the wind?'

'A hundred and eighteen knots, sir. Dead on the nose.'

'*Nonsense.*'

'That's what my fix says.' Douthwaite's face remained detached and unemotional. 'But if you have a different wind in mind, sir . . . perhaps you'd like to come back and take your own fix.'

Cavendish shot the navigator a suspicious glance. Seeing nothing but impassiveness, he exclaimed, 'But that means we're in a jet-stream, Mr. Douthwaite!'

'Might mean that, sir.'

The newspaper was thrust suddenly to one side of the left-hand seat, where it lay crumpled, forgotten. The tea-tray was swept down to the floor. With a tremendous dramatic lunge, the auto-pilot was slammed out.

'Mr. Hooper! Contact Control for descent clearance to 16,000! Winds for all zones at that height!

'Mr. Douthwaite! Revise your flight plan to 16,000 feet!

'Mr. Rawlings! Throttle back for descent!'

Captain Cavendish was *acting immediately*.

Rawlings was the only one who questioned his orders. He looked up, surprised, and asked 'What . . . *now*, Captain?'

'*Now*, Mr. Rawlings!'

'But we haven't got permission from Control yet, Captain!'

Cavendish made no reply. He leant his huge hand on the pilot's set of throttles and pulled them back himself. 'You're here at the right time. Mr. Cruttwell,' he said. 'The time when a pilot has to act *immediately*.'

Grandly, the Emperor's nose dipped downwards. With fixed determination, Cavendish held the wheel just forward of centre, and the aircraft allowed herself to descend for the first two thousand feet without the slightest qualm. Then she plunged into a flurry of dark cloud and started to shake all over in protest. Hail that had been lurking there in ambush now got her range and pinged and peppered her all over.

Behind the concentrating pilot, Rawlings shook his head from side to side, and catching Hooper's eye, looked up at the roof. He muttered to the Radio Officer, 'Always the same with him! Least thing . . . off he goes! Real old shadow-boxer . . . Cavendish.'

Hooper's eyes had widened. ' But a hundred and eighteen knots – '

'We've got the fuel,' Rawlings pointed out comfortably. 'Engines are all right. New York's all right. Why he wanted to go down – '

'And without permission! We might collide!'

'Trouble is . . . he never remembers he isn't the only captain in the sky.'

'He isn't the only captain in this aircraft . . . never mind the sky,' Hooper said. 'Thought on this leg, Bellamy was in command.'

In the rest compartment, Bellamy had been half-way through his steak when he heard the motors change power. At first, he had thought that Control had allotted them a new altitude, perhaps at 22,000, and he'd gone on eating. But as the Emperor dived further and further down into the bumpy cloud, he parked the tray on the seat opposite, next to where Seawood was quietly finishing off his coffee, and opening the door, returned to the flight deck to investigate.

His first glance was at the navigator's altimeter—19,000 feet, and still going down. Cavendish was wasting no time.

'What's going on?' he asked Douthwaite.

The navigator looked up from a fresh set of calculations. 'Jet stream, sir,' he said. 'Over a hundred knots.'

'But why are we going down?'

'Captain Cavendish's orders, sir.'

The altimeter needle flashed past 18,000 like an express train.

'What height?'

'16,000, sir.'

Bellamy's face wrinkled over with exasperation. 'Christ Almighty!' He strode in towards the pilots' seats. 'Captain Cavendish!'

'Ah, there you are, Captain Bellamy!' The older pilot turned his head momentarily from the instruments. 'Here . . . take over for a minute, would you?'

The only alternative left to Bellamy was to leave Mr. Cruttwell, now cowering back from the controls in the right-hand seat, in complete charge. Cavendish had squeezed past him towards Hooper, saying as he left, 'We're taking her down to 16,000, Captain!' Then he bent over the Radio Officer. 'Have you got permission to descend yet?'

But Hooper, bent low over the key with the earphones clamped hard on his head, was trying to listen to morse through a fearful jumble of howling static.

'Permission!' Cavendish cried. 'Have you got permission?' He was feeling a slight uneasiness that more frequently these days invaded his self-confidence. These controls and regulations that now red-taped the free air were a damnable nuisance. They had a habit of catching airmen in their trammels. And he was uncomfortably aware that these turbo-prop engines, unlike their pistoned ancestors, increased their fuel consumption heavily by descending lower, and also lost a considerable amount of speed. Perhaps in this case, immediate action –

From the front, Bellamy called out, 'Levelling off at 16,000!'

Cavendish glared at Hooper, whose face had taken on the vague other-worldliness look of a man in a trance. His eyes had gone up to the duralumin arches on the fuselage above him. 'Permission!'

It was bumpier down here. The hail had changed to electric rain, now washing the black windscreen over with sparkling swirls. In a majestic malaise, the Emperor began to roll.

Cavendish impatiently whipped the headset off Hooper's left ear and roared, 'Haven't you got permission *yet*?'

But Hooper grabbed at his earphones and jammed them back on his head. He took no notice of Cavendish. At a highly-trained racing speed, he began to write plain language in his log.

Cavendish, looking over his shoulder, read the words one by one as they appeared on the white page before him: *Special. New York and Boston forecast, 24.00–12.00. Ceiling indefinite. Sea fog. Visibility variable. 440 yards to nil.*

In the long passenger compartment, everything was quite still and quiet. The only light was right at the back, where Lalette (whose turn it was to be awake) sat at the catering staff's table over which a shaded lamp sent a round yellow patch of brilliance right on the open book in front of her, looking for all the world like a night nurse on duty in a sleeping, contented ward.

Seven of the super luxury bunks had been pulled out of the fuselage wall above the seats, and were now occupied, with the sole exception of Mr. Cruttwell's, and he was preparing very quietly to get into it. He had thought it advisable to leave the cramped confines of the flight deck soon after Bellamy had arrived on the scene, and saying his unnoticed adieux and thanks, he had slipped noiselessly away.

Lalette watched him pull the curtains apart, and climb cautiously up on to the foamy mattress. She had heard the engine power decrease. There was some (but not much) sensation of going lower. Then the engine noise roared up again, and the vibration became more evident.

She stopped half-way down a page and peered out of the porthole at the left-hand engines, out of which two trailing tongues of fire licked unenthusiastically at their burnt-porridge-coloured environment.

They were, anyway, still functioning. Her minute knowledge of engineering thus confirming that everything was all right, she returned to the page, fiddled around trying to find the exact word she had left, found it, looked at her watch, and with a sigh, returned to her novel.

The call bell beside her buzzed. She looked at the indicator. It was the flight deck. Cavendish would be wanting tea *again*.

She went into the galley and poured the still simmering kettle into a pot she had already prepared on a tray with the cups. Then she walked softly up the aisle to the door and into the cockpit.

She noticed the hush straight away. Everyone seemed to be expectantly waiting, except Douthwaite, who was still bent over his calculations, working out now what the wind was at this new height. Even Rawlings, who usually welcomed her with a witticism, this time said nothing. She saw the heavy curtains behind the pilots were drawn, separating them completely from the rest of the flight deck. Pulling them aside to let her tray through, she was surprised to see Bellamy in the left-hand seat.

Rather distantly, he nodded and said, 'Thank you.' Cavendish, sitting beside him, just went on staring into the dark night beyond the windscreen.

She left the tea-tray on the pedestal, a gently chattering reminder that she had been there at all. But after she had gone, neither of the pilots made a sound. There they sat, in this little confession-box at the front of the aircraft, lit by the phosphorescent green glow of the instruments, while the Emperor's propellors churned onwards against the invisible wind.

At last, Bellamy said in a low voice, 'Got the idea I was in command on this leg.'

'So you are, Captain.'

'Then why not tell me before coming down?'

With considerable dignity, Cavendish replied, 'I acted as I knew *you* would have acted.'

'You got it wrong.'

'Captain Bellamy, this is neither the time nor the place – '

'No clearance! Nothing on the winds at 16,000! Worst cruising altitude!' Lowering his voice still further, he demanded, 'What the hell put the idea into your head?'

Cavendish glowered down at him. 'It was necessary, Captain, to get out of the jet stream.'

'Slap into this ice, eh? Look at it!' Bellamy flashed his torch out into the blackness. There, on the port wing, a glistening straight white stripe piped the muzzy line of the leading edge.

Down the airspeed went as the ice built up. Bellamy did not switch on the de-icer boots – he dare not. While the stuff was building up, certainly it might crack it, but with the cunning of heavy ice, it would build up again beyond the travel of the inflating and deflating rubber boots, making them powerless to reach it.

'In the middle of the Atlantic, Bellamy, I have other things to do than to argue – '

'And so have I . . . now! But get this straight, Cavendish. While I'm in command, I have the responsibility. *And I take the decisions!*' And then, as though it was all finished with, he pulled open the curtain, and in a completely different voice, now quite calm and controlled, he turned round to the rest of the flight deck and asked, 'Has Mr. Douthwaite worked out a wind at this height?'

'Just coming up, Captain,' the navigator called back. 'Won't be a minute.'

Bellamy poured out the tea and handed a cup to Cavendish. As he drank it slowly, he was revising the plans he had already made for the crossing. He never regarded the Atlantic as a whole entity, but split it in his mind into various lines of defence away from England, and then various strongholds nearer the American continent. Every degree of longitude had to be fought for, while always in the rear were maintained the retreats and divisions, available if necessary.

This was a situation he hadn't expected – but immediately he had sent messages, probing across the ocean, seeking for a destination, safe from the weather. Iceland, Moncton, even the aerodromes in England might be called in to help him, now that the whole of the North American seaboard was out. He had the answers beside him: English weather was fair, Moncton was on limits with fog, Iceland at present was good, but with the Low rushing northwards, how long it would remain so was problematical.

Douthwaite came up with the wind he had found. 'Ninety-five knots, sir. Still from the same direction.'

Bellamy turned and looked at the man in the right-hand seat. He raised his eyebrows.

'Considerably less than at 24,000,' Cavendish pointed out icily.

Douthwaite said, 'We've gained on the wind. But we've lost fifty knots airspeed, sir. What's more, we're still losing it!'

The ice was building up fast now. Great chunks were being slung off the propellors to bang and clatter against the Emperor's sides. The cloud outside was weaving a white cocoon as though trying to contain the whole aeroplane within it.

Bellamy knew he would have to climb again to get out of the stuff. There was no destination he could find on the other side which was safe from the weather. The Low was rapidly approaching Iceland, his only possible diversion.

He studied the figures of fuel used and fuel available that Rawlings had worked out for him. There was no doubt about one thing – he would have to act immediately. Either he could go back to England, or he could fly north to Iceland, hoping to beat the Low in. He thought for a moment on the two alternatives. Iceland was nearer; it was also five hundred miles closer to New York. And a return to England would be a sad sequel to the glory of that send-off.

He weighed it all up in his mind, trying as he always had to do to find out the safest odds and yet still do his job. He knew that the snowball, the one-damned-thing-after-another that was always a danger signal of an avalanche over airmen, was already rolling.

He rubbed his eyes with his right hand, and then, suddenly vigorous again, he made up his mind. Turning to Hooper, he called out, 'Clearance to Iceland . . . 23,000. And get me every Keflavik weather report you can!'

After Hooper had said, 'Yes, Captain,' a hush descended over the whole of the flight deck, a kind of quiet knell for the proving flight's non-stop trip to New York. Then the Radio Officer's key rattled out, an uneven match against the ice that still clattered against the fuselage. The Emperor, unperturbed but much slower now, plunged steadily through the storm.

Cavendish said, 'Iceland!'

'Only thing to do. Apart from going back.'

'But the Chairman . . . Sir James – '

'What about him?'

'I think he should be told.'

'So do I.'

'And *when* he's told, he – '

'He can go back to sleep again. More than I can.'

Hooper called out, 'Clearance, Captain.' And Bellamy without looking round said, 'Climb power.' The engine noise increased. The pilot moved the stick to the right, and pulled back slightly. The Emperor, responding immediately to the hydraulically boosted controls, veered off her Great Circle into a long climbing turn to starboard. The altimeter needle awakened into life to clock in this extra height, and the whole aircraft, as though anxious to leave this treacherous icy bog, gave a heartening leap upwards, away from the wet tenuous depths of the cloud.

Douthwaite came up with the course for Iceland, 031 degrees, and set it on the compass. And twenty minutes afterwards, the time it took for the pot of tea on the throttle pedestal to go cold and undrinkable, the whole aspect of the flight had changed. Here they were, Cavendish and Bellamy still sitting side by side, the autopilot re-engaged, back at altitude, in the clear with the de-icer boots cracking the ice off the wings. But the Estimated Time of Arrival, 01.51, on the piece of paper between them was for the American air base at Keflavik, in Iceland. And just above it was a square card, made out in columns at the head of which Hooper had written: –

KEFLAVIK 22.30. Cloud 8/8 1500 feet. Wind 180 degrees 20 kts. Visibility 6 miles. Temperature 04. Dew Point 02. Altimeter 29.21.

KEFLAVIK 23.00. Cloud 8/8 800 feet. Wind 200 degrees 28 kts. Visibility 4 miles. Temperature 03. Dew Point 02. Altimeter 29.17.

Cavendish observed, 'Keflavik's going down fast.'

'Yes.'

'Have we enough fuel to go there, and *then* return to London?'

'I doubt it.'

A silence fell between them. Then Cavendish remarked, 'The Chairman will be disappointed.'

'Yes.'

'When are you going to break it to him, Captain?'

Bellamy said, 'I'm just giving myself a rest . . . before the big moment.'

The aircraft flew in a stately progression towards the stars in the north. The Plough was just on the port bow now. Bellamy suddenly moved back his seat. 'Well . . . better get it over, I suppose.'

He climbed out and stretched, watching the excellent behaviour of all the engine instruments. 'Going well, anyway,' he said to Rawlings.

The engineer said, 'Yes, sir,' and went back to his struggles with the fuel figures. Hooper was tensely awaiting the next weather report from Iceland.

Just before he pushed open the door to the cabin, Bellamy heard Douthwaite humming, with the curious unruffled attitude to everything, good or bad, that all navigators have, a rather tuneless version through his teeth of *Here we sit like birds in the wilderness . . . birds in the wilderness* –

CHAPTER FIVE

LYING on his back in his bunk, Sir James had been dozing on and off, still in his clothes. Vaguely, he had heard the engine note change several times, but it had not worried him. The pilots were doing their job of finding the best altitude to fly, and he had other matters on his mind. One of them had woken him up now, and sitting up, he noticed that instead of a dark mass of cloud, now they were flying in the clear black air under the whole panoply of stars.

That was better.

He turned the light on, and leant over to the bottom of the bunk, where he had put his brief-case, anxious to clarify a particular detail (the estimated operating cost of the Emperor per ton mile) which had for the moment eluded his overworked subconscious mind. Pulling it up to him, he started to search through the papers.

In his opinion, he was doing this because of his pride in never leaving a job undone, but really it was in order that he could get some rest, for like most Chairmen of big businesses, his mind was pursued day and night by a swarm of details, each one equipped, until it was taken care of, by a sharp, sleepless sting.

Here it was! Sir James found the fact, broke off the sting. Cheerfully now, because it was less than he had imagined, he was just preparing to lie down flat again when he noticed that the bunk curtains were moving.

A voice said, 'You awake, sir?'

'Yes,' he said, pulling the curtain aside. 'Hello, Bellamy! Nice night outside.'

But the pilot made no comment on the night. He came straight to the point. 'Bad news, I'm afraid, sir.'

His mind now suddenly flooding with all sorts of dire possibilities, Sir James demanded, 'What's the matter with her?'

'The aircraft's fine, sir. Going well. It's the weather – '

'Oh.' For a moment, the Chairman's face relaxed. Then he said, 'But Captain Cavendish told me New York was CAVU.'

'Fog there now.'

'Well . . . where are we going? Boston . . . Washington?' In the dim light that was glowing from the back of his bunk, Sir James searched the pilot's face for the answer.

'We've run into hundred knot headwinds.'

An awful thought suddenly gripped the Chairman's brain. 'Bellamy, we're not going . . . *back*?'

'Not as bad as that, sir. Iceland.'

'*Iceland!*'

'Only thing I could do, sir. I'm sorry – '

But Sir James, with all his plans for the Emperor balanced on the pivot of this proving flight, was not one to accept an explanation like that. 'But there are a lot of aerodromes on the North American seaboard!'

'All marginal now.'

'What does Captain Cavendish say to this?' Watching Bellamy carefully, he noticed a certain stoniness come into his eyes.

'I'm in command on this leg, sir.'

'Surely we can find somewhere better than Iceland! That'll make us hours late! This aircraft is intended to operate non-stop in all conditions! The Reception Committee – ' He was getting really rather angry now. This pilot Bellamy, he had realised yesterday, was not so much *his* man as he had thought. Perhaps it had been a mistake to include him on the same crew as Cavendish. 'The weather can't be as bad as all that, Captain.'

'Worst situation I've ever seen.' The pilot paused. 'The Emperor can operate non-stop in the worst of *normal* weather conditions. But this is phenomenal – hundred knot head-winds, coupled with bad weather at all the terminals and alternates. You can't fight a situation like that, sir.'

But Sir James hardly heard him.

'When are we turning off?' He had started to clamber down from his bunk, all hope of sleep gone now. He seemed just on the point of marching to the flight deck to take over.

'We've turned off, sir. Nearly an hour ago.'

So there was nothing that could be done about it now. He sank into his seat, fingering the fat folds of his chin in furious concentration. 'How late will that make us?'

'At least six hours.'

It was the man's calm that was so infuriating. His apparent indifference to the issues at stake. Joliffe felt as he sat there that he was in a prison – a beautiful airborne prison he had erected himself and had paid for and then handed the keys to someone else so they could lock him up in it. Just as he had not explained the complications in the Emperor's building to the pilots, because they wouldn't understand, now Bellamy did not further elaborate on his decision, assuming with that infuriating airmen's attitude to laymen that *he* wouldn't understand.

And then, realising the impasse, his well-drilled mind refused to try to shift the past. It was Iceland now. And Iceland had to be explained.

'Very well, Captain Bellamy,' he said.

'Pity! Just one of those things.' An observation like that, Sir James thought grimly to himself, gave warning of how much Bellamy understood. And then his parting remark, as he moved away, proved that lack of knowledge and put Q.E.D. on the end of it. 'E.T.A. isn't till 01.51. Time to get a couple of hours sleep in, sir.'

Sleep! He was at that moment busily reorganising in his mind the programme of the proving flight. Already the words *due to the worst weather for many years* had occurred to him to explain the diversion. *The cautious skill of the pilots, sensing trouble ahead* – there were nine more. Wide awake now, he watched the dark chunky shape of the pilot's back go through the door to the flight deck.

Nobody said anything to Bellamy when he came into the cockpit. Hooper, his eyes as wide as saucers, looked up from his set. As he settled himself back into the left-hand seat, Cavendish silently passed him the weather card.

There had been another addition: KEFLAVIK 23.30. Cloud 8/8 300 feet. Wind 220 degrees 30 kts gusting 40. Visibility one mile in light snow. Temperature 01. Dew Point 01. Altimeter 29.12. RAPID DETERIORATION EXPECTED.

The north star crawled higher in the sky. Perfectly at ease, Emperor Able Dog droned on the way Bellamy had pointed her, nearer and nearer towards Iceland. The winds, starting on the beam, were changing continually as the aircraft crossed over the circular pressure pattern of the Low. And every half-hour, Hooper made another addition to the weather card concerning the surface conditions at Keflavik. Heavy snow was now being reported with a visibility of less than half a mile.

Bellamy sat quietly in the left-hand seat, studying the Notams – notices to airmen concerning aerodrome states and the serviceability of blind landing aids. Though the world knows the news about magnificent runways and marvellous scientific devices, it is only airmen who need to be warned to land on the left-hand side of such-and-such a runway, since work-in-progress has dug a deep ditch on the right, or to be told about the height of water towers, pylons and other obstructions, or to be informed of the serviceability of the radio aids.

A near-blind landing would be needed tonight – and the Emperor was equipped with a number of devices for accomplishing it. There was the instrument landing system, whereby the pilot follows two radio beams, one at the angle of his glide path, the other dead in line with the runway direction and called the localiser. If he goes too far to the left, the needle flicks over to a yellow sector on the dial; if too far right, on to a blue. If he goes too low, another needle rises right up the instrument, if too high, it sags to the bottom. The principle is to keep the two needles making a cross in the centre. There is real beauty in the simplicity of its teaching, except that sometimes a combination of circumstances (especially varying changes of gusty wind with height) can make it easier to propel a camel through the eye of a needle than to keep a heavy, wide-turning aircraft in just that descending condition of azimuth and altitude. Then there is the range, down which the pilot follows an audible steady note – but sometimes he can't hear it in the crackling static of a storm, and the needle on the radio compass can be pulled all over the place around its dial. Finally, on some selected stations (for the equipment is very expensive), the pilot can put himself entirely in the hands of other people, and be brought down to earth by the radar screen of the ground controlled approach.

For Keflavik during that night, the Notams stated baldly that the G.C.A. was for the moment under maintenance, the radio range legs had not been flight-tested and should only be used as a beacon. And of the two parts of the I.L.S., only the localiser was serviceable.

Cavendish had changed places with Seawood, and was now pacing up the tiny floor of the cockpit as though it was a quarterdeck. Every half-hour, as though he could influence the instrument, he bent over the radio while Hooper took down Keflavik's latest weather. But his presence made no difference. The Emperor was racing north at a groundspeed of over 300 miles an hour, but the storm had had a long start.

'You'll want me to stand between you,' he said to Bellamy. 'To keep a look-out for the runway.'

'Please.'

There was another three-quarters of an hour to go. Time to descend. Hooper, as a change from his eternal weather reports, obtained clearance, and Bellamy nosed the aircraft gently downwards.

The Emperor seemed reluctant to descend. For a brief space of time, there she had been, her lights adding a new constellation to the glitter of the sky. And now, like an uninvited guest at a party, she had been asked to leave. She had been found out, a usurper whose heavenly body could not indefinitely maintain a fixed position relative to space, but must return to the earth from whence she came.

The dark tops of the cloud came slowly up to meet her. And then, in a great wet welcome, they hugged her all over. Able Dog's wings shivered from the shock. Snow softly flew towards them in a low unending pattern of dots, starting nowhere, like so many white flies banging themselves to death against the windscreen. The altimeter, like a clock going backwards, read 16,000 . . . 15,000 . . . 14,000.

Bellamy had tuned in the radio compass to the range station, but at present the needle was flickering around its dial, unable to make up its mind where to point. But on the V.H.F. voice radio, they could hear Keflavik Tower giving instructions to another aircraft.

Like a radio play whose plot was oddly prophetic of their own future, they heard:

– You are now Number One to land.

– Roger, roger . . . I'm Number One, Tower.
– Keflavik Tower to Six-oh-six. Latest visibility, six hundred yards blowing snow. Runway lights turned full-bright.
– (Laconically) Six-oh-six is on final.
– Clear to land, Six-oh-six.
– Say (in a conversational aside) is this localiser serviceable? Needle's got D.T.'s.
– Flight checked yesterday, Six-oh-six.
– Maybe it's this dam' wind! What's the cloud base? (Pause.)
– (Very loud) *What's the latest cloud base?*
– Hang on, Six-oh-six. We're just checking for you.
– (Very fast) Where-ja-think-I-am-straphanging-in-a-New-York-subway? (Back to a professional rate of speech) For your information, approach speed of a D.C. 6 is a hundred and twenty knots.
– What's your altitude, Six-oh-six?
– Four hundred feet descending.
– Can you see anything, Six-oh-six?
– (Bitterly) Snow.
– Do not descend below Company limits.
– No answer.
– Here is the latest weather: ceiling indefinite, visibility four hundred yards.
– No answer.
– Ceiling indefinite. Visibility four hundred yards.
– No answer.
– Can you hear me, Six-oh-six? . . . Six-oh-six . . . are you
– receiving me?

No answer.

– SIX – OH – SIX!
– (A microphone switch crackle) Kee-*rist*! See anything, Bob?
– (A brand-new voice, almost inaudible) Nuttin'.
– (With relief) Request your position, Six-oh-six . . . (The gentlest of reminders) Your aircraft intercom is on the broadcast position.
– Thanks . . . (Officially) Six-oh-six is overshooting. Now at three hundred feet, climbing east of the field. Request re-clearance back to London at 19,000 feet.
– You're not making another attempt?

– No, sir!
– Climb on course. Stand by for clearance.
– Climbing on course. Standing by for clearance . . . (A long pause, then good-humouredly, philosophically) Know somp'n? Don't believe you *got* an airfield under that stuff. Just don't believe you have!

Bellamy said to Cavendish, 'There's a D.C. 6 gone back to London.'

'Why . . . couldn't he get in?'

'No.'

The altimeter unwound past 5000 feet. The needle on the radio compass was now fluctuating within twenty degrees of dead ahead. It was too far away yet for the I.L.S. to be effective.

Keflavik Approach cleared them to the Tower, and the Tower, having obtained two-way communication, informed them that they were 'now Number One'.

'Isn't this,' Bellamy asked Seawood drily, 'where we came in?'

Faced with a difficult let-down in very bad weather, a pilot's mind, screwed up in a ball of tight concentration, draws itself furthest away from two images at opposite poles of his consciousness. One is a picture that this is a hide and seek game, and he has hidden himself too well: all he has to do is to call out – 'Here I am!' and run out into the sunshine. The other, painted bolder, is a come-on-let's-get-this-thing over-and-done-with-as-quickly-as-possible.

Both are equally dangerous.

Impatient as he was to get down, mindful of the probable increasing violence of the weather, Bellamy nevertheless was carrying out the standard procedure more fully and correctly than ever he would have done in practice. He knew there were no short cuts to safety. The weather and the visibility were almost impossible. Therefore, his flying must be dead accurate, unhurried, his eyes taking in, all at the same time, a many-dimensional scene of instruments, controls, throttles, and co-relating what he saw with his arms and legs.

The Emperor was bumping about much more now. The

new wings shook up and down, protesting. Eased back, the engines grumbled into the cold, snow-filled air.

'Visibility,' the Tower said, 'is now two hundred yards.'

The needle on the radio compass, tuned in to the range station, wavered and hesitated, but Bellamy could get a mean of its position, despite the bad static that was diverting the signal. He saw the I.L.S. indicator move over hard into the blue sector. Then he throttled back further, and descended to 1500 feet with half-flap and undercarriage down, and all landing checks complete.

The I.L.S. needle came over towards the centre again. Wrestling with the controls in an effort to keep a steady course in the bouncing, turbulent air, Bellamy got the nose of the aircraft pointing in the reciprocal direction of the runway, still keeping exactly to the let-down pattern as laid down by the Company route book.

For a full two minutes, he went away from the airfield, and then altered course on a procedure turn, so that Able Dog finished on a course for the instrument runway, eight miles from the threshold.

'On final,' Seawood told the Tower.

Cavendish stood quite still between the two pilots, alternately staring ahead into the snow-filled darkness and looking at the stop-watch, timing them from the Outer Marker. Able Dog was rocking around like a wild thing. Everyone in the cockpit was held by the tenseness of Bellamy's concentration. Slowly, he allowed the aircraft to move lower. The needle on the I.L.S. localiser gradually crept into the centre.

Lower and lower, the aircraft descended into the blackness of the night. The altimeter lazily unwound, 600 feet, 500 feet, 400 feet, 300 feet. Seawood was calling out their height above the airfield.

At 200 feet, they seemed to break cloud. The only difference was that it became slightly less dark and now the red light on the nose did not reflect back at them.

Bellamy had his eyes glued to the instruments, his hands all the time making their disciplined slow movements on the controls.

'Time!' Cavendish called.

'See anything?' Bellamy asked, his head still down.

'Nothing!'

'Gear up! Rated power!'

At maximum continuous power, Able Dog raced back into the night again. Bellamy took her up to 1500 feet, and once again began the complicated manœuvre of positioning the heavy aircraft in line with the invisible runway.

The Tower reported that the wind had dropped a little. There didn't seem to be so much blowing snow. But on the next approach, though Bellamy brought her down lower, nobody saw anything. On the fourth attempt, Seawood caught a glimpse of two runway lights, flashing by in a sodden muzzy glow – so separate that they seemed to belong to another world, an uninterested, placid world which had no business to do with Emperors.

But someone had at last seen something. The runway was *there*. And on the fifth approach, there was more hope in the cockpit.

Sweating a little with the effort of manhandling the aircraft, Bellamy still remained outwardly self-possessed and calm. He knew he had to get in. He knew the I.L.S. was bringing him accurately to the runway. Putting all his skill and experience into following the needle, doggedly he followed its moving indications. He brought the Emperor down past 200 feet, 100 feet.

'Fifty feet indicated,' Seawood warned.

Cavendish called out – 'Five seconds to go.'

Bellamy counted them to himself – one, two, three, four, five, holding the aircraft level on the artificial horizon. 'Any sign?' he shouted.

'Nothing,' Cavendish said. Then, 'Wait! Yes ... *there are the threshold lights*!'

Bellamy allowed his eyes to come away from the instruments and look out. He saw one white light. The I.L.S. indicator was dead centre. He called abruptly, 'My throttles!' and slamming the four levers hard back, he pushed the nose down.

Another white light reluctantly revealed itself, slightly below them and to port, before snuffing out. The speed dropped past 110 knots. Bellamy edged the Emperor's nose higher until she started to sink into the black bottomless pit below her. He opened the throttles so she hung on her propellors.

Then he saw two more lights, one on either side of the runway. More slowly this time, he closed the throttles again and hauled back on the nose.

Slowly, the Emperor mushed on to new-laid snow. Her wheels made a soft crunch, and began to slow up rapidly. Then she stopped.

For a few moments, nobody in the cockpit said anything. Bellamy got a handkerchief and wiped the sweat off his face. Seawood said, 'Nice landing, sir.'

'Well, at least we're down. Problem now is . . . how do we find the ramp?'

Though he knew Keflavik well, in the blind invisibility, Bellamy had to use his compass, and the map of the field in the route book. The Emperor crawled forward from one dim glow to another.

Bellamy tried the landing lights, which twitched on to grey rocks, half covered in snow, and then shone back in his face. 'Hopeless,' he said, as he switched them off. The wind was tearing at the tail, slapping it about as though it was a rigid steel sail. The side windows were open, and both pilots peered out into the night.

'We've sent a Follow-me Van to bring you in,' the Tower told him. 'But I think it's got lost on the way.'

Eventually, over two thousand miles away from where a swarm of high-up aviation officials and representatives were making their way to New York International Airport to welcome her, the Emperor – her four propellors threshing the wet air, her brakes gently squeaking – loomed up out of the snow-storm, bedraggled-looking and half-frozen, to make her first appearance on foreign soil before an audience of three.

One of those three was Murdoch, the Company's one representative in Iceland, warned by wireless, only too unhappily aware of the great honour that had unexpectedly been thrust on his shoulders.

The other two were American A.F. marshallers, each with a torch. They had been on duty most of the day and all that night. The ramp was already jam-packed full of jet-fighters flying to England, troop transports on their way to Europe, diverted commercial aircraft that had been delayed for the night. They took in the unfamiliar outlines of her unorthodox design. They gawped at the great length of wing, mistily indistinct, contained between a muzzy red light on her port side, and an almost invisible creme-de-menthe glow on her starboard.

One of the Americans pulled down the long peak of his cap, tilted up his head and blinked the snow out of his eyes. Then he said to the other, in a voice shrill with indignation: 'Aw, Eddie . . . for Chrissake! What we got here? A flicking flying saucer?'

CHAPTER SIX

In the packed Reception Hall, the inhabitants of the Emperor surrounded Mr. Brocklehurst and the Chairman with a protective palisade against the onrush of humanity. Irritable voices muttered and shouted. Men parked round the bar. Women sat patiently shushing the children. The harsh metallic voice of the Tannoy regretted to announce cancellation after cancellation.

Sir James was drinking coffee, firmly impressing Brocklehurst with the fact that 'it was the worst Atlantic weather within living memory', and adding on the bright side, 'We'll be airborne within the hour. Six hours or so late . . . that'll be all.'

He saw Bellamy struggling through the mob. 'Want us out at the aircraft right away, Captain?' He drained the last dregs of coffee in his cup with an eager relish. Then he put the cup back on the saucer balanced in his hand and saw the bad news in Bellamy's eyes. 'Well . . . ' he added grimly, 'What is it this time?'

Eastlake and Cruttwell, standing in the group as far as possible from each other, individually held their breaths. Then each of them saw the pilot produce the folder he had been given at the Meteorological Office and they could breathe again. Nothing to do with either of their departments after all. Bellamy said, 'The weather . . .' and began to explain.

Sir James waited until he heard the word *night-stop*, before saying quickly, 'Was Captain Cavendish with you at the Meteorological Office?'

'He was, sir.'

'Then where is he now?'

'He's arranging accommodation with Murdoch,' Bellamy paused. 'It isn't going to be easy, with all this crush.'

Sir James said, 'I feel we should discuss this situation together, Captain Bellamy.'

'Can't see there's anything further to discuss, sir.'

He was so glaringly wrong that the Chairman did not

trouble to disagree with him. There was everything to discuss. A discussion between the two of them properly conducted, would take all night – crammed as it would have to be with descriptions of the growing faith he had felt in the Emperor, even before she had been built, of long tramps in search of money and backers, of political arguments with governments, of fights with other airlines, of exhaustive efforts to keep on good terms with the manufacturers, of long nights without sleep when there were labour troubles, delays, unforeseen mechanical snags. There were millions of man-hours filled with sweat, hope and dreams, all of them delicately balanced on the pivot of a successful proving flight. And the man said there was nothing to discuss!

All Sir James did was to call out, louder and more insistent than before, 'Where's Captain Cavendish? I want Captain Cavendish! Ah, there he is!'

One head taller than the sea of faces around him, the older pilot, with Murdoch slightly ahead of him, slowly struggled towards them. The Company representative reached the circle first. He said, 'I've got two rooms, sir.' He had threatened, fought and bribed to get them. 'Mr. Brocklehurst in 21. And you in 24, Sir James.' He turned to the others and ruefully shook his head. 'Nothing else left, I'm afraid.'

But the Chairman brushed the man aside. 'Captain Cavendish,' he said. 'You've seen the weather?'

'I have, sir. A most complex situation.'

'But surely there must be somewhere –'

Cavendish methodically stroked his chin. 'The temperature at Montreal – ' he began.

It was enough. Through the grey overcast, the Chairman had seen the glimmerings of light. A great hand came up under Cavendish's arm. The Chairman started to move forward and the pilot moved forward with him. 'This calls for a get-together. Between the two of us, I mean. Room 24, Murdoch said. This noise!' The Chairman's round face gave a wince of pain. 'Up there, at least we'll be able to hear ourselves speak!'

It was perfectly obvious to the Emperor's crew and passengers, as they left the circle with Murdoch slightly ahead again, that Bellamy was in high disfavour. Cavendish was the

Chairman's man now. Side by side, they mounted the stairs. On the first landing, Murdoch produced the key, installed them in room 24, and left them alone together.

It was very sparsely furnished. There was one chair and a small bed, with a rectangular slab of grey wool, placed like a prayer rug on the plain wood floor beside it. The curtains had not been drawn, and the Chairman, as though the sight of the snow-filled darkness offended him, walked over and flicked them impatiently across the window.

'Cigarette, Cavendish?'

'Thank you.'

'You take the chair. I'll sit on the bed.' Sir James' body dented the clean counterpane. He leaned towards the pilot, and immediately came to the point. 'Now I shall be quite frank with you. A lightning sketch of all the things *behind* the building of an aircraft like the Emperor . . . that's what I'm going to give you.'

His tongue came out of his mouth, as though to oil his dry lips. And then he started.

He had a wonderful control over words. He picked the powerful ones out as easily as an artist chooses and blends the colours from his palette. The spaces, the change of tone, the lines of the long sentences followed by the emphatic dots of the short ones, all vividly contributed to the design of all his difficulties, the invisible blots on the Emperor's silver sides. And right in the foreground, painted a rich overdraft red, was *the money involved*.

He finished by saying, 'And these enterprises are always so uncertain that something quite minor,' he shrugged his shoulders, 'like night-stopping in Iceland, might be disastrous. The Press might take the wrong slant. People might get the wrong idea. Before she had a chance to prove herself, the Emperor might get a bad name!'

A short silence fell between them. Then with eloquent simplicity, the Chairman signed off. 'That's *my* side of the picture,' he said.

Cavendish fingered his grey moustache, preparatory to beginning the pilot's painting on the back of the same canvas. 'Now from the master of the aircraft's point of view – ' he began, but Sir James was too quick for him. 'Now tonight . . .

we managed to land. Therefore the visibility is adequate for the actual operation of take-off. Am I right?'

His paint-brush parried before it could express itself, Cavendish frowned. 'Just. But – '

'From what Bellamy said, I gathered that the forecast weather on the other side is better than here.'

'That wouldn't be difficult, Sir James.' At last his brush has registered – but the colour and shape were transformed by the Chairman's overlaying, '*But we landed.*'

'After a considerable – '

'And forecasters being what they are . . . the American weather might be perfectly all right, after all.'

'Company regulations – '

'But this is no ordinary *commercial* flight!'

'Very high headwinds, of course – '

'But look at the Emperor's range . . . her power! And what a trouble-free performance she's given us from London!'

'She's certainly kept remarkably serviceable.'

'Smooth! Smooth!' Sir James paused, partly for breath, partly as though now he was positively encouraging Cavendish's collaboration. 'And there's the temperature at Montreal you mentioned earlier.'

'Yes . . . interesting, that. A possibility, perhaps, of a fog clearance earlier than anticipated, *provided that* – '

'Quite, Captain.' The reverse side of the canvas was finished now, varnished and framed. With the same eloquent simplicity as before, the Chairman again signed off. 'That's *your* side of the picture,' he said.

There could, of course, be no doubt about it. Painted on the same canvas by the same hand, both pictures conveyed the same message. But Sir James was not one for stopping there. Modestly, he began to disclaim both the credit and the inspiration.

'You're known all over England, Captain Cavendish. Your reputation is bound up in the success of the Emperor. And how long have you been flying now?'

'Thirty years.'

'Thirty years! Very nearly right from the start of civil aviation!'

'*Right* from the start of civil aviation!'

Sir James quickly corrected himself, 'Of course . . . *right* from the start. You've done all the pioneering. Through all the difficulties. Taken all the chances that has made civil aviation advance the phenomenal way it has done. *And it is still advancing!*' Dramatically, the Chairman came to a dead stop. 'And why?' he added, but before Cavendish could say anything, he had provided his own answer. 'Because men like you are still out there in front . . . leading us on.'

A faraway look came into Cavendish's eyes, as though he was remembering: the excitement, the dangers, the early airmen. He said, almost to himself, 'It's been a long time!'

'Twice as long as Captain Bellamy! Not that I'm going to say anything against him. He's a *young* man, not settled down yet. He's a *skilled* man. But still . . . and I'm sure you see what I mean . . . *a pilot*. I was surprised when I found he was in command on the eastbound.'

'I was reserving myself for the homeward trip, Sir James.'

'Quite! But you and I are of the same generation. We know where our duty lies. And I want *you* to take over now. In a difficult situation like this . . . something more than piloting is wanted.' Sir James raised his head, and his eyes glittered with a burning respect. 'Leadership! The pioneering spirit! You . . . Captain Cavendish!'

For a few moments, they sat in complete silence, looking at each other gravely. The smart that Bellamy had inflicted on Cavendish by the argument on the aircraft was cooling now in the balm of this smooth ointment. The pilot suddenly stood up, towering above the round figure on the bed. 'They will have refuelled her by now,' he said. 'We have lost enough time on this flight . . . *already*.'

Sir James reached the door before him and turned the handle. Standing aside, he waved his hand forward. 'After you, Captain,' he said.

They left Room 24 in high good humour with each other, and walked down the corridor. Beside the tubby figure of the Chairman, Cavendish seemed to be taller and straighter than ever.

Half-way down the stairs, the lights went out.

Sir James made a joke about fuses. With difficulty in the

darkness, they located their own kind. Then the lights came on again.

Cavendish was just saying that the Emperor would be taking off immediately, under his command, when Murdoch came up to interrupt him. The short spell of darkness had *not* been fuses. A tractor engaged in towing the snow-ploughs over the runways had inadvertently taken them over the main power cable, cutting it to shreds.

'But the lights have come on again!' Sir James expostulated.

'The domestic supply and the telephones have an emergency system, sir. That's why everything's on now. But there's no emergency system for the field.'

The Chairman suddenly grasped what the man was driving at. 'You mean . . . there's no runway lights now?'

'None, sir. And no I.L.S. and no main radio. Until the cable's repaired.'

'And when will that be?'

'Tomorrow some time, sir. With all the snow, it'll be difficult. I'm afraid it rules out take-off until after the sun comes up.'

The Chairman seemed to change colour. His cheeks went a ripe bulging red. He appeared on the point of bursting. And then, as though with a supreme effort, his lips closed tight, one on top of the other, and his face reverted to its accustomed calm and its usual complexion.

Sir James had fought nearly everyone there was to fight in the British aviation industry. Alternately with the government, he had been down on one knee and up in arms. He had flattered and threatened. He had borrowed other people's money and mortgaged his own. With his employees, he had inspired a few and driven the others. Even now, on the proving flight, he was still battling – against the very elements themselves. Through all that avalanche, he had won through. And yet, after this single arrant piece of carelessness committed by an unknown oaf, there was only one thing on heaven and earth that was left in *anyone's* philosophy.

And that was to go to bed.

Sir James and Brocklehurst departed, with Captain Cavendish in attendance. Left on their own, without a centre, the human circle from the Emperor for the moment looked lost, until Bellamy stepped into the vacant middle to make arrangements for their lodging.

'Looks like the barn for us tonight,' he said. Then he turned to the stewardesses. 'But you two might as well go to bed properly in the aircraft bunks.'

'Yes, sir,' Lalette said for both of them, and they started to squeeze their way through to the door.

Bellamy called after them. 'Don't use the lights! The batteries are low . . . and I don't want you messing around the cockpit, looking for the master switch. You've got torches?'

They nodded at him vigorously and moved on towards the door. Then, huddling their shoulders up and shielding their faces, they dashed through the snow across the ramp and up the stairs by the Emperor's flanks. In the light of her torch, Lalette opened the heavy aircraft door.

Inside, Angela shivered. 'Cold,' she said.

'Absolutely petrifying. I *thought* the men were being uncommonly chivalrous!' Lalette smiled wryly over her shoulder as she closed the door. 'Let's keep some of that air out, anyway.'

She rubbed her hands together and looked around the cabin. It was not quite dark. An opaque bluish light, comfortless as skimmed milk, leaked in through the portholes from across the snow, and the pale paint diffused it around the cabin into a glimmering ghostly twilight.

'Anyway,' she said doubtfully, 'there's plenty of blankets. Look, if you put your torch beside mine, we can see to get the bunks down.' She kicked off her shoes and stood up on one of the seats to tug at the handles. 'Thank the Lord these are easier to get down than the Astroliners'!'

'I thought,' Angela said at last, still standing in the same place as though she had been really frozen on the spot, 'that you were supposed to be the small and helpless variety.'

'Sometimes,' Lalette said. 'But not here and now. And certainly not for your benefit.' She smiled down at Angela, and then went on fixing the bunks into the down position. 'What wouldn't I give for a cuppa! If the Big White Chief hadn't said no lights, we could make quite a cosy brew. Anyway,' she jumped down, 'I'm going to forage.'

She came back, swinging her torch gaily and tossed a packet of biscuits into Angela's hands. Then she curled herself into one of the seats and said, 'You know, it's really rather fun, after all. It's a lovely sight if you look out of the galley window. You can see all the aircraft and the snow and the lights in the hangar. It's quite a picture!'

Angela had slid reluctantly into one of the seats. She sat, her face half turned towards the curtained porthole, her arms hugged tight across her body as though to protect her.

'I don't think it's fun,' she said flatly. '*None* of it has been. And now this cold!' She clenched her fists and banged them together. 'I never could stand cold Never!' She looked across at Lalette. 'I was brought up in India. Daddy was Indian Army.'

'I see,' Lalette said gently. 'But if you got ready for bed, you'd feel better.'

'I can't. Not for the moment. I'm too cold to *move*.' Her teeth chattered together.

'Well, put a couple of these around you.' Lalette pulled down two of the cellular blankets and tossed them over to her.

'And all the fuss there's been all day! That *awful* send-off! Having Sir James on board! And then everyone *knew* something would go wrong. I know I did.' Angela covered her face with her hands. 'I knew! I knew it! I knew it! And then . . . it did!'

She put her hands down in her lap and looked around the cabin with a sudden calm that Lalette found rather eerie. 'And now to sleep in it as well,' she whispered. 'I feel so shut in, as though I'll *never* get out. Just like we all did up there . . . in the cloud . . . seeing nothing. Just going round and round!' Very quietly, she had started to cry. 'And then that awful landing! Five attempts! Worst I've ever been in.' She looked across at Lalette. 'And other people were frightened, too. I *know* they were.'

Her eyes wandered from Lalette's face, beyond the pool of the torch-light that they sat inside to the grey shadows of the rest of the cabin. But it was all quiet and unrevealing. On the ground, the life good or bad had gone out of it, like an empty cinema with a blank screen.

Lalette shrugged her shoulders. 'Well . . . we're here now. That's all that matters. We *did* get down.'

Angela said wearily that she supposed it was. She reached for her expensive fawn leather overnight bag, and then sat staring at it as though trying to remember what it was for.

Lalette unfastened her tie and unbuttoned her blouse. 'You know,' she said, eyeing Angela warily, 'the longer you sit there, the worse it'll get. The cold, I mean.'

Angela whirled round suddenly. 'Leave me alone!'

Lalette looked away, pretending to be absorbed in the unzipping of her skirt. Then she heard a snuffle from Angela. She saw the tears rolling down her cheeks.

Nervously, Lalette edged nearer. She put out a hand to touch the other girl and then withdrew it. After a moment, afraid to speak, she stretched out her hand again and put it on her shoulder and with quite disproportionate relief, she saw that Angela was going to allow it to remain there. Sympathy and the desire to comfort seemed to well up inside Lalette, only to crack the little vessels of conventional phrases and to leave her without anything to say. She wondered if understanding could come out of her finger-tips and she pressed a little harder for them to express it in good measure. Gently, she edged her hand across the back of Angela's neck and on to her other shoulder. Then she drew her closer.

Quiet minutes went by. The nearness of another human being, even the slight warmth from her body, seemed to soothe Angela. Outside the wind was rising. It pushed and nudged the side of the aircraft as though a big animal moved restlessly in a stall beside them. Instinctively they huddled close to one another like a young litter under a strangely comfortless mother.

Gradually Angela stopped sobbing. She gave her face a final scrub with her ball of a handkerchief. 'I'm sorry,' she murmured. 'All this fuss! I don't know *what* you must think of me.'

'That's all right.' Lalette stood up and stretched, her voice quite shaky with relief. 'It's this damned cold.' She peered at Angela's face in the torchlight. 'You look pretty blue.' She pursed her lips. 'You know what? I'm going to boil a kettle!'

Angela smiled briefly as though her mouth were just trying the feel of it. 'I must say, a hot drink *would* be nice.'

'A hot drink and a hot bottle. Absolute bliss! And absolutely essential!' She fished inside her bag and brought out a pair of highly impracticable satin mules, and then, stockinged heels smacking against the quilted soles, she moved gracefully towards the galley.

She was back almost at once. 'I forgot,' she said, 'about the master switch. Now where would it be?'

Angela shook her head. 'I can't remember from the conversion course. Should I know?'

Lalette pursed her lips. 'If you mean would you get a "below average" if you didn't, no. But unless we're to die of cold and thirst and general frustration, yes, you should. Or I should.' She tapped her white teeth with her fingernail thoughtfully. Then she said. 'Well, it's bound to be up at the front. That's one thing.'

Angela looked distressed again. 'But ought we to? I mean, Captain Bellamy did say – '

Lalette said quickly. 'Well, there's no harm in *looking*. It's not sacred up there. Not *quite*. And I *think* I can remember which it is.' She started to move towards the door. 'Come on,' she called over her shoulder. 'Stretch your legs. Come and make sure I don't pull up the undercarriage or something.'

Angela got up and followed her through the flight deck door.

Through the wide front windscreen, a strange glow came from the lighted windows of the Reception Hall which outlined the dark emptiness of the two pilots' seats, glittered here and there on the glass of an instrument, and showed up with a cold, flat light the deserted put-away look of the navigator's table, the engineer's panel and the radio officer's equipment. Hundreds of dark button eyes looked back at them, round dials grinned or frowned or kept blank faces.

Angela shivered. 'It all looks different, doesn't it?'

'Very!'

Lalette scanned the front instrument panel, and then turned and looked at the engineer's. 'Now let me see . . .' She laughed. 'It would be rather awful if I really *did* do something dynamic!' She giggled helplessly. 'Imagine old Bellamy! Only imagine!' She looked in silence for a moment. her finger poised. 'Ah, there it is, I betcha!'

She flipped on a switch with a for-a-sheep-as-a-lamb air. 'I'll wait here if you'll try the kettle and the hot-plate. Will you?'

Angela nodded.

'Oh, and try the cabin lights as you go by.'

Through the half-open door, she saw the long cabin suddenly illuminate. Then Angela put her head round the doorway to the galley, and called, 'Everything's working. Hot-plate, kettle and lights.' She smiled.

'Praise be!' Lalette waltzed herself skilfully round and round up the aisle and into the galley. She screwed her eyes up and rubbed them. 'I say, is it the light? Or do you feel a bit grim?'

'A bit.' Angela put up a hand to her face, and it was still not quite steady.

'Look,' Lalette said, giving her a gentle push out of the galley, 'leave all this to me. You choose your bunk. The ones at the back haven't been used yet. And I'll make you a drink.'

She hummed to herself while she boiled water, filled two hot bottles and put them in the bunks, and made the hot drinks. Five minutes later she put her head round the door. 'Get into bed, I've put your hot-water bottle in. The drink's just coming up.'

She came slowly up to the bunk, carrying one of the Company's cream plastic trays. 'If you wanted tea, I'm sorry but you're going to be disappointed. I thought it would keep you awake, so it's hot milk instead. And there's a couple of aspirins, just to make sure.'

She watched Angela, looking relaxed and comfortable in her demure white nightgown, sip the drink gratefully.

'There's something in it, isn't there? What is it?' She sniffed the beaker that she was holding in both her hands to keep them warm. 'Brandy?'

Lalette nodded and laughed. 'I took some out of the first-aid kit. That will *really* warm you. Now don't say what someone or other'll say because no one will say anything. I'll pop it back when we get the bar tomorrow. Otherwise, they might think Hamilton was having a nip!'

They both laughed heartily at the very idea of Mr. Hamilton breaking the law.

Angela drained the beaker, and handed it back to Lalette. 'You make a good nurse,' she said, 'and I feel much better.' She huddled herself under the blankets. 'But tell me,' she added anxiously, as Lalette turned away. 'Weren't you nervous yourself? I mean, just a bit?'

'Oh, I was terribly nervous at the time. But I knew Bellamy would get us down. If it was possible. And if it wasn't . . . well . . . there wasn't much any of us could do about it.'

'But in here . . . in the cold, thinking about it . . . I was *awful*, I'm afraid. Daddy would have *hated* it. He loathes that sort of thing.'

A ghost of a smile plucked at the corners of Lalette's mouth but was immediately laid low. 'Oh, different things make different people feel miserable. It's the cold that gets you . . . Now with me – '

'Oh,' Angela said a shade disapprovingly, 'I really can't imagine anything getting *you* down. You're not the kind.'

'Well . . . let's hope you're right.' Lalette began to close the curtains of Angela's bunk. 'I don't suppose it'll be a long night, but sleep well.'

She walked over to her own bunk and finished undressing. She folded her clothes with mechanical respect, and then scrambled into bed. Then she rested her body, now suddenly tired, the first humble, unpaying guest on the soft foamy freshness of this much-advertised luxury bunk.

The others had gone to the barn.

This was a disused hangar, separated by wooden partitions into cubicles containing six or eight bunks. When things got desperate, mattresses were taken along there, together with rough brown army blankets, and it served as an overflow dormitory.

Through half a mile of snow, they had battled down the road to pitch darkness, leaving Bellamy and Cavendish behind to wait for the 04.00 Tafors – the long range weather forecasts – due any time now.

The crew knew the place of old, but it was worse than they remembered. The emergency supply did not cater electricity for it, and the place was already full of stranded men of a number of nationalities. A couple of noisy poker games were going on by candlelight. A party over in one corner was guarding its liquor against the invasion of uninvited guests.

'You're sure this is it?' Payton asked Douthwaite.

The navigator smiled. 'This is it, sir.'

They went from cubicle to cubicle, peering into the darkness to try and locate odd unused beds. Riley and the doctor got two bunks, one under the other, in quite the quietest backwater. Payton was not so fortunate. The only bed he could find was in a cubicle larger than the others, in which a crap game was in full swing. He pulled his ration of scrubby blanket around him, and turned his face to the wall.

Hooper and Rawlings found two beds over on the far side, away from the door. Before he got into his bunk, the engineer tested it. Under his weight, it didn't give an inch. 'Christ!' he said.

Fully clothed, they clambered in and lay down. For a number of minutes, they listened to the snores and the talking, while outside the wind howled. Then Rawlings suddenly sat up in bed, and said, 'Hell to this!'

Hooper grumbled. 'Pretty damn bad, isn't it?'

'Bloody awful beds! Bloody awful blankets! Bloody awful noise!' A large leg came over the side, above the radio officer's bunk.

'What you doing, Red?'

'I'm going!'

Hooper sat up in alarm. 'There's nowhere to go!'

'There's the aircraft.'

'But Bellamy said – '

'This is an airline . . . not a school! Girls' dormitory . . . boys' dormitory. Hell – who does Bellamy think he is? The Headmaster?'

'All the same – '

'He won't find out, anyway.' More of Rawlings appeared to Hooper's eyes. The engineer eased his whole body gently back on to the floor. 'Are you coming? Or aren't you?'

'Well, if you're going, Red – '

Outside, they found the snow had turned to hail, coming down thick and fast over the bleak blasted heath of Keflavik aerodrome. They lowered their heads and ran.

The wind, gusting in from the Atlantic, beat strongly

against their half-hidden faces, continuing steadily south-south-west.

The 04.00 Tafors showed that a marked improvement could be expected in the Maritimes around 20.00 next day. Gander would still be out, but Goose was lifting. New York and Boston, recovered from their sea fog, would both be good.

But along the route, the winds would still be against them, in some zones, as much as 90 knots. Cavendish, after considerable thought, had decided on a Composite track, over the Greenland ice-cap till civilisation was reached round the Laurentiens and Montreal. And as Bellamy didn't disagree, he didn't argue, but instead, after Cavendish had set off for the barn, stayed behind to have a chat and a cigarette with Murdoch.

It was very late when at last he said good night and went off to bed. His way led across the ramp. In spite of the icy wind, he turned his eyes up to look at the millions of pounds' worth of aircraft herded there, each under its quilt of snow.

Suddenly a great glow of light shone out into the blizzard. Reflected in the storm, it looked like a bonfire, producing a great falling mass around itself of white ash. He stopped. The Emperor, among all her dark bedmates, glittered from nose to tail in a blaze of glory. Her cockpit lights, her cabin lights, her navigation lights, sent out a flaming glow of warmth into the cold light.

He walked quickly across the fifty odd paces to the aircraft. With a frown, he noticed the footprints in the snow around the steps.

Then all the lights went out.

Blinking in the sudden darkness he ran quickly up the stairs. He banged loudly on the door. 'What's going on?'

There was no answer. He hauled the big door back and stepped through into the cabin.

'It's only us, Skipper,' Rawlings' voice said, half-apologetically, half trying to bluster it out. 'There wasn't a hope of sleeping in that barn, sir. And – '

Hooper interrupted him with: 'Some skippers, sir, they let the crew sleep in the aeroplane.'

'Get your things,' Bellamy said, 'and get going!'

Then he remembered the lights, half-forgotten in the surprise of finding the two men. He tried the switches. The cigar-shaped cabin was flooded with hard illumination. The pilot's face was pale. Hooper and Rawlings looked embarrassed and slightly indignant. And the grey curtains of the girls' bunks were quiet and still, but almost visibly listening like wide-open elephants' ears.

Bellamy looked at the lights. He said, for the first time raising his voice a little as though he was too tired for a moment to control it, 'Who put the master switch on?'

'Not me,' Hooper said quickly.

'Only just got in here. Haven't touched a thing,' said Rawlings.

The grey curtains parted. 'I did,' Lalette said.

Bellamy swivelled round slowly and stared at her. For about ten seconds he kept his eyes on her face. Then he looked away from her and back to the others.

'Sorry, sir,' Rawlings and Hooper said together.

'Turn the master switch off, Rawlings,' Bellamy said, and the engineer hurried up the aisle to the flight deck.

The cabin became once more dark. Bellamy reached over and flicked the switch off. As though he could feel her waiting for him to speak, he said quietly. 'Why did you put the switch on?'

Lalette's voice was low. 'To make a hot drink. I'm sorry.'

Bellamy said nothing. When Rawlings came back, he said, 'I'm sorry, Skipper, we didn't mean . . .'

'I know,' Bellamy said wearily. Then as the two of them shuffled towards the door, he shone his torch for them and said, 'Good night.'

Lalette called out to him. 'Captain Bellamy. I'm very sorry. About the lights . . . and everything. I . . . we . . .'

He shone his torch, a little to one side of her, away from her eyes. Her face was white and strangely pointed with fatigue in the indirect light. Her short hair, rumpled with sleep, was like a flurry of dark gold snowflakes. She blinked her eyes. Just for a second, her mouth trembled.

'You didn't touch any of the other switches?'

'No, Captain Bellamy.' She moistened her lips. 'I'm sorry,' she began again flatly.

'That's all right then,' he said. 'Good night.' He turned towards the doorway.

'Good night,' she said sadly. She sat still, listening to the sound of his steps on the metal stairway. When all was quite quiet, she lay down on the pillow, her mouth pressed into its soft thickness.

'Whew!' Angela sat up in bed. 'I must say, he needn't have made *quite* such a song about it. After all – '

She stopped.

'Lalette,' she said.

There was no answer.

'Come on,' she said. 'You can't be asleep.'

Lalette said, 'I'm sleepy. Good night.'

Angela listened. The wind still thumped and snuffled the body of the aeroplane. Every few seconds a burst of hail like machine-gun fire rattled on the metal sides. But along with the noises of the storm outside went a quieter one – one that kept mood with the snow and the cold.

Someone else now was crying in this damned aeroplane. But not for fear of it, not for the unimaginable things that might happen in the morning.

For something much, *much* worse.

CHAPTER SEVEN

NEXT morning, under a sky filled with the grey remains of the snowstorm, the ramp at Keflavik took on all the appearance of a Martian cattle market. Tethered steel bulls of civil airliners snorted with impatience to be gone. Little lambs of jet fighters gave out curiously ferocious bleats. A pig of an American troop transport (with no manners at all) grunted and pushed its way out first to the front and was off.

Above everything else, like a high-and-dry whale, towered Emperor Able Dog.

Angela and Lalette walked past her on their way to the Catering Section to collect the stores. After a time, Angela broke the regular scrunch of their feet in the snow, with 'Sorry about all the fuss last night.'

Lalette shrugged her shoulders. 'Oh, that's all right,' she murmured. 'My own fault.' She was walking with her head down, holding her forage cap on her head with her hand so Angela couldn't see her face.

'I must say, Captain Bellamy got rather worked up about nothing very much.'

Lalette smiled rather shakily. 'He wasn't exactly in the best of spirits.'

'I wouldn't be surprised if he was mad at himself. About that awful landing, you know.' She paused. Then she asked, 'Tell me, have you seen much of Captain Bellamy before this?'

Lalette's blue eyes appeared suddenly from behind the arm that still held on to the cap. 'We-ell,' – she looked startled – 'he used to come home on leave sometimes with my brother Chris. But then I was still at school. And he's taken me out a couple of times to the flicks since I came on this route.' Then she suddenly stopped, looked at Angela, and said, 'Why?'

'Oh, has he? He gets around, doesn't he?' The other girl drew a deep breath. 'But I didn't mean that sort of seeing actually. Though there's no telling what goes on, *is* there? What I did mean, was *trips*. Have you flown with him much?'

Lalette laughed 'Now I get you. What *you* mean is trips in general and landings in particular?' She shook her head. 'Sorry I can't help. I've done three with him. All as calm as millponds.' She pushed open the Catering Section door. 'But,' she said over her shoulder, 'if it's any comfort to you' – she pointed at the chalked-up notice in front of them on the wall – 'by the look of *that*,' she waved at Captain Cavendish's name on the board, 'Old Father Time himself is taking over!'

'And a good job too, I think.' Angela gave a brief wintry smile. Her first that morning.

After they had collected everything that Hamilton had ordered, they walked back to the aircraft. Lalette said, 'Well, at least they're looking after her!'

Certainly she wasn't being neglected. Men with brooms were sweeping her wings clear of snow. Her leading edges were being sprayed with alcohol. Two bowsers had squeezed their way to her. Cruttwell was giving her engines a loving once-over. Payton was fussing. Cavendish was walking up and down beside her, with his hands behind his back. Rawlings was cursing any ground-staff who came within earshot.

Inside the cold passenger cabin, the Chairman and the Under-Secretary sat silently side by side, waiting for the engines to start.

Able Dog was Number Sixteen to leave the ramp. She had been kept waiting so long, it was past eleven local when her chocks were pulled away. Murdoch, now grey with tiredness, had made a brave attempt to make the pomp and circumstance due to the second send-off of the proving flight sound not too much like the tinklings of a one-man band.

But for all his efforts, as Cavendish taxied out to the end of the duty runway, there was an air of discouragement and irritation through the whole aircraft.

Cavendish ordered the Before Take-off Check. When it was completed, Seawood obtained permission from the Tower.

But Cavendish refused to be hurried. He sat in a study of concentration, feeling his dry fingers with his thumb, as though testing them one by one. Then he donned a pair of immaculate gloves. His eyes staring out at the long empty runway ahead and the sky beyond, he took the throttles and manipulated all four with the delicate dexterity of a surgeon.

The Emperor began to move. Wider and wider the throttles opened under Cavendish's gloved fingers, until, within the space of twenty-two seconds, with the fuselage bumping up and down lugubriously on the oleo legs, he had completed the operation, severing the umbilical cord that held his aeroplane to Mother Earth.

And Able Dog was airborne.

But the change of element seemed to do no one inside her any good. Over the whole aircraft, a depression had settled, a kind of shattering of all codes of hierarchy and social structure, a stripping to the bare skin of that necessary importance that makes men think it at all worth while to work. The snow and ice of Keflavik had somehow got through their bones and into their souls, and they shivered in the unaccustomed cold.

Cavendish climbed steadily away from the course of the other westbounds – for the normal track was via Prince Christian and Gander – and started on the huge Composite to New York, towards the high wastes of the interior of Greenland. The cloud thinned practically to nothing. They were leaving the bad weather well to the north. Apart from the top of the Maritime front that they would hit over Labrador, there was no further high cloud forecast for the rest of the trip. Now in the sunlight, Able Dog was no more than a silver cross in the vast blue bubble of the sky. Her shadow, ringed in a double rainbow, momentarily darkened the small white pebbles of cloud, thousands of feet below her, which gathered into screes and cairns that gradually combined to form a long sunlit shore stretching to all the limits of the eye.

Jimmy Seawood looked down at the cloud and the sea and ran his fingers through the long fair hair, that lay untidily backwards over his head like a field of trampled-down wheat. It was a habit he had, and since he kept his chin up at the same time, his whole attitude implied a slightly sardonic superciliousness which was misleading. In actual fact, Seawood was shy and inclined to be sensitive, and this hair-fingering was nothing more than a fairly common form of nervous tic.

At their cruising altitude of 24,000 feet, Cavendish turned to the engineer. 'Speed on the graph, Mr. Rawlings?'

'Five knots above it, Captain!'

Cavendish rubbed his hands with satisfaction. 'Excellent!' he said. 'Everything else working satisfactorily, Mr. Rawlings?'

'Just like clockwork, sir.'

'That being the case . . . and with no trouble about the weather, I think we can safely leave you on your own up here for the first three hours, don't you, Mr. Seawood?'

Recognising this allusion to his inexperience, Seawood flushed. But all he said was, 'I think so, sir.'

'Did you succeed in sleeping, Mr. Seawood?'

'Two or three hours, sir.'

'Then you were more fortunate than myself. I shall ask Captain Bellamy to do the second three hours. The third three hours will be my watch. I think that's fair, don't you, Mr. Seawood?'

'*Very* fair, sir,' Seawood muttered, already having worked out that such an arrangement meant he was on watch longer than the others. But at least it would leave him up here on his own, and with relief he watched Cavendish climbing out of the left-hand seat to join Bellamy in the rest compartment.

Seawood liked flying. What he was not so keen on, he reflected, were the other subjects in which for his job it was just as important to be thoroughly proficient: psychology: Indian mind-reading: automatic slot-machinery, and a university standard of tact and etiquette. He flew with a varied selection of captains, each with highly individualistic ideas on what he wanted the first officer to do for him. Some of them were all orders, and were outraged if he did anything without being told. Some of them gave few orders and expected him to get on with his job quietly and without any fuss. Of course, Cavendish was more difficult than the average. Harder to please. More inconsistent. More conscious of his own importance. More full of –

'Mr. Seawood! Two degrees off course *already*!'

The First Officer jerked into immediate action. 'Sorry, Captain.' He turned the aircraft the requisite two degrees on the autopilot, as the Captain moved his great height carefully towards the rear. Behind Cavendish's back, the spirits of everyone on the flight deck began to rise.

And in the passenger cabin, too, things were beginning to

look up. In that snug metal world, gradually a proper sense of values was being restored. Everyone started to feel less depressed by the delay and the lack of sleep. And there the man responsible for so miraculous a change was Hamilton.

He did it superbly.

Lunch, he had decided, would be served early. An hour and a half after take-off, he started to serve cocktails and sherry, strutting up and down the carpeted aisle like the captain of a man-of-war.

On most trips, it was hard to convince the passengers that he was indeed not the captain, for he was at least five years older and two inches taller and a dozen times more the air mariner than the average aircraft commander. Now, as though the tall bottle which he carried in his left hand contained the same elixir that had restored Alice to her normal size from the dwarfdom of Wonderland, Hamilton dispensed the necessary recuperative potions to the passengers under his care.

Sailing back into the galley, he said to Lalette, 'Sir James will have another sherry, Miss Greenacres, if you'll hand me the Amontillado!' His smile made a crescent of his pale lips. 'I'll see if I can tempt Mr. Brocklehurst with another cocktail. Put one on the tray, Miss Knight! Oh, and a clean napkin! Hurry, please! Hurry!'

He folded the napkin quickly over his arm, and walked down the now gently swaying aisle like a ballet-dancer. After Sir James, he got customers all the way down the line. As if at a royal reception, they took their drinking cues from the Chairman. One after the other, they held out their glasses like obedient children in a well-run nursery. Only Cruttwell's drink remained untasted as he kept his nose sunk in an engineering journal.

After such an introduction, lunch made a triumphal entry. Hamilton had the inspiration to add the personal touch to the menu, always the secret of good catering. There were Hors-d'oeuvres à Joliffe, Chicken Suprême Flight, Fruit Compôte de L'Empereur.

'Well!' Hamilton said, looking at his work with the pride of a true artist. 'They all seem very cheerful now!'

Up at the front, Rawlings turned round and said to Seawood, 'You know I told the Skipper we were five knots above the graph? Well . . . now, on the same power settings . . . for some damn reason, we're five knots under it!'

In the galley, Angela finished washing and stacking the lunch-trays and poured herself a cup of coffee. Lalette was taking a spell off duty, and was already fast asleep in the back seat.

Hamilton was still pacing the quarter-deck. Most of his charges were now sleeping away the bright landscapeless hours of a sun-filled sky. A drowsy after-lunch contentment filled the cabin. Able Dog held steadily on her course as though fearful of waking her occupants. Her engines hummed a gentle reassuring lullaby, as near to bees-in-the-clover as aircraft engines can get.

Angela looked over the supplies for afternoon tea, wiped and polished all the immaculate enamel and chromium surfaces, and then hovered between the door to the galley and the first of the rear seats.

The sleepiness was catching. Even Hamilton's measured tread weighted the calm, gave it permission to continue. All could rest in the security over which he kept watch. At the next turn, he took in the tail area, including Angela. 'Everything all right, Miss Knight?'

'Yes, thank you.' She smiled, and almost yawned. Last night, with its fears and troubles and discomforts, seemed a long way away now. The sunshine brightened still more the strawberry upholstery, and cheerfully coloured up the whole interior of the cabin.

'Piece of cake for you girls, these sort of trips!' He looked in at the spotless galley, and nodded approvingly. 'Washing-up finished? Crew got all they want?'

Angela nodded.

'Might as well sit down then. Soon as the Chairman wakes, I want to see you girls bustling!' He looked at his watch, timing Sir James' afternoon snooze, as might a nurse the first after-crisis sleep of a very sick patient.

Angela sat down and picked up a magazine. She eased her feet a little out of their shoes which were beginning to feel too tight, and rested her head against the soft cushions at the back.

Slowly, the heavy air and the bright hard light forced her eyelids shut. But after only a few seconds she opened them quickly. Immediately she shut out the cabin with its double row of steady unmoving seats and the glimpse of the wing through the porthole, she had the unpleasant feeling of being swung very slightly from side to side, in a nauseating, frightening motion.

She looked across at Lalette, but Lalette was still peacefully asleep. She looked at the sleeping men, but they remained the same black and brown and blue bundles of a few minutes ago. Hamilton had altered his perambulations only to dab gently at his forehead, and to check his weighty chin for stubble. The door to the flight deck remained closed. Nothing had happened, except she must have been asleep. Like the nightmare of suddenly falling, this was a quick self-waking one. But instead of downwards, the movement had been sideways.

Afraid that she would sleep again, she walked back to the Ladies' Powder Room and filled the small bowl almost to the brim with cold water. She marvelled at the wonderful lack of vibration. The water had scarcely a ripple on it. She creamed the light make-up off her face, and dipped her face right into the bowl, opening her eyes under the water. She gasped, shaking the drops off her chin and nose and rubbed her face briskly with a linen towel. She felt wonderful. She dabbed behind her ears with the cologne in the big blue bottle and let little trickles run down her thin wrists. She smiled at her reflection in the mirror, feeling immensely brighter, more vigorous and alive than the stuffy sleepers in the cabin.

Then just beside her came a soft little noise: slip-slop, slip-slop. She turned quickly. The water in the basin was having a miniature storm. A wave scooped out from the hollow of the bowl flopped over on the port side, to be immediately swung back and toppled to starboard.

She looked at the basin disbelievingly for a moment. Then just as suddenly it settled back to its former sleekness. Its plain blank face said that once more she had been dreaming. But the water was now a couple of inches further down the bowl, and on the steady unvibrating floor were two ragged little puddles.

Mechanically, Angela fetched a cloth and mopped them up. No bottles had fallen over, no powder was spilled. She went back to the mirror and outlined her lips with her lip-pencil and filled them in with her scarlet stick. But her eyes were a slightly different colour now. The black pupils had almost swallowed up the soft sherry-coloured irises. And twice she had to reach for tissue and blot off the lipstick where her not-quite-steady hand had overlapped the careful outline.

Before going back to the cabin, she carefully re-rolled the sleeves of her cream poplin shirt, combed her hair and checked the dead straight line of her stocking seams.

Mr. Hamilton was just outside the galley. Taking a deep breath, she said suddenly, 'Did we hit a bumpy patch or something, a minute or two ago? The water in there . . . it spilled. I wondered . . .?'

'Did it now?' Mr. Hamilton grinned. 'When you've flown as long as I have, my girl, you'll know all sorts of queer things happen in the tail. Always wobbling, the tail is! Least bit of bumpiness and away it goes!'

His eyes travelled beyond her head and suddenly alerted. 'Quick, girl, get your monkey jacket on! Wake Miss Greenacres!' His hand in one great swoop checked his own collar and tie and his immaculate jacket. 'The Chairman's stirring! Hurry, girl, do!'

But the stirring never grew into an actual uprising. The Chairman moved from side to side, pulled down the pillow impatiently and grunted down once more into the depths of sleep. The only one to leave his seat was Mr. Riley. He pulled down his overnight bag from the rack above his head and brought out a bleached pigskin toilet box. He loped slowly to the back, the sunlight catching the smooth sealskin blackness of his bent head.

As he came nearer, Mr. Hamilton, standing very straight, inclined his head slightly and called to Angela, 'Mr. Riley might like a cup of coffee, Miss Knight.' He turned and smiled at the Public Relations Officer.

'Good idea, Hamilton. Very sound!' He grinned and stroked his cheeks. 'Make it fifteen minutes. Must have a shave. Got a beard like a porcupine!'

'Right you are, sir!' Mr. Hamilton rubbed his hands together, and called, 'In fifteen minutes, Miss Knight. *If* you please!'

Angela had been sitting on the high stool in the galley, tapping her heels softly against the metal walls, and watching the little foam flecks of cloud drift and disperse and reform again. She made some coffee and set a small tray with biscuits.

Then Mr. Riley swept the curtain to the gentlemen's room aside impatiently. He held the white handkerchief hard against his cheek, but even so the bloodstains darkened it. 'Got any dressings?' he said. 'Should be some already in there. *Your* job, Hamilton!'

The chief steward's chin rose a little. 'Elastoplast for Mr. Riley, Miss Knight,' he said coldly. 'A small one, I think, will do.'

'Damn large one! Biggest you've got. Here, give it me!'

He took the first-aid box from Angela's hand and went back and drew the curtain.

When he reappeared he said: 'The tail moved. Shook from side to side like a damned great shark!' He patted the plaster. 'I could do with that coffee.'

'Miss Knight will bring it to you in your seat, sir.'

Angela came back, a small worried frown drawing together and levelling her brows. 'Did you hear that, Mr. Hamilton? He said the tail moved. I think I felt it, too. A little while ago. You know, when I said . . .'

'Look, girl!' Mr. Hamilton took her arm and winked. 'When you've flown as long as I have, you'll know! Some folks can take their liquor. And some can't. And our friend, Mr. Riley, is one that . . . ah well! Least said, soonest mended, that's my motto! But what I will say is . . . I don't think you saw him with the Amontillado. The Chairman's *favourite* Amontillado!' He paused for effect, and tightened his lips primly. 'But I did, Miss Knight. *I* did.'

CHAPTER EIGHT

'THIS speed, Mr. Seawood!' Rawlings grumbled. 'We should be doing better than this, you know!'

The First Officer still sat on his own in the right-hand seat. Sweat had begun to run down his forehead. More than ever before, his fingers combed his hair. Things seemed to swim a little in front of his tired eyes, and his arms and legs seemed unbearably heavy to move. Far below shone the endless clear white miles of the high Greenland plateau.

He said, 'I've taken the auto-pilot out. Ought to be all right now!'

Rawlings' beady eyes left the instrument and looked up at him. 'It's worse! Ten knots down now! Can't you see the airspeed indicator?'

Seawood applied himself once more to the business of hand-flying the Emperor. But the engineer's exasperated voice called out again, 'Can't you keep her steady, Mr. Seawood? That's what's doing it. All this yawing from side to side!'

The First Officer had been aware of the situation for some time. Now, the gyro in front of his eyes which had been on a heading of 295 degrees moved round to 298. He edged on a sliver of port bank and a touch of rudder. The gyro shot back, past 295 on to 292.

'It isn't bumpy, is it?' Rawlings asked. 'Looks calm as a millpond to me.'

'Just a bit of clear air turbulence. She won't stay on course.'

Rawlings gave a snort of disbelief, but did not contradict him. Back went the gyro to 295. Stopping itself abruptly, it started to swing back to the left again.

'This thing!' Seawood muttered. 'Nothing but a damned old holy cow!' He spoke the words bitterly and vehemently, but he did not really mean them. Like many first officers, he had way down inside him a deep-seated inferiority complex in regard to his own flying ability, carefully hammered into him by captains, instructors and the accurate hard hits of the weather itself.

A long thick blanket of cirro-stratus came lazily towards

Able Dog, and by degrees enveloped her. Viciously, Seawood jabbed at the right rudder to get back on course. In the clammy greyness of the cloud, the Emperor's nose reeled to starboard as though he'd punched it.

Rawlings got up from his seat and came forward. 'Look, Mr. Seawood . . . I'll help you put in the automatic pilot.'

'I don't see what that'll do.'

'Stop this yawing! Get our proper speed!'

'I don't agree with you at all.' Seawood's chin came right up. 'Only make things worse!'

Just to show how easily he could hold her, even under instrument conditions, Seawood kept his left hand lightly on the control column, and with studied indifference again ran the fingers of his right hand through his fair hair. These engineer officers (the whole crew for that matter) were always criticising the first officer's flying. That was because they daren't criticise the captain's. Joe, that's what a first officer was.

He turned towards Rawlings and with a brave attempt at putting him in his place, observed with a slow smile, 'You engineer officers are all the same! Make a lot of fuss about nothing at all!'

With a sudden fearful jerk, the Emperor whipped over to the left. Seawood was flung against the windscreen. Two route books clattered off the throttle pedestal. A cup by Hooper's elbow rattled to the floor and sent a steaming smell of coffee through the whole cockpit.

Then just as suddenly, like the return swing of a gigantic horizontal pendulum, the nose swung over violently to starboard. Bellamy, staggering through the door from the rest compartment, was hurled against the stacked radio equipment beside Hooper. He shouted to Seawood, 'Here . . . what's going on?'

The First Officer turned a white face round to him. 'I dunno, Skipper. Think an engine cut!'

Bellamy cautiously lowered himself into the left-hand seat, expecting at any minute a new frenzied change in attitude. But none came. Able Dog flew on sweetly and tamely on course. 'I've got her,' he said to the First Officer.

Rawlings exploded, 'Nothing wrong with the engines, sir!'

'You sure?'

'Positive, Skipper! We've been yawing port and starboard for the last hour.' He glowered at Seawood. 'Soon as there was a bit of instrument flying to do . . . got worse.'

Cavendish made a sudden entrance on to the flight deck. 'Well . . . what are we doing up here?' he asked.

Caught between two captains, Seawood miserably tried to explain. 'There was a sort of wobble.' He looked at the still rudder, the unmoving control column. Hopelessly, he burst out with, 'Can't describe it. Sort of wander . . . and then a kind of *twitch*.'

'Kind of inexperience, more like!' Rawlings growled to Hooper behind his hand.

'I expect he's a bit tired,' Bellamy said to Cavendish. Then turning to the First Officer, he asked quite gently, 'You haven't had many hours hand-flying the Emperor, have you?'

'No, sir.'

'The highly boosted controls . . . there's very little *feel* in them. Different from the Astroliners you're used to.'

'Yes, sir.'

'You go back and have a bite of lunch. I'll look after things for a bit.'

Seawood slid out of his seat. The two captains talked over the situation for a while, and then, satisfied, Cavendish followed the First Officer back to the rest compartment.

The Emperor was flying perfectly steadily now. They were still in cloud, but there were no sign of any bumps. A peace descended again on the cockpit. Everyone relaxed. Rawlings lit up a cigarette, and with a sigh of contentment puffed out a great cloud of smoke.

Bellamy, his hands gently moving the very obedient controls, sat thinking. Seawood was a good first officer. Certainly he hadn't had much time on the type. Certainly he was tired. All the same, those were two great flips of the tail.

'Mr. Rawlings,' he said at last. 'Did you see Mr. Seawood get all fed up with hand-flying her?'

'Yes, sir,' the engineer replied promptly. 'Seemed to be having a bit of difficulty.'

'I see.' Bellamy was aware that sometimes tired pilots would give the controls some incredibly rough treatment, out of sheer vexation that the machine wouldn't do what they wanted.

'Engines been all right?' he asked the engineer.

'Couldn't be better, Captain.' Rawlings swept his hand lovingly over his colony of dials, all of them so well behaved that they were reading exactly what they ought to.

But Bellamy went on, 'When this bad yawing happened . . . where were you?'

Rawlings gave a thoughtful chew of remembrance on his cigarette. 'Well, I'd got out of my seat to find out what Mr. Seawood was up to, sir – '

'So you wouldn't be able to see the instruments on your panel?'

This check-up on his movements looked like the beginnings of a ticking off. In an aggrieved voice, Rawlings said, 'I couldn't actually *see* them, sir. But all the same – '

'Nobody, in fact, could tell us if an outboard suddenly cut?'

This was definitely a reprimand. 'But we'd been yawing in dribs and drabs for an hour before that, sir!'

'Only in a very minor way.'

Rawlings said with dignity. 'And everything's all right now, isn't it, Captain?'

Bellamy smiled slightly at the round circles of Rawlings' glaringly innocent eyes. 'Everything.'

Mollified a little, Rawlings asked, 'What makes you think it might have been an outboard, sir?'

The pilot was busy putting the three levers of the automatic pilot back into position. When it was engaged, he turned round to the engineer and comfortably shrugged it off with: 'Nothing. Just checking . . . that's all.'

'Must have stopped a few after-lunch cat-naps at the back,' Rawlings suggested, not without a certain inward satisfaction.

'Yes,' Bellamy said. 'Wouldn't be surprised if it *did*.'

Rawlings was right. The first jolt had wakened most of the passengers. Hamilton kept an anxious eye on the Chairman, who was moving his closed lips up and down like a baby trying to suck at a receding bottle of sleep. It eluded him. Sir James sat up suddenly and blinked his eyes. Mr. Brocklehurst straightened himself and looked around.

Hamilton hurried to the galley for his clean folded napkin and two glasses of fresh orange juice. As he reached out for the jug, he was thrown sharply against the metal wall of the galley. He caught his shoulder painfully against one of the metal uprights of the doorway. Instinctively, he moved round a little and held on. Through the porthole he could see nothing but cloud. Countless grey shapes, disintegrating as they went, fled ghostlike past the windows.

Moving cautiously away from the upright, he rubbed his shoulder, smoothed his hair and walked unhurriedly into the passenger cabin.

Lalette and Angela, both rather tremulously eager, were helping the passengers to straighten themselves. Everyone had been banged against the sides of the seats. A few magazines had spilled on the floor. Riley's glass was rolling about on the carpet.

Hamilton made his way to the Chairman. 'Allow me, Sir James.'

'Thank you, Hamilton.'

'Your paper, Mr. Brocklehurst.'

Sensing the man's uneasiness, the Chairman observed, 'We get some nasty clouds up here.'

Hamilton recognised his cue. Respectfully he made his own indirect contribution to Mr. Brocklehurst's peace of mind. 'And very common,' he said, 'at this time of year, sir.'

CHAPTER NINE

HOOPER took the fingers of his right hand off the radio key to give them a bit of exercise. Like four odd-sized gymnasts, they bent double and stretched up straight in double-quick time, all perfectly in unison. He had just finished sending their position at 19.00 G.M.T. – 57.04 North, 58.16 West. With it, went their height (still 24,000 feet) the outside air temperature (– 41° Centigrade), the fuel available (35,000 lb.) and the latest weather observations by the pilots.

He looked out of his porthole. Little beads of moisture fell down the glass. Beyond, he could just see the two port engines churning their way through a grey mass of cloud that was slowly turning black. This, he thought to himself, must be the front that had been closing down so much of the North American seaboard.

Then he put his hand back on the key and waited, still listening. The message hadn't been acknowledged. Radio conditions were poor. He had had difficulty with Keflavik. Now Goose Bay, south of them, was coming in and out, in a wavering, semi-apologetic way. Then finally, rather faint, in the midst of the crackling and popping of the static, he heard the Emperor's call sign and R. Received.

He sighed. The outside world had now been informed of Able Dog's position. In at least three Control Rooms, it would soon be plotted on large Mercator maps. It was reassuring to know, after that mysterious tail-waggling an hour ago, that the rest of the world now knew where they were. He looked at his watch. It would be past tea-time in his semi-detached house at Hayward's Heath. Jennie would be sitting with one of the neighbours, listening to the six o'clock news. There she would hear of the Emperor's progress, of which he was the spokesman. In the one international language of the world: Morse.

Hamilton passed him, and he said, 'I'd like a cup of tea.'

When it came to him, scalding hot and brown, he thought to himself: the news will be over now: Jennie will have heard about me.

But as it happened, not only Jennie but many people all over the world were hearing and reading about the Emperor, interested in her progress. The British press gave it a column with the nearly unanimous heading: EMPEROR DIVERTED TO ICELAND, DUE HEADWINDS.'

The American newspapers, however, had not been so reticent. Due to the same bad radio conditions that Hooper was experiencing, there had been conflicting reports, muddles, inevitable confusion that took some time to get sorted out. The New York newspapers announced: 'WEATHER SENDS NEW BRITISH AIRCRAFT SKEETERING BACK TO SECOND BASE: WELCOME COMMITTEE UP ALL NIGHT AT NEW YORK INTERNATIONAL, WHILE BRITISH FLIERS KIP DOWN IN ICELAND.'

Able Dog, regardless of the comment and interest of the world, now flew comfortably on under her anonymous grey blanket of cloud. The tea in Hooper's hand was still hot and sweet.

Two tea-leaves floated in it, becalmed in the centre. He bent his head low over the cup, feeling the thin fragrance of the steam on his face. With a teaspoon, he idly netted the two leaves and shook them out in the saucer.

In front of him, he heard Bellamy say, 'Getting darker. Put the propellor anti-icers on.' Out of his porthole now, he could hardly see the port inner engine, the stuff was so thick. He felt an updraft tremor through the wings. He thought to himself: better drink this up quick before it gets too bumpy.

He brought the cup up to his lips and was just sipping at it when there was a sudden violent swing to port, and the whole cupful, burning hot, was dashed over his face. He cried out in pain, but nobody heard him.

Bellamy had slammed out the auto-pilot and was straining his right foot against the rudder pedals. And then, just as suddenly, the great tail swung round again and they careered well over to starboard in a horrible skidding motion. The jolts were far worse than they had been before.

Rawlings yelled, 'It's the engines! The outers are cutting!' He had seen the momentary immense drop on the fuel flowmeters.

Bellamy shouted back at him, 'Throttle them both right back then!'

He watched two levers on the throttle pedestal move backwards. But by that time, Able Dog was flying perfectly normally again.

The pilot turned to Rawlings. 'What the hell happened there?'

'The outboards cut. One after the other. That's why we swung.'

'Which cut first?'

Rawlings fingered his chin and looked at the flow-meters. The needles of both outboards, labelled 1 and 4, used the same dial. 'Difficult to tell, sir. Happened so quickly.'

'One cut out and came on again . . . then the other did the same?'

'Think so, Skipper. Only momentarily . . . both of them.'

Bellamy looked out at the clammy cloud that was now moving Able Dog up and down in unsteady bumps. 'Couldn't be ice,' he said. 'Not at this temperature.' Then he saw the speed dropping rapidly – 180, 170, 160. 'Better bring the outboards in again, Mr. Rawlings. All the instruments reading correctly?'

'All of them, sir.'

'What about fuel?'

'Well . . . we're still on the outer tanks both sides. They're well down, sure. But they've both got nearly five hundred gallons in.'

'And they're running all right now.' Bellamy's face was wrinkled up in worried concentration. 'Damned things . . . what the hell could have happened?'

Nobody on the flight deck answered him. Hooper's eyes, far away from his radio now, were glued to the engine instruments opposite him. Even Douthwaite had stopped work to hear what was going on. Into a tense, expectant silence came Captain Cavendish from the rest compartment. 'What is it *this time*?'

'That's what we're trying to find out.'

'Whenever I go to the back for a minute, Captain Bellamy . . . something seems to happen.' He glared moodily around him. 'What are we doing about it?'

'Nothing. Everything's okay now.'

Bellamy explained the engine cutting. Cavendish listened

with his head on one side, and then said, 'I feel I shall have to stay up here at the front.'

With a shrug, Bellamy relinquished the left-hand seat, and climbed into the second pilot's position. Now sitting side by side again, he suggested to Cavendish, 'How about having Eastlake up? After all, they're *his* engines.'

'You think it might come on again?'

'Might. Better put the seat belt sign on, too. Just in case.' He leant back and turned on the switch, at the same time as Cavendish despatched Douthwaite for the engine designer.

The illumination of the seat belt sign just stopped the Chairman making a determined assault on that last privacy of pilots, the flight deck. Now, strapped in with the others, he sat in a frenzy of concealed irritation, parrying Brocklehurst's questions. The first great lurch had sent him hurtling against the Under-Secretary's sharp shoulders; and no sooner had he disengaged himself than the swing to the right had sent the man's bony elbow like an arrowhead deep into his stomach.

'What could this be, Sir James, do you think?'

It was the same question the Chairman was asking himself. 'Expect someone else sat on the switches!' he said, but his laugh this time rang hollow.

'You think it might be that again?'

'Well . . . everything's going all right now, isn't it?'

'It will not be repeated, I hope?' Brocklehurst's tone implied a surfeit of this aircrew habit of parking on propellor switches.

'Captain Cavendish will want to know the reason why . . . *if it does*!'

'And all this strapping in?'

'Can't you see the cumulus outside, dear fellow? Cavendish is only making *quite sure* that in all this turbulence . . . we don't get hurt.'

Brocklehurst chewed over this information in dubious silence. Like the rest of the cabin behind him, he was still trying to readjust himself to this new situation. Most of the passengers now had decided that *something* was going on under the smooth outside skin of the Emperor. They sat now, staring out of the windows through the ghostly greyness at the unbroken curve of the wing and the silver covers of the engines, striving to pierce through that metal with their eyes in an effort to diagnose that shuddering disease.

The weather on its own could no longer take all the blame. Nor could Hamilton's account of the curious things aircraft tails get up to, coupled with Riley's drinking capacity. And Sir James' propellor switches, even with Brocklehurst, were wearing remarkably thin.

Sitting beside Enderby-Browne, Riley had gone quite white. 'There's probably an explanation . . . perfectly simple, perfectly true . . . to those big shakes,' he said. 'But *I* don't know it. So I just sit here, saying to myself . . . why? It's not knowing . . . *that's* what gets on your nerves!'

The doctor had recovered from the momentary acceleration of his own heart. He said, 'The truth is never so bad as you think it is,' noting down at the same time: *query for aircrew selection boards – Is an imagination an asset to airmen?*

'The *truth*,' Riley said, 'as I was saying to you earlier – '

Two rows in front of him, Eastlake and Cruttwell were arguing with each other over the cause of the trouble. 'It was the engines!' the airframe designer said. 'I tell you . . . I heard them cut!'

'Must have been the controls,' Cruttwell objected. 'You'd never get a swing like that . . . no matter how many engines failed on one side!'

'*But the engines cut!*'

Many rows in front, Payton heard them and another silent shiver went down his already cold spine. The only person who was exactly the same as before was Hamilton. Though he could no longer strut up and down the cabin, he was putting his enforced idleness to good use. 'Tea!' he was saying to the stewardesses. 'Sir James prefers very strong Indian. There are not enough cream cakes to go round . . . go easy on the crab for the sandwiches! Clean cloths – '

On and on it went. Lalette sitting beside Angela, heard the other girl's fast breathing and saw the fear in her wide eyes. 'It's all right now,' she whispered, pointing out at the rotating propellors. 'Look . . . everything's working!'

' – and as soon as that seat belt sign goes off . . . I want to see you girls *moving*! Whether or not the milk – '

By their very ordinary subject, the staccato little sentences were a comfort. Undisturbed by aeroplanes' jolts and jars, Hamilton still went on planning for the essential inevitability of the new meal.

When the navigator came in through the door from the flight deck, Sir James called out to him from his padded prison seat, 'What are you doing up there, Mr. Douthwaite?'

'I think Captain Cavendish will be coming back in a minute, sir.'

'I see! Nothing wrong, of course?'

'Oh, no, sir! At least . . . not that I know of, sir.'

He went on to the back towards the two designers and interrupted their argument. Eastlake was not displeased to discover that the aircrew were calling for Cruttwell – not himself. That meant he was right after all. It was *the engines*.

Cruttwell, called upon to explain the curious behaviour of his engines, stared at all the dials, which now read exactly as they ought, listened to the pleasant purr outside, scratched his bald head thoughtfully, and suggested 'ice'.

Ice is one of the habitual criminals of aviation. It does things in the air that according to all the laws of physics it shouldn't be able to do. Cruttwell had heard, for instance, of one case of kerosene freezing up on the filters, momentarily blocking the fuel to the engines. He said doubtfully. 'Could that be it?' Then he looked at the air temperature gauge. Minus 44 degrees Centigrade now. Cold enough, in all conscience. But not *that* cold.

Then he said, 'Could it be ice on the intakes?' That would prevent the air (which provided most of the combustible materials) from getting into the engines, again causing them to cut.

'Hardly any ice outside,' Bellamy said, and pointed to the few crystal spots that ornamented the windscreen.

Cruttwell hesitated. When he spoke again, he said his words timidly, as though he expected to be contradicted. 'You know . . . back there, it didn't *seem* to be an engine.'

Rawlings growled. 'Well . . . it was!'

'It's all right now, Mr. Rawlings."

'Sure . . . but for how long?'

The weather outside was getting worse. Dense black cloud

like thick smoke swallowed Able Dog up. She bounced. She banged. All her plates quivered and shuddered. A wing dropped to the left, and Cavendish pulled it up on the control column.

Because there was nowhere else to sit where he could study the engine instruments, Cruttwell sat cross-legged on the floor of the flight deck, fixedly staring at the round bland faces of the dials.

'That was a bad bump,' Cavendish was saying when the nose of the Emperor dipped slightly, and then rocketed off to the left.

'Here we go again!' Douthwaite murmured.

The aircraft was behaving as though it had suddenly lost its head. Off it careered, this time to the right. 'Put full left rudder on!' Bellamy called, and the pilots' legs jammed tightly against the dual-control rudder pedals.

'Doesn't move an inch!' Cavendish yelled. 'Can't get it to budge!'

Bellamy's face, screwed up and red with the effort, dripped with sweat.

Able Dog seemed to be flying sideways, like a gigantic crab. Then all of a sudden, as though released from what was holding her, she gave another great lurch to the left. Light hail pattered on the windscreen, and out of the inky-black air, unseen updraughts punched at the fuselage and tilted the wings.

'I'm scared of the tail!' Bellamy shouted through his teeth to Cavendish. 'Won't stand much more battering like this.' And then louder, in anger and exasperation, he yelled, 'Cruttwell! Anything showing on those damned instruments?'

Rawlings called hoarsely back, 'The outboards are cutting again! Then they're coming in again . . . one after the other. That's why we're swinging!' The engineer throttled back engines one and four. Cruttwell hung on for dear life to a stanchion beside him.

The slapping this way and that was still going on. 'Inboards are cutting now,' Rawlings reported. 'Again . . . first one side, then the other.'

'These damn rudder controls!' Cavendish roared. 'What's gone wrong with 'em, Bellamy?'

'How about throttling back all four?' Bellamy suggested. 'See if it stops the swinging a bit.'

But Cavendish was anxious to get out of the turbulent wet air of the cloud. 'I'm going to get on top of this stuff first!' He turned back to the engineer. 'Give me take-off power on all four!'

The motors roared up again, only to die out on the port side. They were still going crab-wise. 'It's the controls,' Bellamy said. 'Must be!' He had already put the booster controls selector into the emergency position, but without the slightest effect, although an entirely separate hydraulic system was now doing the work. Rawlings was still crying out, 'These goddam engines!', his big fingers rushing all over the place, pulling at throttle levers, touching propellor switches.

Inching up through the cumulus, Able Dog struggled, her airspeed dropping further and further back on the indicator as her great sideways sweeps continued. Both pilots, on the climb, now seemed to be having trouble with the elevators as well as the rudders.

But now, as the violence intensified, all that became important was the necessity to survive. What was causing the seventy-ton aircraft to dance this mad witch-doctor waltz became secondary. All thoughts were whistled clean out of everyone's heads but the paramount need to hang on and live.

Both pilots, straining together, each on his own set of controls, tried to curb the Emperor's capers. But still she skidded sideways, skating helplessly in the snow-filled gloom, her motors fluctuating violently, all four engines now cutting alternately in pairs, first the port pair, then the starboard. With sickening judders, her whole airframe rocked and shivered. The wings shimmied up and down, bending and giving in the rough air.

'Christ!' Rawlings gasped. 'This is it!'

White-faced, strapped in his seat, Hooper called up, 'Want me to send an S.O.S., Skipper?'

But Cavendish was much too busy to hear him. The Emperor blundered, tripped, lurched all over the blind cloudy air. It was impossible to keep on course. The two pilots did their best to steer a rough mean. Douthwaite took notes of her nose-nodding plunges – but in a half-hearted way, not really knowing what he could do with them, doubting the position that his pencil at last managed to draw on the drunken, reeling table in front of him. He had found out, just before they hit the bad weather, that there was an eighty-mile wind blowing, somewhere between west and south-west, but he heard nothing but the soft pattering of hail on the fuselage, and the roaring of the engines at take-off power.

Not at all like a heroic picture of a ship's struggle against a storm, Able Dog staggered – choking, gasping, reeling, hurtling to the left and to the right, and then drunkenly moving all ways; more like a grotesque fish being gassed to death in thin air, denied its own element, its huge tail thrashing round in the convulsions of dying. Inside her, thirteen people sat strapped in their seats, and Cruttwell hung on grimly to his stanchion, all quite powerless, all doing nothing; while up at the front, sitting too, the pilots did their best to keep her seventy tons from losing the magic that kept them floating in the air, grimly preventing her from giving up the ghost, from showing her beaten belly to the sky, from hurtling spiralwise through the cold dark air into the endless net of ice and snow that Labrador held beneath her.

But all through her wild antics, the Emperor's wet metal skin was giving battle. The tail might swing. The wings might rock. The plates might shiver and vibrate. But she was strong. Cruttwell, furious that she was twenty knots slower than he had dreamed, had complained bitterly that Eastlake had made the fuselage like a battleship's. Now, that layer of metal fat was an extra safeguard. Everyone inside her felt warmer for knowing it was there. Her paroxysms might be violent and unorthodox; her wings and tail might bang and strain, but all the time, she showed no mark of taking any punishment. Her outside skin was unmarked and unbruised. Just . . . wet.

Bellamy and Cavendish did what they could for her in her paroxysms. Hanging on with a mixed feeling of hope, they straightened her wings when they dropped. They tried to get her to climb higher, to top the bad weather. But her air-speed was too low. In between her skids, she was mushing badly.

At the back, the passenger cabin was heavy with the smell of fear. They all sat, silently now, strapped in, waiting for the end. But then, as the buffeting went on, sick and tired though they were, the fear began slowly to dissolve into an agony of helplessness. They watched the cloud outside. They seemed to tense themselves every time another violent swing was expected, as minute by minute Able Dog lurched onwards, nearer and nearer to New York.

Bellamy's eyes were beginning to ache from staring at the green lighting of the instruments; the artificial horizon that was their yardstick in this topsy-turvy world of whether they were on their head or their heels: the airspeed indicator, its needle fluctuating violently: the gyro compass, and the half-dozen other dials that fed him some clues of what was happening to the aircraft relative to the ground. He closed his eyes, wrinkling his whole face as he did so, and rubbed them wearily with his left hand.

The bumping suddenly stopped. The yawing from side to side went on, but when Bellamy opened his eyes again, magically, he could see. A blinding dazzle of snow and ice showed up five miles below him. Purple shadows ringed the peaks of two mountains that stood out to finger the slanting beams of the sun from the west.

Able Dog, as though the tune of her devil's dance was still inside her head, slid to and fro for a few minutes in the clear air. And then, like a queen caught red-handed in a wild party, she suddenly pulled herself together, and flew on over Labrador, steady and stately.

Bellamy watched her with wary disbelief. There was a clear horizon ahead, full of greens, yellows and blues of the northern sunset. They had passed the front now – the air temperature had shot up 14°. Gradually, the darkness was closing in on the hundreds of square miles of cold desolation below.

But inside the Emperor, the lights were full on, people began to recover, ask questions. Life revived. For nearly an hour more, Cavendish kept them all strapped in, just in case Able Dog suffered another outburst. But everything went on smooth and calm and untroubled. And he reached up his right hand and flicked off the seat belt switch.

The Chairman was up at the front first, at last able to burst in to this topsy-turvy pilots' world from which he had been so long excluded. In his agony, he couldn't wait to reach the pilots' seats, but from the cockpit door burst out to Cavendish, 'You didn't radio that anything was wrong, did you?'

Cavendish turned round, surprised at the loudness of Sir James' voice. 'No, sir. I didn't.'

The Chairman gasped with relief. 'Thank God for that!' he said.

CHAPTER TEN

COMING down from the north, leaving the cold Atlantic and Labrador way behind them, it was warmer now. The outside air temperature around Able Dog was only −22° Centigrade. As though a child's pencil had moved over an enormous blank piece of paper, the white landscape below her had disappeared under a dark lead-coloured scribble. In the quiet evening air, with the sun paying its last respects to her with a coating of gold on her silver tail, the Emperor flew majestically south towards civilisation, with not the slightest tremor in the whole of her huge frame.

But inside her fuselage, the sixteen souls were without her resilience and magnificent aplomb. Most of them had been thoroughly frightened. Angela's hands were still shaking, and her eyes were wide with fear. Riley's lips were a kind of frightened blue. Even the doctor's heart thumped out at well above its usual speed. And when, somehow or other, the frantic caperings had ceased, and just as they had thought life was about to end, life began again, their relief was boundless. But after talking it over, and trying to smile, they remembered the miles yet to go. And everyone retreated into his own private thoughts, fearful that at any minute she should start acting up again. There was something wrong. By now, all on board were convinced of that. A flood of questions had flowed from the Chairman's lips. 'What is it?' 'How bad is it?' 'Can it be rectified in New York?'

To all of them, the technicians had shrugged their shoulders and said they didn't know, they couldn't say exactly.

Sir James had observed grimly that they damn well better find out, and had stumped back to his seat in angry silence. Hamilton, seeing the need for his services yet again, his own private feelings as inscrutable as ever, strutted up the aisle, as though nothing untoward had happened at all. 'The Amontillado!' as he said briskly to Lalette, and looking both girls up and down as though they were about to take part in a Regimental Parade, he uttered the evening orders: 'Dinner will be early tonight! I want everything served . . . eaten . . .

washed up . . . *and put away* . . . by the time we reach New York!'

But the Chairman, though conscious of the minute steak and potatoes which he ate, was busy trying to catch up on his dreams, now fast dissipating to nothing in his mind. He was thinking that if the uncontrollable yawing started up again, the pilots might well decide to land at the nearest suitable airport – Montreal – instead of proceeding to New York. And then, there would have to be explanations. If the Press didn't worm something out of somebody, they'd make up a story even more lurid, even more damaging to his much publicised plans for the Emperor.

Up at the front, Bellamy stared out at the beginnings of the night, looking anxiously for signs of bad weather. There was a wisp or two of cloud, nothing more. He turned over in his mind what could have caused the Emperor's dangerous antics. The really bad swinging had started only two hours ago. Seemed like two years. Moodily, he hauled out a packet of cigarettes and offered one to Seawood, who had replaced Cavendish in the left-hand seat.

'Have one?'

'Thank you, sir.'

Bellamy passed over the packet. Seawood took one, and said, 'Nasty while it lasted.'

'Very nasty.' Then he added, 'Must have been pretty vile at the back, wondering what the hell was happening.'

'But what *was* happening, sir?'

Bellamy shrugged his shoulders, and jerked his thumb backwards to where Rawlings, Eastlake and Cruttwell, their voices raised, were arguing hotly about the same subject. 'I think it was the boosters . . . but the engines *were* cutting. Anyway, I'm not going to compete with the experts.'

Eastlake, not having been up at the front and hearing the engineer's evidence that the engines were fading out, said, 'Well . . . that's it!' Cruttwell's eyes, however, went wide with indignation at so facile an explanation, and brought in the boosters. Rawlings, listening to them both, said belligerently, 'You can keep the whole damn box of tricks! Me for a posting back to Astroliners!'

Unconcerned with the fears and worries inside herself,

Able Dog slid into the slowly forming night, as darkness came up like a black tide from the ground to reach them at 24,000 feet. High above their heads, the same old stars trooped out again, bright and beautiful as ever.

And then, one by one and isolated, below them the little lights pricked through. Trappers' cabins in Northern Quebec showed up their tiny yellows; a mining village made its minute Milky Way on the ice and snow. Gradually, civilisation came towards them. Able Dog flew high above the beginnings of the Laurentiens. Ski-lodges showed up gaily. St. Jovite, St. Agathe and St. Adèle blazed one after the other like signal bonfires leading to the great glittering sea of every-coloured lights that was Montreal.

The Emperor passed to the left of the great cross of lights on the top of Mount Royal, made no attempt to divert to the airport at Dorval, and joined the Airway for the last hour's flying to New York. Cavendish came up to replace Bellamy for the final finish.

Everybody had had a wash and a clean up. Everybody had eaten Hamilton's dinner. Everybody looked down at the lights, now bearing them company all along their route, and thought warmly to themselves: this is almost as good as being down on the ground.

Brocklehurst coughed. Then he spoke for the first time in two hours, nodding his head at the illuminated ground beneath. 'Awfully pretty sight,' he said, '*Awfully* pretty.'

High in the sky, for many miles around New York, hangs a complicated network of invisible roads. The pattern of their whereabouts, printed on a plain piece of quarto size paper, is included in every airman's route-book (no matter his nationality), who flies to the civil airports of Idelwild, La Guardia or Newark, and is called the New York Holding and Area Facilities. A lot of different coloured lines go criss-cross in an anatomical jumble of innumerable four-legged Radio Ranges, all pouring the secret position of their dead straight limbs into the ears of airmen who listen on the right frequency; keeping him in the steady note of the middle of the road by whispering Dit-Dah when he's on one side of the leg, and Dah-Dit when he's on the other. Here and there, on that same map, a lozenge shape denotes a Fan Marker, where, as an extra aid to position, a light will flash on and off in the cockpit of an aircraft dead overhead, identifying itself by various combinations of dots and dashes. More frequent as the airports are approached, minor race-tracks make their appearance, innocent-looking and anti-clockwise, tucked in at the intersections of range legs, especially ordered for airmen to mark time there – the inevitable companions of bad weather over the terminals, the hated Holding Points.

Along the tortuous by-lanes of this giant Snakes and Ladders Board, south-west to Philadelphia, north-east to Gander, north to Montreal, south-east to Bermuda and north-west to Chicago, flow the world's airlines out of New York, and especially dog-legged to avoid collision, the arrival traffic pours in.

On that night, along the north-east leg of Mitchell range were four Idelwild-bound Astroliners, flying above 6,000 feet, separated by a three-minute time interval. Three D.C.6's were coming up from Bermuda at differing heights. Half a dozen Constellations were checking up to Gander along the Fire Island route. And dotted all over the area, being kept a strict watch on by New York Control were a gaggle of D.C. 3's, Stratocruisers, D.C. 4's, all being kept skilfully separated by being detailed to fly on different lines of the chequer board. And right at the topmost edge of the area, flying into the game on the north-east leg of Poughkeepsie range, after eleven hours flying on the Composite, Iceland to New York, came Emperor Able Dog.

Over Poughkeepsie's cone, Cavendish checked in, and Poughkeepsie replied with a cheerful American Roger, stand-by for clearance. But when it came, to Peekskill only, tagged on to the end of an instruction to maintain 24,000, was New York's latest weather: wind south-east, five knots: visibility half a mile in slight drizzle.

Cavendish said furiously, 'Stuff's come in off the sea again! After all that, they're going to stack us up!' He stared moodily down at his copy of the Holding and Area Facilities Chart already on the pedestal between the pilots, his eyes paying particular attention to the wretched race-track Holding Points. Then he turned to the engineer. 'What's the fuel state?'

Sweat rolled down Rawlings' face like water running down red standstone. 'Well . . . these gauges aren't good, as you know, Skipper –'

'*How much fuel?*'

'Less than three hours, sir.'

New York came up with their clearance, first in a slow drawl, 'A-bull Dawg – ', and then crisp and clear and very fast, 'Able - Dog - cleared - to - Westchester - direct - Glencove - direct - Idelwild - range - direct - Scotland - cross - Glencove - 22,000-Idelwild-19,000. Hold-in-the-pattern-at-19,000. Expected-approach-time-02.14.'

With some prompting from Seawood, Cavendish repeated it back. Then he snapped, 'Zero two one four! That's a long time to wait!'

'Must be a full stack,' Seawood said. 'All that bad weather, I suppose. Flood of delayed aircraft converging on Idelwild.'

Cavendish started to let down. Over La Guardia, suddenly all the lights on the ground went out. Now and again, in the clear darkness, the navigation lights of other aircraft showed up a vivid red or green. They, too, went out as Able Dog once more nosed into cloud.

At Scotland, Cavendish dutifully reported at 19,000, and throttling back to save as much fuel as possible, started to go round and round the mulberry bush of the Holding Pattern, while the pilots listened to an eternal spiel of orders to other aircraft from Idelwild Approach Control, waiting patiently for the open sesame of 'Emperor, Able Dog' preceding an order from the ground.

Screams, shouts, a rapid fire of angry American and hesitant, un-understanding mixed up echoes in some language with a heavy coating of French round it, denoted the fact that a foreigner had made a missed approach on the runway, and now floating, lost, in the stack, was snarling up the system, endangering hundreds of lives by not carrying out the proper overshoot procedure.

Cavendish gave a sigh of exasperation. It was over a quarter of an hour before they were cleared to descend to 18,000 on the first leg of their descent.

Gradually, Able Dog crawled downwards, while her occupants, tired out, could do nothing but sleep and wait. The doctor was making up notes on the effects of an emergency in the air on the human body, and had underlined *causes sudden and excessive aftermath of tiredness.* Bellamy had closed his eyes in the rest compartment, his arms and legs stiff from battling with the controls. Cruttwell and Eastlake, who had been arguing with each other over the cause of the Emperor's curious behaviour, began to feel too fatigued to continue.

But the Chairman, stirring a cup of coffee Lalette had given him, was methodically and grimly sorting out in his mind the innumerable problems that awaited him, when at long last Able Dog set her wheels down on American territory.

One by one, the aircraft in the stack, separated by 1,000-feet intervals, and helped in the end by the Instrument Landing System, touched their wheels down on Runway Zero Four (named after the magnetic course of its north-easterly direction) through the thick grey mist that came rolling in from the sea.

The time crept slowly by.

'Anyway,' Hooper said with relief, when at last they were cleared to the range station. 'One thing we can be thankful for. We've stopped bumbling around from side to side. That's something!'

But there he was, in a sense, wrong. Cavendish was very tired. His instrument flying wasn't what it was. Keeping a heavy aircraft dead in the centre of an I.L.S. radio beam can be very difficult. The needle on the round-faced instrument had flicked hard over into the blue sector.

Cavendish turned to the left. The needle accompanied him, passed the centre, and finished hard over in the yellow sector. Cavendish turned to the right.

Zigzagging painfully from side to side, Able Dog, at last Number One to land, her wheels down now, her landing check complete, flew lower and lower into a woolly, unseen, unwelcoming world. Her rudder twitched. Her ailerons moved up and down continually, as though she was waggling her wings. A moist dew of rain (as though it, too, was sweat) spattered on the brow of her windscreen.

Two and a half miles from the beginning of the runway, still left of the beam in the yellow sector, but at the prescribed altitude of 700 feet, the needle on the radio compass did a complete half circle. Seawood reported over the range station.

'Come right on in, Able Dog,' said the new, friendly voice of Idelwild Tower. 'Clear to land.'

Cavendish punched the stop-watch on the instrument panel, and put down flap. Able Dog descended.

Half a minute went by. The aircraft was still in a grey-black stew, with no meaning, no beginning, no end. Her navigation lights reflected back on themselves in a mizzly gloom.

At four hundred feet indicated, there was still nothing. Cavendish was now exploring the blue side of the I.L.S., and Able Dog, with her left wing down, was straining through twenty degrees in an effort to get back into the middle of the beam.

The speed fluctuated round 125 knots. Then Cavendish, noticing how low he was, started to pull the nose back.

Discouraged, the needle fell back further – 122, 118, 116.

'Approach Lights!' Seawood shouted. 'Starboard! Starboard!'

Cavendish raised his eyes from his strict surveillance of the instruments and looked out. Below the nose, a few hundred yards ahead, a portion of the dark air had smouldered into a sullen red, and then two stubby lines, slightly inclined towards each other, seemed to burst into flames.

The pilot swung the Emperor to the right. As he did so, the speed dropped to 110 knots.

Cavendish, lined up now with the lights, and anxious to be down, called to Rawlings to reduce power to 7,000 compressor r.p.m.

Seawood murmured, 'You're undershooting!'

Able Dog wallowed. The tail began to swing again. Before reaching the first approach light, that jutted out 700 yards into the water, the aircraft started to sink. Cavendish pulled the nose up, and called for 7,500 r.p.m.

Rawlings, to be on the safe side, as he always did, gave him an extra thousand. But Able Dog still sank.

The first light went by, apparently just under the wing. Douthwaite saw it, with a little ring of reflected light round it in the still water. Hooper got a glimpse of it, too, and muttered, 'God . . . we're low!'

Cavendish called for 8,000 r.p.m. Rawlings gave him over nine thousand. The speed flickered round 100 knots. At that low speed, with the heavy drag of flap and undercarriage down, there was difficulty increasing it. They seemed to be skimming just above the water. Four more lights went by. In the gloom, they could see the beginnings of the runway lights now. Seawood saw in horror that they seemed to be *above* the aircraft.

Runway Zero Four at Idelwild juts out like a breakwater, dropping at its beginning a clear twelve feet down into the sea. Able Dog struggled just above the water. Only two of the red lights remained before the threshold, shining misty and green a hundred yards away from them.

The aircraft's tail frantically juddered. Her nose came up. Cavendish called for 10,000 r.p.m. What he got was nearly all the power available in Cruttwell's immense engines.

Seawood was sure the aircraft started to climb *up* to the runway. He saw a black wall, perpendicular and unyielding, dead in front of them. He thought to himself: there goes the undercarriage on that sharp cutting edge. The nose was shaking to and fro as though it was in a fit. The whole aircraft was in a begging attitude. The Emperor was on the point of stalling.

Then somehow or other, shuddering all over her body, Able Dog started to climb. She rose above the wall. The threshold lights flashed by.

Cavendish, realising they were climbing, called out 'My throttles!'

'Your throttles,' Rawlings echoed him.

Cavendish was surprised to find the four throttle levers so far forward. He took them in his gloved hand and pulled them suddenly back.

Able Dog seemed almost to stop dead in the air. Deprived suddenly, a dozen feet above the ground by now, of all the immense power by which she was literally hanging on her propellors, the Emperor shook and shivered. Then the left wing dropped. Everybody on board had a horrible sensation of going down and down and down.

Then the port wheel connected with the wet runway, giving it a tremendous thud that made the whole aircraft quiver like a leaf, only to be followed, a second later, by an even more fantastic noise as the starboard wheel thundered on to American soil.

Douthwaite peered out into the night to make certain that the undercarriage legs hadn't crashed right through the wings. Then in his log, he wrote: '*Touched down Idelwild*, 02·31.

As soon as they had slowed up at the end of the runway, Rawlings said, 'I want to look at the port gear, sir.'

'Why, Mr. Rawlings?'

'We're skee-whiff, Captain! Something's gone! We'll collapse in a minute!'

Glowering at him, Cavendish stopped. Rawlings produced the Aldis lamp, and in its light studied the left undercarriage leg. He said gloomily, 'We're at least six inches down on this side. Might get us to the ramp . . . if you go carefully, sir.'

'It's only the oleo leg, Mr. Rawlings,' Cavendish called out, gingerly taxi-ing forward again.

They were a long time reaching the ramp. There was no doubt about the fact that they were certainly tilting to the left. And then there was a further delay when they at last reached the tarmac.

The Company steps were missing. In the pandemonium of so many arrivals, everyone was using everyone else's.

That was all right normally. But steps are part of an airline's advertising equipment. Knowing that Very Important Persons will be photographed on them, the Company's name is always most prominently displayed in order to claim a modest share in the ensuing press publicity. That night, with a battalion of photographers waiting to take pictures of the Chairman disembarking from the Emperor, it was unthinkable that he should make his descent on Pan American, or K.L.M. or even B.O.A.C. steps.

The station manager, red in the face even under the glaring neon floodlights, was shouting into the rain, 'Where the hell are our steps?' even as Able Dog came up to a brake-squealing halt by the chocks.

The Medical Authorities' doctor mounted by courtesy of

Scandinavian Airlines System. He asked Hamilton the routine questions: 'Everything all right? Nobody sick on board?'

The cabin kept quite quiet as the Chief Steward shook his head. Brocklehurst jerked round suddenly in his seat when the American went on: 'When did you let the bomb off?'

But Hamilton replied with an expressionless face that he'd let the aerosol bomb off an hour before landing. The air still reeked with its pungent disinfectant. The doctor left, satisfied.

Anxious to put their two feet back on to the ground, everyone got up and crowded round the door behind the Chairman. Then Sir James looked down and saw a sheer drop of twenty feet where the steps had been taken away with the doctor.

Below, the ground engineers, working feverishly, had located the Air Enterprise steps at the far end of the ramp, in the process of being used by Italian Air Lines. They swooped down on them and bore them away amidst shrill cries in several foreign languages. Pushed by a squad of men in their best white overalls (now soaked in the rain), they came weaving through the crowded ramp like an odd-shaped float at a carnival.

But all the same, when the Chairman walked out into American air, smiling, as shutters clicked and movie cameras whirred, on every step he took downwards was painted for all the world to see: *Air Enterprise Limited.*

Once more on the ground, he turned to his companions. Jovially, rubbing his hands together level with his chin in a more decorous version of a boxer's overhead victory shake, he cried, 'Come on, come on! We're all in this together.'

He shepherded them himself in front of the cameras. 'Captain Cavendish!' he shouted up to the cabin, 'Captain Bellamy!' and then, in an aside to the photographers, 'Must have those important people, the pilots.'

Eventually, then, they were all grouped together at the bottom of the steps, slightly behind Sir James, Angela and Lalette pushed to the front, Cruttwell and Eastlake at opposite ends of the untidy little knot; Rawlings expecting the undercarriage to collapse at any minute, the rest of the crew bringing up the rear; while in the shadows behind the arc lamps and the cameras, the good-humoured welcoming Committee of important American aviation experts stood watching and still waiting.

Sixteen flash-bulbs exploded simultaneously.

It was that picture which was immediately wired to three hundred papers in America, and which eventually travelled all round the world. Against a background of the immense unorthodox flanks of the Emperor, and in support of the confident good-humour that stretched from ear to ear on the Chairman's face, her designers, her crew, the doctor, the future Line Manager, Mr. Brocklehurst and the Company's Public Relations Officer all contributed their mixed British assortment of bravely sheepish smiles.

CHAPTER ELEVEN

NEXT day, the American Press surprised everyone (including itself) by being both gentle and generous.

The assumption had been, before the Emperor had left England, that the newspapers' attitude would be one of guarded and unenthusiastic interest. Photographs of the unusually designed aircraft had been published, and representatives of shopkeepers, manufacturers and householders around La Guardia and Idelwild (considered to be the probable target areas) had written indignantly to their Congressmen to forbid the passage in the air above them of an article of foreign manufacture, likely at a moment's notice to turn into a missile.

The Civil Aeronautics Board, the lawgivers of the American air, had expressed understandable concern that a projected London-New York scheduled non-stop service might very likely mean (bearing in mind the strength of the prevalent westerly winds) that Emperors would sometimes arrive over Idelwild in bad weather with insufficient fuel to take their rightful turn in the stack; and by necessitating an immediate landing, would thereby avail themselves of an unfair advantage over other operators.

The airlines of the U.S.A. (all highly prized advertisers in the Press) had made it plain that they were very, very lukewarm about such a service until they had an aircraft with sufficient range to do it themselves. That aircraft American manufacturers, naturally and vehemently, wanted to be the first to build. And the Government had blessed them both in a double benediction by letting it be known (unofficially) that for world prestige purposes it would be an excellent thing if such a landmark in the history of the sky was first undertaken by an American airline in an American aircraft.

Then the delays, the diversion to Iceland, the muddled arrangements for the arrival at Idelwild had reached the headlines before the Emperor touched down. Feeling had hardened from an off-cold shoulder to unveiled suspicion. When the Emperor arrived (if she *did* arrive) certainly she would be received by an official committee, by photographers, newsreel cameras and television, but in the columns of the newspapers, in the air-correspondents' first-hand summing up of her, in the highest aviation circles, it was now perfectly obvious she was to qualify for the old Bronx cheer.

And yet she received a thundering welcome. Such a reversal of popular expectations, unprecedented since Mr. Truman's election as President in 1948, happened quite simply. There was, in any case, after a particularly unfriendly fracas over China, a feeling in the air that the time was overdue for the two allies to smoke a pipe of peace together, and late that night, New York editors, red-eyed with fatigue, and with no other news on their plate, looked at the curiously sad little picture of the Emperor and her sixteen inhabitants, and recalling what they were in for from other city editors, had taken the traditional cigar out of their mouths, and had all said benevolently, 'We'll play it up and give 'em a break.'

In the second-best suite in the Grand-Plaza Hotel, Sir James was over the moon. With a slight head from the whisky of last night's large-hearted American hospitality, he had rung for all the morning's papers. They had come to him in a stack so big it almost covered the diminutive bell-boy who brought them.

For five minutes, he grimly surveyed them. Sir James was a business-man, brought up in a hard school. Whiskies, buffet suppers, kind words and back-slaps were expendable and deductable items he'd used too many times himself to be at all impressed about receiving. He'd smiled; he'd laughed; he'd talked. He'd been confident, enthusiastic and determined. But all the time he'd had a feeling, a sixth sense, that all this was the gilt on some particularly inedible gingerbread. The day's papers, he reckoned, would probably confirm that feeling.

He shrugged his shoulders and reached for the silk dressing-gown his wife had given him only last week for his birthday. Ah, well! He'd expected a fight during the four days. Naturally, the Americans wouldn't give in easily. He thought wryly to himself of the diversion, the delays, the still unexplained behaviour over Labrador. He tied the green cord tightly round his middle and compressed his lips. One thing, anyway, he knew he could do (and he squared his tough shoulders defiantly), and that was to fight every inch of the way.

He reached over and took the paper that was sticking out half-way down the pile.

He opened it.

Headlines on the front page cried, 'Welcome, Emperor!'

Excited, his eye scanned two whole columns, below the photograph. The delays and difficulties were minimised. The storms over the Atlantic were stressed as being unprecedented since meteorological records had been kept. Ships had sent distress signals. No other aircraft had attempted the westbound crossing. It had been appalling bad luck to choose that night for the non-stop proving flight of the Emperor to New York. But the cautious, common sense attitude to possible hazard—shown by the diversion to Iceland—showed this was no desperate, flash-in-the-pan bid for supremacy over the North Atlantic sky, but a well-balanced, well-planned confident campaign that boded well for the future of the aircraft and the service. It was a great step forward. Sir James Joliffe and the British were to be congratulated.

He could hardly believe his eyes.

Quickly, he tore through a dozen others. Though the language varied, the tone and the friendly feeling of all of them was unmistakable. As he sat down on his bed to read through each one of them very carefully, there was one thing about the strange and inexplicable existence on this earth of which Sir James was absolutely certain.

Life was wonderful.

He went down to breakfast in excellent spirits. In the restaurant, he joined Brocklehurst, who was sitting on his own at a table, and said enthusiastically, 'Seen the papers?'

Brocklehurst said, 'Yes, Sir James.'

'Excellent, aren't they? Excellent!' He rubbed his hands together, then he took the menu. He felt suddenly hungry. He went through cereal and bacon and eggs in double-quick time. Then feeling inwardly and outwardly completely satisfied, he suggested, 'Toast, Brocklehurst?'

'Thank you, Sir James.'

'Don't bother with that sort of thing, old chap,' the Chairman said, as he passed the sparkling silver toast-rack across the breakfast table. 'Call me Joliffe.' He forked the last piece of bacon into his mouth. He smiled kindly, 'Or James... Jimmy... anything like that. This is the land of informality ... friendliness.'

He had expected today to have to strip (metaphorically) off his coat, roll up his sleeves, and go into this strange American boxing ring to fight sceptic and scoffer, Government red-tape, C.A.B. regulations, other airlines' antagonism and aircraft manufacturers' jealous mistrust. Subconsciously (for his well-drilled brain planned ahead as automatically as a machine) he had planned a campaign where fierce, back-to-the-wall speeches, and swift denials that the delays and diversions had been anything but a shrewd weather sense on the part of the pilots (coupled with bad luck) joined hand in hand with performance graphs and running costs. For in this struggle, the prizes of success were large and glittering. The Americans must be made to realise the need to have Emperors of their own. They must clamour for them, while all the time being unable to get them. For the first twenty were on contract to Air Enterprise; and the earliest possible American delivery date was a British aircraft manufacturer's promise of three years. During that decade, Air Enterprise would lead the field, well ahead of all competitors, with the public knowing that, far from operating an aircraft nobody else wanted, everyone wanted Emperors, but couldn't get them. He knew he had to (in a sense) sell the Emperor over here, in order to sell the new service.

And now, it looked as though he'd already sold it. He rolled the last drops of his excellent second cup of coffee round his mouth, reached for his cigarette-case, took one, and then (he could be forgiven a slight forgetfulness on manners today) saw Brocklehurst had finished his toast, and passed over his case, saying fervently as he did so, half to himself: 'A wonderful country... the great United States!'

His right hand still stretched across the table like one half of a supplication. There it stayed for a quarter of a minute, un-sought, apparently ignored. Surprised, Sir James' eyes peered myopically through a honey-coloured haze of well-being at the Under-Secretary of State.

'Want one, old chap?'

Brocklehurst said stiffly, 'Thank you, no, Sir James.'

The cigarette-case shut with a loud snap before being bustled back into the Chairman's pocket. 'You're very quiet this morning. Sleep all right last night?'

'Not particularly well, Sir James.'

The Chairman laughed out loud his rich round laugh. Studying Brocklehurst's thin face more closely, he saw the wintry lines of discontent running downwards from his nose nearly to his chin. He had heard somewhere (the Minister, wasn't it?) that Brocklehurst was hen-pecked. You'd think a trip like this, off on a spree by himself to New York, no responsibility really, just coming along for the ride, was just what the doctor would order. And yet, the man was as sour as an unripe guava.

'Should have thought after all that whisky last night... you'd have slept like a top. What's the matter? Feel a bit sick?'

'Nothing like that, Sir James.'

'Should have opened the window. This American steam heating – '

'As it happened, my window was wide open.'

For a moment, the Chairman looked puzzled. Then: 'The traffic! Hell of a noise isn't it? Better get a room on the inside of the hotel. Round about the thirtieth floor. I'll see to it myself.'

'Very kind of you, Sir James. But I prefer to stay where I am. The traffic did not disturb me.'

'Well... in heaven's name, dear fellow, what on earth kept you awake?'

'I was thinking, Sir James.'

'You were!' The Chairman exploded genially. 'After all that whisky! Brocklehurst, old chap, you're a better man than I am!'

Frigidly, his small eyes unamused, unappeased, Brocklehurst said – 'I was thinking about the aircraft... the Emperor.'

Immediately, the Chairman's immense mental powers came turning out at the double. Somewhere inside him, a fire-alarm had sounded. In quite a different tone of voice, he said very quietly, 'What d'you mean... the Emperor?'

'Well... there's obviously *something* the matter, isn't

there? Something serious.' Then he added a dig at the pilots, 'I mean, apart from the undercarriage trouble caused by that *terrible* landing.'

'My dear chap,' said the Chairman rather acidly. 'Don't exaggerate! Don't get the wrong idea!'

Brocklehurst asked point-blank in his thin, high voice, 'What *was* wrong over Labrador, Sir James?'

'Nothing serious.'

'Does anyone other than those on board know what happened?'

'No . . . and under the circumstances, it would be most unfortunate if anyone did. We are in the delicate process of making the Emperor into a success. My employees . . . the aircraft designers . . . all know they have a duty to perform.'

'And I have a duty to perform, too, Sir James.'

Irritated by the man's prim pomposity, the Chairman said, 'This is *not* a government aeroplane, Mr. Brocklehurst. After backing so many long-range losers at the public expense no doubt the Minister wishes it *was*.'

'I have a duty to the British public.'

'And I have a duty to them, too.'

Brocklehurst leaned right across the table. In a half-whisper, he went on, 'Suppose that swinging should develop on the way home. Only worse. We'd disappear without any message . . . nothing. The Minister . . . nobody . . . would know what had happened. They might send up another Emperor. And the same thing might happen again.'

Sir James said grimly out loud, 'I don't know which to congratulate you most on . . . your public-spiritedness or your imagination.'

'It is my duty to tell the Minister, Sir James.'

Like twin visors, the Chairman's lids almost completely closed over his trustfully wide-open eyes. 'And it would be *his* duty to tell someone else, whose duty it would be to tell another. Until it would be common gossip . . . a little latitudinal swinging distorted . . . magnified . . . a travesty of the truth published . . . a stab in the back to us as we strive for the nation's good in this foreign land.'

'Such eloquence at the breakfast table!' The Under-Secretary gave the Chairman a starved smile. 'You should have been a politician, Sir James. However, in spite of it I still feel – '

'You mean you'd telephone him . . . letting half a dozen operators listen in at the same time?'

'I see no other available form of communication.'

The Chairman carefully wiped his mouth with his napkin. When he began to speak again, he had managed to pump back into his voice some of his earlier friendliness. 'Aren't you rushing your fences a bit, old chap? They're working on it right now. They'll find what's wrong and put it right quicker than you can say Minister of Civil Aviation. In fact, I shall be very surprised if they haven't rectified it *already*.'

Brocklehurst looked at him for a long time. Then he suddenly burst out with, 'And I shall be very surprised if it isn't a major fault in the design!'

'Nonsense, Brocklehurst!' Sir James threw back his head and laughed. 'You do get the queerest notions into your head, old chap!'

'You think it's something quite small?'

'I *know* it is.'

Brocklehurst studied the rosy well-being of the face opposite him. 'You're very confident, Sir James.'

'*Of course* I'm confident, old chap.'

The Under-Secretary paused. 'There would be no question, would there,' he asked tentatively, 'of going off . . . *without the trouble having been put right*?'

'Good heavens above, man!' Sir James' eyes went twice as wide as usual with astonishment. 'That wouldn't be legal!'

'No.' Brocklehurst reflectively contemplated the weave of the white tablecloth. 'I'd forgotten that point.' When his eyes came up again to face Sir James, they were more cheerful and friendly. 'I thought perhaps the importance of maintaining your schedule – '

'So you won't phone the Minister?'

'I'll *think* about it, Sir James.'

'Think seriously,' the Chairman advised. 'Take your time.'

Brocklehurst rose from the table, 'The urgency is not . . . is *perhaps* not so great as I at first feared. Good morning to you, Sir James!'

' 'Morning, Brocklehurst.'

The chairman watched the straight figure in the black and white striped trousers walk across the restaurant and out of the swing door into the body of the hotel. An odd character, he decided. Civil-Service mind, of course, coupled with the high ambition of keeping well in with his boss. But you'd have thought that the R.A.F. would have taken some of the starch out of that high, stiff collar.

He sighed. That was the trouble with people – you never could tell what on earth they'd do next. How easy his single-minded track through life would be if it was a strictly private road! Brocklehurst might phone; he might not. But the assumption must be that he *would*.

There was not a moment to lose.

He returned to his suite in a thoughtful mood. There, waiting on his desk were two envelopes. The first was an invitation to speak at the American Aeronautic Dinner that night. The other requested his presence at the American Aircraft Manufacturers' annual cocktail party.

Both were unexpected. Both had a hidden treasure of potential publicity.

He slapped his plump thigh with delight. 'Excellent!' he murmured at the Gothic gold lettering and the expensive paper. By what devious means the Emperor had tickled the American fancy, he did not even consider. The possibility of Brocklehurst phoning the Minister, coupled with these two important invitations on top of the welcome in the papers, galvanised his whole armada of energy into immediate operation.

Speed was essential. On one side lay defeat, on the other – victory.

It would be a fight, of course, and he would have to do most of it himself. But that did not trouble him. This was the sort of battle he knew of old, from the very moment he started selling motor engines at the highest possible price to a choosy British public and a parsimonious government.

Now the publicity ball had started rolling, there would, he knew, be other invitations, other opportunities to spread the Emperor's good name far and wide over the American continent. Too many for him alone to handle.

But he had help. He had a number of his fellow-countrymen

on hand. More important still, they were also on his payroll. This afternoon, he would summon them to his suite for (that favourite word of his) a *get-together*.

As he made his plans, the New York air was like the smell of blood in his nostrils. He walked up and down the room, joyfully jiggling shillings and sixpences and dimes and quarters indiscriminately in his trouser-pockets as a tambourine background to the tune he was humming—a very discordant but powerful rendering (as though wasps and bees and bluebottles were all buzzing in the same hive together) of *Men of Harlech . . . are ye waking?*

In the Coronet Hotel, the men of the Emperor were, as it happened, all awake. Most of them were dressed. Some had even had breakfast.

But none of them was thinking of any form of advance. The first lap of the proving flight, no matter what it said in the papers, could hardly in their eyes be described as a triumph. The trip had created for each of them their own particular personal problems – all different, and all needing for the moment their undivided attention.

Payton had woken from a particularly unpleasant nightmare in which not only was he Line Manager of the Emperors but also in some curious way the pilot in charge of every one that took off on its gibbering, juddering junket across the Atlantic. He had got out of bed and was washing away the taste of the dream with ice-cold water, shivering and still a little dizzy from his dream ascent of the high ladder of success.

Hamilton – up, spruce, and as always in New York, alone – was having a quiet late breakfast in a drug-store, considering with concern a possible interruption to the schedule of a private business he conducted, out of Air Enterprise's bread-and-butter hours, to provide himself and his family with cake. Dr. Enderby-Browne was scrupulously writing up his notes on the trip in the quietness of room 3165, so high above New York that he had the advantages both of being airborne and of being in blessed stationary peace on the ground. In their separate rooms, nine flights below him, both girls were still having their beauty sleep. And much nearer the ground, in room 1016, Douthwaite was phoning Rawlings in 603 and suggesting the usual economy, on the $10 a day that Air Enterprise allowed them for meals, of combining breakfast and lunch: 'Ready to eat, Red?'

'Will be, Alex, in a couple of minutes.'

'Come up to 1016, will you? And I'll give Jimmy Seawood and Hooper a call.'

A quarter of an hour afterwards, all four of them were in Douthwaite's room. There seemed to be no hurry. Though it was past eleven, none of them expressed hunger. Seawood sat gloomily on the navigator's bed. Hooper asked, 'Well ... you haven't really told us, Red. What do *you* think it is?'

Rawlings shrugged his massive shoulders. 'Could be any number of things ... now.'

Douthwaite put in with, 'What d'you mean ... now?'

'After Cavendish's performance last night. He's broken one of the undercarriage struts, you know.'

Simultaneously, Hooper said, 'I've been in a good few bad landings but – ' and Douthwaite observed, 'The weather wasn't too pleasant.' Seawood still said nothing.

The engineer looked down at the First Officer, 'Couldn't *you* see we were undershooting?'

Seawood put his hands up to his hair, and started to comb it ferociously with his fingers. 'I ... eh – '

'Why didn't you *do* something?'

Seawood muttered something about Captain Cavendish's long experience.

'So rather than trust your own eyes, you'd land us all in the drink? Well, it's a good thing for the lot of you *I'm* not like that! And d'you know what happened last night after we got back from that party? Cavendish catches me up in the foyer. "Mr. Rawlings," he says. "I'd like a word with you." '

Hooper asked, 'What time was that?'

' 'Bout one in the morning. I said, "But Captain, I'm just going to bed." He said, "I insist, Mr. Rawlings." So I stopped. To tell you the truth, I thought he was going to say thank you for helping him out with the landing. Then I looked at his face. Death warmed up, but the eyes fairly blazing.'

Douthwaite said mildly. 'He was a bit upset with himself about the landing.'

Rawlings snorted impatiently. 'Wasn't upset with himself

at all! He was mad. Mad with . . . with . . .' – he stuttered with furious astonishment – '. . . with me!'

Hooper's eyes opened wide. 'Why ever you, Red?'

'He said to me straight away: "That landing tonight was your fault!" "What d'you mean, Captain?" I said. Then out he comes with a most extraordinary story. "You were giving me at least a thousand r.p.m. more than I asked for. When I came to pull the throttles back, I must have had just about take-off power. Naturally, when I took it off, we came down with a bang." '

Hooper said, 'Trying to blame it on you, eh? Bet you were wild, Red!'

'Wild! I was tired. I'd had a few drinks.' Rawlings, remembering it, went pink with rage again and waved a fat finger in the air like a wand re-creating it all in front of them. 'I said to him: "Look, Captain, I agree I gave you more power than you asked for. And if I hadn't, we'd have made our landing in the water, a good half-mile from the beginning of the runway! The Emperor may be a lot of things, Captain," I said, "but she's not a flicking flying boat!" '

Hooper said, 'I thought we'd had it! I tell you . . . I looked out of my window and I swear I saw the wheels touch the water!'

'We were pretty low,' Douthwaite admitted.

Seawood still said nothing.

Rawlings thought such comments meagre, considering what he'd done for them. Glowering at the three of them, he went on, 'Well . . . of course he blew his top at that! Said, "Mr. Rawlings, I shall report you for disobedience to orders, impertinence and gross insubordination. I shall write a full report of the incident the moment we get back." '

Hooper asked him sympathetically. 'What did you say to that, Red?'

'I just said, "*If* we get back." Shut him up like a clam.'

Even in repetition, ten hours later, the same magical quality had not worn off the words.

It shut them all up like clams.

'E,' the gruff voice muttered through the grey moustache, 'A . . . L . . . P . . . R . . . I.'

There was a moment's pause. Then: 'Either C or G . . . difficult to tell.'

At the far end of his room, Captain Cavendish was standing with his back against the wall. His left hand covered his left eye, which gave him a slightly menacing, piratical appearance. Propped against the closed window was a copy of the *New York Times*.

But Cavendish was not reading about the Emperor's success. With immense difficulty, he was identifying each letter of one of the smaller headlines.

One edge of the paper flapped over. It fluttered feebly, like a dying bird's limp wing, and then the whole paper, with no more pretence at flying, dropped headlong down from its perch and spreadeagled itself on the carpet.

The pilot walked across the room and bent down to pick it up. He studied the words in question, now much more closely. 'Of course, it's very small print,' he said.

As though the time had come to examine, not the products, but the instruments themselves, he went into the bathroom and inspected his grey eyes in the mirror.

There was no getting away from it, they weren't new. There were little red lines running through the whites. The first bright translucent varnish had worn off them. The brown skin in the corners had warped into a number of little grooves to produce two arrow-heads that boldly pointed out his eyes so that nobody could possibly miss noticing their age.

He moved them up. He moved them down and sent them sideways. He put his finger in front of him and watching it all the time drew it slowly towards his nose, making him cross-eyed in the process. Anyway, they still *worked.*

He went back into his room, and sat on the bed. Now that the first furious indignation with the engineer over giving him too much power had worn off, he had analysed that bad landing, worrying over it as pilots often do, and had come to the conclusion that his judgment had been out. In fact, if it hadn't been for Rawlings, the accident might have been very much worse.

He'd banged them down before, of course, but he'd never bent anything. The incident to a pilot of his reputation was both mortifying and unexpected. Bellamy had now and again criticised his instrument flying on check-outs, but nobody had liked to say (it was a thing nobody *could* say, bearing in mind his long service with the Company) that his reactions were slowing up and he should watch himself carefully.

Now that fact had been hammered home to him by two sickening thuds, made by the Emperor's main wheels on the runway at Idelwild. He began to remember other things. For the last few years he had been gratified to discover that he always was given a most experienced First Officer on his trips, and he had thought that the Company hadn't liked to affront him with the sight of the new raw recruits which were the only reinforcements it could get in a pilot-hungry world. Perhaps there was another reason.

All of a sudden, the whole six foot two of him seemed very lonely, very unsure of itself, not nearly so tall. If he did it this time, he might do it again. And again. Until –

He saw his immaculate gloves on the dressing table, the uniform jacket on the chair, and he turned away, as though now the sight of them sickened him. He picked up the receiver and dialled the number of Bellamy's room. This was the second phone call he had had that day. Earlier, he'd been speaking to Sir James.

A voice in his ear said sharply, 'Yes?'

'Captain Bellamy,' he said. 'This is Cavendish.' Without its normal distinctive vanguard, the three little syllables of his name seemed to shiver in a cold world.

'Yes?'

'The Chairman rang me this morning.'

'Yes?'

'He said that under the circumstances on the return journey perhaps I should concentrate on' – he could not somehow give the words the same confident importance of two days ago – 'my advisory capacity.'

'You mean . . . he wants me to do all the handling?'

In the silence that followed, Cavendish was thinking bitterly to himself how strained was the quality of mercy of young pilots towards their elders. A little sympathetic understanding, a considerate admission that all pilots (even Training Captains) held off too high now and again was too much to expect these days. 'Yes,' he said heavily. 'That is . . . if you agree.'

'I'll agree to that.' There was surely no need for Bellamy to leap quite so readily at his chance to assume full power. 'But what's worrying me is this Labrador business. Did he mention it?'

'As a matter of a fact, he didn't.'

'I told Cruttwell I thought it was in the rudder controls somewhere.'

'They might find the trouble there.' Cavendish's mind was not, however, in Labrador. It was milling round and round New York, banging down at Idelwild and bouncing up into a dark, uncertain future. He had screwed up his left eye, and with his right he was reading a notice pinned on the far wall: *The Management will not be held responsible for –*

'What was that you said?'

'I said it'll be a long job whatever it is.'

For once in complete agreement, Bellamy immediately reiterated: 'It'll be a long job, all right.'

That opinion was echoed in all the rooms of the Coronet Hotel occupied by the Emperor's inhabitants. Whatever their personal problems, and however diversified – there at least was common ground. Schedules would go out of the window. They would be safe from another berserk imperial ballet-dance for many days to come.

It would be a long job.

At Idelwild airport, Cruttwell spoke triumphantly into the telephone. 'Well, sir . . taken us all night, but we've fixed the undercarriage! We've done a retraction test. Everything worked perfectly.'

Sir James' voice came echoing back to him immediately, warm and generous-hearted. 'Excellent . . . excellent, Mr. Cruttwell. That's splendid! I always knew I could rely on the two of you.'

A pleased smile cut more lines than ever in the engineer's wrinkled face. There was a moment's pause. 'And the other little thing, Mr. Cruttwell?'

His brain fuddled by lack of sleep, the engineer did not quite catch on, 'I beg your pardon, sir?'

'You've found out the cause of the trouble over Labrador?'

Confident of sympathy under the circumstances, Cruttwell

said frankly, 'We haven't had time to get around to that, sir.'

'*Get around to it immediately!*'

Pained and surprised, Cruttwell pointed out, 'That's not so easy, sir.'

'Why isn't it?' The voice was now as cold as the Arctic air.

'Well . . . everyone has a different idea of exactly what *did* happen. It's always the same in these emergencies. People are so busy that nobody can take any notes. The Flight Engineer and Mr. Eastlake seem to think it was the engines. I think it was more likely something to do with the rudder controls, the boosters or – '

'You *think*! Mr. Eastlake *thinks*! Think is a word I have no time for, Mr. Cruttwell! I want to *know*.'

Stung into raising his voice, Cruttwell replied, 'We can't do everything all at once, sir.'

There was a very long pause. Then, with deadly quietness: 'We have a much advertised schedule to maintain.'

'We're both aware of that, sir.'

'We have also a great opportunity for promoting the Emperor over here. All that publicity *your* Company will receive gratis through *our* hard work. I had enough trouble in England with costly delays while the aircraft was being built. I have no intention of standing for a repetition of them over here.'

'We'll do our best, sir, but – '

'And another thing! There is to be no mention of the trouble over Labrador, even to our own hangar personnel. Tell them it's an extra safety check.'

'There's more to it than you seem to – '

'Don't manufacture your own difficulties, Mr. Cruttwell. Makes your work twice as hard. You've got my orders quite clear in your mind?'

Through the engineer's tightly compressed lips, a sound came out just recognisable as an affirmative.

'Good!' The Chairman's voice became once more as balmy as a Bermuda breeze. 'Then all you have to do is to carry them out. Thank you, Mr. Cruttwell.'

The receiver at the other end clicked. The engineer stood,

swaying a little, listening to the empty line. Then he went out of the telephone box, and said bitterly to Eastlake, 'Better get on with the job. Better find out what's wrong with these controls!'

Just as bitterly, Eastlake reiterated, 'You mean, what's wrong with those engines!'

CHAPTER TWELVE

Sir James Joliffe gazed round his suite at the Air Enterprise men on his payroll – the Emperor's crew, Riley, Payton, Dr. Enderby-Browne – and said, 'Well . . . now.'

He rubbed his hands together vigorously, as though he was hoping to create fire by friction, to envelope them all in a great warmth of enthusiasm.

None came.

He looked round at them again, rather more closely, as though he was examining their texture, the ingredients in their make-up. Clay certainly, and meant to be moulded, but not exactly the sort of clay God would have chosen to make the Garden of Eden. He tried again. 'Now I regard all of you,' he said, 'as potential salesmen.' His eyes travelled over to the two stewardesses, the blonde and the brunette sitting side by side on the sofa, and they brightened perceptibly as he added, 'And potential sales-*women*.'

After they had arrived, he had put a glass of sherry into everyone's hands. Then he came straight to the point. There was no need, he had said, to tell them that now was not the time to talk to anyone who was not a fellow-traveller of the little spot of this and that which had occurred over Labrador, and which at this very moment was being rectified.

'So they've found the trouble, sir?' Riley had asked, but he remained unanswered as Sir James proceeded to point out to them the Emperor's triumph in America. After an advance like this had been made (he was speaking to them like a general) the important thing was *the follow-up*.

That was the moment he had reviewed his troops available for this operation, and for once his voice had hesitated.

They were so very English – not at all bad in what they had called a war of defence, but unaware that the real battle, the struggle for survival, went on every day of their lives, and they must attack or die. He would have preferred a show of horseplay, even of vulgarity, a bouncing up and down to demonstrate at least that the energy was there, a slap on the back and someone to shout, 'C'mon, boss . . . we're right behind you, Jimmy.'

Nobody said anything like that, of course. In fact, nobody said anything at all. In a dignified professional silence, they peered mistrustfully into their sherry as though searching it for grains of poison.

'Now don't get the idea,' he said to them, 'that I'm asking you to go round from door to door, peddling brushes.'

There was a rustle of polite laughter.

'Since this morning's great publicity in the papers,' he went on, 'invitations have been pouring in to me. To make appearances on the radio, on television. To meet politicians . . . the press . . . business organisations. I shall do my best to attend as many of them as I can. But obviously, in the limited time available, I can't go to them all. And that' – he leaned towards them with his never-failing smile – 'is where *you* come in.'

He had worked it all out before they arrived – who was going where and why. But now, after what his eyes had taken in on their inspection round the room, there was a last-minute alteration to the command decision. On the flight over, the Chairman had certainly noticed among the smartly uniformed men on board the undoubted prettiness of both Miss Knight and Miss Greenacres. There had been a limpid liveliness in the blonde's blue eyes, a kind of dreamy softness about the brunette's small heart-shaped face. But now, with everyone out of flying fancy-dress, the contrast between a smart green frock and a plain red woollen dress against a background of brown suits and black suits and grey flannel trousers was more marked and *much* more flattering.

If the men, the Chairman thought to himself, were really rather a scratch crowd for this sort of thing, there were real possibilities in the women.

A pretty face could sell anything, couldn't it? Cigarettes, whisky, toothpaste, books and cars. There was no reason on earth, especially in America, why it shouldn't help to sell Emperors, too. He had planned to use the girls in rather a minor way, a ·5 c.c. injection of sugar and spice into the puppy dogs' tails of technical get-togethers. But now his eyes and his nose (for their combined perfumes had a considerable range) told him instinctively that he'd been wrong.

His brain ticking over in double-quick time, he made eleventh-hour changes to the battle-order, withdrawing the men a fraction and promoting the girls to the front of the firing line.

'Now let me see . . . the American Aeronautical dinner. I shall be going there.' The Chairman looked over to the prospective Line Manager whose position in the plans remained unaltered as Little Sir Echo, the knight's page. 'With Captain Payton. Likewise the aircraft manufacturers' do. Mr. Brocklehurst may be coming with us, he may not. It all . . . depends. Mr. Eastlake and Mr. Cruttwell may be able to attend various technical functions' – in his thoughts, he saw them with their coats off, still working in the hangar at Idelwild – 'it all depends, again.'

'However' – and he included them all in a beam, chockful of trust and confidence – 'I am lucky to have *you* always available. And now' – he picked up a piece of paper and made lightning alterations to it – 'I am ready to read out a list of names and times and places, if you would be good enough to note down the ones that concern you.'

With Enderby-Browne, Joliffe did preserve a certain face-saving impression of free speech and free will: 'I wondered, doctor, whether you could possibly fit in tea tomorrow with the Daughters of the American Air?'

The physician bowed his head.

And with Cavendish, the Chairman remained tactfully considerate. It would be a pity, wouldn't it, if the Americans missed having a radio interview with one of Britain's pioneer airmen? And the idea had struck him (the sort of novelty New Yorkers liked), of having the most senior captain of Air Enterprise make a T.V. appearance with one of the most junior employees, Miss Knight – air experience and air youthfulness side by side, so to speak, if Captain Cavendish could see his point.

The iron-grey moustache in front of the mask-like face seemed to twitch an affirmative.

But for the rest of them, it was orders. Rawlings and Hooper would attend a rally of Air Scouts in Central Park. Douthwaite and Seawood would help each other out at a reception given by aircraft instrument manufacturers. Hamilton would go to a dance held by the American Customs and Immigration people. Bellamy would be present on his own at a meeting of American pilots.

There were other functions which he listed to fit names he read out. But the two most important ones he kept till last. He would have liked to have attended them both, but unfortunately they clashed with the coveted invitation to attend the American aircraft manufacturers' party – which he had decided after considerable thought was just that jot more important.

The question was – who to send in his place?

Sir James Joliffe had not got where he was without knowing how to deal with potential trouble-makers, with the ears of corn in his cornfield which for the time being stuck up further than their fellows. You either cut them off sharp, or under your very eyes you cultivated them carefully with the manure of responsibility. Such as being your personal representative at a vitally important function.

He glanced across at Bellamy. The man was keeping extraordinarily quiet, content with his lot of having to contribute nothing to the negative atmosphere of the audience. Lying low, no doubt, for the slightly sardonic look on his face seemed to say plainly to the Chairman . . . well, *you've* got us into this, and now *I've* got to get you out. Certainly, he was a good and conscientious pilot. Certainly he appeared to keep his counsel. A useful piece of corn and one which for the moment had to be spared – but, whatever it was feeling about itself, a piece of corn, nevertheless.

'And there are two other functions,' Sir James said. 'Rather important ones. The Air League's gathering. And our Manager's party for the American Press. To this last, of course, since he will know so many of his colleagues there, Mr. Riley will be *one* of the guests who must go. But I've been thinking that it might be an excellent idea – '

He gave the appearance of musing, but he had as a matter of fact already made up his mind. He had taken rather a fancy to Lalette Greenacres on the way over. Rather more than the other girl, she seemed to possess life and an attractive initiative. He had noticed how she altered her approach to her various passengers: the way she had tactfully kept Riley rather shorter of whisky than he really liked.

She would, he decided, do very well for both of them – as a lightener to Bellamy at the aircraft manufacturers' party, and as a beautiful sobering influence on Riley, let loose among his fellow journalists.

He confided in them his excellent idea.

Bellamy appeared to take the news indifferently. But Riley looked pleased, and so it seemed was the girl. She smoothed her hand over her skirt and looked across at Bellamy, and the Chairman saw a half-smile curl round her rather nice lips.

'Has anyone got any other suggestions to make?'

Sir James gazed round his suite again. He had been hoping, now that the campaign had been explained to them, now each man had his orders, they would grasp this opportunity to fulfil their masculine selves with at least one of their two hands. But there they all sat, exactly as they had sat when they first came into the room. The only difference was – they had all finished their sherries.

'Well, that's the lot, then.' He was dismissing them now. 'Oh . . . one more thing! I know the ladies' – and he nodded graciously at the girls – 'dislike regimentation in their dress. And I think it would a shame if Air Enterprise's feminine contribution to colourful gatherings was just dark blue. But it would be better' – he was protecting his other aircrew, if they did but know it, with the only battle-armour he could: superbly cut cloth, brass buttons and gold wings – ' best – ' he corrected himself, lest they failed to realise that this was in effect an order, ' – if the *men* attended their various functions *in uniform*.'

With Payton a respectful two feet behind him at the window, the Chairman watched his employees spill out of the hotel entrance into the bustle of Fifth Avenue. Seeds, he thought, English seeds, sowed by himself all over New York to reap a hopeful dollar harvest.

His eyes watched Hooper, Rawlings, Seawood and Douthwaite, lost in serious grumbling about the functions they had to go to, disappear into the Snack Bar on the other side of the street. There, far away from his ears, Hooper studied the menu and remarked, 'Making a fair old song and dance, isn't he?'

'One thing.' Rawlings said, 'is as plain as the nose on your face.'

'And what's that, Red?' Hooper asked.

'He's had the undercarriage fixed. He's landed himself all this hoo-ha over here. *He's going to go!*'

Seawood said comfortably. 'He can't . . . if the aircraft's unserviceable.'

'You can bet your sweet life he would . . . if he could get Bellamy to take it!'

'Which he won't be able to do,' Douthwaite said.

'No . . . he won't. Bellamy may be a lot of things . . . but he's not a fool.' Rawlings paused for a moment and surveyed his audience. 'There's one thing *we* can do, though.'

Hooper again asked his favourite question. 'And what's that, Red?'

'Claim Emperor operational pay! That aircraft's still in the development stages . . . we know that now. We've got an excellent case for a test technician's bonus!'

The waitress arrived and they ordered coffee and doughnuts. A silence fell over them as they considered the engineer's proposal with respect. Even Douthwaite seemed impressed. 'How much d'you reckon, Red?'

'Twenty pounds a month.'

'Rather a lot.'

'Fifteen then.'

Seawood suggested, 'Wouldn't it be better on a trip basis? So much for each Atlantic crossing?'

'Far better to have it in an annual lump sum,' was Hooper's advice.

'It should *vary*,' Rawlings said. 'Chief engineers should obviously get more than seconds. And so much extra for each year served with the Company.'

Douthwaite said doubtfully, 'That'd take an awful lot of argument to settle. Among ourselves, I mean. Wouldn't it be better to save our breath for the argument with the Company?'

Rawlings sniffed. 'Oh, the Company'll agree to it fast enough. When it's put to Sir James, he won't be able to do anything else!'

'Will *you* put it to him, Red?'

'I thought Jack Seawood, as he's the First Officer – '

'But I haven't had half the time in the Company that you three have had!'

Douthwaite said, 'It's *your* idea, Red. You should follow it through.'

'After all I've done already!' The engineer's face turned an indignant scarlet. 'My name's Red Rawlings! Not Joe Soap!'

Cavendish and Bellamy passed the outside of the Snack Bar on their way to the hotel. Bellamy was saying, 'The Old Man's going to sell the Emperor to the Americans . . . even if he busts it and us in the attempt!'

Cavendish, relieved that the broken undercarriage was no longer a stumbling block to success but still worried over the accident, said, 'I feel we should be very thankful, Captain, that Sir James Joliffe is *on our side*!'

'But a trip like that . . . and then these damned functions!'

Cavendish had never been averse to a bit of publicity. 'All in a good cause.'

'He's taking us in deeper and deeper! We haven't even a serviceable aeroplane! And he's selling them a magic carpet!'

'I shouldn't worry about it,' Cavendish said. 'Sir James is a very capable man.'

'Sir James isn't flying the thing back!'

Enderby-Browne accompanied Riley back to the Coronet. They walked slowly. Riley was saying, 'You saw the big splash in the papers, doctor?'

'I read about our arrival with considerable interest.'

'And now . . . all this extra publicity!'

'Now that I *do* find a little tiresome.'

They had arrived at the glass doors of the hotel. Both pushing in the same segment, they were quickly deposited on to the marble lobby floor. 'At least you collected some valuable, accurate facts for your thesis, doctor.' Riley gave a thin smile. 'As for me . . . I'm further from the truth than ever!'

'I think you're exaggerating, Mr. Riley.' Then on a kindly impulse, the doctor added, 'Come along to the lounge and have tea with me.'

'Tea!' The P.R.O. shook his head. 'Whisky for me, doctor.'

The cornstuke eyebrows shot up. 'So early?'

'Early or late, makes no difference to me.' They began to

divide – Enderby-Browne to the left and the lounge, Riley to the right and the bar. 'In vino veritas,' the P.R.O. called over his shoulder. 'Or in plain English, doctor – truth will out . . . *of a bottle!*'

Angela Knight had hurried away from the get-together on her own. She was not altogether displeased with her assignment. She couldn't help being conscious of the fact that to be chosen to go with the most senior pilot in the company was no mean honour. Nevertheless, the implication that the whole business was still going on was a disturbing thought. She lit a cigarette and stared out listlessly at the rusty white tiles of the opposite side of the hotel. She ran her hand through her hair, and then walked over to the mirror, to comb it carefully back into place.

She noticed that her face was paler than usual, and that her eyes seemed darker, but otherwise there was nothing to suggest the hopeless mixture of thoughts and ideas that pulled her now this way, now that. She accorded to Sir James as Head of the Company her wholehearted confidence and support. Yet, there was a feeling, not confined to herself, that the whole enterprise was ill-starred. Bound to end in disaster. If she closed her eyes, she could almost see the headlines in large black type, and, in smaller print, their own names in the list of casualties. When you came to think of it, even the names they had were the sort of ones that figured in casualty lists. They had the right ring about them.

And the name of Bellamy no longer sounded, as she had once thought, strong and assured, a big name of the future in aviation. She could see it: 'The aircraft was piloted by Captain Andrew Bellamy.' Just as it had been when the trouble started.

The telephone rang. Impatiently, Angela picked up the receiver. It was Lalette. Would Angela like to have tea with her? No, Angela couldn't.

She put the receiver down, and wished that she'd said yes. But the wretched girl had sounded so full of beans. A cat-that's-swallowed-the-mouse sort of voice, that she couldn't have tolerated spending an hour and a half in company with it.

And then Angela remembered. Of course, Lalette had been

teamed up with Bellamy. She smiled to herself. She probably wanted to see just how Angela was taking it. Probably imagining a discomfited rival. Well, as far as she was concerned, she wished them joy of their evening together.

She sat down at the writing-table and tried to do a few letters, but it was useless. The room was as cramped as a condemned cell. She got up and went down to the hotel coffee bar for tea.

But there she got no comfort either. She wished she could close her ears to the cheerful sound of American voices, so out of tune with her own mood. The sight of men as old as her father eating ice-cream and drinking cartons of milk with ridiculous looking straws, moved her to almost hysterical anger. The bustle, the crisp clatter, even the smell of coffee at a time when all civilised people drank tea, made her feel as homesick as a missionary in darkest Africa.

She thought of tea-time at home. Molly wheeling in the trolley close by the fire. The gleam of silver, and the beauty of old lace. The sight of Daddy coming in gravely from the library, still preoccupied with the highly important work that made even his retirement so rich in service. Herself sitting down and lifting the heavy silver teapot that her mother and her grandmother had poured from with dignity and elegance. It was all a tradition. A way of life. Just as her mother had deferred to her father, so now she did. And just as in the days when they had servants, they had known their place in the ordered household, so Molly, the last survivor of better days, went about her daily duties with modesty and respect.

And that, in a way, was why she had found her job in flying so eminently suitable. True, she had fairly menial duties, but she had only to speak for people to realise that she was of good education and culture. And most people realised that a stewardess's job was sought after, important, and taken up more often than not by girls of the better families.

And the whole set-up was rather like service tradition. The captain was the captain. In the air, he was all-wise, all-powerful. And under him, the crew became like a large well-ordered family. Each knew his place, his exact position in importance, and each owed implicit obedience to the man in command. On the ground, of course, it was different. But even there, rank was obvious. Everyone was labelled with the requisite number of gold leaf bands round their arms, and rank and seniority made a safe and ordered sanctuary in a world which, as her father so justly remarked, was throwing off all bounds of decency and self-control.

But now, all that had gone. Angela took a sip of the cool brown liquid and put her cup down with a frown of distaste. The little world that she was in, the hierarchy of the Emperor, to all appearances was out of hand. And here she was, isolated from all she knew, unable to get back home without another trip in that nightmare contraption. With Bellamy, the supposed crack pilot.

Angela gave her head a little flick at the thought of him. Impatiently, she pushed the cup away from her and walked out of the coffee bar. Half-way across the foyer, she saw the man in person.

She was in no mood right then to talk to him, and it was unlikely that he'd seen her. She turned away and stared into one of the show-cases. It was full of costume jewellery laid out on black velvet shelves. After a second or two, she saw a head and shoulders reflected back at her from the case. 'Hello, Angela,' Bellamy said. 'Can I buy you a cup of tea?'

She turned round slowly. Bellamy had a queer appraising way of looking at people as though he was checking them for accuracy and reliability. 'I've just had some, thanks.' She shook her head, and attempted a friendly smile.

'Then have another.' He put his hand under her elbow and turned her round. 'D'you want to have it here or somewhere else?'

'Well, I don't really – '

'Here, then?'

'Yes, I suppose so.'

She walked back to the same table in the coffee bar, while Bellamy went to fetch the tray from the counter.

With the tea in front of them, they sat in silence. Then Bellamy handed her a cigarette. 'Your hand's trembling,' he said as he lit it. Then he said, 'So you're going to appear on television? With Cavendish.' His voice sounded mildly amused.

'Yes.' She stirred her tea. 'And you're going with Lalette, to the party. That should be quite nice.' She paused. 'For you.'

'Very nice.'

'It must have been quite hard for Sir James to decide which one of us to send with you.'

'I don't imagine he lost much sleep over it.'

'Nor you, apparently.' Her anger against Bellamy was unaccountably rising again.

'Meaning exactly what?'

'Meaning I know you've been taking Lalette out. *And* me.'

Bellamy frowned. 'Did I ever tell you I hadn't?'

'You never told me you had, though.'

'Because it was nothing to do with you.' More gently, he added, 'I've known Lalette's family for years. And you know you don't really give a damn.'

'I know *you* don't.'

'Maybe not.' He drew on his cigarette. 'You see, I happen to believe it's up to me whom I take out . . . where, when and why. And nobody else.' He smiled. 'That's if they'll come.'

'But I don't like people thinking I'm – '

'I don't suppose right now anyone's giving you much of a thought.' He leaned forward. 'Look, Angela, you're tired and strung up. Finish your tea and then go and lie down. And if you feel like a drink later on, give me a ring, and we'll go and have one.'

'I don't think you understand – '

Bellamy leaned forward. All sympathy had gone out of his face. 'I don't understand because there isn't anything to understand. Except that you need to take a hold on yourself. Calm yourself down.'

'I *am* calm.'

'Look, Angela. You've got yourself all mixed up, and you're fastening on something to cover it up. I've seen it happen with men in the air. And I imagine it works much the same way with women.' He paused for a moment, before adding wryly, 'Only worse.'

Angela got up. 'From what I saw coming over,' she said with acid dislike, 'it's *you* that got yourself mixed up!'

Bellamy said nothing for a moment. Then he narrowed his

eyes. 'That's what I mean,' he said softly. 'Glad you've got the real trouble off your chest . . . at last.'

That evening, as all over New York his employees cautiously and rather shyly tried to carry out their social orders, Sir James Joliffe was standing above a hundred seated diners under a high-ceilinged banquet hall.

He swung himself back on his heels and placed the tips of his fingers carefully together. The pleasures of the Aeronautical Association's dinner, the rich food, the wine, the drone of voices, the compliments as delicately succulent as the roast young pig, and the listening ears of authoritative men, left a well of sweet saliva in his mouth that to contain, he must always keep the corners of his mouth upturned in a gentle smile. All through his speech he could taste it, and now, as he paused for effect before his final, grateful words, it produced a smile of the utmost benignity.

'Gentlemen,' he said gently, 'may I say that *your* encouragement, *your* enthusiasm, has moved me more than I can say. You are business men. Hard-headed, efficient, the backbone of this great country. Most of you are aviation operators or have wide interests connected with aviation. Therefore, gentlemen, *you* understand. You know the difficulties, and you can't be deceived by the finished product. All the enthusiasm we have had up to now, heartwarming though it has indeed been, and grateful, immeasurably grateful as we are for it, cannot compare to the *informed* enthusiasm which you have so touchingly displayed tonight.'

He put his hands behind his back and leaned forward, so that every diner could see his bright eager face.

'I could – ' He paused again, and his eyes were earnest. 'I could even go as far as to say that this journey, with all its planning and all its anxieties – ' He stopped and raised one hand slightly. 'This may sound sentimental to you.' He looked around the granite-jawed faces watching him. 'But I know that with your hard heads you conceal some very soft hearts.'

A pleased and deprecating murmur ruffled round the tables.

'So, I say it, without hesitation, that the whole enterprise, gentlemen, yes, the whole enterprise, would have been well worth while to me for the moment when the business brains of this wonderful country set the seal of their approval upon it.'

He looked down at the table as though overcome by his own emotion. Then he looked up and said, quite simply, 'Thank you.'

He sat down while a roar of applause like a tropical storm burst around him. Under the shelter of it, J. G. Carruthers, of All-American Inc., screwed up and threw away the little speech containing a quiet warning on forcing the pace too soon. To produce it now would have been worse than tactless, it would be sheer discourtesy. Appleside of Electra Aviation added a few very's and immense's and complete confidence's to an otherwise lukewarm speech, and Donald Prescott decided, after all, he would say nothing.

Sir James kept on staring at the intricate patterns of the damask cloth. The lobes of his ears had reddened as though they had been smartly boxed, and as the clapping continued he darted from time to time a small deprecating, gratified look at his immediate neighbours. It took several smart raps of the gavel before the next speaker could be announced, classified and labelled and prepared for their ears like a joint for the table.

Sir James raised his head, squared his shoulders, and let his eyes rest as though absorbed on the high ornate ceiling. Out of its excellent training, his head nodded judicially at the right pauses in the current speaker's sonorous rumble, his mouth pursed and smiled and looked aggressive at the unheard cues. Now that he came to think of it, there had been really nothing to worry about. If he had felt a bit put out by the Emperor's tantrums, by the landing at Idelwild, it was all over now. After all, he smiled grimly, they'd arrived, and that in the aviation business was a sure sign of success. And Cruttwell and Eastlake, still hard at work at Idelwild, would have produced the answer by now. Victory wasn't just round the corner. It was *here*.

Just as he had cleared the Company sky of every trace of cloud, a little pencilled note was handed to Sir James. He read it. It was signed, Hal Matherson, and it went, 'How about looking round this old bucket of yours?'

Delighted, Sir James smiled across the table a few chairs further down at Matherson, the President of World Travel, the power behind Sky-Am, one of the largest share-holders in Invincible Steel Inc.

He put up his thumb, and wrote back. 'Delighted, when?'

Hal Matherson mouthed, 'Tomorrow,' and Sir James nodded again. He would get the press in on this. He put his fingers together, enthralled with the picture of Matherson and himself, arm in arm on the Company's steps.

And as if to give body and meaning to Sir James' pleasant dreaming, as the speaker sat down in his little cloud of applause (happily very much smaller than Sir James') Hal Matherson despatched another note. Sir James unfolded it with the pleasurable anticipation of a child unwrapping a toffee whose prototypes he has seen, sampled and approved. It said, 'Better still. How about me coming with you? Will you let me hitch a ride to Bermuda?'

He looked down at it, and read it again, just to make sure. He turned it over and studied its blank back. There was no doubt that it was an innocuous piece of paper that had once been part of an envelope; and yet now, as Sir James rubbed its surface with his fingers, he knew that just those words written across it in pencil had changed its composition into potential dynamite. That was if Matherson really meant it. He looked up, hoping to see the good-humoured American grin that would tell him it was all just good clean kidding. But Matherson's eyebrows were raised, and he was smiling with genuine eagerness.

Sir James grinned at terrible expense to his aching face muscles. Very thoughtfully, he wrote, 'Would be most honoured. But afraid impossible. Formalities.' And then as a brilliant after-thought: 'Will present you with first ticket on our scheduled service.'

In return he got: 'To hell with formalities! Can I? And I'll take a rain check on that first seat.'

Sir James read it twice before he ventured to look up. The applause was petering out, and a slow pleasant buzz of talk filled the long glittering tables. Matherson leaned over, pushed aside a graceful fluted vase of silver filled with red roses, and said, 'I'd get a helluva kick out of it.'

Sir James didn't doubt it. He fingered his tie. He stroked his chin. He laughed. Then he hedged with: 'The regulations, and – '

'Never heard of 'em.' Hal Matherson grinned. 'Am I on or not? Is it okay with you if I fix the rest? I'll sign anything you want.'

Sir James just shook his head vigorously. He was still shaking it when Matherson got up to make his speech.

'I guess you boys don't want a spiel from me.' He was interrupted by loyal shouts of dissent, but he shook his head at them like a big good-humoured dog. 'We-ell,' he went on 'I'm not gonna make one.'

He crumpled a piece of paper, tossed it on the table and pushed his hands in his pockets. 'I can only say what you can see with your own two eyes far better.' He waved at Sir James. 'The achievement of yesterday's flight, and meeting our honoured friend and hearing him, has just left me nothing to say, except thanks for coming . . . thanks for what you've done for aviation . . . come again soon!' He paused and winked. 'And good show!'

He held his hand up. 'But before I sit down, there's something else. Sir James has invited me to accompany this historic flight to Bermuda.' He gave a wry smile. 'When I say invited, mebbe he didn't exactly twist my arm. But the fact is . . . *I'm going!*'

There were cheers. Hal Matherson held up his hand again. 'And looking at our friend, I don't think somehow he's the sort of guy who'd say no to a lady, so I wouldn't be at all surprised if Mrs. H. Matherson didn't find herself included on that invitation, too!'

Sir James sat there, with a stupefied smile glazed on his face. Automatically he joined in the applause, and in the after-dinner get-together, he was passed from group to group like a prize to be raffled at the local bazaar.

But the glory had gone from his evening, and he was glad that it was obviously his turn now to listen. He heard a number of interesting theories on why British airlines didn't make enough profit, received a string of useful hints on how to handle strikes, communist agitators, troublesome shareholders and balding hair, and listened to first-hand spirited accounts of brilliant financial coups d'état. Nevertheless, he trailed behind him now the vision of Mr. and Mrs. Matherson accompanying them on the next leg of this increasingly bothersome journey. More and more it became necessary for his current addresser to say to him, 'Now as I was saying,' to extract even a fraction of bemused attention for the subject on hand.

As the hands of the enormous figure-decorated clock befriended him, pointing ever nearer to the blessed hour when he could lay aside his glass slippers and return to his pumpkin of an aeroplane, his mice and his bevy of ugly sisters, his spirits rose a little.

There was just one more hurdle. And that was the photograph.

It was the sort of picture it would have done any business good for the boss to be seen in. Top executive arms were draped round one another, firm mouths grinned confidently and contentedly, and well-filled, well-clothed stomachs jostled one another like a clutch of black swan's eggs. And Sir James' grin was the most confident, the most contented of all. He kept his smile like a white flag of truce across his face, while behind it he busily rallied his forces. He was composing an aural version of his quarterly pep talk for Air Enterprise employees, as the little group's smiling lips were licked and gummed into position.

'Now, Sir James . . . what'll it be? What's your message? The real secret of success?' The reporter was bundling up his apparatus. He flung an impatient glance at Sir James' smiling absent face. Recalled from his pep talk, Sir James brought forth the word so unhappily occupying the intricate tracts inside his impressive head. 'Co-operation,' he said firmly, 'co-operation. The *get-together*.'

He gathered the remnants of jollity around him for the farewells, the humping on of coats, and the leisurely descent down the marble steps to the waiting cars. From a group just a little way behind, Hal Matherson's voice boomed out.

'You know,' he was saying to some anonymous grunter of assent, 'there's just one thing'd make me happier about this Bermuda trip. My two little ladies. Y'know Clare and Janine. They'll be hopping mad if their Mum and Dad make that first Emperor trip . . . and they get left behind!'

'Guess so.'

Hal Matherson ruminated for a moment. 'Reckon it was a pretty open invitation.'

'Guess so,' said the voice.

'Wouldn't be surprised if the whole Matherson family is meant to be included on that invitation!'

By the time the other voice said 'Guess so', Sir James was safely in the car.

By an odd coincidence, as the engine woke into life with a low throb, a clock on the corner of the block distinctly struck midnight.

The telephone was ringing when he let himself into his suite.

He picked up the receiver. 'Joliffe,' he said.

'Cruttwell speaking, sir.' The engineer's voice sounded elated. 'At last, we're really getting somewhere!'

'Fine work! *Fine work!*'

'Been working all day, sir.'

'You and Eastlake must be tired.'

'All in a good cause, sir.'

'Of course . . . of course! And what have you found?'

'It's not the engines, sir.'

'What was that you said?'

'It's not the engines, sir. We've been right through them and – '

'I don't want to know what it *isn't*! I want to know what *it is*!' There was a very long pause. Then the Chairman asked, more quietly, 'Cruttwell . . . *what is it?*'

'Well . . . we can't tell yet, sir. That'll take time.'

'I *must know*.'

'I realise that, sir. We'll start work again first thing tomorrow.'

'*I must know by tomorrow!*'

'Eastlake and I have to get some sleep, sir. After all – '

'Cruttwell . . . this has now developed into an affair of national importance. D'you hear what I'm telling you? *National importance!*'

'But, sir!'

'Don't waste your time arguing with me, Mr. Cruttwell. Get back to that aeroplane! I'll give you twenty-four hours flat to get the Emperor serviceable!'

CHAPTER THIRTEEN

It started off blustery on Tuesday morning, full of wind and the sky grey with rain. But Sir James was unaware of the weather outside. He sat in his suite, with Payton by his side, only aware of his own utter isolation in a foreign land.

He was like a general who had advanced too far ahead of his own troops. This was the sort of victory that turned out in the end to be a smashing defeat. All yesterday evening, while at the Aeronautical Association's dinner he had effortlessly carried the fort, his employees had been obeying his siege orders in the usual plodding, scrupulously honest, not very exciting British manner.

But, as far as he knew, they had, in fact held the line where he had told them to hold it. It was he himself, by that unexpected leap forward in the dark forced on him by Matherson, who had exposed the Emperor's flanks to acute danger from attack.

'A triumph . . . last night!' the Chairman said to Payton, perhaps just to hear the reassuring sound of that victorious word again in his ear.

'Certainly was, sir! You had them cold!'

The Chairman looked sharply across at the future Line Manager. 'They became most interested in the Emperor . . . if that's what you mean, Payton.'

'That's what I mean, sir! You had them really warmed up!'

'I can't remember when I've seen such enthusiasm.'

'That's what I mean, sir! You had them absolutely bubbling over!'

'They were generosity itself! The least we can do now is to give Mr. and Mrs. Matherson a ride down to Bermuda on the Emperor.'

'The *very* least, sir,' Payton paused before asking tentatively, 'You've phoned the airport this morning, sir?'

'They're still working,' Sir James said shortly. 'No change.'

'I see.'

They lapsed together into a gloomy silence. Outside the open window could be heard the roar and hustle of New

York's traffic – all very busy, racing around to get things done, while here in this quiet suite, the Chairman sat doing nothing, watching success, laurels and honour being thrust into his lap. What some people might call, Sir James thought ruefully to himself, *winning the easy way*.

The telephone by his side rang out, loud and confident. 'Perhaps it's the airport,' Payton said, brightening.

But it wasn't. It was Amos Appleside, Electra Aviation. 'You remember me, Sir James, last night?'

'Yes,' the Chairman said. 'I remember.'

'You've got a mighty fine aeroplane in that Emperor, sir! That's my belief!'

'Yes,' the Chairman said. 'That's my belief, too.'

'Big, too.'

'*Very* big.'

'How many passenger seats did you say you had, sir?'

'A hundred and sixty on this luxury version.'

'Holy smoke!' There was a long whistle on the other end. Then suddenly, unexpectedly, pointedly, 'You must have a lot of empty seats down to Bermuda, sir.'

Too late, the Chairman said quickly, 'I don't think you quite understand, Mr. Appleside.'

'Oh, yes, I do, sir! You told me you'd got seven passengers with you. I heard Matherson bum a ride from you last night. That leaves you a hundred and fifty-two buckshee seats to Bermuda!'

'Mrs. Matherson will be coming along, too.'

'Well . . . a hundred and fifty-one then.'

'And their two daughters.'

'Well . . . a hundred and forty-nine then. Now I've got a free couple of days . . . and we're very interested here in Electra in turbo-props . . . bit cold in New York . . . hear they're having a heat-wave in Bermuda. Now I'm going to be what you English call blunt, and come straight to the point, Sir James. Since you're letting the Mathersons in on the ride, perhaps – '

Knowing he was trapped, the Chairman tried to bring a gracious lilt into acknowledging a reverse: 'Of course, Mr. Appleside. We'd be glad to have you with us. One o'clock. Thursday – '

' – and my wife and young Amos. That little boy is . . . as

you can guess, sir . . . mighty keen on aeroplanes. Just the three of us in our little family.'

'We'd be delighted, Mr. Appleside. Delighted.'

When he put the receiver down, the Chairman just had time to say, 'It's getting more important than ever to get that aeroplane fixed,' when the telephone rang again.

It was Silkenstein of Sky High Octane Fuels.

'Yes,' Sir James said. 'Yes . . . yes . . . yes . . . yes. Delighted. One o'clock. Thursday.'

Moodily, he rang off and made a note of it. 'That's another four,' he said. 'Certainly gets around.'

The telephone pealed out again. Zweigler of Deep Tread Tyres. Within a minute, he was on board, too.

As Sir James said to Payton, 'Nothing else I can do! I can't accept one . . . and turn down another!'

'Of course you can't, sir.'

The telephone rang again. For the next hour, as Payton sat there, it was constantly ringing. Sir James was fully occupied: but it left the future Line Manager with little to do. He stared at the carpet – but this time, there was no pattern of promotion to be seen. Instead, the design was all higgledy-piggledy, as though an aeroplane had crashed from a very great height and had strewn itself before him. And when he lifted his eyes away from the scene – there, outside the window was Manhattan, its skyscrapers like stones so square and straight and flat that together they made up a gargantuan Stonehenge, standing there as though waiting for the hour to strike for some gigantic sacrifice.

Within that hour, half the Emperor's seats had been taken. The smooth plumpness of Sir James' forehead was now wrinkled with lines. 'One thing's certain, Payton,' he said, 'We can't let a little yawing over Labrador stop us now!'

For once, Payton said nothing. He was still sitting there, as though hypnotised by the weird giant's circle outside. It was Sir James who continued the conversation.

'Wonder how the others are getting along with their little publicity jobs,' he said, in an effort to get back to his old joviality. 'Let's hope they're keeping their end up!'

'Well, Miss Knight,' Captain Cavendish said, gallantly

opening the taxi door, so that the girl could step out first, 'after that . . . I think we *owe* ourselves a drink.'

While he paid off the driver, Angela stood quite still on the sidewalk, her hands clasped in front of her. He could feel her eyes on him, just as he had felt them during the television interview, gentle and helpless as two soft brown animals, waiting all the time for his protection.

He strode over to her and took her arm, half to steer her through the crowds as they bustled on every known compass heading towards lunch, half to shield her from them. 'A bit overpowering at first . . . all this coming and going.'

She nodded and smiled up at him rather shyly and primly, as they twisted their way in and out of the crush. She kept the elbow that he was holding very stiff, leaning her body towards it, as if afraid that his hand, if jolted or jogged, would break away.

'Not far now . . . just down here and to the right . . . there's a little place . . . nice and quiet and – ' He had almost added *refined*, a word he abominated, but somehow a rather suitable one to use to Miss Knight, 'And restful,' he finished.

'Good.' She let him usher her in to the warm dusk of the bar, so different from the noise outside and the lights and the voices of the television studio. She stood for a moment, not sure, he knew, whether to choose a table and walk towards it, to let him guide her, or to await the orders of the head waiter.

'I think over there in the corner would be pleasant enough. What d'you think?'

She nodded. Now that he had told her what to do, she did it well, moving across the polished floor with quietness and grace.

When the waiter came, he guided her choice to a good dry sherry, and then sat back in his chair watching her pale face, her rather large nervous hands, and the little way she had of flicking her head back as though her hair, instead of being cropped to a fashionable and regrettable half boy-cut, was a long silky mane that she kept tossing behind her.

It was a long time since he had protected, guided, advised a young and attractive woman. It took him back thirty years to his own courtship with his wife. To the first glass of shandy she had ever sipped in the riverside pub at Barnes. She'd been shy, like this. He had too, of course, but he hadn't been able to show it. He was, even then, the sort of man that *looks* as though he knows his way around. And just because he did, sooner or later he'd had to find out how to live up to it.

'Cheers!' Angela said, just as Mary had thirty years ago, and sipped a lipful of the stuff with ladylike distaste.

'Cheers!' Captain Cavendish said, thinking that now it was Mary who was the expert on liquor, as indeed of most other things, not excluding airlines.

The thought of aircraft recalled him to less pleasant thoughts. He took a mouthful of the sherry and gazed moodily across the table at Angela. Immediately, as though it was a cinema screen that reflected the powerful beam of his projector, her own face clouded over.

Minutes passed by. At last, Angela looked up at him, and said timidly, 'D'you think it was all right, sir?'

He looked at her silently for a moment. Then he said broodingly, 'Was what all right?'

'The television interview. D'you think Sir James would be' – she was going to say *pleased*, but after looking at his face, she finished with – 'satisfied?'

Cavendish gave his shoulders a shake, and as the waiter passed by, ordered two more sherries. 'Oh, the television . . . of course! Yes.' He stroked his moustache and nodded. 'Indeed yes, I do. I should say Sir James would be satisfied. More than satisfied. Pleased!'

It had, after all, not gone off badly. As always, the producer had had a pow-pow with them beforehand about interesting things to say. 'Now what, Captain, was your most exciting experience in the air?'

'Perhaps Miss Knight could tell us how she likes her job, why she chose it, what she thinks of American men, and what was *her* unforgettable moment?' Miss Knight had blushed quite obviously at that, though why on earth, he couldn't, then or now, decide.

'And tell us,' the interviewer had gone on, 'just what it feels like on the newest and fastest airplane on the North Atlantic?'

The interviewer had sat between them. Captain Cavendish had at first kept his eyes on the polished tips of his own black shoes, then let them hop on to the interviewer's sporty suedes, and, a bit higher this time, to Miss Knight's high-heeled courts and well-shaped ankles. Then, remembering the eyes of America, he had managed a few straight looks at the camera, and then gone back to his own large (heaven knew) capable-enough looking hands, and then across to Angela's, so calmly folded in her lap, while all the time, surreptitiously, the thumb-nail of her right hand dug – it was painful to watch – into the pad of her first finger.

There was only one moment when he'd realised she'd been tongue-tied. Her small mouth had opened and closed and then wobbled terrifyingly, but he had managed to come forward with an experience of his own – a dust-storm in the desert or something – and had then brought her in neatly at the end with, 'Of course you weren't with me then, Miss Knight, but you were that time we flew to Montreal with the load of . . . ' And she *had* remembered, and she *had* smiled, and then she had managed to add some quite apt remark of her own.

He had felt good about that, about his little effort for her, and like donors of good deeds the world over, his own heart had warmed towards her.

'If he is,' she said suddenly. 'If Sir James *is* pleased . . . it's you that . . . well, did it!' Her eyes, her voice, her mouth, were all very earnest.

'Come, come, Miss Knight!' He laughed, and the warmth of his own pleasure ran through him, more kindly and pleasantly than the comfort of the liquor. 'I hardly think Sir James would agree. Or the viewers. I'm not,' he said, 'exactly photogenic.'

'Oh, but you are!' Angela said, so vehemently that he raised his iron-grey eyebrows and they both laughed.

'But . . . well,' the girl went on, 'you look so . . . so . . . '

Cavendish said, 'You're making me quite nervous!'

'So strong! Someone to trust! Like . . . like – ' She was going to say *like Daddy*, but then, with an instinctive feminine tact, she said instead, 'Like a rock!' Her eyes were misty. 'Who'd always be there' – her voice was quite definitely husky – 'when you need them.'

Surprised by an outburst like that, it did not occur to him to lay the blame for it on the Emperor. He kept quite still for a moment, eyeing her bowed head a little anxiously and thoughtfully. He was allergic to weepy women, but there was something about her sincerity that had touched him deeply.

Her hands were folded on her lap now. As she sat there quite silently, not moving, her whole body looked as though it had been exploded from within, and there was nothing of her left but the same timid shell he'd known before.

At last, she said, 'I'm sorry. I'm afraid I said too much. If I offended you – ' The little brown animals peeped out of their shelter for a moment, and then scuttled for cover again.

'But you didn't at all!' He smiled. 'It's just – ' Memories of the landing leapt up in his mind, dissolving his pompousness, his dignity, his pride. 'Not true,' he added quietly.

'Oh, but it is!' she said hotly. 'It *is* true. I feel . . . *safe* when I fly with you.'

He drew in his breath and frowned. With a trace of his usual self at Operations or Met, he said almost sharply, 'You are not exactly an expert in flying, Miss Knight!'

'No,' she said. 'I know. But all the same, I get a feeling. Call it anything you like. It doesn't matter . . . it's still there. And I'm not the only one. Lots of the girls in the catering section . . . they try to fly with you. I've heard them ask!'

She watched his face triumphantly.

'Well, let's not argue!' He smiled across at her, and on an impulse patted her hand. 'That was one of the nicest things anyone has ever said to me.'

'And the truest,' she said, as though now she had been started, nothing could stop her.

They sipped their drinks companionably. 'If I was to order lunch in the dining-room, would you care to have it with me, Miss Knight? I know the food here. It's particularly pleasant.'

'I'd like that . . . very much.'

They finished their sherries, exchanging rather tentative smiles across the table.

As they walked through the glass doors into the grill room Cavendish said, 'You know, I'd enjoy my lunch a great deal more if we dropped all this Captain Cavendish stuff. My name's Charles.' He gave a little bow as he said it, as though the captain had left the room and he was introducing a new and more interesting creature for her delectation and amusement.

'And mine –'
'Is Angela. I heard you tell the producer. It suits you admirably.'
The girl's face was a little pink as she allowed the waiter to settle her in the chair.
They talked about this and that over the shrimp cocktail and the fried chicken. Over the ice-cream, airline personalities were beginning to crop up. And above the smooth surface of the coffee, the Emperor had begun to cast the shadow of her wings.
It was inevitable, he supposed. The raison d'être of their lunch, indeed of their new friendship, was bound to be mentioned. But momentarily he wished, though not so vehemently as he might have done earlier on, that it *hadn't*.
'You weren't nervous?' he asked, stirring an extra lump that he didn't want into his coffee.
'Oh, but I was!' Her eyes looked across at him almost indignantly. 'Nearly all the way over. When we were in Iceland . . . I felt like asking not to go on!'
'Whatever for?' Cavendish's voice was rich and steady. 'Because it was a new aeroplane? Was that it?'
She nodded. 'Partly. But that wasn't all. And anyway . . . I was right! There was trouble in the end. Wasn't there?'
He drew a deep breath. This was more or less where they'd come in. Where he came in, at any rate. So they'd felt that bump just as badly at the back. Even now, perhaps people were talking about it. Sir James had obviously been thinking over the age of his most senior pilot. Rawlings and the rest of the crew, too, no doubt. He screwed up his left eye and read in small print on the top of the menu *Consommé Vermicelli*.
He swirled his coffee round and round with his spoon until the middle of his cup was a little open concave circle, a round mouth that went on talking and talking – about ageing pilots and slow reactions, and retiring ages, and all the unfair pitfalls of this job that snatched the fruits of a lifetime's toil and plumped them into the hands of a young and inexperienced man.
He looked across at her gravely. 'You felt it very much at the back, did you?'
She nodded. 'We were strapped in, of course. Even so,

some of the passengers fell heavily against each other.' She put her hand to her mouth, as the picture of the cabin and the fear and the disorder filled her mind. 'And we didn't know how far away from a landing field we were . . . you remember?'

As a matter of fact, he hardly did. It had taken him a moment to realise that she was, after all, talking about the happenings over Labrador. Not about his own mishandled landing, which like a great smudge of failure had blotted out all the previous frets and worries of the crossing. His face cleared. Nothing that had happened up in Labrador could be blamed on him.

'You see, it doesn't worry you, because you've been through it so often before. But I was frightened! I thought we'd never make New York!'

'And then the weather there was bad,' he smiled grimly. After all, it *was* an extenuating circumstance.

'*Awful*,' Angela said, and shuddered.

'And we were piled up in the stack!'

'Yes, we seemed to go round and round. In cloud . . . all the time!' Angela took a sip of her coffee, and coloured a deep pink. He watched her carefully. Already he had learned this faint blushing was a sure and certain prelude to making a remark that had touched her deeply. Now would come the question of the landing. For a moment he chided himself that the most senior member of the Company's aircrew should be watching with anxiety for a remark from one of its most junior. But he excused himself with something about out of the mouths of babes and sucklings, and waited.

'But I wasn't afraid, then,' she said. 'I knew *you'd* get us in safely.' She hid her face again in her cup. 'And you did!' Her eyes were shining. 'You brought us in! First time! Straight on to the runway!'

With a great crump at the end, he thought grimly, that cracked a strut on the oleo leg. But perhaps after all, it hadn't felt so bad in the cabin. It was just possible that they'd hardly noticed it. It felt worse to him, because he'd been so keyed up about it all. And that man Bellamy certainly hadn't made it easier for him.

'Not a very smooth landing, I'm afraid,' he said.

'I could see the lights come up from out of the mist, and then . . . suddenly we were safely on the ground!'

And that, of course, *was the whole point.* He had got them in safely. After a gruelling flight. In a brand new aeroplane. In bad weather. With fuel running low. As he'd often said, on the North Atlantic it was experience that counted. That sixth sense that put safety first. A polished smooth landing was often the most dangerous. What did a bump or two (or a cracked strut that could be replaced in a few hours) matter? He'd been getting things out of proportion. And now, at last they were settling down again into their right perspective.

Nobody, when you came to think about it, could *really* call him old. He looked across the table at this twenty-four-year-old girl, and realised that certainly he was experienced, but for all that – he was still in the prime of life.

The coffee was finished. The bill on the plate was hinting at departure. Angela Knight was putting on her gloves. But Cavendish did not put on his own. Postponing their parting, he suggested, 'How about an hour or two in the cinema, Angela? Let's watch someone entertain *us*!'

It was pleasant to have his invitation accepted so readily and with such touching gratitude. They swung along in step down the sun-bright sidewalk, and went inside the first cinema they came to, without looking to see what was showing.

Inside, once more in the darkness, he took her hand. It lay quietly and trustfully in his. And as though she had deposited all cares and worries with it, she gave her undivided, rapt attention to the screen.

It was evening by the time they came out. And now it would have seemed churlish to take her back to the hotel without tea. He knew just the place where they served real English teas. Best of all, the manageress knew him personally.

A kind of gentle authority, a feeling of maturity and wisdom was over him now, like a comfortable garment. His age remained unalterable, but the residue of the years was no longer a clogging metabolism that was slowing his brain and his muscles and his mind. It was a fine mature wine . . . a liqueur . . . an essence. Rich in experience and thought. It was only this supersensitive thoughtfulness which had made him so touchy about the landing. He was a perfectionist. After all these years, a bad landing *hurt* him. Any of the youngsters, with the exception of Bellamy, would have passed it off and forgotten all about it.

He saw Angela looking at him over the homely tea-table, and he smiled. Fifty-odd wasn't old, he thought, if a man was fit and virile. Her eyes were no longer timid. They watched him openly and happily. He held out his cup for more tea, so that he could watch her while she poured.

Half an hour later, they were almost back at the hotel. There was no reason that either of them could think of now to prolong their outing together.

The rush hour was petering out. Under the black sky, the neon lights drenched the sidewalk with squirts of red and green and dead white light. They both walked slowly. At the corner, just in front of the hotel, they paused. They were oddly at peace. They seemed to fit in so well, both giving and taking, one to the other, one from the other, each other's separate, single need.

Angela's face was turned up to the pilot's, and he could see how well the clear skin, the dark eyes and the red mouth kept their youthful prettiness even in this harsh, unkind light.

With almost ponderous courtesy, he took off his uniform cap and bent down to touch his lips gently on her white forehead, just before the beginnings of her black hair. It wasn't the sort of kiss Mary, his wife, would have minded in the least if she'd seen it. It was, if he'd known it, just the sort of kiss Daddy would give her at this sort of time and in this sort of place.

He could hear the movements of people along the sidewalk, the almost rhythmic roar of the traffic. But he only really knew the touch of her cool skin, the hand laid on his arm, as though to hold him a second or two longer, and the pleasure of this day.

Then they both drew back and smiled without embarrassment.

'Thank you for a lovely day,' she said.

'Thank *you*,' he said.

In the mid-afternoon, the doctor held the telephone receiver against his ear with his left hand. In his right was a single sheet of dazzling vellum, beautifully typed in blue.

There was a click. Then: 'Joliffe.' The Chairman's voice sounded much further away than the eight hundred odd yards that separated the two hotels.

'This is Enderby-Browne, sir. I have some *extraordinarily* good news.'

'*You have?*' The words came rushing down the line with the speed of an express train.

'I think we can say that it seals the success of – '

'Fine, doctor! Fine! When did they tell you?'

'About an hour ago, sir. I don't know why they should pick on me – '

'I've been out all afternoon. Lunch with All American Aero lasted late. That's why.'

'The only trouble is . . . maybe it means an alteration in the programme.'

'I won't hear of it, Browne, I tell you! *Won't hear of it!*'

There was a frigid, painful silence. Then, in a flat, disappointed voice, Enderby-Browne said, 'Oh.'

'Well . . . come on! What did they tell you?'

'It doesn't matter now, sir.'

'Of course it matters now!'

'They didn't *tell* me anything. The Canford Institute *invited* me. My lecture . . . the earthly body in the sky. On Saturday.'

The silence this time was longer still. It was a full minute before the Chairman said, 'I'm sorry, doctor. You had me mixed up for a moment.'

'I thought in any case there was a good chance of the Emperor still being *here* over the weekend,' Enderby-Browne suggested eagerly.

But the Chairman did not apparently hear him. 'I know you'll be disappointed to miss the flight. However, an unexpected chance like this – '

'I can assure you it was *quite* unexpected, sir. I met a Mrs. Lepage at the convention of the Daughters of the American Air which you asked me to attend. We had a most interesting talk. I had no idea that her husband was the president of the Canford Institute.'

Rather surprisingly, what sounded like a low chuckle came from the other end of the line. 'You can thank the Emperor's success for the invitation, then, doctor. You see now, don't you, how one thing brings on another?'

Enderby-Browne did *not* see it, either now or before. He had never considered the co-relation of the Emperor's publicity and this sudden, belated recognition of his efforts. He said stiffly, 'It's a very great honour, Sir James, rarely bestowed on foreign – '

'Of course it is! The Company's very proud of you, doctor. I insist on you staying. We shall have to manage without you.'

'Thank you, Sir James.' Enderby-Browne's voice glowed with gratitude. 'Thank you very much indeed.'

Immediately he put down the receiver, the doctor went over to the top drawer of the desk to get his notes. He became so engrossed in sorting out his work, he did not hear the first knock on the door.

The second was very much louder.

'Come in,' he called.

Turning his head, he was surprised to see Captain Payton.

'I wonder, doctor,' the future Line Manager said, his voice lowered, as though every tightly closed door guarded a sleepless patient, 'I wonder if I might have a talk with you?'

The doctor waved him in. His pleasant smile was more than words of welcome.

Payton came to the point fairly slowly. He talked about this and that. He inquired after the doctor's researches. Then he said, 'It's really about myself, doctor.'

Enderby-Browne's little yellow cornstukes became stacked even higher below the furrows of his reddish forehead. He pursed his lips professionally. 'Yes?' he said.

Payton took out his cigarette-case. His hands weren't quite steady. 'This may surprise you, doctor. But I feel a bit . . . well, strained. Tired. Off my food, Shivery. Jaded.'

The doctor nodded his head at the end of every symptom that Payton produced. Puffing hard on his cigarette, the man went on: 'Not at all myself.' *Puff.* 'Bad taste in my mouth.' *Puff.* 'Heartburn.' *Puff.* 'Nausea.' *Puff.* 'Headache.'

The doctor kept his head on one side. 'Mmm,' he murmured thoughtfully. 'Mmm – go on.'

Payton looked slightly put out. 'Well . . . that's about it.'

He rubbed his forehead, now a little damp, as though trying to scrape the bottom of the barrel. 'Oh,' he puffed again nervously, 'and last night I had a pain across here.' He rubbed the area around his waist.

'Mmmm,' Dr. Enderby-Browne said again. And then, after a pause, 'Worried about anything?'

'Well.' Captain Payton waved his hand, and smiled thinly. 'Of course I am. I mean . . . '

'You mean about the flight over?'

'Oh, not *that*, doctor!' Captain Payton laughed. 'But I do think,' he said slowly and judiciously, 'that maybe at my age, you feel this business of pressurisation and long hours a bit more. What would you say? I've lost my acclimatisation. Being tied to a desk. All that sort of thing. Am I right, doctor?'

The doctor nodded his head vigorously. He had arrived at that part of his thesis which dealt with the extra red corpuscles in the blood that regular fliers acquired, and his theories were very fresh in his memory. 'You're probably still a bit tired.'

'That's another thing, doctor,' Payton said eagerly. 'Can't get any sleep.'

The doctor corrected himself, '*Over*-tired. Not surprising. Your body hasn't made up the sleep you lost on the trip over. And now, all these parties! All this excitement! All the same . . . if you'd take off your jacket and shirt – '

As Payton did what he was told, he explained with an off-hand grin on his face, 'Thought I better get this seen to right away. Might need diet. Rest.'

The doctor examined his patient with infinite care. At the end of an exhausting half-hour, he said, 'Captain Payton, there's only one thing I'm going to prescribe for you.'

Payton said quickly, 'And what's that, doctor? '

'You're going to the American Airlines' party tonight?'

'Of course. There's a number of highly influential – '

'Don't go.'

' . . . the Chairman will expect . . . perhaps for my future job – '

'Don't go,' the doctor said, a little more loudly.

' . . . to get acquainted with other managers . . . '

'Captain Payton,' the doctor said very decisively, 'my prescription is *not to go to the party tonight.*'

Payton looked at him hard. 'You mean – '

'I mean there's nothing the matter with you a night's rest won't cure.'

'That's good!' Payton laughed a little shakily. 'For an awful moment, I thought you were going to say I'd better go into dock here for a week's observation. I'd have missed the Emperor's biggest moment.'

Enderby-Browne went into the bathroom to wash his hands. 'How d'you mean . . . biggest moment?'

'Haven't you heard?'

The doctor returned, wiping his fingers carefully with a face towel. 'Heard what?'

'Half the American aviation industry are trying to come down with us to Bermuda on Thursday.'

'They are?' The surprise on Enderby-Browne's face changed to cautious inquiry. 'Have they . . . have they found out the trouble?'

'With the Emperor?' Payton shook his head. 'Not that I know.'

'Yet she'll still leave on Thursday?'

In a perfectly deadpan voice, as though all feeling had been anaesthetised out of it, Payton replied, 'She'll leave on Thursday, all right. With a full load.' He rose to his feet. 'Well . . . thank you, doctor. I'll stay in tonight, then . . . if you say so.'

Encouragingly, sympathetically, Enderby-Browne said, 'That's the ticket! Early to bed! Good night's sleep!'

Just before he closed the door, again Payton said mechanically, 'Thank you, doctor.'

Left on his own, Enderby-Browne shook his head thoughtfully. Of course, it was perfectly obvious. The man was worried sick that Sir James would leave on schedule, serviceable aircraft or not. He'd had a bad fright over Labrador. He didn't want another one.

First Riley and his obvious fear of flying. Now Payton. Probably a good many more among the Emperor's inhabitants – if the truth were known. That dark-haired girl, for instance, Eastlake didn't look too happy. Even some of the crew –

All of them crying out to be encouraged. Nothing much you could do, of course. Jolly them along. Tell them to keep their peckers up. Boost their morale.

There was no doubt about it, life was queer. Here were a lot of people trying to get on something at the same time as a lot of others were trying just as hard to get off it.

It was an observation well worth noting. He crossed over to his desk to put it down. Here I sit, he thought to himself as he wrote, like a Greek chorus – commenting on the vagaries of mankind, preserving them for posterity.

This man Payton, for instance. His case was a kind of Pavlov's experiment in reverse. The mouth did not water at the sound of a bell that had always before meant food. But the nerves shook in apprehensive anticipation of Able Dog shaking again. The man's fingers had shivered as though they were freezing.

That was curious. At the thought of Able Dog flying again, even *his* hand had shaken a little as it continued with his notes.

Impatiently, he gripped his pen more firmly. This trembling was ridiculous. In any case, he wouldn't be *going* on the Emperor on Thursday.

Finishing his notes, he began to rearrange his lecture for American consumption. The very first words were difficult. How *did* one address a gathering of such an assembly as the Canford Institute?

Ladies and gentlemen? – too formal, much too cold. Physicians? – there would be a good many surgeons there. Fellow doctors? – not accurate, there would be research workers, scientists. American colleagues? – too like a business organisation.

A smile lit up his face. Of course! That was it! In a surprisingly neat hand, he began to write on the very top of the blank sheet of foolscap.

And then he stopped. His hand rubbed his chin. All of a sudden, his mind had been flooded with the picture of the other fifteen inhabitants of the Emperor, his charges, going off into the unknown without him.

He gazed round the room. He stared out of the window. He looked at his pile of notes. At last, very reluctantly, he allowed his eyes to drop down on the page in front of them, to re-read the words he had just written: *Fellow servants of humanity . . .*

High above the hum of Fifth Avenue that evening, Lalette finished her dressing and make-up with a kind of uninspired precision. Outside, the heavier sky had shrunk in on the city. There was no natural illumination now, only the pink reflection of neon lights on the clouds, and the cold white tide in the streets below. A different New York was coming to life, paler and darker and more exciting than the loud-voiced friendly hustle of the day; as different as the faces and clothes of the people, made into black and white portraits by the high hard lights.

Lalette walked away from the mirror and leaned her elbows on the window-sill, gazing down at the small figures moving in the street below. Cars slid in to the curb, and spilled out well-groomed and much-furred figures; others hooted their way swiftly along and out of her sight, bound for unknown and exciting evening assignations. Inconsequentially, she pitied Bellamy. Somewhere, underneath twenty or so layers of iron and concrete and the overheated air between them, he would be moving slowly and reluctantly, to his evening assignation with *her*.

In spite of the fact that he didn't want to, and in spite of the fact that, anyway earlier on, she did.

And all because a chubby, not over-large man, with square busy hands had pulled yet more strings, and everyone had once again immediately jumped.

She moved away, glanced at the alarm clock on the mantelpiece and decided it was just a bit too early to go down yet. If she had been a bit nicer, or a bit more strong-minded, she would have telephoned Bellamy and told him she had a headache. And if he'd been a bit nicer, he'd have telephoned *her*, and told her he was looking forward to it. Maybe even, although that was stretching the imagination rather far, sent her a corsage. She smiled to herself. Then seeing that it was close on seven-thirty, once more she felt nervous and shy, and wished she wasn't going.

After she closed the door behind her, she thought: I wonder how I'll be feeling when I open it again? It was something she often felt these days, a result of flying, she supposed. A result of closing up her small flat behind her, and then suddenly being whirled halfway across the world. The Mediterranean, the Far East, India, Australia and America – she'd had a brief taste of them all. Anything, she felt now, could happen to her in the space of a few hours. Every time she set out, she must surely come back – just that much different.

She pressed the button for the lift, watching with pleasure, as she always did, the doors part to show the mixed box of human beings it had inside. In the brief descent, she tried to partner whom with whom, to decide where they were going and why.

She got out at the Mezzanine, and walked with exaggerated slowness towards the first door. She felt a reassuring number of heads turned as she went, noted them, counted them up, clasped them around her for decency and protection as though she had arrived at the lounge underclad. Inside the Mezzanine lounge, the atmosphere had turned a deep electric rose. More people in their smarter clothes drank more and smiled more, and filled the air with a perpetual simmer of conversation. For a moment, she felt rebuffed by the noise and the smoke and the groups of people, all knitted together in an unnoticing, indistinguishable mass.

'Hello, Lalette, there you are!' Andrew Bellamy came up behind her and took her arm. 'On time, too!'

'Hello.'

'You're looking pretty nice.'

'Thank you, Andrew. That makes me *feel* nice.' She let him lead her to a table just inside the door.

'Come and sit down, and I'll buy you a sherry. On the Company.' He grinned down at her. 'If you're good.'

'I am.'

When he had ordered whisky for himself, sherry for her, he said suddenly, 'You know something, Lalette?'

'No.'

'You always make me feel better.'

'Do I?' Her mouth curved gently. 'Quite often . . . you do the same to me.'

'Heaven knows why!'

'And it won't tell.' She looked at him out of the corners of her blue eyes. 'Not always, though.'

'Not always what?'

'Make me feel better.'

'Like Iceland for instance?'

She nodded her head gravely. 'Like Iceland.'

'That's because you were wrong.'

'I know. That makes it worse. Much worse.' She gave him a little sideways smile.

'Drink up your sherry, and let's get off on the job. How's Chris?'

'Fine.'

'And your mother?'

'The same.'

'And you?'

'Am I forgiven?'

'Yes.'

'Then I'm the same too.'

He lifted his whisky. 'Cheers, then!'

'Cheers!' she said, and then still in the same voice. 'Disappointed it isn't Angela?'

'No.'

She finished her sherry slowly, watching the ebb and flow of the room's mixed tide, hearing the sugar-waterfall roar of dozens of cocktail-time talks.

Bellamy looked at his watch. 'Like another before we go?'

Lalette shook her head.

'In that case . . .' Bellamy got up, and held out her coat. Then he followed her down the staircase, and across the foyer.

Once inside the taxi, she settled in her corner and looked across at him. Even if he hadn't been in uniform you would have known that that was his normal dress. The thick strong neck, the clean line of his jaw, and that economy of movement produced that indefinable air of authority that uniform was supposed to give. Sometimes, she thought rather sadly, it was as though the uniform had irretrievably moulded the man.

'Lalette?'

'Yes?' She turned to him. He was back on the job now. She could see it in his eyes and the set of his mouth. Duty had to be done. A job lay ahead. He had metaphorically put his cap back on. She might have been any female sitting there, so long as she was not improperly dressed. She might, for that matter, have been Hamilton.

She folded her hands in her lap, eyed her faultlessly groomed and unnoticed hands, and waited patiently for the briefing.

'You've heard about the Air League?'

'A little. Only vaguely.'

'It's an organisation of aircraft manufacturers and airline executives.'

'I see.'

'Now, when we get there – '

'Yes?'

'I'll introduce you around. You won't be lonely.'

'No.'

'And . . . I shouldn't drink too much if I were you.'

'No.'

'And don't talk too much.'

'No.'

'Don't say anything much about the Emperor.'

'No.'

'Nor about the trip over.'

'No.' Then after a moment, she said in a deceptively meek voice, 'Is there anything I *can* do too much?'

'Nothing.'

'In other words, I'm to be the usual stuffed shirt?'

'Nicer shirt,' Bellamy grinned. 'And better stuffed. But that's more or less the idea.'

Lalette paused. Then she said, 'They should enjoy that.'

In the silence that followed, she turned her head away towards the long inviting display of the shop windows. Only the reflected lights of the neon signs changed the pale cameo of her face from white to pink to green to blue, and back again to white.

The cab slid in front of the Fourth Avenue portico of the Van Dyck hotel. Bellamy said, 'Well . . . this is it.'

The big glass doorway was full of syrupy peach light. Two green-uniformed porters stood waiting like hungry grasshoppers on the pink-stained pavement outside. Gathering her skirt up daintily, Lalette stepped down from the cab.

They both watched the lift-indicator in silence as it marked them up to the second floor.

'Sure you're all right?' Bellamy looked down at her. 'Not nervous or anything?'

She half shook her head and smiled. As they walked down the corridor towards the Connaught suite, they could hear a soft sustained murmur leaking out from the solid oak doors.

'Anything more you want me to tell you?'

This time Lalette shook her head vehemently. She put her hand on his arm. 'Andrew.'

'Yes?'

'I'm not exactly bubbling over now,' she said half wryly, half sweetly. 'If I get any more advice . . . I'll get pricked like a balloon.'

Bellamy frowned and went on staring at her. With his hand on the door, he felt suddenly impatient and tired. The noise of the party became a meaningless drone, and Lalette's eyes, clear and blue as summer skies, looked as good and sweet a place as anywhere for a weary airman to rest. He frowned more deeply, remembering the taxi ride, its dark seclusion, the heavy smell of Lalette's perfume.

Then he opened the door to the reception. The steady noise swelled and disintegrated into all its various ingredients: male and female voices in talk and laughter, soft movements of feet on the sponge-thick carpet, rustling of dresses, clinking of glasses, the rattle and rasp of crushed ice in the silver bowls and the frosted jugs. But as though the party was geared to a mechanical inhibitor, the voices, the footfalls and the laughter never rose above the rich discretion of the room.

Lalette, after walking the ten-mile-long few paces into the room, stood a little behind Bellamy – one foot slightly in front of the other as though she were dipping her toes in the sea to test if the water was warm enough.

'And this is Miss Greenacres,' Bellamy was saying to Mr. Isherwood, Manager of Atlantic Airways.

'Well that's a very pretty name for a very pretty lady! But I guess her other is prettier still.'

'Lalette,' she said simply.

Mr. Isherwood slapped his thigh. 'Say now . . . didn't I tell you! Lalette! Well, fancy that! French, isn't it?'

'I had a French grandmother.' Lalette smiled up at him. The water was beautifully warm.

'I knew it! Cutest name I heard in a long, long time!' He gave Bellamy a grin. 'Now Captain Bellamy here will be talking with these other guys about what keeps aeroplanes moving. You and me, Lalette . . . we'll go and meet Mrs. Isherwood. Laura!' He led her away, like a collector that has netted the bird of rare plumage.

But their passage was disputed. There were introductions, compliments, half-completed conversations. As if to wipe away Bellamy's prosaic and bread-butter advice, every voice seemed to tell her she was pretty, every face that they liked her. Her head whirled with countless Sid's and Mac's and Dan's and Eddie's. She broke off half-way through answering one question, to start on another by someone else. She couldn't remember why she became an air hostess, whether she liked flying, how long she'd been doing it, what she thought of the Emperor, or if all the girls back home were like her. What she could remember was that they were loving her, and that Andrew Bellamy must see, at least in some men's eyes, she was pretty and attractive and good to know.

Eventually they made the small table where Laura was in a huddle with two other wives. Laura raised her hand, heavy with rings and said, 'Say, we might have known Brett wasn't wasting any time, eh?' And they all laughed.

'This is Lalette!' Brett Isherwood put his arm round her waist and gave her a little push forward. Laura put out her hand and said 'I'm glad to know you,' and squeezed so hard that Lalette could feel the rings cut into her fingers. She couldn't remember the other names. But they all smiled and nodded and welcomed her as though they really meant it.

Under their exquisite dresses, their so-real jewels, the beautiful hair-do's and the expensive corsages, they were cosy and warm and human. Among business and aeroplanes and pay loads and passenger psychology, they formed a happy oasis of delightful femininity. As one cocktail followed another, they talked of shops and bargains and dresses; nylon pleating and its permanency, shampoos, diets, babies and husbands.

'And now, dear,' Laura Isherwood said, as Bellamy came over to stand beside them, 'I do believe your boy friend's getting out of patience waiting for you!' Bellamy was talking cautiously about the Emperor to a couple of airline presidents, who had expressed the possibility of buying a few; but from time to time, he had been looking over at Lalette.

The few feet of floor that separated them seemed to have grown. It was as though, for the first time, he was seeing her clearly. Before tonight, the vision of her as Chris' younger sister on brief leaves in the R.A.F. had overlain every more recent one. Even the sight of her, neatly dressed in the same company uniform as himself, being on the same crew, had not altered it.

He had taken her out from time to time, as he had taken out lots of girls. Or he'd bought her a beer, or a cup of coffee on different trips. That is, if she'd happened to be around, and if he'd happened to think about it.

And now, he was noticing her tight-fitting dress, and seeing the line of her throat, and the redness of her mouth, and for some inexplicable reason it made him irritable and angry. Not with himself, but with her.

There were several more men who wanted to meet her, and after a while he reluctantly fished her out of her small safe backwater and launched her once more into the noisy stream. He stuck it for about half an hour. The monotonous sameness of the compliments got under his skin. So did the sight of Lalette rather enjoying it. So did the knowledge that there was a lot to be done, if this trip was to be completed successfully and safely.

'Time we went,' he said to Lalette at last, and walked over to make his good-byes.

The comfort of being liked had warmed Lalette in its deceptively rosy glow. The good-byes and see-you-again's were the triumphant finale. She took her coat from the cloakroom, and let Bellamy put it round her shoulders.

Inside the taxi, she said, 'Did we do all right?'

'I think so.'

'Did *I* do all right?'

'Yes.'

'Did you enjoy it?'

'No.' Bellamy leaned forward. 'I kept remembering something I hadn't done.'

'That's not like you, Andrew.'

'And I couldn't wait to put it right.' He put his arm round her shoulders.

'What was it?'

'I'd never kissed you.'

'No.'

'Never really before.'

'No.'

'Only at that party of Chris'.'

'And that can't be counted.'

'That's what I mean,' he said. 'Not *properly*.'

After a moment, she said softly. 'D'you know something, Andrew?'

'No.'

'I'm awfully glad . . . you . . . remembered.'

Just on midnight that night, Eastlake leaned against the telephone box outside the deserted hangar, his eyes closed, his head on his chest. Inside, Cruttwell was saying, 'We've been through everything, sir. And we can find nothing wrong!'

'There *must* be something wrong!' The Chairman's voice, very quick, very cross, came immediately back at him. 'You don't have that caper over Labrador without *something* being the matter.'

'We're trying to work out a theory, sir – '

'I don't want a theory! I want the facts!'

'You've *got* the facts, sir,' Cruttwell put in. 'At present, the Emperor is perfectly serviceable.'

'That's because she's on the ground. In the air . . . it'll be a different matter! I can't tell you, Cruttwell, how important it is that nothing goes wrong on Thursday!'

There was a pause. At his end of the wire, Cruttwell was dispiritedly considering the uncertain future; while Sir James, in his suite in the Grand-Plaza Hotel, was remembering the terrible day behind him. Never alone for a moment, ceaselessly subjected to a withering fusillade of notes, messages, requests and phone calls, which had only ceased when it became known that the Emperor's capacity had been reached. She was full up. A hundred and fifty-three Americans would be accompanying the proving flight down to Bermuda.

Cruttwell said, 'I don't see what else we can do, sir.'

'You can go over the aircraft again. *Very* carefully.'

'But Mr. Eastlake and I have hardly had a wink of sleep – '

'This is a matter, now, of the *highest international importance*!'

'I can't see that it's *that* important, sir. I mean – '

'Every precaution *must* be taken against a repeat performance.'

'If we're not certain what caused it . . . that's difficult, sir.'

'*It's what's got to be done!* Get back to the aircraft, Mr. Cruttwell! Go through her with a fine tooth-comb! I shall hold you and Mr. Eastlake *personally* responsible . . . if anything happens on Thursday!'

Cruttwell came slowly out of the telephone box. 'Did you hear that, Alan?' he asked.

'I've been asleep.' Eastlake rubbed his eyes. 'Can we go to bed?'

'He says we'ev got to go through the whole thing again.'

'*No!*'

'Fact.'

They walked together towards the snack-bar. 'For a sheer, honest-to-God nigger-whipper,' Cruttwell went on, all his mildness vanished into exasperation, 'I don't suppose that man Joliffe has an equal in England!'

Eastlake nodded in perfect agreement.

So far apart before, now both the designers had been brought together by their mutual hatred of Sir James Joliffe. Apart from the aircraft (and they had reached the stage there of even expressing admiration for each other's work), the Chairman and sleep were the only subjects they talked about. Victims under the same lash, they were fast becoming friends.

Over coffee and sandwiches, Eastlake said, 'I mean to say . . . we're professional men! Not slaves! Who does he think he is, Douglas?'

'Impossible to find the word in English.' Cruttwell paused. 'Or in French.' Cruttwell paused again. 'Or in German.'

'I believe the Russians have a word.'

Cruttwell thought for a moment. He took a bite out of his sandwich and munched it slowly. 'Yes,' he said at last. 'Looking at it logically, Alan . . . I suppose the Russians would *have* to have.'

CHAPTER FOURTEEN

ON Wednesday morning, in the Chairman's suite, Bellamy was saying, 'I'll give you an outline of our theory, sir. Then perhaps we can discuss what can be done.'

'What does Captain Cavendish say to this?'

But Cavendish had nothing to say. Nor had Payton. Nor had the last two people in the room – the two tired designers.

'Well,' impatiently Sir James turned back to the younger pilot. 'Let's hear the theory.'

There was no getting away from it now. In spite of surface similarities, this was not, after all, an ordinary Air Enterprise *get-together*. Though everyone was still preserving the most cautious respect towards him, it was obvious that Sir James Joliffe was being brought to book. He had piped a particular tune that nobody in the Emperor wanted to follow. And he was going to be asked to change it. Or else –

The Chairman, however, did not concern himself with that other alternative. His large blue eyes narrowed slightly as he looked across at Bellamy, analysing the young self-confidence on the pilot's face. This particular cornstalk, the *ghost* pilot at London, had grown alarmingly in the past few days. There seemed a danger now of it taking possession of the whole cornfield.

'Difficult to reconstruct exactly what *did* happen,' Bellamy continued. 'Same with any emergency. Everybody's got their own ideas. I've discussed it thoroughly with the crew. And with Mr. Eastlake and Mr. Cruttwell here . . . when they haven't been working.'

He looked up to give the two designers a sympathetic smile.

'The engines cut . . . *fact.* The controls, especially the rudders, got stiff . . . seemed to stick. *Fact, too.* This last points to hydraulic booster trouble. As I said from the beginning.'

The Chairman noted the pilot's underlining of his own rectitude, but the expression on his face did not change.

'But then . . . why did the engines fade? Why should the boosters right themselves? That's what was troubling us.'

Sir James murmured, 'Two questions that were also troubling *me*.' But all around him, all attention, even Payton's now, was fixed on Bellamy.

'We can't prove it . . . but now we think the answer's in the very low temperatures. Just before the front over Labrador, it was—44° Centigrade.'

'You mean . . . that after all this, it's just *ice*?'

'No, sir. The *effect* of the cold on the booster cylinders . . . contracting the metal so the piston was continually jamming inside. In the air, two of us were straining on the controls to shift the rudder, jammed over hard on one side. When it did move . . . it jammed over on the other. And so on – '

'And the engine cutting?'

'We were on 1 and 2 tanks. There was still a good deal of fuel left in them . . . but the level was low. In the sudden swings, kerosene was being washed away from the collector boxes in each wing root by centrifugal force – causing the motors to cut from fuel starvation and then come on again.'

Sir James' face had suddenly brightened. 'Then there's nothing wrong at all now?'

'Of course there is, sir,' Bellamy retorted. 'They shouldn't do that! In his Mark II booster cylinders, Mr. Eastlake has used a different alloy for that very reason.'

'You remember, sir,' the airframe designer put in. 'Before we set off, I told you they were just about ready. I did suggest a day or so's delay – '

Sir James said abruptly, 'If I'd adopted everyone's suggestions, the Emperor would still be on the drawing-board!'

'And now tomorrow's trip to Bermuda, sir – ' Bellamy stopped short. In the brief silence, Sir James could feel that the tenor of the meeting had changed. The allegiance had shifted. They'd been getting together. There was some sort of conspiracy. Just before Bellamy opened his mouth again, the Chairman knew he was going to say, 'Under the circumstances, would it be wise to go?'

He said very coldly, 'And what would *you* propose to do, Captain Bellamy?'

'Wait here for the Mark II boosters to be sent over.'

'Have you any idea of the boomerang effect bad publicity would have on the Emperor . . . *now*?'

'This isn't a sales promotion matter, sir. It's a matter of life or death.'

'Bellamy, you're exaggerating!'

The Chairman's pink face had flushed an angry red. He'd had enough to put up with from the pilots already without this bid to usurp his authority. For that's what it was. He could recognise a trial of strength as soon as he saw one. He drew in a deep breath. He put his plump chin higher in the air, till his eyes looked down at them all.

He seemed just on the point of blasting the lot of them out of the window.

And then, as suddenly and as quickly as the Emperor had stopped thrashing about over Labrador, the Chairman's shoulders sagged. The round head dropped. In a surprisingly quiet voice, he asked Bellamy, 'Now tell me, Captain . . . just as a matter of interest . . . if we kept *low* on the way down to Bermuda, we wouldn't run into any cold temperatures, would we?'

Bellamy said warily, 'No, sir. We wouldn't.'

'So the present booster cylinders would remain serviceable?'

'Might. Might not. It's still only a *theory*.'

'But it *does* seem to suit the facts.' Sir James looked up at the ceiling and rubbed his chin. 'On the New York-Bermuda route, you're never more than an hour from an aerodrome.'

'A lot can happen in an hour, sir.'

'And a lot *will* happen if we stay in New York.' A gentle smile of resignation came over the Chairman's face. 'Nothing in this world is *completely* safe, Captain Bellamy. We've got to weigh the risks against the rewards. Now – are we going down to Bermuda tomorrow . . . or aren't we?'

It was all done in the quietest way. Sir James and Bellamy talked – about the ethics of going, about conflicting responsibilities, about the consequences of *not* going. And as every minute ticked by, the Chairman seemed to retreat further and further from the centre of the stage, joining the onlookers around the pilot, leaving Bellamy alone with the question that he had intended Sir James to answer.

The pilot was speaking more slowly now, weighing what he said with care. He was so absorbed, he did not notice that now he was doing the talking. Sir James' replies had got shorter and fewer, as though they were in any case only noises made to cover up the soft sounds of his retreat. Bellamy's forehead was furrowed as he struggled to solve, more and more on his own, the intermediate problems before the final question would be posed. And when, having taken everything else into consideration, at last he reached it, and again he questioned, 'Would it be wise to go?', it was assumed by his audience as rhetorical, asked by himself to himself. For nobody said anything.

Looking up, surprised, he saw that the circle around him, including the Chairman now, were quietly and attentively waiting for his answer. And suddenly conscious of the isolation of the leadership that had stealthily been left in his lap, he tried to go back on his tracks, to lead up to the vital question yet again, this time more slowly, hoping for help. 'Of course, on this flight . . . there's a good deal at stake.'

Nobody said anything.

'It's only a short hop down to Bermuda. Not like an Atlantic crossing.'

Nobody said anything again.

The pilot turned to the Chairman. 'If you sent a cable now for the Mark II boosters to be sent to Bermuda – '

This time, Sir James came bounding forward with the quick suggestion: 'They could put them on the Bermuda service leaving London tomorrow. We could have them by Friday.'

'We *must* have them before the Atlantic crossing on Saturday.'

'Of course we must, Captain. *And we will have.*'

'We could fly tomorrow,' Bellamy said reassuringly, 'low down. Avoid the cold temperatures.'

An hour after what had become Bellamy's *get-together* broke up, and half an hour after the cable for the Mark II boosters had been sent to England, the Chairman ran into Brocklehurst in the lounge of the hotel. Considering his recent reverse, Sir James seemed to be in excellent spirits.

'All set for tomorrow?' he asked the Under-Secretary.

Brocklehurst's eyes looked at him suspiciously. 'What did they find wrong, Sir James?'

'That's just it . . . nothing!'

'But the trouble over Labrador – '

'Caused by cold, dear fellow! Bellamy's going to be careful not to go too high tomorrow.'

Brocklehurst scrutinised the Chairman's bland face. He had attended one or two functions. He had been impressed, in spite of himself, by the American enthusiasm for the Emperor. Now he had just read in the evening's paper that half the high-ups in the American aircraft industry would be accompanying them to Bermuda.

Sir James would never dare to allow that, if the aircraft wasn't serviceable. In spite of her early reverses, the Emperor looked like being a success, after all.

'That's good news, Sir James.'

'Yes, isn't it?' The Chairman seemed to have divined the reason for the sudden reappearance of Brocklehurst's party political smile. 'Saves you the price of a transatlantic phone call . . . into the bargain!'

As the day wore on, the other inhabitants of the Emperor learnt that nothing could be found wrong with the aircraft and they would be leaving on schedule.

The news affected them each in their different ways.

It made it immediately apparent to Enderby-Browne that a decision was imperative. For a whole day, he had been vacillating, first one way, then the other. The first few words of the lecture still lay on his desk – *Fellow servants of humanity*. He had been pondering their meaning ever since he wrote them. They always showed up in his mind against a background of the faces on board Able Dog over Labrador, Riley's obvious nervousness, Payton's slightly shaking hand.

Was it enough, he asked himself, to be a Greek chorus? To note all these things down, and yet not be involved in the plot? He had always before rather wistfully regretted the lack of co-operation among the aircrew in his efforts to help them. They could hardly be blamed if now, at the first real opportunity of sharing some of their trials, it had been conveniently necessary for him to be off-loaded.

Being a direct, methodical man, he reached out for the telephone, and dialled the number of the Canford Institute. As the ringing note sounded in his ear, other words came to the tip of his tongue: *appreciating the honour . . . not at this moment . . . pressure of urgent business.*

Two floors below him in the hotel, Payton was packing. Cavendish was brushing down his uniform. And in the coffee bar on ground level, the crew interrupted their long argument over Emperor operational pay to consider the news that the Emperor was serviceable with considerable scepticism. As Rawlings said, 'We'll find that out tomorrow!'

'I suppose Bellamy's agreed to it?' Seawood asked dubiously.

'Must have done! And we all know why!'

'*Why*, Red?'

'Wants to get back in with the Old Man!' Rawlings snorted. 'That's why!'

The Operations Room at Idelwild had been phoning Riley's room all afternoon to tell him. It was evening before they finally contacted him, as he changed for the Manager's party for the Press.

His face went pale. A slight sweat broke out on his brow. One thing was certain – it was now or never.

But now he was finding that his courage had set with the sun. The telling phrases, the sentences with which he hoped to illuminate the Emperor's secret were losing their light and shape and colour like a darkening landscape.

And just as, with nightfall, millions of people turned on the artificial lights, so Ralph Riley reached his arm for the bottle of Scotch.

Half an hour before the party, not much light or life had returned. He padded about his bedroom, jotting a few words on a pad or an envelope from time to time. Then he sat down at the writing table and read his carefully prepared notes. And that was the hell of it—the one really hundred per cent true story he'd written since he came into this racket, and every damned bit of it cried out it was a lie!

He moved over to the window, staring out gloomily at the steady unnatural brightness in the buildings and along the sidewalks. Pipped at the post Riley, that's what he was. Good start, bloody awful ending. He'd never quite made it. Not his fault of course. But always something had happened. That was why he was still just a P.R.O. in a private outfit when with a bit of luck, he might have been right at the top. And after tonight, if he could only put it across, he wouldn't be even *that*.

The thought depressed him even further. He walked into the bathroom to get some more water for the latest glass of Scotch. He stood in front of the mirror and watched himself slowly gulp it down. That way, it was more companionable.

He refilled his glass and said 'Cheers,' waiting hopefully for some sign of good cheer in his companion in the mirror. But there was none. Two more whiskies, their heat and energy wasted in lighting up the red filaments at the corners of his eyeballs and in the tight skin over his cheekbones, joined their companions in an ice-cold effluent in his guts.

He looked at his watch and swore. Downstairs in the foyer, the little blonde would be waiting. Ready to laugh and simper and flutter her eyelashes like blondes (or brunettes for that matter) the world over. As though all life's problems could be solved by the right dress, soft lights, sweet music and the latest style in hair.

And maybe they could. For *them*.

He had one more for the road. One for the corridor and another for the lift. For when it all worked out, the things that really solved your problems were the little ones. The things no one actually noticed. Like just having the correct amount of whisky inside you. Or arriving at the right time, or saying it at the crucial moment. Reluctantly, he drained the glass, bowed to his reflection, and closed the bedroom door behind him.

Down in the foyer, he walked slowly and very carefully towards Lalette. 'Good evening, my dear,' he said, in the kindly, slightly familiar voice he used for young female subordinates, 'You're looking very lovely.'

But he didn't like the way she sat well over to the far side of the taxi which the doorman found for them. He could have used a bit of light-hearted feminine chatter. Instead, he could feel her eyes moving over his face slowly and searchingly like geiger counters.

'Is there anything particular you want me to do at the party, Mr. Riley?'

'The name's Ralph.'

'Is there, Ralph?'

He stared at her owlishly. Something in her feminine security, the unshakeable belief in life of a young and attractive girl, made him ache to blow it sky high.

He drew up his head. Choosing his words, he said meaningly, 'No, there's nothing you'll be needed for. I intend to make' – he paused and leaned forward so that all he could see were her wide-open eyes – 'a very full and frank statement.'

But all the time he was saying to himself: if I can count ten before she says, 'Whatever d'you mean?', I'll know it's no good.

Counting like this was a trick he'd learnt as a child. If I can count ten, I won't get it . . . they won't allow me to go . . . *this* won't happen.

He counted ten. He counted twenty. He was well up into the hundreds in no time.

At the other end of the seat, the girl sat quite still by her window, saying nothing at all.

Hamilton had been out all day. The news reached him by way of a note in his letter-box, when he returned to the hotel after eating a late supper, as usual by himself.

It set him thinking even deeper than he had been doing these past three days over what really amounted to the same problem that had been bothering Sir James and Bellamy – only on a different plane.

For Hamilton had two jobs. He was the most up-to-date kind of Jekyll and Hyde. In the air, he kept his mind strictly on the duty of making every passenger's wish his command, as the very best steward on the run. And on the ground, apart from competently and correctly attending the particular function to which Sir James had sent him on this particular trip, he regarded himself as a courier for those organisations that were finding it increasingly difficult to transport their freight from one country to another.

He had the highest sense of loyalty to both his professions; their ethics were immaculate; and he kept them strictly apart.

That had been the trouble this time. They were overlapping. For an hour, he paced the carpet of his room, up and down, his usually straight figure bent a little as he concentrated on obtaining a decision. Then very suddenly, he reached out for the grey trilby that he had carefully perched on the hook behind the door, and adjusting the brim over his eyes, set off for an area round Third Avenue, where his ground headquarters were located.

It was not a very salubrious neighbourhood. Dark, rather dirty. Full of bars in which silent men sat by the hour, busy slaking the thirst of their dry sorrows; the streets cobbled; the jampacked traffic a continual hooting nightmare; scraps of newspaper fleeing from cremation; a Chinese laundry or two, fiercely flying the American flag; and a number of antique shops, their wares behind the windows untouched for years, dusty, as though they were embalmed in a huge glass coffin for the century that would at last appreciate them.

It was to the back of one of these antique shops that Hamilton went. He knocked three times. He knocked three times again. It was eventually opened by a little old man with a nut-brown chubby face. 'Back again, eh?' he said. 'Still stallin'?'

Hamilton drew himself up to his full length. 'I can give you my decision now, Joe.'

'Glad to hear *that*.' The little man led the way to a small parlour. Rummaging in the middle of a pile of papers on the desk, he produced two bottles of beer and two glasses. Then he went over to a rusty safe and said, 'I'll give yer them now.'

'No need to, Joe.' Hamilton compressed his lips tightly. 'I can't take the stuff.'

'Whassamatter?' the little one snapped out in a remarkably loud and aggrieved voice. 'Not 'nuff in it for yer? Is that whassamatter?'

Hamilton said sorrowfully, 'You know me better than that, Joe.'

'Whassamatter, then? Yaller?'

'After all I've been through for you, Joe!'

The little man croaked, 'Thought you were my friend!'

'That's it!' Hamilton said with dignity. 'That's why! You *are* my friend! So I'm *not* going to do it!'

Exasperation showed on the wizened face. 'I spent every bean I got on this stuff. Once I get it over to Lefty in London, I'm made!'

'I can't,' said Hamilton. 'For you, Joe . . . I *can't*!'

'There ain't anyone I can trust but you!' the little man pleaded. 'The rest of the bunch are nutting more'n a pack of thieves. And if I lost this lot, I'd be sunk! Out on my ear! Nutting left! But you – ' Suddenly dipping his nose into his beer, Joe's face came up quite different, the creases in different places, a smile decorating the colourless lips. 'My friend! My pal!'

Hamilton finished off his drink. 'I'm sorry, Joe.'

'Call yourself a friend, and yet yer won't do this for me!'

The Chief Steward said steadily, 'We've been in this too long to quarrel, Joe.'

'I'll quarrel when I damn well wanna!' The wooden chairs shivered and trembled. Unwillingly, even the dust moved.

And then, with a disappointed flatness, the little man said, 'Throwin' away a chance like this! I'm surprised at yer! Customs won't trouble yer . . . with this proving flight lark!'

Hamilton said nothing. His code of loyalty still held fast. He would not have dreamed of divulging any of those professional secrets of his courier career to Air Enterprise. In exactly the same way, it did not enter his head to acquaint Joe and his friends with the Company's secrets. Both were excellent jobs. In both he gave excellent service.

He put out his hand. 'Well . . . so long, Joe.'

Grumbling, the little man took it. 'Can't understand why yer won't take the stuff. Don't weigh much! Just a few jools for yer pocket!'

'I'd have liked to, Joe! Believe me, I'd have liked to! But not on this trip, Joe . . . not this one!' Momentarily, Hamilton's big brown eyes misted over with emotion. 'Some *other* time, perhaps.'

Later that night, Bellamy sat in his room, watching an all-night marathon television performance. It wasn't a particularly good show, but he was perfectly contented.

By the Chairman's whole attitude that morning, the authority for the proving flight had shifted. The pilot's ultimate responsibility had been recognised. *His* advice had been taken. The future of the Emperor now lay on *his* decision.

It was in fact, from that angle, quite a satisfactory state of affairs, considering the position when this trip had started. And Bellamy, now the future was cut and dried, was both pleased and relieved.

Just before one in the morning, when he was about to go to bed, a slight scuffle in the corridor began to develop into a hubbub outside his door. There were voices, one high and sweet, one low and slurred. A man started singing drunkenly. A girl said, 'Shush! Now come on, behave!' Heavy uncertain feet thudded beside the tapping of high heels. The song got louder. Then Bellamy heard the girl say. 'What's your room number?'

There was no doubt about whose voice that was. Bellamy flung open the door. 'What the hell's going on here?'

The little procession outside came to an uneasy halt. One of Riley's arms was draped around Lalette's shoulders. He raised the other in a swaying Fascist salute. 'Ish the gallant captain himself!'

Then he gave Lalette a great urge forward. But the girl stood quite still, and pressing on perilously without her, Riley fell flat on his face.

Bellamy folded his arms. Across Riley's prone body on the floor, he regarded the girl coldly. 'Quite a party!'

She nodded her head.

'You drunk, too?'

'No.'

'You made a very loving couple. Sorry to break it up.'

The eyes that had looked at him, half embarrassed, half penitent, suddenly blazed. 'Don't just stand there looking like the Inquisition! Help me get him to his room!'

'I should imagine you've woken half the hotel.'

'Come on . . . help me!'

'You were making a hell of a row! You'll have got the Company a thoroughly bad name.'

'Stop preaching! *Do* something!'

'Damned well deserves to lie where he is.'

'If that's the way you feel about it . . . I'll get the night porter.' She turned back along the corridor, but before she had walked more than a few steps, Bellamy had been galvanised into action. Quickly, he followed her and caught her wrists. 'No, you don't! This is a respectable hotel. Not used to this sort of behaviour. D'you want the Company turned out as undesirables?'

'*Then help me.*'

The two of them went back to the body. Riley was asleep. Bellamy went through his pockets till he found his room key. '2155,' he said. 'Just down to the left.' Then he put his arms under the man and pulled. 'Weighs a ton, too.'

'I know.' Lalette knelt down on the other side. Between them, they got him to his feet. All the way just on the point of collapsing, they managed to reach his room.

Bellamy put the key in, turned it, and pushed the door open with his foot. Before they got him through the threshold, Riley let out a whistling gasp, like all the air going out of a very big bladder. 'Ish the condemned shell!'

They turned into the room and deposited Riley flat on his back on the bed. Then Bellamy briskly brushed his hands together as though shaking off the man's dust, and turned towards the door.

'Aren't you going to undress him?' Lalette asked.

'Good Lord, no!'

'I thought that was what they usually did with drunks.'

'I don't care what they usually do with them.'

'He'll feel awful in the morning.'

'Might do him some good.' Then seeing Lalette walk up to the head of the bed, he said sharply, 'Come on . . . we'll both get out of here!'

'I was only loosening his collar. He might strangle himself!'

'Why worry about that?'

'And I thought you were always so concerned about people's safety!'

'If he did it on my aeroplane,' Bellamy said, 'that would be different. And now . . . quick march! Out!'

Obediently Lalette preceded him through the door. They walked side by side down the corridor in silence. Then in a quiet voice, Bellamy said, 'I'm ashamed of you.'

'Why?'

'You know perfectly well Riley drinks like a fish. You were sent to keep him sober.'

'Nobody briefed me.'

'You could have kept your eye on him. Seen what he was up to.'

'I tell you, I hadn't a chance! When we met before the party . . . he was very mysterious. And very drunk.'

'God knows what sort of impression you made on the American Press!'

Lalette drew in her breath sharply. 'Quite a good one, I think.'

'And coming back at this time of night!'

'I've tried to – '

'With a man like Riley!'

'He wasn't my choice! Sir James – '

'In this sort of state.'

'Oh, *shut up!*'

Bellamy stopped dead. Roughly, he swung her round to face him. He looked at the curiously dead-pan face in which only the eyes were alive and angry. He moved closer to her and bent his head. The eyes changed from anger to surprise. They softened. Then Bellamy sniffed. 'You may *look* sober,' he said. 'But all the same . . . I can tell you've had too much to drink.'

Without a word, she turned away from him and went hurrying down the corridor. He heard the furious hiss of her skirt. 'Here, wait a minute!' he called out after her, but already she was at the lift, pressing the button. 'Where d'you think you're going.'

'To bed. Good night.' The lift door shut behind her.

Angrily, he started to rush up the stairs to the next floor. He turned the corner into the corridor just in time to see her step out and disappear to the right. 'Lalette! I haven't finished with you yet.'

'I've finished with you.' She was turning the key in the lock of her room, as he came up and caught her arm.

'Look, Lalette,' he said quietly. 'I'm responsible for you just as much on the ground as in the air.'

'Either the Big Captain. Or the Kindly Uncle.' She sighed. 'That's all I get.' She turned to look at him, now that she had stepped inside the doorway. 'Don't you see me . . . as . . . just a girl?'

'That's what I'm trying to tell you. You're a nice girl, but – '

'I'm not a nice girl, but *anything*! Just let me tell you about *you*. You've always been so good, haven't you? The youngest Wing Commander in the R.A.F. The youngest senior pilot. Then the youngest training captain.' She was speaking so fast, she was breathless. 'But you didn't have time for any fun. Life's got the laugh on *you*. You're the *oldest* man of thirty-two I've ever met in my life!'

'And you're just a nice young girl,' he said coldly. 'And nice young girls . . . don't know very much.'

There was a quick rustling of taffeta. He caught a last glimpse of a white face, and a flash of fair hair. Then the door was shut in his face. Behind it, he heard the bolt click.

He tapped on the wood. 'Come on, Lalette. Open up! I'm not angry.'

'*I am*.'

'Whatever for?'

There was no answer from the other side of the door.

'Can you hear me, Lalette?'

Airily, a voice floated back at him. 'Loud and clear.'

'Then open up!'

'No.'

'I want to know what happened at that party. And I want to know – '

'Not now.'

'Look Lalette, it's very late – '

'I know, I'm getting undressed and going to bed.'

'You don't want the whole corridor to hear.'

'I don't mind.'

In a voice of quiet exasperation, Bellamy said, 'Would you please be good enough to open up this door.'

'I wouldn't be good enough.'

Bellamy rapped loudly. '*Open this door!*'

'Go away.'

He rattled the door handle. 'For the last time – '

'And for the last time . . . *go away!*'

'You're getting *me* angry now.'

'And you're making an awful lot of noise.'

'I've told you to open it. If you don't . . . I'll break in."

With his shoulder against the door, he was so busy pushing and banging at the lock that he did not hear the soft padding up the corridor behind him. But he felt the tap on his back. Looking up, he saw a round middle-aged face under a balding head of mixed grey and white hair. Two eyes looked at him with considerable disapproval. 'Mister,' a rasping voice asked, 'whadjer think *you're* doing?'

Rather sheepishly, Bellamy stood up. 'I don't think you quite understand.'

'You underestimate me, mister.' The man rapped authoritatively on the door. 'This is the house-detective on his rounds. This man bothering you, lady?'

There was dead silence at first from the other side of the door. Then, defiantly, 'Yes.'

'Come on, mister,' the house-detective said. 'Let's walk.'

'Lalette,' Bellamy called back furiously, 'what the hell d'you think you're doing?' But the only answer came from the house-detective. 'What's your room number, mister?'

Arm-in-arm, the Englishman and the American began the promenade down the long deserted corridor. 'I'll go back to my room now,' Bellamy said, trying to get his arm free. 'Don't trouble to come with me.'

'No trouble.'

'I can find my own way, thank you.'

'No doubt you can, mister,' the house-detective said placidly, 'but my job is to see you get in it. And stay in it.'

'There's been some misunderstanding – '

'Always is. *Always* is. Too bad.'

They walked in silence to the lift. 'It's only the next floor,' Bellamy said. '2117.' The house-detective pressed the button and the lift descended.

As they were walking back along the 21st floor, the American said, 'You're one of the English pilots, aren't you?'

Bellamy nodded.

'Thought you were.' The man seemed to be musing on the many things foreign airmen got up to. 'This is a good, respectable American hotel, you know.'

'I know.'

They had reached 2117. 'By rights, I should tell the management about this,' the house-detective said. He looked at the pilot's stony face, as he deftly inserted the key in the lock and turned. 'But don't you worry . . . I won't.' He gave Bellamy an understanding pat on the arm. 'I was young myself . . . *once*.'

CHAPTER FIFTEEN

'Now tell me,' Mrs. Matherson said, her bright eyes on the Chairman. 'Where *is* this wonderful aeroplane I've heard so much about!'

Idelwild airport looked as though it was giving a house party. A great warm wave of gaily-dressed friendliness was lapping at the feet of Sir James Joliffe. The Matherson family, as the influential cause of this happy fusing of Anglo-American relations, stood at his right hand.

Nodding and smiling at his guests for the flight, he led her to the open window of the inner office. There on the tarmac, a little apart from a congregation of D.C. 6's, Stratocruisers and Constellations, the wind swirled a grey drizzly mist round the curious contours of Emperor Able Dog. She stood there, out in the cold, as patiently as a huge silver dumb animal. Harmless, tethered, groomed and exhaustively doctored. It was only to the Chairman's over-anxious eyes that a sardonic smile seemed to curl round the perspex panels on the underside of her nose.

'My!' murmured Mrs. Matherson with conscientious enthusiasm. 'What a *bew*-tiful airplane!'

Hal Matherson looked at the Emperor with keen professional interest. 'What height will we be going down at, Sir James? Twenty-five thousand?'

The Chairman had been informed that the height would be nine thousand (where the temperature would only be a few degrees below freezing) and had accepted it without question. When he told Matherson, the American looked disappointed. 'I'd been hoping – '

'Airways,' Sir James said swiftly. 'Control's orders. Very busy route.'

And while Matherson was saying, 'But surely – ' the Tannoy mercifully announced their departure.

True to the Station Manager's expectations, shutters clicked and ciné cameras whirred. In twos and threes, the passengers mounted the Company steps to disappear into the square mouth that opened in the Emperor's side. Lalette and Angela helped everyone off with their coats while Hamilton, as though in compensation for the lack of precious stones in his pocket, carefully placed each American in his or her seat like a jeweller a gem in its own particular setting. He beckoned. He smiled. He was the perfect airline steward.

The doors shut down on a full load in the cabin. Innumerable perfumes fought each other for precedence. Dresses and costumes rustled expensively. The whole passenger compartment bubbled over with the joy of living.

Before the engines started, Bellamy came to the back, his blue raincoat still over his uniform. The Chairman jumped to the conclusion at first that the pilot was going to have a word with him. But he went further aft, and spoke to Hamilton. The only words Sir James caught were 'Emergency hatches'.

As Bellamy went back up to the front, Amos Appleside, who had had a snort or two and a snifter, and was now looking forward 'mightily' to his lunch, his flight, and his two days in Bermuda, turned to the wife by his side and jovially remarked, 'Say . . . that limey sure looks sour!'

The main wheels left the ground. Hesitating twice, reluctantly they allowed themselves to be tucked inside the inboard engine nacelles. Sir James heard the motors throttled back from take-off power, and felt the Emperor swing steadily up into her climb.

The cloud outside was moist and grey. Now and again, the tail gave a wag or two in the uneven air. The Chairman held his breath. But with airy unconcern, back it went to its orthodox position, with no more than the slightest flicking movement at the back.

All the same, he was unhappy. He talked to Matherson about the likely operation of the Emperors across the Atlantic. London-New York, against the persistent headwinds, would usually take about eleven hours, while with those same winds behind them, the return journey would take less than nine. Such an operation would crush all other competitors by a matter of several hours. But he talked completely mechanically of things he knew by heart. He smiled through long habit at the right places.

Every tremor the Emperor made, the slightest pitch or yaw

seared into his nerve ends like a succession of red-hot needles.

Appleside came over to have a drink and a short discussion on fuel consumption. As he leaned beside the Chairman's seat, Able Dog slid into heavier cloud and started to roll. Appleside grinned and said, 'Certainly takes it nicely, Joliffe,' and he would have gone on but Hamilton, always there when he was most wanted, was at his elbow, with the information: 'Lunch is being served, sir.'

And it was a wonderful meal. No expense had been spared. Caviare, smoked salmon, lobster, turkey, mousse, fresh fruit salads – what more could anyone want? The aircraft droned steadily on through the cloud, her four motors purring sweetly, till finally she broke through the last soft layer of eggshell round the yellow yoke of the sun. The light shimmered and danced on her wings. Pausing for a moment as they ate, people pointed out the freakish colours on cumulus heads. Odd shapes and shadows on the horizon were admired. There was a triumphant hilarity about the meal, which Lalette and Angela, unobtrusively walking up and down the cabin, so efficiently served.

It was all a very splendid advertisement for the Emperor and Air Enterprise Limited.

But while the American guests were thoroughly enjoying themselves, their British hosts sat in taut silence. Cruttwell and Eastlake, still exhausted, were continuing their sleep right at the back. Enderby-Browne had put away his notebook, and was keeping an anxious watch over his charges. Payton had retreated into the background, unusually well away from the eyes of the Chairman.

Riley was nursing once more his own sense of failure in the only way he knew how. Once again, he'd been pipped at the post. Through the shocking headache that had clamped over his head, he remembered the Manager's party without enjoyment; the words on the tip of his tongue about the Emperor over Labrador that simply would not come; the girl Greenacres hovering round him while he fortified himself to make the great effort; and then, after hours and hours it seemed of the Emperor's good points being discussed with his full, rather slurred agreement – oblivion.

Of all the inhabitants of the Emperor, only Brocklehurst was really entering into the spirit of the thing, behaving himself among the American ladies with traditional English gallantry, all thoughts of Ministers and machinations for the moment forgotten. Whenever the hydraulic pump whined out, he took no notice; it was Sir James, this time, who stirred in his seat. Beside him, Hal Matherson lay sprawled back comfortably, his hands in his trouser-pockets, while his eyes leisurely inspected every bit of the cabin interior. That finished, he stared out at the wing, holding a course, steady and majestic, against the clear blue welcome of the sky.

Then he smiled, and nudged Sir James. 'How about the grand tour?'

'What was that, Matherson?'

'Trip round this bucket of yours. I wanna see what *goes on*!'

The Emperor gave a sudden lurch to the left, and the Chairman started. 'Of course,' he said, when everything was level again. 'Where would you like to begin?'

'The tail,' the American said decisively. 'Right at the back, eh? And work forwards?'

Sir James shot a glance at the shrewd face beside him; but he saw only good humour. He got up and smiled. 'Certainly,' he said.

Together, they walked towards the rear. Matherson inspected the galley and joked with the catering staff. Then casually he asked, 'Rudder's worked by hydraulic boosters, isn't it?'

'Yes,' Sir James said. 'I don't know if you've noticed the way this refrigerator – '

'Where are the actuating cylinders?'

'In the rear of the tail cone.' Before Matherson could make any further remarks on the subject, the Chairman said, 'And now, I want you to have a look at the holy of holies. The flight deck,' and this time, scrupulously sent Hamilton to the front to get Captain Bellamy's permission.

On the way up the aisle, Appleside joined them. To others, who asked if they could come, Sir James said, 'If there's time later – '

In the cockpit, he stood unobtrusively in the background

while the pilots explained the lay-out. Appleside was taken by the excellent view afforded by the wide window. Matherson asked Rawlings some technical questions on turbo-props, which the engineer skilfully stalled and then, as though the bee was still in his bonnet, harked back to the subject of hydraulically boosted control.

'You've got an emergency system, of course?'

Seawood pointed to three red levers on the side of the throttle box.

'But still on the hydraulic principle? No direct mechanism?'

'That's right,' Bellamy said. 'No simple system on this aeroplane!'

'Of course, over here . . . we now prefer servo tabs. There's very little *feel* as a rule in these boosted controls.' He turned to Seawood, who was hand-flying. 'May I?'

The First Officer said, 'Of course, sir,' and took his hands off the control column. Sir James quickly pointed out the new style gyro-compass, but Matherson was not to be diverted. Putting his hands on the stick, he moved the nose up and tilted the wings. 'Mmm.' His forehead wrinkled up in a frown. The Chairman watched him anxiously. 'You got a feel mechanism incorporated in the system?'

Bellamy said they had.

'Not bad . . . not bad, at all!' He went on to discuss the problem of controls on a large aircraft. Sir James was glad enough to let the pilots do the talking. But he was gladder still when Bellamy said, 'It's time for our descent. I'm afraid – '

Sir James looked at his watch, and saw with relief that in just over half an hour, they should be on the ground. 'The crew will be very busy now,' he said to the visitors. With warm-hearted thanks all round, he led them back to their seats, while the Emperor flew smoothly through the clear air, without a tremor in her huge frame.

Back in the cabin, the Chairman felt the nose dip. With relief, he turned to his porthole and was lost in the wonder of the view outside. As delicately as a well-made fabric, the crêpe-de-chine sea stretched nine thousand feet below Able Dog's silver wings, changing from grey to ever-deepening blue, until, free of every soft drift of intervening cloud, it threw back again the sky's own shade of clear tranquillity. Shallower near the islands, the water was shot with mauves and purples and milky turquoises. The aircraft was descending slowly, as though lazily savouring the warm calm air, and around the rocky islands he could see the clear water ruffle back and forth over the irregular submerged reefs that gleamed up into the sky like amethyst and aquamarine.

No more than a grey chalk mark, a child's clumsy outline on the blue of sky and sea, Bermuda filled itself in as the aircraft rode down to her, with hills and houses, skeletons of cedars and thick dark bushes. Low over the creamy yellow shore, he could see into the small shallow valleys filled to the brim with every shade of green, with whites and yellows and blobs of red, carefully prepared like so many giant-sized salad bowls. Then Able Dog drifted quietly down to a surprisingly naked airfield, dotted around with huts and hills and half encircled by water. Sir James kept his eyes continuously on his watch, counting the minutes of flight that were left. One, two, three – they were nearly through now. He watched the port wheels glide over the threshold, straighten up with a comfortable aplomb a few inches above the runway, and then gently brush the tarmac with their tight rubber skins.

They were down! With unconcerned majesty, Able Dog rumbled round the airfield until she was neatly in front of the airport buildings. Once more the steward and the two stewardesses formed up in a row, to bow the passengers off the aircraft; while at the bottom of the steps, yet another reception committee waited, curved in an inescapable crescent around the bottom rung of all.

But before the passengers could engage in the tepid official handshakes, the warm air of an unusually early heat-wave embraced them in a hot hug that gummed their clothes to their bodies, and laid a burning arm across their necks and shoulders. The bright light ricochetted from the concrete apron, and the air was heavy with honey-sweet words. In a cocoon of officials and porters, the Chairman and the Under-Secretary, together with Matherson and several of the most important Americans, were led away to the Governor's waiting limousine.

Just before they got into the car, Matherson laid a hand on the Chairman's arm, and said, with a chuckle: 'There was only one thing wrong with that flight – '

He paused, and fixed Sir James, as though pinning him to the wall with a clear gimlet blue eye. The Englishman waited for the sword of Damocles to fall. He had heard these Americans were pretty shrewd. Had those X-ray eyes of Matherson's pierced through the booster cylinders? Had he discovered the facts of the Emperor's secret of which her inhabitants still only had a theory?

He waited. He saw the American pass his tongue over his lips, as though preparing the way for words that would be both dry and salty. Then with a burst of kindly good-humour, Matherson added, 'It was too short!'

CHAPTER SIXTEEN

Now they were back on the ground, a wonderful feeling of relaxation came over all the inhabitants of Emperor Able Dog. It was partly the sun, partly the heat-wave, but mostly because that particular trip, which had gathered as dangerously as an avalanche in New York, had, after all, touched down at Bermuda as softly as a snowflake. Everyone felt a gulp of exhilaration. Two days from now, they would be heading off north-east, back over the three thousand miles to England. But for the present, to all of them, those two days were an eternity.

The Bermuda authorities, not to be outdone of their share of the attendant publicity, had arranged various little functions. There was a cocktail party in a few hours' time, and a dance the following evening. Close behind the Governor's car, the American passengers scattered to various hotels, while close behind *them* came the Emperor's crew, bumping over grey roads prickly with dust.

Long, low houses glared white in the sun, while pinks and reds and oranges of tropical flowers boiled over their garden walls like overflows from enormous vats of jam. And when they drove in through the hotel gates, all over the lawns and under the palms, the sun had lured out the drifting blossoms of candy-striped, be-flowered and polka-dotted young girls.

Rawlings nudged Hamilton, as they both waited in a glass-sided foyer for their rooms, and waved his eyebrows at a colourful little cluster on the loggia outside. 'Are they reserved?' he asked. 'Or can anybody have one?'

Hamilton squared his shoulders. 'It's just coming up to the season, Mr. Rawlings. Easter time. When you've come here as often – '

'I *have*. And twice as long. So don't give me *that*.' He tried a tentative wink at a nut-brown brunette, a smile at a honey-blonde. Then he said crossly to Hamilton, 'Trouble about this place . . . they don't give a damn about aircrew. Service is terrible. *Terrible*.'

He got his key, grumbled that the room was at the back of

the hotel, over the kitchens, and far too small, and shambled off up the elegant white stairs.

Already unpacking in her room, Lalette smelled the strong salty tang of the sea, and heard the slight wind rustle the palms in the garden and all along the shore. She peeled off her uniform and put on a ruffled cotton bathing-suit with a dress to match, and went out into the corridor. She banged on Angela's door. 'I'm going to bathe. Are you coming?'

'Will be in a minute. I'm still unpacking.'

'I'll be by the slipway, when you do come.'

She swung her raffia bag as she walked down the stairs, imagining she was on an expensive holiday, that she didn't know a soul, and that around every slender white and gold pillar, behind every slatted blind or under every striped umbrella awaited some kind of deliciously tropical adventure.

The sand was warm even through her thin shoes and was as clean and crunchy as lemon-tinted sugar. The little wooden pier with the hotel flag on the end was crowded with bathers, and the grey coral reef at the far end of the bay had a multicoloured growth of dresses and bathing-suits and bare brown legs. And on the beach itself, as though butterflies had torn off their wings, dresses and skirts and scarves and wraps lay beside the thin brown swim-suited bodies slowly deepening their colour in the rich steady sun.

She found a small unoccupied area, and ashamedly stretched out her indecently pink limbs. She fished out her impedimenta from her bag – dark glasses, her sun lotion, a headscarf and her latest book. She buried her toes like scarlet-backed armadillos into the warm sand, and hugged her knees and savoured the thought of a swim.

The sea was lazy calm. Hypnotically, the little waves ran up the sand, turned a somersault and drifted away again. Bright-sailed boats slid over the sleek water, and loud voices clamoured above the hushing of the sea and the palms.

Then she sank back into the warm bed of soft sand and closed her eyes. Under the shelter of her sun-glasses, the world was dark and warm and empty. The distant noises, without her eyes to pinpoint them, merged together, revolving around her like a gently playing gramophone record.

Like everyone else, she felt the tension ease out of her now that they were here. Above them, the empty sky smiled down as though it spread its arms in a wide friendly gesture to show them it hadn't a speck of a cloud in store for them. It circled the world with benignity, offering only the gentlest of breezes to puff into tiny sails, sun and warmth to make them forget there was such a place as Labrador, such things as ice and snow.

Lalette sat up when she heard a long unmistakable shout from the hotel. She blinked her eyes behind her glasses, and shook the sand out of the back of her hair. Just inside the hotel, in an orderly line, headed by Douthwaite, with Seawood a close second, the crew were preparing to take to the water. Followed by Angela in a smart scarlet swimsuit, they made their way in a bunch of assorted whiteness to the shelter of the sea.

They shouted to her to come on over. Very slowly, making sure that Bellamy wasn't with them, she pulled on her cap, walked down the strip of sand and splashed into the water. All the way down from New York, when she had been up to the front, he had treated her with normal, distant courtesy. Not even by the most fleeting expression in his eyes, had she been able to find out his reaction to the night before.

Now, she swam and jumped and turtle-dived with the others, seeing everyone through sun-warmed droplets of shimmering water.

Someone came swimming under the surface and pulled her ankles from under her. The sea roared in her ears and she swallowed great mouthfuls of water. Recovering, she dived under herself, and swam around, catching hold of a foot whenever it came within reach. The water was churned up into a liquid form of the laughter that floated above it.

Then she surfaced again, rubbing the sea-water out of her eyes, and laughing with the feeling of sheer well-being. Then she stopped laughing. Her under-water swim had brought her up right in front of Bellamy.

She blinked up at him, screwing her face up against the sun. 'Hello,' she said slowly.

'Hello, Lalette.'

She lowered herself further in the water, prepared to move away. She wished he hadn't his back to the sun. She could see his mouth wasn't smiling, but she couldn't read his eyes.

'I'd like to talk to you.'

Lalette drew in her breath sharply. 'About . . ?'

'Yes.'

She made a little choking noise that was half nervous laughter, half apology. 'I can't see if you're angry. *Are* you?'

'I am.'

She gave a quick dive under the water, and swam for a few yards, surfacing a little over towards the reef.

A hand caught hold of her. She kicked hard, but it still hung on to her ankle. 'All right,' Bellamy said, letting go, and coming up beside her. '*We'll both* go to the reef.'

They swam in silence for a minute. Then Bellamy helped her up on to the rock. She sat down on the prickly surface, and squinted up at him anxiously. Across the water came the sound of the rest of the crew at play.

'Well,' Bellamy said, still standing up. 'What've you got to say?'

'I thought you wanted to do the talking.'

'That'll come later. Right now, I'd like to know what you've got to say for yourself?'

'About last night?'

'Yes.'

'With Riley? Or with you?'

'Both.'

'Oh.' Lalette put her arms round her legs and rested her chin on her knees. 'I don't know where to start.'

'I can believe that.'

Lalette looked up suddenly. 'You see, *there* you go! You put me off to begin with!'

'Like last night, I suppose?'

'Yes. Like last night. You should have guessed that Riley was drunk to start off with. He managed to get through his party pieces about the Emperor all right, but I could see it was a struggle.'

'You should have bundled him back home earlier.'

'I *couldn't*. He insisted on staying and staying and staying. And if you weren't always the captain . . . on the ground and off . . . you'd have been a bit more understanding.'

'How?'

'Oh, I don't know.' Lalette stood up. 'I can't explain.

Not properly. But I never know when you're off duty. Sometimes . . . well, it's difficult to tell where the uniform ends, and the man begins.' She made to move past him, but he caught hold of her arm.

'Don't you see?' she went on. 'Last night it was all a case of letting the side down. Coming in late. Being with a drunk.' Her voice shook. 'Nothing about how it *felt* like to be with a drunk. All evening. And on duty more or less.'

She didn't look up at him.

'You've got it all wrong,' he said slowly. '*Quite* wrong.'

She raised her eyes cautiously. 'What, then?'

'Look, Lalette, your whole attitude last night – '

'Oh, I *thought* so. It's the captain himself.' She drew a deep breath. 'Well, I'm sorry if I was rude. And I'm sorry if I lost my temper. And I'm sorry if I've got the wrong attitude. But one thing I'm not sorry for.' Her voice rose to a furious crescendo. 'And *that's* for handing you over to the house detective. Not a bit sorry.' She shook her head vehemently. 'In fact, I'm glad. *I'm glad.*'

Immediately, Bellamy caught hold of her wrist, and gave her a small, rather grim smile. Then the next moment, he seemed to spin her suddenly around, so that she was lying over his bare wet knee, the tip of her nose almost touching the rock. '*Let me go!*' she shouted. 'I'll scream!'

'Scream away,' he said equably. 'You've had this coming . . . for a long time.'

He pushed aside her heels which were kicking up against him. She felt his hand smack hard against the still-wet seat of her swimsuit.

'Let me go! You're hurting me!'

'For your information, this,' Andrew Bellamy said, 'is where the uniform ends . . . and the man begins.'

But when that day was nearly over, life was not quite so carefree and boisterous for one of the Emperor's inhabitants. Payton sat in his bath, getting ready to go to the Governor's for dinner, and he was by no means pleased with himself. He had listened all afternoon to the Chairman, now imminent disaster had again flowered into a beautiful victory, expand exuberantly on the immense potentialities of Emperors.

He expected a clear field on the Atlantic. Other airlines might take the crumbs that dropped from his table. At no extra charge, three to four hours knocked off the time, and super service and comfort, who would travel any other way?

Sir James did not boast. He had no need to. He steered the conversation into the right channels and let his American passengers do that for him. They would be going back Saturday on a chartered Astroliner. And meanwhile, Payton thought to himself, Sir James was certainly seeing to it that unconsciously they paid the full fare for their ticket.

And the future Line Manager was beginning to resent it. His own doubts about the Emperor were still there. He still considered that he should have seen to it that Sir James waited for the Mark II boosters in New York. Payton was not a particularly brave individual and had used as many tricks as the next man to get himself comfortably where he was, and when they didn't come off, as they hadn't with Enderby-Browne, he could usually think out another one. But there was a curious, undefined limit beyond which he knew he couldn't go.

Between the fish and the roast beef at the Governor's that evening, he came to it, stopped and dug his heels in. He had, as usual, been very quiet, just answering with a nod of the head, and confirming the Chairman when he said, 'That's so, isn't it, Payton?'

Then Appleside asked casually, 'And when d'you expect the first scheduled service to operate, Joliffe?'

Straight away, Sir James shot back at him, 'We'll have two services a week opening in less than a fortnight. Won't we, Payton?'

There was a pause that developed into a silence. Everyone looked in his direction. A waiter served him with a plate of meat, and he helped himself to mustard. Then he said, very clearly, 'I doubt it, Sir James.'

The Chairman laughed. 'Thing I like about Payton. Very cautious.'

'Well . . . when d'you think it'll be, Mr. Payton?' Matherson asked him.

'In my opinion,' Payton said slowly, 'I doubt whether we'll be able to do it this summer.'

Sir James opened his mouth and then shut it abruptly. He looked surprised. Even a little hurt. Payton could see what was going on behind his eyes: we've *got* to put up a front with these Americans, otherwise they'll grab the trade themselves.

There was something else in those eyes Payton thought rather wistfully. They kept coming over in his direction, moving from the top of his head to the toes of his shoes, as though they were measuring him, seeing if he was after all such a good fit for the Line Manager's chair on the Emperor's Atlantic route.

CHAPTER SEVENTEEN

AFTER a late breakfast next morning, Andrew Bellamy lay back in an armchair just beyond the verandah. Already it was warm. The sun struck the white face of the hotel, and glittered on the blue semi-circle of the harbour below him. At the other end of the garden, somebody was cutting a privet hedge. Very slowly, very lazily.

It was the kind of day that is all the sweeter for having been well-earned. Bellamy's eyes were closed. For once, he was not thinking about the Emperor – the difficulties and dangers of Able Dog seemed now to have been pretty well wrapped up. The trip to England tomorrow with the Mark II boosters fitted would be plain sailing, with all the decisions (as they should have been in the first place) left entirely to him.

With a mixture of tenderness and amusement, he was, instead, thinking about Lalette.

He heard a click that wasn't the shears and wasn't a cricket. He sat up and took a sleepy, contented look.

It was Eastlake, taking photographs.

'Am I in the way here?'

'No, no, Captain,' the airframe designer said genially. 'I like a figure in the foreground.'

He bent over the view-finder. The shutter clicked again.

'Thought you'd be out at the airport.'

Eastlake pulled a face. 'Cruttwell and I are having a rest from airports.'

'London service late?'

'No. Came in on schedule. Saw the crew a couple of hours ago.'

'Don't tell me you've fitted the Mark II boosters already?'

The designer put his camera back carefully into its leather case. 'They didn't arrive.'

'But they were practically ready last Saturday!'

'Weren't on board.'

Bellamy got up from his chair. The air had suddenly gone chillier. The view was not nearly so pleasant. 'But there isn't another service for three days!'

'Isn't there?'

'Does Joliffe know?'

Eastlake shrugged his shoulders. 'I suppose so.'

'He wouldn't be thinking of going off *without them*?'

But the languorous expression on the designer's face did not change. After hell in New York and a good trip down, this Bermuda air was heaven. 'I'm sure I don't know, Captain.'

Half to himself, Bellamy said, 'I'll bet he knew all the time the damned things wouldn't arrive!'

'Hangar doors! Let's close the hangar doors!'

'If he *doesn't* know . . . somebody had better tell him.'

'Oh, he'll *know*, all right!'

Bellamy said nothing. He was staring down at the clipped green grass round his feet. Eastlake was already walking away from him, down towards the path to the beach. 'Promised Douglas Cruttwell I'd have a bathe,' he called over his shoulder. 'Pity to waste the only bit of summer I'm likely to see!'

Left on his own, Bellamy started moodily to walk up and down the lawn. Far out in the bay, a ship hooted mournfully as it trailed its white wake out of the harbour towards the open Atlantic. A very slight wind was beginning to ruffle the potted palms on the verandah.

The pilot turned abruptly on his heel and walked up to the hotel. Sir James was not in his suite. When he asked at the hotel desk, the receptionist said, 'He went out over an hour ago.'

'Did he say where he was going?'

'He said something about whacking a ball about.'

'Whacking a ball about? You mean . . . on the golf course?'

'Yes, Captain. Told me he was slicing them. Had to get in some practice before his club tournament on Monday.'

Dressed in a faded blue shirt and brown cotton trousers, Sir James Joliffe addressed the teed-up ball with considerable care. Then his pudgy arms swung the club as far as it would go behind him. There was a momentary flash as the steel shaft caught the sun in the downstroke, and a smart click as the wood connected.

'Damn,' he said out loud, as he watched the tiny white blob soar into the air and plummet into the dead cedar trees, far to the right. 'I've done it again!'

He picked up his clubs, and started to walk in the direction of its landfall. His shoes sank a little every time he took a step over the springy turf. He was just entering the rough before the copse, when he heard the longer grass being brushed briskly aside behind him. Turning his head, he recognised the chunky figure in the grey lightweight suit. 'Ah, Captain Bellamy,' he called. 'You couldn't have come at a better time! Come and help me to find my ball!'

He stopped to allow the pilot to catch up with him.

'I've been looking for you, sir.'

'You have?' Side by side now, they moved towards the brambles and wild rhododendrons that bushed up round the dirty-white trunks of the skeleton trees. 'Well, you've found me. Now all we have to do is to find my ball!'

'About those Mark II booster cylinders, sir – '

'You look over there, would you?' The Chairman pointed to a bosky clump of brambles. 'And I'll look over this side.' He plunged into the undergrowth, and started to beat it around with his club. Bellamy peered unenthusiastically into the gaps between the thorns and kicked the tall grass flat.

'I hear you're in your club tournament on Monday, sir.'

'That's right.'

There was a silence, broken only by the rhythmic threshing of the Chairman's club. Then the pilot said, 'Pity you'll miss it, sir.'

'Miss it! Miss it! Who said anything about missing it?'

'Haven't you heard, sir?'

'Heard *what*?'

'The boosters weren't on the London service.'

The massacre of the foliage still went briskly on. 'Mmm . . . yes. They did tell me something of the sort.'

'Well,' Bellamy said slowly, 'we'll have to wait now till the boosters *do* arrive, won't we, sir?'

All executions ceased abruptly. Reprieved for the moment, but still shaking from the shock of previous near-misses, rhododendron leaves and bramble branches quivered for the future together.

Bellamy had been under the impression that the trial of strength had already taken place in New York. But now he recognised he'd been wrong. This was the critical point over which of them, ultimately, was *really* in charge of the proving flight – who was the indispensable instrument whose decisions must be taken as gospel.

He waited, digging his heels further down into the turf, as though preparing his foundations to stand his ground for the onslaught. It would come, he had already decided, from one of two directions. Either it would be the big laughing-off act. Or it would be the whip. He studied Sir James' eyes carefully, watched which way the flesh round his lips was moulding.

The Chairman's mouth opened. Then it opened wider. Here it came!

But just like a dove it came. Almost meekly. Even across the short distance between them, the words were hardly audible. 'Will we, Captain Bellamy?'

'That was the idea, when I agreed to fly down to Bermuda.'

'You mean . . . that we'd have the Mark II's fitted before the Atlantic crossing?'

'Yes.'

'And now . . . we haven't got them, have we?'

'No.'

'We couldn't press on with the old boosters?'

Bellamy gave him a guarded look. 'I said not, sir.'

'Even though they worked all right coming down here?'

'The Atlantic is a very big ocean.'

'You're right. It is. Ah, well!' He stood there quite still, a crumpled, tubby memorial to the end of an aeroplane.

And then suddenly, as though someone had just poured coals on the furnaces, the power inside Sir James revved up again. The steam pressure, which had dropped on the gauge, now shot up again to that red line, known to ships' engineers as *the blood*. 'Now let's get down to business,' he said. 'Where the hell's this ball?'

And the club started to thwack at the survivors in the bushes.

'I reckon you've lost it, sir.'

'No such word as lost in *my* vocabulary, Captain.'

The Chairman led the way further into the bushes. Bellamy followed. The fight, after all, had been a friendly one. He had not expected Joliffe to give in so easily. By accepting the pilot's decision, Sir James had admitted that no matter what the consequences were, the expert technical opinion of the man in charge of the proving flight was the only one that mattered.

'One thing, anyway,' the Chairman said. 'By the time they get around to delivering the boosters here, I *should* be able to drive a straight ball.'

'All this would have been avoided if they'd arrived.' This time, it was the pilot's turn to be indignant. 'Damned inefficiency!'

'Mustn't be too hard.' Sir James shook his head resignedly. 'Manufacturers have their difficulties . . . too.'

'Pity we're so near New York.' Bellamy thoughtfully picked away a very large bramble, and scrabbled around in some grass behind it. 'I mean . . . after that big boost-up we got.'

'Yes.'

'And now to be . . . sort of ship-wrecked just off the coast like this.' Bellamy paused. 'I can appreciate your disappointment, sir. You've done absolutely everything in your power for the Emperor's success.'

Sir James said nothing. Just went on endlessly slashing at the bushes. His very silence seemed to emphasise the depth of his feelings. Bellamy began to feel uncomfortable. A fight was a fight, but a walk-over was unfair. Especially when the man had so much at stake. He said, more stiffly than he intended, 'I hope you don't think I'm being unco-operative, sir.'

'Good heavens, Captain Bellamy! *You* unco-operative!'

'This is a minor thing. But in aeroplanes, minor things – '

'I understand completely. If there was only yourself to consider, it would be a different matter.'

'Of course it would, sir.'

'You've got the responsibility of everybody else.'

'That's the trouble.'

Bellamy stopped kicking away at the undergrowth to watch a grasshopper give a joyful jump on to a twig, ten times its length above its head. Then he said slowly, 'I think there is *one* idea we might try.'

Like a flash, so quickly he seemed almost to have been waiting for it, Joliffe came back with, 'You can keep us moving, Bellamy?'

'It struck me that if we off-loaded everybody but a skeleton operating crew, under the circumstances the risk of flying her back would be justified.'

'Oh.' The Chairman's voice sounded disappointed.

'The others could come back on the Astroliner service, sir.'

'They'd be off-loaded for their own safety?'

'Yes, sir.'

'Me, too'

'Well, sir . . . it's all rather difficult – '

Suddenly, the thwacking went on twice as vigorously as before. 'I see your point, Captain.' *Thwack*. 'I see your point completely.' *Thwack*. Leaves fell. Branches snapped. 'But it strikes me – ' *Thwack*. 'Since it's *their* safety that's involved.' *Thwack*. 'They should be allowed some say in it themselves.'

'How d'you mean, sir?'

'Well,' the Chairman said. 'The whole thing should be put to them. The safety angle . . . everything. This isn't an ordinary service. In a sense, we're explorers . . . pioneers. Every one of us. And everyone should be allowed their own choice.'

Bellamy considered the proposal for a minute. Sir James had accepted his decision. What he was suggesting was only a modification of the pilot's own idea. And there was sense in what he said. Not that it would make the slightest difference, in any case, to the vast majority. Unlike Bellamy, the Chairman had not been in a position in New York to hear Able Dog's inhabitants talking about the Emperor.

And there was one thing of which he was absolutely certain. They'd jump at the chance of an honourable exit.

'Seems fair enough, sir.'

'Does . . . doesn't it?' Sir James sounded much more cheerful now, as he busied himself in the greenery around him. 'Then everybody will be satisfied. We'll have a get-together in my suite. Say two this afternoon.'

There was only one bush left now, and that was bending

under the onslaught of his club. Bellamy was still searching the grass just under his feet, when there was a shout of victory. 'Got it!'

'Good show, sir.' Friendly now, he was nevertheless relieved (the Chairman's persistence being what it was) that the battle for the lost ball was over.

'It was down there, just under that cedar root.' His face red, sweat pouring over his forehead, Sir James held the ball aloft in triumph. 'Play,' he said happily, 'can now be continued.'

Sitting on the grass-covered earthwork in front of a tumbled-down fort, built by their ancestors three hundred years previously to repulse other pirates, Brocklehurst and Sir James pensively studied the bubbly white clouds that seemed to rise from the sea and drift in the evening sky, high over their heads. The Under-Secretary was feeling mellow, perhaps from the sun, perhaps from the young blaze of colour on the beaches below him.

'This *get-together* idea of yours, Sir James,' he said. 'I must say it impressed me.'

The Chairman had specially asked the Under-Secretary along to see what he described as the 'workings of Air Enterprise'. Brocklehurst had expected that, at such a meeting the whole atmosphere would have been dominated by Sir James' powerful personality. And yet, practically all the talking had been done by one of his employees, propounding a scheme that must surely have been anathema to his press-on spirit towards unconditional success.

After explaining the technical side, Bellamy had emphasised that this was no ordinary flight, but one that still could be considered as the last of the trials' programme, and he had strongly impressed on them the advisability of being off-loaded. Apparently on purpose, Sir James had kept in the background. Before the meeting broke up, he had told them in a mild voice that it might be embarrassing for them to answer in front of everyone else: that either decision would not make the slightest difference to his outlook on any of them: and that they must go away and think about it, and then let Captain Bellamy or himself know what each of them thought it best to do.

'You won't mind me saying so, Sir James,' Brocklehurst went on, 'but I always had the idea that you were one of the tough old school of business-men. A driver, if you see what I mean. What *I* say *goes*.'

The Chairman laughed. 'These notions of yours, Brocklehurst!'

'Socialism hand in hand with free enterprise, democracy – ' Brocklehurst began, but he was interrupted by a shout from behind. Walking towards them, up from the path to the beach was Riley. He appeared a little breathless, but there was no doubt about it, he was perfectly sober.

'Sir James,' he said to the Chairman. 'I've already told Captain Bellamy. But I thought I should let you know, too.'

'And what's that, Mr. Riley?'

'Can't understand anybody hesitating about going, sir. After all that publicity we put in at New York – '

'I must congratulate you on the way you apparently handled the New York press, Mr. Riley.'

The carefully measured mead of praise was drained thirstily, and the empty handed back for more. 'They're tough, American journalists. Very shrewd. I – '

But there wasn't even twopence on the bottle. 'The Under-Secretary and I, Mr. Riley – '

'Of course, sir. Sorry to interrupt.' The Public Relations Officer started to move rather lamely away. 'I thought you should know that I will be coming.'

'I never had any doubt that you would,' the Chairman said, and seemingly satisfied with this show of confidence, Riley said his au-revoirs and sheered off down the path, back to the beach.

If Brocklehurst had been impressed by the *get-togethers*, he was even more impressed by Riley's cheerful acceptance of his lot for the morrow. With an acute vividness, he remembered the man's white face over Labrador, the trembling that had made it difficult for him to get out of the aircraft at Idelwild. And yet now –

It made you think, he said to himself. It was another little piece in the jig-saw of making up his own mind. Sir James' unshatterable confidence had left its mark. The generous enthusiasm of the Americans had not failed to catch his eye.

After his will-I-won't-I performance, like a girl with a dandelion puff, over phoning the Minister, he was beginning to congratulate himself now over doing the right thing by doing nothing, especially after the smooth trip down from New York.

'You know, Sir James,' he said suddenly. 'I'm thinking we've got a winner in the Emperor.'

The acquisitive pronoun was not disputed. 'I *know* we have.'

Brocklehurst plucked a piece of long grass and thoughtfully shredded it between his small teeth. As a politician, he was skilful at recognising a band-wagon when he saw one. This aircraft had not at first shown the usual resemblance to that indispensable method of political transport. But appearances were deceptive. And to be the first Under-Secretary to hammer home in the House the immense potential of Emperors –

'It goes without saying that I shall be accompanying you tomorrow, Sir James.'

If the Chairman was surprised, he didn't show it. All he said, with quiet friendliness, was, 'You must please yourself, Brocklehurst.'

'Hand to the plough . . . Lot's wife,' he said vaguely, looking at the vast flat floor of salt that lay, wet and waiting; from a few yards below him all the way unbroken to England, three thousand miles away. 'Well . . . at least that's Riley and myself – '

'They will all come,' the Chairman said.

'All of them?' Brocklehurst asked incredulously.

'*All* of them,' he repeated. 'What you're forgetting is the wonderful esprit-de-corps in Air Enterprise, dear fellow. The one for all, and all for one spirit. *That's* what will do the trick!'

But other factors were in operation among the inhabitants of Emperor Able Dog – some individual, some communal.

In the end, it was *these* that did the trick.

Most of the people who had wavered in New York – first this way, then that – now found their minds suddenly harden into a decision. The feeling towards Bellamy was far from a warm one for having their safety nearest his heart. Forced into going, with no exit allowed, that was one thing. But when an honest exit was provided, and they were bidden, almost pushed, out of it – that was a different thing all round. It implied they were dumpable salvage anyway, and they resented the high-handed notion that they could easily be removed without for a moment being missed.

Go? *Of course they'd go.* The Bermuda sun had melted the icy memories of Labrador. In this balmy air, it was impossible to imagine catastrophe.

And it was, in any case, a call to their democratic conscience – an almost heroic choice was offered them, and, wide-eyed, they were all for accepting it, carrying as it did just that pinch of braving the elements and fighting the good fight that has always kept every pilgrim happy along his progress.

Then they'd turned the corner, with a good start from New York. They were on their way home. Most of them felt that even if the Emperor should fail, they could somehow still fly to safety within the ample bosom of Sir James Joliffe.

There were a number of particular private reasons, too, for weighing the scales further down to an affirmative. Payton, having braved Sir James earlier by contradicting him, and rather liking the new flavour of independence in his mouth, tackled this second obstacle with a fresh determination. He might have come unstuck from the Line Manager's chair, but no one was going to say that made the slightest difference to his sticking to the Emperor through thick and thin.

Cavendish, a measure of his confidence having already been restored by the rejuvenation in New York, was even more anxious to get back on the aircraft – the only place where he could recover the rest of it. He knew that as far as the Emperor went, he was dead as a pilot until he flew her again. Not with the same smoothness as the youngsters maybe, but within his limitations that had been hammered home on this trip, as safely and surely as his long experience taught him. And Angela Knight faced the flight back with much more equilibrium, now she knew he would be on board.

Riley was too feverishly pleased to find that he was still an accepted (paid) member of the community, and not an outcast from the herd, to allow him to contradict by any word or action any of the nice things said about the Emperor by the American press.

The two designers, now welded together in an amiable whole by their mutual feelings towards the Chairman, hotly contested the slur cast by Bellamy on the serviceability of their combined product. Hamilton had already in New York decided the question of how far his two businesses could ethically go side by side with each other in mutual safety to both. And the doctor longed no longer for the rostrum, knowing now that his real duty lay, not in lecturing laymen on the organic behaviour of airman, but by taking the chance, whenever he could, of being beside them in their curious perambulations through the beginnings of outer space. As he told Bellamy – where the wind whist, it listeth. And whichever way the wind blew the Emperor to-morrow, it would also blow Enderby-Browne.

The operating crew would have had to go, anyway. But they resented this choice that was offered to the others of being volunteers, because it hit at the very roots of their scheme for Emperor operational pay. It was still on what could be called a discussion basis. Neither the vital question of how much should be asked for, nor who should be the person to put it to Sir James had yet been decided. But the fact that the others were coming regardless made it impossible, as Rawlings indignantly pointed out to Hooper on the beach, for them now to say they weren't coming unless –

Bellamy, when they told him, had enlarged on his advice, thinking perhaps they didn't grasp that what had happened over Labrador might happen again tomorrow, until he saw that their minds were completely made up. He saw other things, too. He had a shrewd suspicion that he had been led along an already predestined path, following a carrot that the Chairman had been trailing behind his ample coat tails. The Iceland incident, the New York publicity, the Mark II boosters at Bermuda, votes for the passengers – the man had been playing one thing off on another, one person against the other all the way along the route to get his own way, knowing already by some diabolical means how each would react, and being all the time two jumps ahead of everybody else.

He went up to the Chairman's suite just after dusk.

Throughout all the hotel, there was an air of expectancy. Strung along the terrace, the coloured lights had taken the place of the blazing flowers, now hidden by the darkness. But their scent was everywhere, mixed with the cedars, sweet in the windless air. A dance band in the empty ballroom chimed softly in with the cries of the crickets outside.

Sir James, immaculate in a dinner-suit, greeted him with a warm smile, which was not returned.

'Whisky, Captain Bellamy?'

'No, thank you, sir.'

The Chairman pulled at the white cuffs of his shirt under the beautiful black cloth. He raised his eyebrows. 'Well?' he said.

'As far as I can see, they're all coming.' Bellamy was watching Sir James carefully for any sign of surprise. But there was none. The eyebrows went back into their normal trim position above the bright blue eyes.

'Excellent!' The expected adjective for the expected news. The Chairman turned towards the cigar-box on his desk, as though the interview was now over.

'There's one more thing, sir.'

Immediately the eyes came back in a middle and off stance to face the bowling from the gas-works end. The brown cigar looked like a cartoonist's cricket bat in his hand.

'This choice, sir. I suppose . . . now . . . it applies to me as well?'

There was a break on that ball. Very likely a googly. He started to play back to block it. 'I hadn't thought of it that way, Captain.'

He put the cigar carefully into his mouth.

'There's something odd about that aircraft. The boosters – '

'Forewarned is forearmed, Captain! We won't get the cold temperatures this side of the Atlantic. And by flying low – '

'We can't fly really low on a long leg like Bermuda-London. You know as well as I do, sir, with these turbo-props we use ninety-five per cent of take-off power *whatever* altitude we are. Instead of a piston engine's sixty per cent. If we fly low we lose so much range and speed, it may make the operation marginal.'

'I didn't mean as low as that, Captain! I just meant you should fly *lower than usual!*'

It was perhaps exasperation, perhaps impetuousness that provoked Bellamy to try this last wild fling to get the Chairman out. 'That's just the point. If I'm to be allowed the choice, too . . . *I* won't be flying her. At any altitude.'

'You mean . . . you'll off-load *yourself*?'

'That's what I mean.'

It wasn't a googly. There wasn't even a curve on it. It was a straight fast ball, a badly pitched body-line, execrably bowled. Without the slightest hesitation, the Chairman lifted the cigar out of his lips, and hooked the thing straight over the pavilion for six. 'That's perfectly all right, Captain.'

Bellamy had expected hesitation. After the Chairman's ruling on who was to handle the aircraft, he had not anticipated quite such an immediate hit. 'You'd go on . . . without me?'

'Certainly! There's Captain Cavendish – '

Bellamy stood looking across at the bland, unruffled face. If the man's will to win was as ruthless as that, nothing short of firearms would stop him. He was thinking of Cavendish's flying, of the lives that would be entrusted to it in a problematical aeroplane on which the older man had had little experience. Whatever had been said in the past about the possible non-existence of a pilot's conscience, it was alive and kicking in Bellamy. With a sudden dignity in defeat that had not been evident in attack, he said, 'I'll be coming, then . . . after all, sir.'

'Make up your mind, man!' The unconditional surrender must be hammered home. No noble hearts must crack over this particular Hamlet.

'I have done, Sir James.'

The game was over now. Stumps were drawn. And with victory, the Chairman's mood changed completely. As though he was looking over the cricket field, now neatly trimmed and emptied of all possible pretenders to the captain's cap, he said genially, 'Well, that's fine, Bellamy! Tomorrow . . . we'll be the same big happy team that set off from England!'

The sky, too, had decided to change its mind. That evening,

the stars still shone down over Bermuda, but the eastern horizon was rimmed with a heavy line of black, cracked every now and then by a jagged fork of lightning.

But with the unpredictable cussedness of human nature, most of the Emperor's inhabitants were in a party spirit, now their decisions had been taken. The heat-wave was not yet quite over; and the last sun-drenched day and a half had done much to disperse the traditionally British fog of doubt and pessimism. Beneath their skins, the blessed warmth of sea and sun and extravagant food met and swelled the optimistic tide of their belief in Sir James Joliffe. Somehow, he'd get them there. Such bounce, such energy, such determined jollity and force could never end up sloshing around the cold wastes of the Atlantic. They gravitated towards his warmth and confidence like flowers to the sun.

All except Bellamy. He stood on the edge of the dance-floor that night, while the singer in front of the band crooned the delights of *A Bermuda buggy ride*. He was talking to a group of American passengers who had come over to the hotel for this farewell party.

Certainly he was doing the Company no harm. The Americans were enjoying the sulky-looking Englishman's intermittent smiles with the added respect that they always accorded to rarities. And they rewarded his rather dry remarks with considerably more than their due mead of laughter.

But the British, who were used to working with him, watched his face as they watched the outside air, and read the signs of the times. There was no mistaking the fact that he was registering less than the requisite party temperature. And because his own coolness menaced their warmth, the opinion of the party was against him.

Lalette's vision of the dance was made up of small fragments snatched from just over the tops of various partners' shoulders. Framed by here a bony uniformed one, there a well-padded, well-tailored one, she saw Hamilton sipping soft drinks and talking to one of the older American ladies, Mr. Brocklehurst dancing competently with another, and some of the crew disappearing on to the terrace with a selection of Bermuda's colourful season's visitors. The hours of the evening spun themselves away as though they were maypole ribbons unwinding to the time of her whirling feet.

When there was very little of it left, Bellamy asked her to dance. They both held themselves stiffly against one another. There was no mention now of yesterday's carefree beach, as they walked gravely around to the time of the music. Then, just as they were beside the glass terrace door, Bellamy danced her through. She dropped her hands quickly from him as soon as they were outside in the darkness.

'Let's walk,' he said, and started across the terrace towards the dark, sweet smelling lawns. Side by side, they walked slowly out into the night. The walls of the storm were fortifying the eastern sky. A faint roll of thunder was muffled by thick cloud, as the bright lights from the ballroom threw their shadows in their path like black cats of ill-omen. Behind them the music swelled in gigantic jollification.

'It's like the night before Waterloo,' Lalette said softly and looked up at his face. It was grave and preoccupied. Heavy with trouble like the sky he stared at. There was no relating this person to the man on the reef. There was no relating herself. In an unconscious metamorphosis, she took the colours of her personality chameleon-like from the night.

Very quietly, she let him slip her arm through his, and then lengthened her stride to walk in a melancholy slow march across the grass and on to the sandy roadway by the beach. The thin western starlight grew in strength as they moved away from the hotel.

Before them in the blue-black, gently breathing sea, a few heads bobbed up and down as some bathers took a midnight swim, their voices rising high above the rhythmic rustle of the white waves and the longer sigh of the palms.

Lalette glanced up at Bellamy's face. He was looking away from the lighted island behind them, with its little toy lighthouse, and a big fat moon above it. Away to the east, to the huge cloud build-up in the sky, lit by odd lightning flashes, and beyond that to a black nothingness.

Abruptly, he dropped her hand and turned away from her. His eye took in the three different sides of the scene around him: the lighted hotel, as a massive glittering centrepiece, sending its sweet music softly over the garden and the beach to the shadowy paths beyond: the moonlight on the right, and the thunder on the left.

Here it all was – yesterday, today, tomorrow, crammed into the same landscape, a warning for all to see. And being, it seemed, the only one to see, the anger mounted inside him: against Sir James for a defeat where there had been no visible battle: against the rest of the Emperor's inhabitants for their smug blind obedience. He said fiercely, 'Puppets . . . all of them!' Then seeing the girl look up at him in surprise, all his pent-up fury seemed to concentrate on her alone, and he added, 'You, too!'

She said nothing. Her eyes left his face and dropped downwards to the dry dark grass round her feet. They stood, side by side like that, for more than a minute, until Bellamy went on, 'In New York . . . damn well falling over themselves to get off the aircraft! And now' – his voice rose above the music, the sighing of the warm breeze through the leaves, the soft shushing of the sea – 'they know there's trouble. They're given the chance to get off. And what happens? They fall over themselves to get on!' He paused. '*You* included.' He stopped again, to let his words sink in, before crying out in irritated exasperation, 'Why? That's what I want to know. Why?'

The girl did not answer. Bellamy, looking down at the slight figure in front of him, saw how taut it was, how high her head was held, the hair glistening fair towards the moonlight, dark towards the storm. And then suddenly, as though he understood at last the reason for this anger, the cause and the cure, he reached out to take her small left hand in his, and gently pulling her nearer, put his arm round her shoulders and held her close to him. He could feel the silky smoothness of her bare arms, and smell the newly-washed fair hair against his face. He took hold of her chin in his fingers and turned her face round. Her eyes looked wide and dark in the moonlight, and her mouth had a strange sad softness.

'Don't come tomorrow,' he said, much more quietly now.

'Why?'

'Don't you know?'

'No.' She hardly moved her mouth when she spoke, and her eyes kept on gravely looking into his. He moved his head nearer to her own and kissed her. 'Not now?'

She drew away from him, and gave a sudden little smile. 'Not yet.'

He kissed her again. 'Now?'

She nodded her head, and put up her face towards him. 'Almost.'

He put his arms round her, and kissed her slowly and gently. In the shadow of the palm trees, between the pink and blue and yellow fairy lights of the hotel garden, and the silent ominous illumination in the sky in front, they held to one another in their own moment of quietness and joy.

Then she drew away from him. He looked down at her, and smiled. 'Now you know.'

'Yes.'

'And tomorrow?'

Instinctively, she turned and looked towards the high black plumes of cloud in their tomorrow's sky. She put out her hand and he held it in his. 'Now it's my turn,' she said.

'To what?'

She stood on tiptoe, and pulled his face down till it was level with her own. 'I have to come tomorrow.'

'Why?'

She put her lips on his and kissed him. 'Don't you know?' she said softly. 'Can't you guess?'

CHAPTER EIGHTEEN

THE thunderstorm broke in the late afternoon. Clouds formed up like a herd of mammoth grey elephants on their way to a Valhalla, and pushing and shoving each other, disintegrated over the island. Rain poured down. The sharp lines of Emperor Able Dog being towed from the hangar were softened by a translucent fur of fuzzy water, as the heavy raindrops splashed all over her fuselage. Spasmodic lightning momentarily cracked open the unnatural darkness. Bermuda's farewell to Air Enterprise Limited got literally washed away.

It had not, in any case, been intended to make too much of a song-and-dance. The aircraft had been looked over. The unexpected arrival of so many distinguished American visitors had used up the furore. They had gone just after lunch in a chartered Astroliner: a lively departure made all the more memorable for Matherson's last remark to the Chairman – 'Wouldn't be surprised if Sky-Am order a couple of dozen of those Emperors of yours!' But in the flatness that they left, the proving flight's departure took on all the appearance of a second feature. The Governor's aide-de-camp came down. A number of wet flowers made the air in the small Passenger Reception Hall smell sickly sweet. There was a reporter or two and a photographer. Most people, looking out, saw that Bermuda had suddenly been transformed to the bottom of a curious sea and stayed in their own dry glass tanks. Five small taxis, shiny as black-beetles, took the crew and the passengers out to Kindley Field.

In the almost empty terminal, the aide-de-camp did his best, talking to Sir James loudly and rather fast, in much the same rhythm as the rain on the roof. The pilots climbed into the Company station-wagon and were taken over to the Met office on the other side of the field. Hamilton fussed round about the catering, while the others quietly waited, some drinking coffee at the counter, some just sitting in the armchairs round the wall, for permission to board the aircraft.

When the pilots came back with the Met folder, Douthwaite started on the flight plan at 17,000 feet. Bellamy was again purposely keeping low to avoid the really cold temperatures. The winds were nearly on the beam and of little help, but few cloud build-ups were forecast beyond the thunderstorm over Bermuda. A weak front, dividing the warm air from the cold – that was all. Sir James excused himself from the aide-de-camp for a moment to ask Bellamy how the weather was; he brightened perceptibly when he heard no cloud was expected above 16,000 feet.

'All set, sir,' Douthwaite called out. 'If you'd care to sign the flight plan. Ten hours, fifty minutes.'

Bellamy added his name at the bottom of the sheet. Then he signed the load and trim sheet produced by the Operations Officer. Seawood and Hooper collected their brief-cases and drew up the collars of their raincoats.

'Can I put the passengers on, Captain?' the Operations Officer asked.

'Yes.' Bellamy peered out at the rain and the gusting wind. 'Well,' he said to the crew, 'I suppose we might as well get mobile.'

A procession of umbrellas already preceded them. The raindrops beat down so hard on the concrete, they sounded like a barefoot army running away. The wind caught at the umbrellas, twisting them out of shape. Eastlake and Cruttwell, under the same one, ran together to the shelter of the Emperor. The aide-de-camp, holding an extra specially large one over Sir James, walked the twenty-odd paces to the foot of the steps with suitable slow solemnity.

There, as Lalette looked down from the open doorway, they stopped. With the rain dripping from his young nose, the aide-de-camp began the little speech he'd been saying to himself all afternoon. 'Air Enterprise,' he started, but his words were howled down by the weather, '. . . . inspiration . . . the British Empire . . .'

'My dear fellow,' Sir James said. 'Don't stand there getting wet!'

He put out his hand. The aide-de-camp, not half-way through, felt his hand shaken in a firm wet grip.

'Good trip, sir!' he said, much more naturally, as the Chairman scuttled up the steps into the shelter of the cabin.

Then helter-skelter, his white suit soaked, he ran back into the terminal, and watched the engines start one by one, the chocks get whisked away, and the Emperor move slowly off on the long journey home. From where Bellamy and Seawood sat, it was difficult to see anything. Rain danced up and down on the windscreen. Though the wipers clashed to and fro, it still seemed as though the whole aircraft was under water. The wind clutched at the huge tail, banging it this way and that, and her plates shivered as she taxied. Plunging through pools in the uneven concrete, little hissing wings suddenly sprouted from the wheels before being smashed up into thousands of water drops. Around them, in the grey gloom of the rain, the aerodrome looked gutted. No living thing was in sight. No cars, no other aircraft moved. The grass, overwhelmed by the wind, lay flat on its back on the soaked sandy soil. Bumping a little, alone but unhurried, Emperor Able Dog proceeded to the take-off position.

The mile-and-a-quarter-long runway, straight as a die, cut off as sharply as a knife, lay before them, the wide short road to anywhere in the world.

'Able Dog,' Seawood said, 'is ready to roll.'

A voice from far away said: 'Able Dog is cleared Great Circle to London at seventeen thousand. Climb on course. Report fifty miles out and again at cruising altitude.'

Seawood repeated it back. Bellamy's right hand gripped the four throttle levers. Over his shoulder, he called, 'Ready for take-off, Mr. Rawlings?', and when the engineer echoed him, he said more quietly to Seawood, 'Well . . . here we go!'

The throttle levers advanced until they were hard against the stops. Even above the engines, the sound of the tyres could be heard swishing over the water-logged runway. Bellamy kept the nose-wheel hard on the ground to correct the Emperor's urge to swing to the right, as the beam wind tried to weather-cock the mainsail-size surface of her tail. Speed quickened into life the feel of her controls. Rhythmically, she moved up and down on her oleo legs.

He pulled the nose-wheel off the ground, and pressed harder with his left foot on the rudder pedal. The wet world outside grew further out of focus. Speed blurred everything. As the airspeed indicator touched 120 knots and the Emperor left the ground, Kindley Field turned into a pale grey smudge behind her.

Up came the wheels, then the flaps. The uneven turbulence slammed at the Emperor's wings, increasing in ferocity as she slowly climbed into the ill-defined opaque outlines of clouds that trailed their wispy tentacles down towards the sea.

For a moment, as Able Dog banked to the right, Seawood caught a glimpse of a coastline metamorphosed from coral and green and sand and clear water into a rugged grey cliff, standing rock-strong and spiky against the thick long ranks of the waves that one after the other swarmed over them. Then the bottom of the thunderstorm swallowed up the Emperor, and rolled a black-out curtain of steamy-grey down all her windows.

'Set the first course on the compass, Mr. Seawood!'

The First Officer set up 069 degrees magnetic. Bellamy banked. The needle on the gyro compass came closer to the twin parallel lubber lines, and then allowed itself to stay steadily imprisoned between them. Able Dog began to climb at over a thousand feet a minute.

Upwards, washed by the cloud they went, until noiselessly, the nose of the aircraft emerged into the clear again. But it was a new world this time.

They were in a valley, it seemed, surrounded on all sides by immense great billows of smoke. And yet, in an uncanny way, the smoke did not move. It did not boil and unfold and sway as smoke does. It was a Pompeii of a smoke-scape – as though lava had rolled down on the smoke as it climbed and curled in the sky, and petrified it then and there. It did not move or resist as the aircraft plunged in and out of it. Hard to look at, it gave softly when it was explored; the gloominess only becoming more clammy; the updraughts a little more violent; the streams of electric rain dancing brighter and more frequent on the windscreen in front of the pilots.

Douthwaite called from the navigation compartment: 'Fifty miles out,' and Seawood, his eyes still fascinated by the peaks, diminishing now as the aircraft climbed higher, reported to Control.

At the back, Hamilton had thought of serving tea, but was waiting for the turbulence to stop, for the aircraft to disentangle itself from the bad weather. The tail still swung, as the bumps hit. But each time, after a little initial waving this way and that, it quietened down.

And then suddenly, the mountains and valleys disappeared. The last remaining cloud tops were tinted blonde from the dying sun. The Emperor, in a final frenzy, shook and rattled in the invisible bumps of air. The great tail swayed one last long time. Mounting above the clouds, subduing them under her wings, the cumulus heads as innocuous-looking behind her now as the curly mops of children, Able Dog climbed into the clear. Everything on board seemed immediately to go quite still. High above, an immensity of deep blue sky darkened towards the east as night came up from the sea to meet them.

'Seventeen thousand feet,' Bellamy said. 'Report at cruising altitude.'

With his face pressed hard against the windscreen in front of him, Seawood studied the dark eastern horizon, as he made up their third hourly weather report. 'Bit hazy tonight, sir.'

'Yes.'

'This warm air from the south?'

'Yes.'

'Can't see a damned star ahead.' He turned to Bellamy doubtfully. 'I suppose it *is* haze, sir . . . not high cloud?'

Bellamy looked up through the perspex panel over his head. A glitter of tiny pieces of light reassured him of a clear sky above; but the horizons right round the aircraft were indistinct and muzzy – all the stars except for this circular patch above their heads were completely obscured.

'Haze,' he said.

Then they relapsed into the same silence that had lasted all the previous hour. Bellamy studied the forecast folder on the throttle pedestal beside him. A weak, rather narrow front was marked at longitude 40 West; but the cloud tops were marked clearly at 16,000 feet, one thousand feet below their present altitude.

Not that he took that as gospel. His eyes were continually watching the small round dial on the bottom left-hand corner of the instrument panel where the outside air temperature gauge now registered a placid – 13° Centigrade, well below the – 40 odd that might have been at the root of the Labrador trouble.

On this trip, he had taken more chances than he cared to think about. He didn't want any more. At this comparatively low altitude for gas turbines, the fuel consumption per nautical mile was high. There was no help from the winds, now mainly blowing on the beam. The responsibility for all on board still weighed on his mind. He had thought over various courses of action, should the boosters start acting up again: but what he most feared was that the gigantic rudder should jam hard over, one side or the other. He was treating the rudders with extra special respect, and when Seawood accidentally banged his foot on the left pedal, he gave a quick start.

'Sorry, sir.' Seawood was just passing the weather pro forma back to Rawlings.

'That's all right.' With an effort, Bellamy relaxed and smiled. Seeing the First Officer's anxious-to-please face under the fair hair, he was suddenly mindful of how much he took his crew for granted. He rarely chatted to them, as they sat together up at the front, watching the night hours go by. He knew nothing of Seawood, except that he was a good, unobtrusive First Officer. 'How long before you get a command?'

'Oh . . . years and years, sir.'

'Not if the Emperor's a success. Twenty new aircraft ordered. They'll be needing a lot of new captains.'

Seawood paused. 'I'd thought of that, sir.'

'You mean . . . you're not counting your Emperors before they're hatched?'

'Well . . . there've been so many others that were going to be so good. And on this trip – '

'Able Dog is only the prototype, don't forget. Not that I'm saying there aren't a few things I'd like to see done. Foolproof booster system. Hot air instead of these antiquated wing de-icing boots. Various little economies done away with.'

'And the Mark II boosters fitted?'

Bellamy grinned. 'Yes . . . the Mark II boosters, of course. But otherwise, she's strong: she's fast: terrific passenger capacity and good engines.'

'So you think she'll reach the Chairman's expectations?'

'I'm not saying anything more till we reach London. All I'll say now is – your command course mightn't be so long away, after all!'

The First Officer seemed pleased even to have his name in the same sentence as a captaincy. Bellamy went on, 'Married?'

Seawood said, 'Not far off, sir.' For half an hour, they went on talking about the outside world on the ground: about cars; films; living in London. But all the time, Bellamy's eyes were watching the air temperature gauge.

It was going up quite fast. Now it was only – 9°. Not a very good temperature, if they should run into cloud.

And ice started to form.

It was the quietest dinner ever.

Though outside in the clear black night, the engines hummed on steadily eastwards, there was rarely a sound in the passenger cabin. Just after take-off, perhaps in a flurry of satisfaction with themselves over their own decision, there had been some quite animated conversations. Enderby-Browne had gone over a number of points in the lecture that hadn't been delivered to the Canford Institute with Riley. Cruttwell was assuring Eastlake of his complete confidence in the toughness of the airframe.

But the talk died down as they drew further away from Bermuda, into the Atlantic. Now the catering staff were serving the meal, they were all silent. The footfalls of Hamilton were muffled into nothing by the thick pink pile of the carpet in the aisle. Angela's voice, as she went round with the wine, was almost down to a whisper. When Payton dropped a fork that clattered down among the plastic plates, at least three heads turned quickly round to see what had happened.

Only the hydraulic pump, unaffected by atmosphere, let out its thin whine whenever the system's reservoirs needed replenishing.

Even Sir James was well on with his sweet before he spoke. Then, perhaps remembering his obligations as a host, he turned to Brocklehurst, and said quietly, 'Comfortable?'

'Very,' The Under-Secretary was still picking at his steak.

'I've noticed you're not eating much. Food all right?'

'Delicious!'

'I can recommend the hock. Have some.'

'Thank you – no.'

'Help your appetite.' But as Brocklehurst showed no signs of being tempted, he changed the subject. 'Very pleasant at Bermuda, I thought.'

'Extremely so.'

'But pleasanter still to be home-bound. On schedule. Eh?'

Brocklehurst said nothing. Instead, he looked at his watch, which he had never altered from English time. Past midnight. It was another day already in London, and here they were still having dinner. His wife would be sleeping alone under the green satin eiderdown of their enormous mahogany bed. While he sat in his seat, with three hours and fifty minutes gone, and another seven hours to go.

He could not fail to notice the air of expectancy in the cabin, as everyone watched and waited. Turning to the Chairman, he asked, 'You did say the weather was good?'

'Not a cloud above us all the way . . . Bellamy told me. This is the fair weather route!'

'A bit off the shipping lanes, though,' Brocklehurst pointed out. 'Very isolated.'

Sir James shot him a sideways glance. The stewardess was just passing, and he signalled to her. 'I insist,' he said, 'on your having some of this hock, Brocklehurst. I'd value your opinion.'

On his tray, the Under-Secretary's glass was filled. Mechanically, he lifted it to his lips.

'Very nice,' he said. But all his attention was outside. Not on the engines, or the cheerful wash of flame tagged on behind them. Nor on the steady length of wing. Much higher still – on the sky high above them.

'I'm glad you like it.'

Brocklehurst continued to sip abstractedly. A frown had come over his face, and his eyes were continually looking sideways and upwards through the round dark porthole beside him. Suddenly, he said, 'Odd.'

'Is that sediment I see in your wine, dear fellow?'

'Just before our meal, I had been watching the stars, Sir James.'

'Well?'

'Now I can't see any.'

'So?'

'I thought you said we'd be in the clear all the way. Above the stuff.'

'It's the cabin lights, Brocklehurst! They've turned them up full bright for dinner.' The Chairman sent his tongue sweeping over his lips for the last crumbs of strawberry meringue pie. 'Say the word *immediately* . . . if you find them too dazzling.'

Up at the front, past the flight-deck door that divided the dark and the light, in the dim navigation compartment, Douthwaite was taking a sight through the periscopic sextant. He had already got one of Altair. Its altitude, 37° 21′ at 01.21, lay scribbled on scrap-paper on the table behind him.

Nearer to the nose, Hooper took off his headphones to grumble at Rawlings, 'Hell of a lot of static, tonight.'

He had not been able to get any information of value from the outside world. By diligent tuning, he had learnt that Russia had set off another hydrogen bomb: a war was brewing in South America: the French government had fallen again: a Member of Parliament had expressed concern at American policy in the Far East, and a senator had accused Britain of having no policy at all in Europe. No football results. No racing news. No winds at seventeen thousand feet.

But Rawlings was quite satisfied with the calm faces of the dials in front of him. 'Engines are bang on.'

The Radio Officer turned to look at the heads of Bellamy and Seawood, still talking side by side at the front. 'Pilots seem to be having no trouble, Red.'

'No trouble at all.'

Suddenly, a very slight vibration shook the flight-deck floor. From the top end of Douthwaite's long body came an exasperated explosion.

'Damn!'

Hooper half-jumped from his seat. 'What's up, Alex? What's up?'

'Capella.' The navigator's head appeared from behind the mask of the sextant. He rubbed his hand over his screwed-up eyes. 'Bloody star just went phut in my face!'

CHAPTER NINETEEN

CAVENDISH had seen the cloud from the rest compartment, where he had been eating a solitary dinner. He walked up to the front and stood between the two pilots.

'There seems more in that weak front than they forecast, Captain Bellamy.'

'Yes. I've been watching the temperature going up over the last hour.' He pointed it out. Only — 7°. 'Might have to climb . . . if we get any ice.'

'One thing.' Cavendish said in a reassuring tone, 'if we *do* have to go up, in this warm air, we won't get anywhere near — 40.'

'I'd have gone up anyway. Except there's that cold air on the other side of the front.' Bellamy turned to Seawood. 'You go back and have dinner now.'

The First Officer carefully got out of the right-hand seat. Just as carefully, Cavendish settled his huge bulk down on the cushion, as soon as it was vacant. Bellamy was looking up through the panel, hoping to see a star or two to prove this sudden darkness was just ragged, unimportant layer cloud. But there was nothing. Only solid blackness, and the tiny reflection of the green instrument lighting on the glass. He took a handkerchief from his pocket and wiped the sweat off his hands. The Emperor had started to rock very slightly from side to side. As a precaution against sudden turbulence he had disengaged the automatic pilot.

Cavendish peered out into the night. 'This haze makes things difficult.'

'Yes.'

'We're not in cloud.'

'Not *yet.*'

The temperature gauge had gone up another degree. They sat together in silence; Cavendish watching out for the slightest sign of heavy cumulus that might mean ice, Bellamy's eyes alternating between the blind flying instruments and the temperature.

Cavendish said, 'Mind if we have all the lights out?'

'Go ahead.'

Cavendish pulled the curtain behind the pilots tight shut. Then he turned out the tiny glow over the instruments. Only the phosphorescent numbers and needles stood out now.

Cavendish still kept staring ahead. He said suddenly, 'Isn't that a cumulus head?'

Bellamy looked up. 'Where?'

'Over to starboard.'

Bellamy turned his head. 'Can't see anything.'

'No.' Cavendish relaxed a little. 'Impossible to tell, really. Pitch black outside. Just thought I caught a shadow that was blacker than the rest.'

'All the same,' Bellamy said. 'I don't like it. I think we'll climb.'

'Temperature still going up?'

Bellamy was just about to answer, when a sudden overwhelming clatter of ice and rain broke in a great splintering mass over the nose. In two seconds, the windscreens changed from black to white.

Cavendish shouted, 'Clear ice!'

It was as though an iceberg had disintegrated on top of them. Though the pilots had immediately switched on all the alcohol anti-icers, all the windows were tightly bandaged up. Nothing could be seen but wet shining whiteness.

Bellamy knew he had to act quickly, before the whole aircraft was suffocated. This was the most dangerous form of ice – almost perfectly clear, heavy and quick-forming. He said to Cavendish as he pulled back on the stick, 'Let's get out of here!'

'Want me to take her up?'

'Please.'

Cavendish put his hands on the control column and moved it even further towards him. The rate of climb shot up. Bellamy went back to tell Hooper to get a clearance to 25,000. This was very definitely a time when immediate action, permission or not, was essential. There were few aircraft on this route, anyway; but all the same, he would feel happier when Control had cleared them. Rawlings had already put on the fractional increase that separated cruise and climb power on Cruttwell's jet engines.

Unseeing, blinded by ice, Able Dog's nose rose up steeply as she started a powerful leap upwards through the freezing air. As Bellamy stood impatiently beside the Radio Officer, still keeping an eye on the temperature gauge, Cavendish edged the control column further back, anxious to shake off the icy clinging fingers of the cloud: up into the colder, drier air where the ice would lessen.

The Emperor responded magnificently. Her propellors slashed through the stuff, sending it clanging in great chunks against her metal sides. The altimeter needle never wavered as it clocked in each thousand feet of height gained. The vibration inside the aircraft increased. She shuddered a little. That was all. And the temperature gauge, very reluctantly at first, started to go down as the altimeter went up: —11, —12, —13. Every degree meant less of this throttling wet ice.

Bellamy came back to the front for a moment. 'All right?' he asked Cavendish.

The older pilot pointed to the altimeter, already at 22,000 feet. 'Climbing well.'

Then Hooper called out, 'Got clearance, sir'; and Bellamy felt that the sudden crisis was over. They would probably be clear of cloud now, if they could see out. The tension on the flight deck relaxed as he went aft to the navigation compartment. Leaning on the table, with his chin cupped in his hand, he discussed with Douthwaite the flight plan at the new altitude. The temperature was still only — 20°, well below the suspected danger point for the boosters.

Bellamy said, 'Of course, the temperature'll go down sharply past this front. May have to go down. But I'll keep my eye on it.'

Alone in the curtained-off tip of the nose, Cavendish relaxed his tight grip of the stick. The needle on the altimeter was still gaily turning. They were past 24,000 now. Only another thousand feet to go – they'd done it easily.

He watched the pointer pass the new altitude. Then he eased gently forward on the control column.

Nothing happened. Only the altimeter moved – up and up, past 26,000, pressing on tirelessly to 27,000.

He called, 'Cruise power.' Not that the small decrease would make much difference, but with everything set up, he could devote all his attention to the problem on hand. Very slightly harder, he pushed forward on the control column.

It still didn't move.

Incredulously, he looked to see if the automatic pilot was engaged. But all the levers were back. Out.

He pushed forward again much harder. The metal stick quivered a little under the pressure. But it stayed where it was.

Then his eye caught the altimeter reading. With the present high angle of the wings' attack, they were still shooting upwards, just passing 28,000.

Settling himself lower in the seat, with all his might, he strained against the control column. But he could not shift it. He tried the ailerons. Then, more gingerly, the rudders. Both were working perfectly normally.

Sweat began to pour down his face. He leant his whole big body against the damned thing. Still nothing gave.

He turned his head and called, 'Captain Bellamy!'

Bellamy came up to the front immediately and leapt into the left-hand seat. 'What's the trouble?'

'These damned elevators!'

Bellamy tried them. Both pilots pushed together. 'Stuck solid!' Then he saw the reading on the altimeter: 31,000 feet and still going up. 'Christ!'

Cavendish said, 'I think it's ice over the hinges of the elevators. Jammed them solid in the up position.'

'Hope to God it's not the boosters.' He tried the emergency position; but there was no change. Only the windscreens were altering: the alcohol had eaten away at the ice, clearing a hole in the centre through which the stars shone, bright and alive around them. But they could also see the lumps of jagged ice, inches thick on the wings.

'I think you're right,' Bellamy said.

He put the de-icer boots on, to get the ice at least off the wings and tailplane. Then he saw the temperature gauge: −32° Centigrade, and still going down. 'Mightn't be the boosters now,' he said grimly. 'But if we don't watch out . . . it damn soon will be!'

He put his hands on the throttles. Very cautiously, he was bringing them back. Cavendish said, 'For God's sake, don't stall her!'

'We've *got* to stop her climbing.'

At the best of times, the Emperor's stall was vicious and sudden. In this nose-up attitude, with the elevators locked, what would happen was best not thought about. To make matters worse, with the ice they still carried, the stalling speed would be anybody's guess.

They had passed 34,000 feet now, but as the power from the engines was reduced, they were slowing up. But at the back of Bellamy's mind was the certainty that now they were passing the front, the temperature up here would take an alarming drop, way past −40°. He watched it going back on the dial, as he reduced power on the engines.

The climb had slowed up to a lazy progression upward. He eased back the four levers just a fraction further.

And then, suddenly, with no warning at all, a great shudder ran through the whole aircraft. She quivered and wobbled like a giant jelly. Bellamy slammed all the throttles into the take-off position.

He yelled to the crew, 'Strap yourselves in!' and switched on the passenger seat belt sign.

The trembling continued. Without the use of the elevators, there was a lag on the speed building up. The Emperor tottered at the top of the sky, trying to make up her mind what to do. Her metal plates seemed to go mad and melt into a shivering, clanging mass of metal.

And then, only seconds after the first tremors but like years to Bellamy, she gave up the ghost. The juddering ceased abruptly. With a whimper, the huge nose dropped. The navigator's pencils bounced off the table. As though suddenly deprived of all air to fly in, Emperor Able Dog plunged like a stone down towards the sea.

Payton was the only one in the passenger cabin to notice the seat belt sign come on. Feeling the juddering, his mind harked back to Labrador. Immediately, he felt for the webbing straps.

But it was too late. Before he could fasten them, the aircraft had lurched forward at an alarming angle. He was hurled against the seat in front. Tightly, he clung to the strawberry-pink upholstery; while the others, caught more unawares, were spilled like dice on the floor in all sorts of attitudes.

Eastlake had crashed over two seats, and was upside-down with his legs in the air. The Chairman hung grimly on to the arm of the vacant chair across the aisle. Brocklehurst had smashed his face hard against the porthole. Hamilton, who was standing up at the time, was knocked nearly unconscious against the rear bulkhead.

After the first cries of surprise, nobody said anything. Unsure whether they were upside-down or sideways, they lay where they had been thrown. Riley gave a groan, but it was the bump on his head that he was groaning about. Cruttwell had a gash right down his cheek that was now red and bleeding. The two girls, flattened on the galley floor, had their eyes tight closed.

They were all in such unlikely attitudes, that there could now be no remedy. They knew they were going downwards. The engines were curiously soft; but a gale seemed to whine and howl against the outside of the fuselage.

Sir James tried to get straight, but he fell back. Only Enderby-Browne was still upright, his legs propped hard against the seat in front of him.

But this descending motion was not an unpleasant sensation. As the seconds went by, they became, one by one, past being afraid. An inability to do anything anyway made them lie there passive, warm, comfortable even in the mêlée of bodies around them, waiting for whatever power there was that controlled these things to do what he wished with them.

The seconds stretched into minutes. They were still going down. And now they were turning. Right at the back, Lalette and Angela began to feel giddy and sick. Their eyes watered. Their heads went round and round. Everyone was conscious that somewhere, at some time soon, the air must end with the hard surface of the sea.

But the minutes passed, and nothing happened. Hearteningly, the engines started to roar up; yet the twisting and turning still went on; they were all pinned where they were by the invisible rotating strength of centrifugal force.

Up at the front, strapped in their seats, both pilots fought to make the Emperor recover. Bellamy yelled, 'Is she spinning?'

The turn indicator was rate four to the left.

Cavendish shouted back, 'God knows!' The turn indicator had swung central again.

'Can't feel anything in the rudders.'

'Nothing in the ailerons, either.'

Bellamy flung himself against the control column with all his might. 'These damned elevators! Won't shift an inch!'

He had tried full travel on the trimmers. Nothing seemed to make any difference. The Emperor, descending now past 11,000 feet, had lost over three miles in height. She seemed to have forgotten all sense of behaving like an aeroplane. More like a huge hunk of metal, irregularly shaped, that twisted and turned, slowed up and spurted down: up on the port wing one minute, starboard the next: skidding and slipping in the darkness, the airspeed fluctuating wildly: now seemingly on the point of recovering, flat and much more steady, until once more the nose dropped violently, the shuddering started up, and she heeled over again, hard on her side.

Bellamy called out, 'She's turning to the left again! I'm trying power on the port engines. Throttle back the starboards!'

He was trying to stop the spinning motion by counteracting it with asymmetrical engine power, now the rudders and ailerons were flabby and unresponsive and the elevators solid in the up position.

The nose steadied a little. The speed built up. Then up on her right wing she went. The altimeter needle unwound past 9,000 feet. There was a mile and half of air left before the cold waters of the Atlantic began.

Bellamy still attempted to help her out of her paroxysms with the motors. Sometimes there was more feel in the rudders: once, just on 5,000 feet, well below the freezing level now, they seemed to respond normally. But it was only for a moment, before the giddily shimmying rotation continued.

Cavendish said quietly, 'Three thousand feet. Turning to starboard now!'

In a last desperate effort to right her, Bellamy tried take-off power on the starboard side, none on the port. Full rudder was already rammed hard on.

The aircraft went down another thousand feet. But she was descending slower. Bellamy saw the speed build up. Abruptly, the turning ceased. All juddering stopped. He banged the four throttle levers wide-open; and at last he felt life flowing back into the rudders and ailerons. The Emperor seemed to stop quite still for a moment. A calm descended over the whole of her fuselage. And then, quite undisturbed, she roared majestically up into the night, while the hard-working hand of the altimeter began rapid amends for butter-fingering five miles' worth of thin air.

The Emperor had reached 6,000 feet before either of the pilots spoke. Then Cavendish observed drily, 'This aircraft continues to astonish me, Captain Bellamy.'

Bellamy could still feel the emptiness inside him; the hard hammering of his heart. He turned his sweat-soaked face towards the older pilot. 'She has her moments.'

He saw Cavendish was smiling: the unperturbed, patient smile of long experience with fractious aeroplanes. 'On top of her other virtues . . . what do we find but a remarkable gift for aerobatics!'

In spite of himself, Bellamy smiled back. His mind had been a blank over what he was going to do, still stunned by that terrifying spiral through the sky. Cavendish looked completely calm, as though he had been immunised against any feelings of near-disaster. His indomitable attitude, as he sat in the right-hand seat unmoved and unshaken, was in itself an immense encouraging comfort.

Bellamy said, 'She'll be wanting to do an encore . . . if we don't watch out.'

'I'd been thinking about that.'

'It can't be ice now.' Bellamy banged at the elevator control column, still stuck fast. 'We got way below the freezing level.' He took out his torch and shone it on the wing. 'Not a sign of the stuff out there now.'

'It was ice to begin with. Then I fancy when we got beyond 33,000 feet the elevator booster cylinders contracted in the cold temperatures. And jammed the pistons.'

'Thank God the rudders didn't join them!' Bellamy bent over the throttle levers, bringing back the power on the engines. There was a greater feeling of security, now they had some height beneath them. But the angle of attack of the wings was very steep, causing an immense drag as the pilot tried to make the aircraft mush. 'We've got to get the nose down somehow!'

They talked it over while the aircraft climbed, slowly and steadily up into the clear sky. The front was behind them now, and they were flying in a cold airstream from the north. When they had agreed on a course of action, Bellamy climbed out of his seat and went aft. He had a word with Douthwaite, Hooper and Seawood; the First Officer opened up a hatch in the floor for them, and all three disappeared into the baggage compartment.

In the passenger cabin, everyone had picked themselves up, and in a dazed silence had obeyed the sign to strap themselves in. Enderby-Browne had taken out the first-aid kit, and now Cruttwell's cheek had been dressed, sat with it on his lap, waiting like everyone else for the next plunge downwards to the sea.

Immediately Bellamy came into the compartment, the Chairman called out, 'What's happened, Bellamy? What's wrong?'

The pilot told them all as briefly as possible. Then he explained what they intended to do. 'As you can guess, the important thing is to *stop climbing*. All the same, we're going up to 19,000 feet, where we'll get a reasonable speed and where the upward effect of the elevators won't be so great. We can't go higher, in case of colder temperatures.'

He paused, looking at the anxious faces around him. 'But fortunately, the Emperor is very sensitive on fore and aft trim. All the cargo in the holds is now being moved forward. I want you to bring everything movable in the cabin and the galley up front. And then come up yourselves too. We want every available pound we can get crammed into the nose. That way, we may be able to balance out the up effect of the elevators.'

'Like a pair of scales, Captain,' Riley suggested.

Bellamy nodded. 'Something like that.'

Everyone in the cabin set to with a will, glad at last to be able to do something to help themselves, pushing and pulling everything that would move as far forward as they could. In a forlorn hope, Bellamy sent Rawlings and Eastlake back into the tail cone, to see if they could do anything about the jammed booster cylinders.

They were down there fifteen minutes. By the time they returned, dirty and dusty, all the other inhabitants of the Emperor were squeezed tightly together on the flight deck.

'Manage to do anything?' Bellamy asked them from the left-hand seat.

Eastlake shook his head. 'Nothing.'

But there he was wrong. By moving their combined weights of 331 pounds from the tip of the tail to the front of the nose, they achieved at last in the Emperor that balance that had been wanting. The altimeter stopped turning. Throttled back a little, certainly, and in rather a begging attitude, Able Dog was nevertheless staying perfectly level around 19,000 feet, and yet still maintaining a reasonably good airspeed.

'Nice to be able to work,' Douthwaite observed, as he sent up through the throng a new course of 072°, 'without going round in circles!'

He saw Lalette, squashed against Cruttwell, and grinned at her. She tried to grin back.

But now that the emergency was apparently over, and there was nothing else to do but stand waiting in this crush, she felt her body take the delayed shocks of the past half-hour. She was suddenly cold. She hunched herself over her folded arms, as though to conserve the dwindling heat of her body, pressing her legs against the metal sides of the cockpit to stop their shuddering.

Instinctively, she pressed herself as far as possible into the dimly-lit, frighteningly crowded flight deck until she stood close behind Bellamy's seat. His nearness gradually comforted her. If she put out a hand, she could touch him. But because she knew she could, she no longer needed to. Instead, she looked along the shadow of the port wing, watching the red navigation light on its tip join the pattern of the stars.

She shifted her half-numbed foot. Around her, heads were bent, eyes peered only half-seeing at the endless black future that stretched in front of them. In the pale green glimmer from the instruments, the faces and hands of the pilots shone as though carved of undersea rock.

Lalette said to Bellamy, 'Would it make a lot of difference if I went to the galley for coffee?'

'It would make some.' He turned and smiled at her. 'But I think it's worth it. So long as you're quick.'

She was back soon, with the first tray. She reached her hand out for a cup for Sir James. 'Two lumps for you, isn't it, sir?'

But he waved the cup away. 'Workers first!' He nodded at the pilots. Lalette put in one lump of sugar and passed it to Bellamy. 'Your coffee, sir.'

As he took it, for a moment his fingers pressed over hers. 'Thanks,' he said. 'Just what we all needed.'

The cockpit began to be filled with conscientious human jollity, as Lalette went aft for the second tray of cups.

But after the coffee had gone, silence descended once more. There was an almost itching discomfort in so many people jam-packed together.

Bellamy rubbed the side of his head and the back of his neck. Then he straightened his shoulders as though throwing off the weight of the anxious souls behind him. For a second, he spared a thought for the girls, hoping that neither of them would feel this suffocating claustrophobia and become hysterical. When Lalette began to speak again, he listened with an ear trained to the nuances of dangerous vibrations, searching in the even tenor of her voice for the too high pitch, the confused hesitations, the beginning of the breaking point into tears.

But there was nothing. She was asking Captain Payton about the stars. Her voice was quiet, polite, interested. He could feel her lean forward a little. He could imagine her hand moving lightly, pointing across millions of miles of darkness to the ordered pattern of the now clear sky.

'Altair,' said Payton. 'Now look up! No, a bit to your right.'

'That bright one? Beyond the Little Bear? Yes? What's that?'

'Deneb.'

They were all looking out now. As if the whole sky were open to them, as if the cabin had been flung wide open, the heavy silence broke, the tenseness eased and flowed away.

Bellamy bent forward and looked at the instruments. Sir James leaned across to him and asked, 'Did we send an emergency signal, Captain?'

Bellamy shrugged his shoulders. 'No point. State we were in, nobody could have helped us. And now' – he looked out at the steady wings stretched out under the orderly sky – 'There's no need.'

'How are we doing?'

'Not bad, sir. Considering everything . . . she's going very well.' He put out his hand for a piece of paper on which Douthwaite had written: *25 West. Course 078° to 20 West. Estimate 06.10.*

Bellamy pursed his lips as he read it. They were going slower than he'd hoped. There was still another eight hundred miles of sea to go.

It was like that, all bunched in the nose of the Emperor, that dawn discovered them two hours later. The door to the passenger cabin swung to and fro, disclosing the empty cabin beyond them. Finding that the Emperor stayed where she was without her yen to climb, they found also that the close proximity was even comfortable. Riley made some crack about coming home with the milk. Eastlake (whose shiny hair was ruffled, his immaculate appearance spoiled) pressed close to Sir James, and said wryly, 'It's my boosters again. Jammed pistons. On the elevators. And this time, they haven't come unstuck.'

But it was no time for recrimination, for allotting the blame. Sir James recalled the whole question of the Mark II booster cylinders – from London through New York to Bermuda – very vividly in his own mind. Thoughtfully, he looked out of the port windscreen, and watched the red line on the eastern horizon gradually disappear, and a pearly grey explosion of light take its place. The cabin, before a small black hole with the flickering dials of the instruments as the only illumination, became a strip of metal with too many people standing on it. Beards began to show; the deep lines of fatigue cut into the faces of all those around him.

Looking at them, he was touched by the rather ragged scene before his eyes, all bunched together behind the pilots, everyone contributing their assorted weights to the eventual home-coming, while above them, glittering in the colours of a new day, the immense universe lay unbroken for millions of miles above their heads and below them washed the waves of the oldest ocean in the world – as though they were poised on a scale between the disaster of going too high, and the disaster of going too low, by the odd counterbalance of the tight-packed weight of humanity on the flight deck.

There was still cheerfulness. The aircraft seemed quite content to go on flying like this, without giving further trouble. Her ground speed, reduced by her begging attitude and the slight hindrance of a beam wind, was over 200 knots. Two hours from the estimated time of arrival over London, Bellamy obtained descent clearance, and by throttling back the engines still further, managed to begin a very slow descent.

The sky had lightened. Down below them now, they could see the slightly ruffled surface of the sea. Everyone immediately started to look at their watches, waiting for the moment when the coast of England would come out of the morning mist to greet them.

The time passed more slowly, now they were counting the minutes. Once or twice, small chunky clouds, low down, seemed to look like hills. And then suddenly, Seawood, squeezed behind the right-hand seat, stretched out his hand and pointed out to starboard. 'Land!'

A craggy piece of rock came jutting out of the horizon. It grew larger and longer – a cliff edged with green, with a beach in front of it and a chequer-board of fields and hills beyond. As they flew over the yellow stretch of sand that stretched like a winner's tape below them, everyone's spirit soared. The Emperor had at last come home.

And then, invisibly as a germ, a thought crossed their minds. Though the present danger had been overcome, and everyone was safe and comparatively comfortable, ahead lay the best-not-thought-about hazard of coming in for a landing at London.

CHAPTER TWENTY

THE sun crept off the line of the horizon, bringing all the dark instruments on the flight deck out into the mundane light of day. Bellamy sat with his hand continually moving the wheel on the left-hand side of the throttle pedestal – testing the effect of the elevator trimmer on the attitude of the aircraft.

Cavendish asked, 'Any luck with it yet, Andrew?' For the last half-hour they had been discussing between themselves the delicate question of the landing.

'A little.'

They were still managing to descend, with engines throttled well back and half flap extended.

But now, there was a little more control. As Bellamy wound the trimming wheel back, very slowly the nose dropped further.

'I trust it will give us a trifle more co-operation at London.'

'Should do, Charles. We're getting less tail heavy all the time.' Every hour, the engines were devouring two tons of fuel: and since the tanks were placed aft of the centre of gravity, as their contents disappeared, weight was being continuously subtracted from the side of the scales that was tipping the nose up.

'Only half an hour to go.'

'Yes.'

Again, Bellamy tried the trimming wheel, this time the whole length of its travel backwards. These trimmers could be called the elevators of the elevators. For they were exactly like very small hinged controls, fitted on the outside edge of the elevators proper, and worked by that ancient and honourable device, a pulley and wire mechanism. Their main purpose was to make the pilot's life easier. If he was forced to exert pressure on the stick to prevent the nose dropping or the tail from going down, a certain amount of movement on the wheel would make the trimmers change their position so that the slipstream hit them; and then they would raise or lower the elevator the necessary amount to relieve the continual pressure on the control column. With the elevator jammed solid, the trimmers could not, of course, move it; but they could to a very limited degree be used as baby elevators, acting in the opposite sense to their much larger parents: that is, if it was required to put the nose *down*, the trimming wheel must be wound *backwards*, and vice-versa.

'Went down more that time, Andrew.'

Bellamy grunted, 'Getting better.'

As Emperor Able Dog lowered herself carefully over the woods and fields of Southern England, she stamped her black shadow on their green and brown surfaces. At this early hour on Sunday, few people moved beneath her. Quickly, she left a railway engine, puffing white smoke, far behind. Two steeples, close together, pointed her out to the houses that huddled sleepily around them.

On the R/T, London Approach Control told Cavendish that the visibility was unlimited, the wind light and variable. 'Well, anyway, the weather's being co-operative for a change.'

'Still going to be tricky.'

'Yes.' Cavendish paused, before going on in rather an off-hand way, 'I did a landing with the elevators jammed a couple of years ago. Rigger left the locks on.'

'Then you're an old hand at this sort of thing?'

'Hardly an old hand. Once was enough. An experience I had hoped would not be repeated.'

Bellamy looked across at the older pilot in the right-hand seat. The iron-grey moustache still bristled immaculately below the aristocratic nose. 'Now it has been . . . you'd better do the landing at London.'

Cavendish said quietly, 'If you wish.'

As the pilots changed seats. Rawlings' eyebrows shot up. Hooper, who had heard their conversation, started to be concerned with the safety straps round his seat, and began to measure the distance to the nearest emergency exit, a red-painted round porthole behind Douthwaite's head. Knowing some of the difficulties involved, he felt the corners of his mouth go down; but he saw the two pilots exchange a glance of complete and friendly understanding, as Bellamy said briefly, 'I'll tell Control we'll be doing a long final approach.'

Gradually, the shapes on the ground grew larger. The great

loop of the Thames glittered to the north of the red rash of Reading. Able Dog was still descending at 300 feet a minute.

'Can you see the field?' London asked them, when Bellamy reported over Woodley beacon.

'We can see the field.'

There it was, the long grey arms of the runways outstretched to welcome them home. 'Then you're cleared final, cleared Number One. Runway 28 left.'

Just after Cavendish had made a long down-wind leg over Staines reservoir, he turned to the passengers and crew that still crammed in the cockpit behind him. 'This is where we'll be using *human* elevators. When I want to flatten out, I'll be sending some of you back to the tail to get the nose up for me.' Then he said crisply to Bellamy, 'Gear down! Before landing check!'

Out of the corner of his eye, Rawlings watched him fearfully. He couldn't help with the engines this time. But Cavendish seemed still to be preserving around himself his usual aura of authoritative calm. Only when at last he had lined himself up with the runway, as his hands lay limp on the useless elevator controls, did his eyes narrow as though they were continually measuring the four miles that still separated them from the threshold of the runway.

Able Dog lumbered on down, her speed flickering around 120 knots. Once, after going too low, Cavendish suddenly whipped the trimming wheel fully forward. Then, as the nose slowly came up, he started to wind it off again.

But past the outer marker, again they were low. Cavendish shouted out, 'Two to the back!', and Eastlake and Hamilton hurried to the tail.

Then it seemed to Rawlings they were getting far too high. The pilot was keeping in line with the runway, but the aircraft had slowed up her descent.

A mile before the threshold, they still seemed a long way from the ground. Cavendish wound the trimmer fully back. Lazily, the nose dropped – but the aircraft was now wallowing badly from side to side. Using too much aileron, Rawlings thought to himself, hope to God we overshoot on this one.

Cavendish called back at him, '8,000 r.p.m.!'

Promptly, Rawlings reduced the power on the engines.

The end of the runway was coming up much more quickly. Cavendish was really committing himself this time.

'Another one to the back!'

He was flattening out his glide as best he could.

'Another two!'

The Emperor was flying almost level now, still a quarter of a mile from the threshold. Cavendish was winding ferociously on the trimming wheel. 'Full flap!'

Just as the hydraulic pump whined out for the very last time, four more were sent to the tail. The pilot's gloved right hand took the four levers on the pedestal. 'My throttles, Mr. Rawlings!'

'Your throttles, sir!'

The engineer reluctantly took his hands right off them. Out of his side window, he could see that they were at least fifty feet up. *Much* too high. He'll be cutting the motors in a minute. And then –

But Cavendish did not move the throttles. Instead, he sent the last of his human weights, including Sir James Joliffe, to the back of the aircraft.

The nose came up higher. It seemed to Rawlings that they were sinking very slowly. He heard all the engine noise die down, and a second later, the Emperor's huge tyres softly brushed against the hard surface of the runway.

The fuselage settled gently on to the oleo legs; the needle on the indicator dropped well below flying speed.

In a voice filled with admiration and relief, mixed half and half, Rawlings said, 'Bloody good landing, sir!'

Riley had been expecting all the time as the Emperor had been taxi-ing (with majestic normality) from the end of runway 28 left to the ramp at London Airport, that the Chairman would be wishing to have a few words with him. In his past associations with Sir James this had so often been the case. The design, the angle, the headlines, the omissions, almost everything except the written words themselves were normally pre-ordained in the P.R.O.'s releases to the Press.

But Able Dog's brakes squeaked her wheels to a full stop, chocks came rattling over the ground, the steps banged against her side, the cabin door was flung wide open, and still there had been no summons. Looking out of his porthole, Riley saw a little knot of people waiting to welcome them. Without Sir James there to whip up public enthusiasm, the safe arrival had stirred far fewer hearts than the hazardous departure. And this, after all, wasn't Saturday afternoon, but lie-abed time on Sunday morning.

The Chairman picked up his brief-case and walked so briskly out through the door and down the steps that the others had difficulty keeping up with him. The photographers only got a blurred photograph of a plump, firm-chinned man in a hurry. He seemed pre-occupied, impatient with the recorded talk, with the film cameramen, the little bit of publicity, even the flowers in the Company colours which the Station Manager had felt sure he would appreciate.

Noticing these signs and interpreting them as the klaxon for the boats, the Minister advanced with his hand outstretched and the friendliest 'My dear Joliffe' those thin lips had the capacity to enunciate, and 'You have had an excellent trip, I am sure!'

Sir James stopped. Riley, by his side, thought: now for the big effort, the spurt before the tape, the jovial super-confidence with which the Chairman was so abundantly endowed. His eyes widened with surprise as he heard Sir James say tersely, 'We had a number of teething troubles. Nothing fundamental. Subject to some minor modifications, I am perfectly satisfied.'

The Minister studied Sir James closely. He knew that the Chairman was as well versed in the double talk of politics and economics as he was. He walked up with him to the Very Important Persons' lounge where drinks had been laid out thoughtfully by Air Enterprise's Operations staff. Though there was champagne, the Minister was not surprised to see Sir James take a whisky with very little water.

The crew came in with the rest of the passengers. 'Why, Brocklehurst!' the Minister said, as though surprised to see him back, and put his arm round him and drew him to one side, and Riley heard a lot of whispering, and out of it all, in a loud clear voice, the Under-Secretary say, 'A very good trip indeed!'

Rawlings and Eastlake and Cruttwell drank champagne together and talked the friendliest sort of aviation shop. Seawood was paying careful attention to Doctor Enderby-Browne. Payton was chatting amicably with the two Captains.

And then, in a flood, the reporters swarmed round Sir James. When would the first passenger service leave? Was the reported huge success in America true? What about the record?

He waved his hand to quieten them. Immediately, a hush came over the room. With a smile he said, 'Aren't we rather jumping the gun?' And then he explained, 'This is only the prototype Emperor, gentlemen. We had expected to make changes after the teething troubles had been discovered. It has been brought home to me on this trip how very important the millions of small things are to the smooth functioning of the whole.' He added that Mr. Eastlake was going to incorporate an emergency system of manual controls – 'for in an age of complications it is sometimes forgotten how rarely simple things go wrong.' And additionally, the rubber boot de-icing system had proved a false economy. Hot air along the leading edge would be used in future. And afterwards? Well, a few months' freighting on the North Atlantic so that all teething troubles (for like babies, there had never been an aircraft invented without them) could be finally overcome.

There was an aghast silence among the aeronautical experts. To them it seemed a bitter bombshell. Freight... that was for old clapped-out aircraft. Not new ones. 'But the delay, Sir James! The Americans might establish the fast passenger non-stop service before us.'

'And what if they do?' was his answer. 'Jolly good luck to them!'

There was whispering among the journalists. Then they asked, 'What is your opinion of the aircraft's performance, sir, now the proving flight is over?'

Sir James said, 'Better ask the pilots. They're the people who really know the answer to that one.'

Bellamy said, 'This flight has proved everything we wanted to find out. She's fast. She handles well. Take-off and climb are phenomenal. Above all, she's strong.'

And Cavendish added authoritatively, 'We have complete confidence in her. Subject to the modifications Sir James has outlined, she has been proved an *excellent* aircraft.'

And Riley, standing just behind them, felt a sudden surprised elation at the thought that, despite his fears and depression in New York, he had apparently at last succeeded in telling the truth, after all.

The Chairman went on to discuss with disarming frankness a number of points connected with running a large aircraft over the North Atlantic. And those who heard him couldn't help thinking that, compared to the super-luxury bunks, the eight-course dinners, the orchids, the expensive flannel with which so many of the world's airlines disguise their unattractive limbs, here was a man who knew what he was talking about, and who really meant what he said.

The reporters wrote it all down. Several went to the telephone. A feeling of spontaneous gaiety took over the party. Everyone seemed to be talking and laughing at the same time. Glasses clinked. The champagne ran out and everyone switched to sherry.

Just before the party broke up, Sir James raised his hands for silence, and when he had got it (for everyone had expected a speech full of achievements in the past and successes in the future) said rather diffidently, 'I would like to thank everyone who came down here this morning to meet us. And now . . . if you don't mind . . . before I go, I want to have a few words with the passengers and crew who were with me on our flight.'

Good-humouredly, the crowd finished their drinks and started to move towards the door of the V.I.P. lounge. The Minister laid his beefy hand on Sir James' shoulder and whispered (he was one of those men addicted to whispering), 'Splendid show!' The station manager bowed, but the Chairman did not see him. He was looking out of the window to where fifty yards away two tractors tugged forwards the silver bulk of the Emperor, baptised now in North Atlantic air, her strong flanks reassuringly unscathed and unperturbed, her whole fuselage glittering in the Sunday sun.

Sir James, lost in thought, watched the aircraft disappear round the corner of the taxiway on her way to the hangar. Then, conscious of the silence in the V.I.P. lounge, he turned and found he was alone once more with the fifteen other inhabitants of Able Dog. They looked towards him expectantly.

Bellamy thought to himself, not unkindly, feeling that in the great man's position it was the only thing he could do: here comes the lecture on taking a Sensible Attitude: no need to talk of the alarms and excursions of the last flight, lest people outside the Company got the Wrong Idea.

Sir James cleared his throat. 'I just wanted to say,' he said, 'how much I appreciate you all being behind me these last few days. Nobody, I feel, could have had more co-operation than I have had. In the end,' he smiled, remembering the scene of only a couple of hours ago, 'we were all needed to bring the Emperor back home!'

And then, looking at the faces in front of him, he became suddenly aware that each must, in the scheme of things, go their separate way. A shadow momentarily crossed his face as he assumed that responsibility for everything that was indeed his rightful privilege. In this aviation Follow-My-Leader through the brambles and the nettles, trying to get in rabbit holes and up impossible trees, his position was there, right up at the front. Rather apologetically he said, 'Rather a dance I've led you!'

And Hamilton, answering for everyone there, for the crew, the designers, for Brocklehurst, Riley and Doctor Enderby-Browne, interpreting accurately the thoughts that were now passing through their minds, immediately flashed back: 'Never mind, Sir James. We are ready to do it again!'

There was a murmur of assent. A splendid feeling that the aircraft was better, not worse, for all the strains and stresses of the flight. That in this most severe of tests she had indeed proved herself, filled every male mind. The dregs of the remaining bottles managed to top up the glasses. The Emperor had really arrived.

Lalette looked around her. A long way away, somewhere on the outer perimeter of her consciousness, she was pleased about the aircraft, she caught the feeling of pleasure and congratulation, part of her brain appreciated some of the plans, the proposed schedules for some months hence, the talk of loads and modifications. But somewhere deeper inside her, like a powerful dammed-up spring of joy, not to be touched or opened in the noise and the hubbub and the presence of so many others, was the quiet certain knowledge of her own homecoming, Very quietly, Andrew Bellamy's hand moved across the table they leaned against. Very slowly hers, too, half-closed the distance between them. And once they had found each other, there they stayed, while the Emperor began her inspection in the hangar, while the Chairman was bowed into his waiting car, while the experts planned, while the publicity men explained.

And while the tumult died away.